Dear Reader,

I wonder what you have heard of the British rebel queen, Boudicca? She is famous for taking on the might of the Roman Empire in the first century and – almost – liberating the Britons from colonial rule. Boudicca's rebellion was profoundly shocking to Rome, not only because she won a string of devastating victories, but because she was a *woman*.

As a Londoner, I have always been fascinated by her monumental, belligerent statue which stands on Westminster Bridge, facing the Houses of Parliament. One of its peculiarities is that it looks as if Boudicca is about to drive her war chariot straight at the heart of the British government, in an attack upon her own. On reflection this is more fitting than it first seems. In her rebellion against Roman rule, Boudicca sacked London, burning the city to ash. Many Britons will have been killed in that assault, the line between colonised and coloniser blurred by ties of marriage, trade and proximity. The statue's position is a reminder that Boudicca's resistance to foreign invasion is not always a simple tale of villains and victims.

Another peculiarity of the statue is that the number of people you can see changes depending on the angle from which you view it. Standing behind the queen are two young women. They are Boudicca's daughters, who both played a key role in the revolt yet were left unnamed by Roman historians. It is their unknown story which has long fascinated me. What might it have been like to be

Boudicca's daughter? And what would it have meant to survive her?

This book is my answer to those questions. I want to tell you the story of Boudicca's eldest daughter, who I have named Solina, a woman who lived in revolutionary times and faced extraordinarily challenging choices. I invite you to ride with her through Britain's ancient forests and to travel to Rome, walking the glittering – yet deadly – corridors of the Emperor Nero's palaces. Sometimes I will change the angle from which you see Solina's story, shifting the focus to her mother Boudicca or to Paulinus, the Roman general who fought them both. All three characters inhabit a world that is morally grey, where virtue must be abandoned if you are to survive. There are no straightforward heroes or villains in these pages; it is for each reader to decide where they stand.

Solina's time was radically different to ours in so many of its customs and attitudes, but human nature is less changeable. The desire for freedom, for love, for justice, for vengeance are all impulses the ancients felt too. And like us, sometimes these impulses would have been in conflict within a person's heart. On her journey, Solina comes to realise that both revenge and redemption exact their own cost. I wonder, reading this story, which you might choose?

I am immensely grateful to you for supporting my book – and I hope you enjoy Solina's adventures.

Elodie Harper

28 August 2025

229x148mm • 480 pages

HB • 9781804544631 • £18.99
XTPB • 9781804544648 • £14.99
E • 9781804544617

Publicity
Kathryn Colwell • kathryn@headofzeus.com
Kate Wands • kate.wands@headofzeus.com

Sales • sales@headofzeus.com

Boudicca. Infamous warrior, queen of the British Iceni tribe and mastermind of one of history's greatest revolts. Her defeat spelled ruin for her people, yet still her name is enough to strike fear into Roman hearts.

But what of the woman who grew up in her shadow?

The woman who has her mother's looks and cunning but a spirit all of her own?

The woman whose desperate bid for survival will take her from Britain's sacred marshlands to the glittering façades of Nero's Roman Empire...

Born to a legend. Forced to fight. Determined to succeed.

Meet Solina.

Boudicca's Daughter.

ELODIE HARPER is the award-winning author of the bestselling Wolf Den trilogy, set in ancient Pompeii. The first book in the series, *The Wolf Den*, was a Waterstones Book of the Month, and the second, *The House with the Golden Door*, was a *Sunday Times* bestseller. Her standalone, *Boudicca's Daughter*, is out in August 2025. Alongside her career as a writer, Elodie has worked as a reporter at ITV News and producer at Channel 4.

Follow Elodie Harper at:
X: @Elodie_Harper
Instagram: @elodielharper
elodieharper.com

Boudicca's Daughter

Elodie Harper

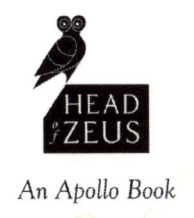

HEAD OF ZEUS

An Apollo Book

UNCORRECTED MANUSCRIPT

Note to reviewers: This is an uncorrected advance reading copy. Please check all citations against a finished copy of the work. This copy is not for sale or resale.

First published in the UK in 2025 by Head of Zeus,
part of Bloomsbury Publishing Plc

Copyright © Elodie Harper, 2025

The moral right of Elodie Harper to be identified as the author of this work has been asserted in accordance with the Copyright, Designs and Patents Act of 1988.

All rights reserved. No part of this publication may be: i) reproduced or transmitted in any form, electronic or mechanical, including photocopying, recording or by means of any information storage or retrieval system without prior permission in writing from the publishers; or ii) used or reproduced in any way for the training, development or operation of artificial intelligence (AI) technologies, including generative AI technologies. The rights holders expressly reserve this publication from the text and data mining exception as per Article 4(3) of the Digital Single Market Directive (EU) 2019/790.

This is a work of fiction. All characters, organizations, and events portrayed in this novel are either products of the author's imagination or are used fictitiously.

A catalogue record for this book is available from the British Library.

ISBN (HB): 9781804544631
ISBN (XTPB): 9781804544648
ISBN (E): 9781804544617

Author photo copyright © Paula Majid

Bloomsbury Publishing Plc
50 Bedford Square, London, WC1B 3DP, UK
Bloomsbury Publishing Ireland Limited,
29 Earlsfort Terrace, Dublin 2, D02 AY28, Ireland

HEAD OF ZEUS LTD
5–8 Hardwick Street
London EC1R 4RG

To find out more about our authors and books visit www.headofzeus.com
For product safety related questions contact productsafety@bloomsbury.com

Boudicca's Daughter

For Juliet, Fiercest of Friends and Queen of the Literary Agents

Dramatis Personae

Solina – Boudicca's daughter
Catia (Boudicca) – Solina's mother, a warrior
Prasutagus – Solina's father, client king of the Iceni
Bellenia – Solina's sister
Riomanda – Solina's aunt, a warrior
Isarninus – a warrior
Diseta – distant cousin to Catia
Caratacus – leader of the failed uprising against Rome
Vatiaucus – a warrior, Solina's ex-lover
Cunominus – Catia's younger brother; Riomanda's husband
Aesu – Solina's cousin, of the Horse Tribe
Cartimandua – Queen of the Brigantes
Vassura – Aesu's mother, sister of Prasutagus
Senovara – a young warrior

Mandubracius – Catia's chariot driver
Lais – a Greek woman in London
Saenu – Druid, advisor to Vassura
Andraste – Iceni Goddess of the tribe
Esus – God of rivers and the rising sun
Epona – Goddess of horses, moon and souls. Bride of Esus
Taranis – God of the Sky

Suetonius Paulinus – Roman Legate of Britannia
Agricola – Paulinus's tribune
Pliny – Paulinus's old friend
Fulvia – Paulinus's wife (deceased)
Catus Decianus – Roman Procurator of Britannia
Matu – Paulinus's translator, Catuvellauni tribe

Alpinus Classicianus – Britannia's new procurator, from Gaul
Cosmus – Paulinus's steward in Rome
Thais – Paulinus's former mistress
Julia Pacata – Alpinus's wife
King Togidubnus – client king of the Atrebates
Nero – Roman Emperor
Tigellinus – head of Nero's Praetorian Guard
Octavia – Nero's wife
Poppaea Sabina – Nero's wife
Claudia Augusta – Nero and Poppaea's infant daughter
Otho – Poppaea's former husband, later Emperor
Ressona – a Briganti slave girl
Corbulo – a Roman general
Secundus – Pliny's steward
Alexios – a Greek slave boy
Lucan – a poet
Polla – Lucan's wife
Vespasian – Paulinus' old friend
Antonia Caenis – Vespasian's lover
Henna – a German slave girl
Frida – a German slave girl
Messalina – Nero's mistress
Fabius – a slave boy
Calpurnius Piso – a Roman senator
Vestinus – a consul
Vitellius – former consul, later Emperor
Aulus – estate steward, Pisaurum
Tita – Aulus's wife
Galba – Roman general, later Emperor
Camilla – Italy's mythical warrior queen
Silvanus – Polla's steward
Gaius – an unruly soldier
Verania – widow of Galba's appointed heir
Caecina – Vitellius's general
Atalanta – mythical female warrior from Greek legend
Mars – Roman God of War
Diana – Roman Goddess of the Hunt
Salus – Roman Goddess of Safety

"Virtue is incompatible with absolute power. He who is ashamed to commit cruelty must always fear it."
                                     Lucan, Pharsalia

PROLOGUE

Her name is rarely spoken, and yet I know people remember. Her shadow lies across me still.

It is there in the suspicion I see in men's eyes, in the flicker of their fear.

Boudicca.

I remember when that one word had the power to drown out every other sound, when the ground shook with it, the raised voices of thousands, chanting her victory. She terrified me, the way she fought, lit by the rage which consumed her, and yet I could not look away. Not even when she burned the temple, when the air was thick with smoke and the screams of those trapped inside.

A monster. That's what they called her. And perhaps she was.

But I have other, earlier memories. The lightness of her laugh, the way she spun when she danced, so fast nobody could ever catch her. How she crouched down to meet a child's eyes, and the warmth of her smile, when all you wanted was the sun brought by her presence.

This is the story I want to tell you. About the time before she was Boudicca.

When she was a woman called Catia.

When she was my mother.

PART ONE
VIRAGO

"They do not distinguish between the sexes when choosing commanders."
　　　　　　Tacitus on the Britons' military tactics, *Agricola*

"All this ruin was brought upon the Romans by a woman, a fact which in itself caused them the greatest shame."
　　　　　Cassius Dio on Boudicca's rebellion, *History of Rome*

1

SOLINA

The twisted branches flash past, swift as shadows, yet solid as spears. I don't have time to feel afraid of falling or being struck by deadly low-hanging trees. Instead, I cling to Tan's mane, my heartbeat racing to the thunder of his footfall. A horse gallops faster than thought, and nothing exists for me but the exhilaration of his speed. The force of it hits me like fire, filling me with joy. Around us the wild wood, stripped of its leaves, glows green from the moss which rolls over waves of roots and stone in a luminous sea. Then Bellenia's scream rings out, startling Tan, sending the last of the birds scattering. I turn in the direction of her cry. My sister has managed to overtake me, weaving dangerously through a narrow gap in the woods, more reckless than I would ever dare to be. Before I can urge Tan to go faster, Bellenia's horse Kintu shoots onto the path in front, kicking up clods of earth, blackening the way. I don't have the guts to try and shoulder her aside – either of us could be snared in a savage tangle of roots and whip-like boughs. Anger fills my heart as my vision shrinks to Kintu's powerful haunches, the dark rope of his tail, the gold of my sister's blonde hair.

White sky burns through the thinning trees, the green glow fading, then we burst out onto the plain. Open space excites Tan, giving him another burst of speed. Bellenia is ahead but not out of reach. I shout at my horse, encouraging him to gallop faster, but Kintu is still swifter, and the two waiting figures grow more solid in the distance. Beyond them the target also looms, the curved husk of a wide, blackened log, upended in the boggy ground: a dark imitation of a Roman invader. I see Bellenia hold out her spear, poised, an image of grace before she throws. Iron sinks into bark and she wheels off, screaming in triumph. I raise my own arm, bracing against the weight of the weapon, urging Tan to gallop directly at the target. He shears off at the last minute, but I ride him so close I hit the chalk daubed at its heart.

Unlike my sister, I canter towards Riomanda and our mother in silence. They sit tall on their horses, watching. Tan's breathing is heavy, sweat lathered into foam at his sides, his coat drenched. Bellenia is already dismounted, weapon drawn, leaving Kintu untethered, the horse's sides heaving like bellows. I leave Tan, drawing the weighted wooden sword from my back. Not a real weapon but still banned, still reason enough to train out here, where the grey fingers of the sea reach into the land, and no spies will watch us.

"The aim is to disarm," Riomanda says, raising her voice over the wind.

I glance over at Riomanda and my mother, sisters by marriage and two of the most formidable warriors of the Wolf Tribe. Rome has forbidden the Iceni from bearing arms, but my mother once told us this is like commanding the sun not to rise. She has brought my sister and me here to learn how to fight, just as she and Riomanda once learned, tracing the thread of their knowledge back through time to the god of our people, Andraste. Riomanda's dark hair is tied in a knot of plaits, her face hard, like the one shaped in metal on the hilt of her knife. My mother, Catia, is cloaked in a wolf pelt, its fur grey as winter clouds. Her eyes are on Bellenia. As always.

My sister's cheeks are flushed red, eyes bright with excitement as she waits for me. We circle each other. She strikes first, as I knew she would. The force of her blow jars up my arm, but I keep hold of my sword. Bellenia begins to shout, aggression transforming her beautiful face, making her look as vicious as the carved head of a carnyx.

"You are slower than a badger, Solina! Even if I cut off one of Kintu's legs, I would still beat you!"

I circle her, dodging another blow.

"Are you silent like a Roman?" she taunts. "Perhaps you are not Iceni at all."

I say nothing, knowing that will enrage her more, and keep my eyes on her blade. The next time she hits out, I dodge in anticipation, and she lurches forward. Before she can recover her balance, I knock her over, sending her sprawling into the mud. Then I pounce, resting one boot on her stomach, the other on her weapon.

"Who's slow now?"

"You sneaky piece of shit!" she exclaims, angrily wiping the mud from her trousers as I help her to her feet. Then she catches my eye and laughs.

"I'm glad you both find fighting so amusing," Riomanda's voice is ice. "Solina, that is a poor way to win, without daring to strike a single blow. Bellenia, if you fight like a fool, you will fall like one."

I look over at our mother. She says nothing, which is even more ominous. Eyes narrowed, she dismounts, murmuring something to Riomanda as she hands over the reins of her horse. She walks over to Bellenia.

"Raise your weapon." My sister swiftly obeys. "You strike

well but you lack sense," she continues, drawing a wooden weapon from her own back. "Fight me now, without signalling where you will hit."

I watch them both, envy burning in my chest. Nobody can handle a sword like our mother, not even Riomanda. Yet, somehow, when Bellenia faces her, my sister draws strength from the encounter rather than falling to pieces as I do. I watch my sister's thrusts and parries grow bolder and know how much pride our mother must feel; I know exactly why she will never love me as much as she loves Bellenia.

They end their bout. My sister did not manage to score a hit, but still, she came close. Our mother's face is lit by an affectionate smile. "Better," she says.

I brace myself, knowing it is now my turn. "Solina," my mother turns to me. "You fight like a coward. In silence. Without striking a blow."

The unfairness stings. "And yet I just won."

"You have no fire," she replies. "How would you survive in battle?"

I hit out in rage. She blocks my impulsive blow with ease, then rains down on me, just as she did with Bellenia. But while this inspired my sister to fight back, it only makes me shrink, my moves becoming ever more defensive.

"Do you have no insults?" my mother shouts. "Where's your passion? Where's your fury? What sort of warrior comes to battle like a mouse?"

"*Quasi tuba inanis!*" I scream back, swinging the sword at her, nearly scoring a hit. I see her face flush red – not at the words, which she would not understand, but because I have spoken in Latin. She knocks the sword from my grasp as if it were a reed, then slaps me across the face.

"Never speak their tongue to your own with a weapon in your hand," she says.

Shame floods through me, scalding my face. Latin is the language of our enemy, the language used by the centurion who murdered Riomanda's brother. I want to apologise but cannot bring myself to do it. My mother's face hardens at my lack of remorse, then she turns her back. I stare after her, watch her swing herself into the saddle, then startle at an unexpected punch to my arm. It is my sister.

"Why would you do that?" Bellenia hisses, her voice low. "How could you shout at her in Latin? Like one of *them*. What did you even say? It sounded so ugly."

"You would know what I said if you had paid *any* attention to our father's lessons!" I snap back. "It was nothing that bad, anyway. I just told her she sounded like an empty trumpet."

Bellenia can't help snorting. "That's a pathetic insult. Just as well nobody understood."

I roll my eyes, but I'm grateful to her for lightening the mood. Tan edges away from me when I go to fetch him, tired from galloping through the woods, but I seize him by the reins. He lets out a long, heavy sigh when I swing myself up onto his back, sounding like a phlegmy old man. Bellenia laughs.

"Tan sounds ready for battle."

I wallop Tan on the backside so that he lurches towards my sister, who trots off with a shriek. I laugh, then look nervously towards our mother and aunt, who have already set off. They do not turn around.

We ride together across the marshland, back towards the Town of the Wolf, through the northernmost edge of Iceni territory. Our mother sets the pace, picking out the path over the wooden causeways, guiding us through the treacherous, watery ground. It is not long past midday and yet the sky has a washed-out look, as if the veil to the Otherworld were already thinning. By nightfall it will be no more substantial than the mist creeping over the plains, and the spirits will walk with us. I stare out over the marshes, at the feathered reed beds which stroke the low-lying cloud, and the iron grey of the sea which lies beyond. I think of Esus the river god, squinting to see if I can glimpse one of his birds, the long-legged herons which wade through his waters.

I have long since abandoned hope of meeting Esus himself – though perhaps this year, at the Winter Solstice, one of the gods will finally speak to me. As Solina, the daughter of Druids, I still lack the *sight* to match the meaning of my name. Riding beside me, her golden hair brighter than sunlight, Bellenia looks the very embodiment of her name: *strength*. I glance down at Tan's neck, my heart heavy, ruffling his mane. His coat is white and red, both colours which mark him as a servant of the Otherworld. But Tan has never led me to any gods.

The closer we come to the town, the more marks the landscape shows of the mortal realm. Salterns stretch towards the horizon, and here a few men, women and children bend over pools and smoking fires, extracting white treasure from the bog's briny water. I see a girl grasping a bucket with red chapped hands, and feel thankful to be safely up on my horse instead of toiling in a freezing trench. The Romans pay dearly for our salt: my father told me once that their soldiers even measure their wages in it. *Salarium.* I murmur the foreign word under my breath, feeling its shape.

"What are you mumbling about?" Bellenia demands, always too sharp-eared to miss anything. She has always been this way, my little sister, full of curiosity and mischief.

"Nothing," I say.

"It sounded *foreign*." Like our mother, Bellenia cannot speak Latin. She has no patience for my interest in the Roman settlers who have seeped into our country, embedding themselves in the land like leeches. They invaded when my sister and I were small children, and now I cannot remember life without their shadow, their casual violence and endless theft. We were raised to hate them, and I do. Yet, unlike Bellenia, the invaders also fascinate me. Our father was gifted slaves when he agreed to serve Rome, and I became fond of one, a woman named Salvia. But while I sat beside her as a child, encouraged by our father to learn about her language and her gods, Bellenia refused to join me. Salvia is dead now, as is her knowledge.

"It was a prayer to Esus," I say. A lie, but not an unlikely one. Bellenia used to tease me for my love of legends about the handsome river god. So many stories tell of him walking among mortals, as if he were an ordinary warrior, granting gifts to his favourites or inviting them to the Otherworld. I spent years hoping I might find him.

The track becomes a road, marked by wheel ruts, boots and hooves. We pass a cluster of roundhouses surrounded by fields, and a gaggle of foraging children run to the roadside to watch us, firewood clutched to their chests, their faces eager. My mother lays her hand over her heart in greeting, bowing her head as if they were kings. The children grin, nudging each other in delight, making me smile too.

On the vast, flat plains of our kingdom, covered by an even vaster sky, the town is visible long before we reach the gates. It rises above the fields, surrounded by steep earth embankments and wooden walls. Sheep graze up to the edge of the settlement's encircling ditch, and thatched rooftops peek over the top of the ramparts, like sentries keeping watch. Travellers grow in number the closer we get, a stream of farmers and traders from nearby villages, heading here to celebrate the week-long Feast of Darkness. A few stare at me, giving Tan a wide berth. One old man even makes the sign of the evil eye. His fear doesn't offend me. I know I make an uncanny sight at any time, but especially today. White skin, red hair, eyes dark as a raven's wing. Marked in the colours of the Otherworld, like my horse.

A growing hubbub of human voices drowns out the birdsong. We ride through the deep trench that cuts through the town's defensive ditches and reach the wooden gatehouse. The beast of my mother's people is painted at the top as a mark of respect for the goddess Andraste, giving the place its name: *Town of the Wolf.* I look up as we pass underneath. Seven human heads hang above the wolf's back, some so decayed they have shrivelled like rotten apples. They are the remains of thieves and murderers, staked here as a warning, even though everyone knows we lack the power to punish the worst criminals – hanging a Roman on our gates would be taken as an act of war. Still, my mother says the heads are a reminder to Rome that our patience should not be tested too far. And my father's presence, as Rome's client king, is an effective deterrent from their violence.

Inside the town, clamour and warmth engulf us. Smoke rises from the roundhouses, making the grey sky above shimmer a darker shade of blue, and my spirits rise with them. We weave our way past traders at the gatehouse, men and women jostling to sell baskets woven from marsh-reeds, or clay pots, or fabric. Further into town, grain stores stand on stilts, hovering like herons. Their height offers protection from vermin and damp, though not from Roman tax collectors.

Bellenia and I ride single-file through the milling people, dogs and pigs, following the loud clanging of metal which marks out the blacksmiths' quarter. This part of town was once the armoury, where people and horses were equipped for war, before it was banned. We pass the forge, where beautiful metal masks sit either side of the door. They are for horses, horned and inlaid with silver. I try to imagine

Tan wearing one, how fearsome he would look riding into battle, and picture myself charging over the field like a warrior of legend, as glorious as Esus's bride, Epona. I pat Tan's neck. "Maybe one day," I murmur, as if he might hear my thoughts.

Our home lies at the heart of the town. My mother's family have ruled here for generations, cousins and kin all living in a vast painted roundhouse, its hall big enough to hold hundreds. Today, the clearing outside our home is crowded with visitors who have not only come to celebrate the feast, but also to bring their grievances to my father. I dismount, watching one of the servants lead Tan to the stables, suddenly nervous. I have lived most of my life in the south, with my father's people. The Wolf Tribe are tougher, harder to read, more prone to fighting. More like my mother.

Even though his rule has brought us peace, many here have never forgiven my father for making our kingdom a client state of Rome. My mother resents his choice most of all. She beckons now to Bellenia, who walks beside her into the hall, their hair the same shade of gold, while I follow behind with Riomanda. Dust motes dance in the dimmer light, and our father Prasutagus sits by the red glow of the hearth, pressed close by men and women, the leaders and warriors of surrounding settlements. High above them, carved wolves' heads are shaded by the fire's rising smoke, and the walls glint with the metal of a hundred shields.

Our father rises as he watches us approach, holding out his hands to our mother. "Catia," he says, embracing her. She draws close to him, resting her forehead to his. He might be king, but everyone watching this performance of unity knows their rule is like a rope, drawing its strength from weaving together the warriors of the north with the Druids of the south.

My parents stand apart, his grey hair at a height with her gold. I try not to notice how much older my father looks. He gestures for me to come closer, laying a hand on my shoulder. "Solina will lead the ceremony tonight," he declares, looking round at our guests. I force myself to ignore my nerves and meet the assembled warriors' eyes with a show of pride, as my parents expect.

"May the gods guide you." The words are spoken by a tall, blond warrior, with a chest as broad as one of the shields on the wall. I recognise him as Isarninus, the leader of a settlement near Andraste's sacred hill. He is the man Bellenia has her eye on.

"I pray they bless the feast," I reply. Even though we are standing near the hearth, the hall feels chill. I fold my arms, not wanting to shiver.

"Your daughters wear warriors' clothes," says another man, dressed in a wolf pelt, his expression as unfriendly as the beast he wears. Bellenia pulls her own cloak closer around her thighs, perhaps hoping to hide the mud stains where she fell. "Yet you have not called for arms against Rome?"

"We still hope for peace," my father answers, not rising to the man's tone.

"They leave *us* no peace," snaps an older woman, deep grooves cut through her weathered face, like wheel ruts in the road. I know her as Diseta, one of my distant cousins. Like my mother, Diseta wanted us to join the rebel Caratacus ten years ago in his doomed uprising against Rome. I remember Caratacus coming to our home at the City of the Horse, a glorious warrior in a cloak of gold, making promises of freedom. My father refused to help him, to my mother's grief.

"They are demanding money from me, from all my kin," Diseta says. "Roman filth turn up at my home without shame, then the bastards make off with whatever they can grab. Demanding we return loans they never even gave us. Stealing our cattle! Even our men are being kidnapped, forced to fight in *their* armies. Yet we do not fight back to defend ourselves? Why?"

I glance anxiously at my mother, whose hand now rests on Bellenia's shoulder just as our father's rests on mine. Her lips are pursed in a hard line. I know she agrees with Diseta, that she would have us go to war. But she will not say so here. It is more important to give a pretence of unity between herself and my father.

"Diseta, I know they are arrogant," my father says. "I know they demand too much. But we are not enslaved, like the Trinovantes. War would risk the loss of every remaining freedom we have."

"We don't yet have the means to fight them," my mother adds. "Too many have forgotten how. It is a question of timing."

There are nods of agreement at this – my mother is always closer to the mood of her own people. "So that is why they are training." Isarninus gestures at my sister.

"Our daughters have always trained in the old ways," my father says, unwilling to give any quarter. "Nothing has changed."

"Everything is changing," Diseta snaps. "Prasutagus, you have given your life to peace, and we have trusted your guidance. But that season is ending. You cannot keep Rome at bay forever, their violence grows daily. They are stripping the land like rats in a barn. Their greed will never be satisfied."

"Do not invite the Darkness," my father says, a note of command in his deep voice, a reminder of his divine status as a Druid. "Tonight, of all nights."

"We share your anger." My mother turns to Diseta whose mouth is already open, ready for a furious retort. "Feast with us tonight. And we will ask the gods to guide us."

At the back of the hall, screened from sight in a chamber under the eaves, Bellenia and I dress for the feast. Through the wicker slats, we can see a few guests still gathered around the hearth, arguing with our father.

"Will Roman soldiers come this far north in winter, do you think?" Bellenia whispers to me. "Surely not with the king here?"

She has voiced my own fear. "Not tonight, they won't," I say, trying to sound less afraid than I feel. "And Diseta would see them all off, anyway."

Bellenia smiles. "She gets more like a forest troll every year."

I can hear one of the maids scolding the children playing knucklebones in the hall, then she is inside the chamber, bringing a bowl of water for us to wash our hands and faces. "Naughty little mice," she says. "Running around, getting in everyone's way." The girl cannot be much older than a child herself, and I remember being her age, wanting to join the adults. "Will you be getting married this year?" she asks, yanking my hair back into plaits. "Imagine all the dancing and feasting!"

"Solina won't be happy unless Esus himself swoops down to claim her," Bellenia teases. "I'm not sure a mortal man will ever be good enough."

"I don't have to find a man of any sort," I say, giving her a withering look. "I will serve the kingdom as a Druid, like father, and marry or not as I please."

"You see." Bellenia smirks. "I told you. She's holding out for Esus, himself. Though failing a god, there's always Vatiaucus." I shove Bellenia, who laughs but then shoves me back, hard, and there's a moment when I know my sister, like me, is thinking of throwing a punch. I picture our mother's fury if we were to be caught brawling and lower my fist.

"Vatiaucus might not even be here," I say unconvincingly.

Last spring, I chose Vatiaucus as a lover, dazzled by the sight of him on horseback, but after a few intoxicating weeks, I realised his body was by far the most interesting thing about him. I managed to disarm the poor man once when we trained together and took this as an excuse to end things – as the king's daughter, I have the right to an unconquered warrior. Now, whenever I see him, Vatiaucus gazes at me with large, sorrowful eyes like a cow stuck in brambles, much to my sister's amusement.

"It's Bellenia you should watch," I say to the serving girl. "She's got her eye on Isarninus."

"The tall one, with the lovely eyes?" the girl exclaims. "What a match that would be! He's blond as a haystack, isn't he? And almost as big." I try not to snort at her ridiculous description.

"He's handsome enough," Bellenia says, with a smug little smile. I roll my eyes. I have no doubt she could claim Isarninus if she wanted. Bellenia has always been more beautiful than me, with our father's fine features, while I take after our mother – tall and striking, but unlikely to steal a man's heart on sight. Even Vatiaucus used to stare at Bellenia when he was mine. I think of the reassurance Riomanda once gave me. "*You have a beauty that grows, an acorn that will become an oak in the soil of the right heart.*"

"Perhaps you and Isarninus will dance together tonight!" the maid says to Bellenia. "A shame there are no flowers for your hair. Will you kiss him or take him to bed? I'm sure he couldn't refuse!"

The girl has now lost interest in helping me dress, fluttering around my sister. I wrap myself in the heavy robes I will have to wear for the ceremony later, woven in a shifting pattern of red and white. Horses run around the borders, stitched in gold. I lift my arms, wanting to see the colours of the fabric shimmer. My chest feels tight – although I always stand beside my father at the Feast of Darkness, I have never led the ceremony. He will take over from me after the invocation, but I am unsure I deserve the honour. Father has reassured me there are many ways to be a Druid; some serve through learning, others through visions or prophecy. Yet I still feel crushed by my inability to see beyond the veil, to walk in the Otherworld as he does.

The maid is now gawping, awestruck, at the sparkle of my robes. "Do you think the gods will speak through you?"

I catch Bellenia's eye. My sister sees my fear and steps forward to take my hand. She is always there when it truly matters. "Solina is a gifted Druid," she declares. "She is blessed by the gods. That is why our father chose her to cross to the Otherworld tonight."

I squeeze my sister's hand, hoping she understands the gratitude I cannot express in front of the maid. Bellenia turns and kisses me quickly on the cheek. "The gods will speak to you this evening, Solina," she says. "I feel it in my heart."

2

CATIA

Catia watches her daughters, their figures lit by flames, her heart gripped by pride and pain. In their faces she still sees the babies she nursed and held, the children they have so recently been and the women they are becoming. Impossible to imagine all the winters that have passed since she carried them. Now they stand, surrounded by hundreds of their people, in the divine clearing between town and wilderness, greeting the Darkness with fire. It is the most sacred night of the year, when the veil between worlds thins, allowing spirits to walk in the mortal realm. Sacrifices made tonight will ensure that the gods will allow the rebirth of spring.

A giant bonfire for Taranis, God of the Sky, burnishes Bellenia's hair to a brighter shade of gold, outshining the priceless torc around her neck. Her youngest daughter is so beautiful, sometimes Catia cannot believe she birthed her. She is a child who has brought nothing but joy. Beside her, draped in ceremonial robes, Solina is clearly Catia's daughter – no other woman could have carried her. That distinctive tall stature, her uninviting frown. Their similarities don't always endear Solina to Catia – it is disconcerting to meet her own stubbornness in another. She frowns, remembering how her eldest child cursed in Latin earlier, like a Roman brat.

Solina moves to stand next to her father. Other Druids who have gathered for the ceremony make space for her, allowing the king's daughter to take precedence. Nothing Catia has done in life has ever pleased Prasutagus more than this child she gave him. She feels a flicker of resentment at her husband's favouritism for their firstborn. He has never believed Bellenia to be as intelligent as her older sister, forever telling Catia that Solina is the one destined for greatness. *He has seen her spirit soar over the rooftops of Rome. He has watched her rise through his black crow's eye, the form he wears in the Otherworld.* There is no arguing with the gods, Catia supposes, but it still rankles, her husband's inability to realise Bellenia is just as special.

In the darkness, Prasutagus looks more like the man Catia met as a girl. His face glows red as blood in the flames, silver horns are set upon his head, and his sacred authority makes him appear ageless. Her husband is not one man to her, but many: the Druid who speaks as a god, the warrior she fell in love with, and the man who betrayed her. Their marriage brought the Wolf Tribe under his control, a gift she should never have bestowed, and he repaid her by becoming a client king to Rome, defying her wishes. Prasutagus succeeded in achieving the prosperity which he promised the gods had foretold, and Catia thought she had managed to make peace with his decision, but now Rome is growing bolder, and the king is weakening. She knows her husband is losing his power to old age, like an oak stripped of its leaves, naked against the coming cold. Rome is a darkness which frightens her more than winter ever could.

Sacred mistletoe is thrown on the fire, and the silver mirror to the Otherworld shines bright on Solina's face, illuminating an expression of fear. Catia's resentment melts into tenderness at the sight. Solina is not Prasutagus, however close the pair may be. Instinctively, she murmurs a prayer. "*May the goddess of souls speak through my daughter, may her vision be true.*" Solina holds out the mirror, its surface representing the veil between worlds, and begins to sing. She invokes the birds of Epona, creatures with the power to wake the dead and send the living to sleep. All eyes are upon her, none as intent as those of Prasutagus. His lips move, silently mirroring her words.

Solina stops singing. Her voice when she speaks sounds harsh and unfamiliar. It is Epona speaking through her, addressing the spirits.

"*For one night you may walk among the living. For one night you may leave the Otherworld. For one night the veil is lifted.*"

There is silence. Catia stills her breathing, hardly daring to make a sound. She can see Epona's horse, inlaid with gold on the back of the mirror clasped in Solina's pale fingers. Her daughter is staring into the glass, waiting for a vision that might guide them through the year. Solina frowns as if surprised, her eyes searching the silver surface, her expression intent. Then her shoulders droop, and she hands the sacred object back to her father.

"I see only darkness."

Catia tries not to let the disappointment show on her face. So many are watching to see her reaction. It is not a terrible vision – the dark of winter is indeed here, and on many occasions, Prasutagus has seen nothing more than this. And yet, they had all hoped Solina might be blessed with more tonight.

Solina steps back. Prasutagus takes over the ceremony, heaping dried mistletoe on the fire that sends up a shower of sparks, calling for the bull to be brought forward for sacrifice.

He is swiftly surrounded by other Druids, a circle of white robes and long hair, chanting their prayers to Taranis. Catia realises Solina is trying to catch her eye, seeking reassurance. It takes Catia by surprise. Solina is so much her father's child, she has long since given up hope the girl really cares what she thinks. Before she has time to nod in encouragement, Solina looks away, mistaking her mother's blank expression for a coldness she does not feel.

In the great hall, the noise of the feast is so loud it eases the weight of Catia's fears. The day's tension is released in wild celebrations, guests laughing and singing, drowning out the musicians. Catia's fingers are sticky from honey cakes, and the tables are strewn with holly and evergreen. At the hearth, the sacred cauldron of Esus and Epona hangs from iron firedogs, whose wrought wolves' heads are familiar to Catia from her childhood. She can remember when she was the same height as those dogs, when she was able to look straight into their carved eyes, poking her small finger into their snarling mouths, until her grandmother warned her they would come to life and bite off her thumb. She had believed that tale for years, even told her own children the same story.

Blood from the sacrificed bull smokes in the cauldron, scented by rosemary. The huge bronze bowl is another treasure Catia knows from childhood, used only at this feast of death and rebirth. The legend on its sides shows slaughtered warriors restored to life by the gods after being submerged in their divine cauldron's depths. Catia stares at the men, riding out on their resurrected steeds, mouths sealed shut as payment for leaving the Otherworld.

"You look very serious, sister. Are you planning to disrupt the feast with a fight?"

It is the familiar boom of Cunominus's voice. Catia turns to her younger brother and laughs. She can still see traces of the mischievous child she once knew in his weathered face; they have sat together at so many feasts in this hall, including the one he is teasing her about. Many years ago – and encouraged by their mother – Catia had challenged a warrior who slighted her. Since the man was built like a mountain, it had been prudent to wait until he was drunk, to be sure of winning.

Both their parents are dead now, but Catia knows they live on in Cunominus's memories, just as they do in hers. Riomanda – his wife – sits beside him, the swell of her pregnancy starting to show. After a decade of marriage, Riomanda is with child. Cunominus will finally be a father.

"I was remembering when we were children," Catia says to them both. "And soon there will be another wolf cub in this hall. Though hopefully not as badly behaved as *you* were." Her brother's grin is half hidden by his thick red moustache.

"We will be blessed if our child has Solina's intelligence or Bellenia's fire," Riomanda says. "I cannot believe they are women now; it seems they were children only yesterday."

They all glance over to where Catia's daughters are dancing. Solina looks awkward, as if she would rather fight her dancing partner than bed him, which amuses Catia. She had feared the Vatiaucus affair might land them with a particularly foolish son-in-law, but Solina was crafty enough to extricate herself. Beside her sister, Bellenia is stamping and twirling with the warrior Isarninus, flushed with happiness. She looks extraordinarily beautiful, but Isarninus is a little too lustful for Catia's liking. He should show more respect in front of Bellenia's parents. Across the table, which is littered with the remains of a giant roasted hog, Prasutagus is also gazing at their girls, his pride seemingly unclouded by any concern. For a Druid, her husband can often be quite oblivious.

The pulse of the music is infectious and Catia sways to its melody, longing to join in. Dancing always brought her such joy. When they were younger, she and Prasutagus would have been first among those whirling around the fire, but even as she yearns to jump to her feet, Catia knows her husband has lost the speed and grace of his youth. It would be unwise to expose his weakness in front of so many. She glances over at Riomanda, knowing how much her friend also loves to dance, suspecting she is only staying seated out of kindness. "You should make use of your time before the baby comes," Catia says. "Don't stay for me."

The pair do not need a second invitation. Catia watches them join the others, her heart full. Inside this hall, on this night, the most sacred of the year, it is possible to forget that Rome lurks outside in the darkness. It is possible to believe that the Town of the Wolf will never change, even though Catia knows, deep in her bones, that change is coming.

Alone with his wife after the feast, Prasutagus finally allows his exhaustion to show. They are cocooned together in the loft chamber, tapestries muffling the noise of the hall below, and within this dimly lit space, he seems to diminish. Catia watches as he eases onto the bed beside her, too worried to ask if he has suffered more pains to his chest. She knows his breathlessness is growing worse. When she married him, Prasutagus had been much older than her, but still god-like in appearance, the most handsome warrior she had ever seen. She had not considered back then that he would reach the winter of old age so many years before her. He catches the expression in her eyes and forces a laugh.

"Don't look at me like that, woman," he says. "You make

me feel even more ancient!" Catia does not reply, only takes his hand and lays it across her heart. "I'm sorry," he murmurs, stroking her fingers. "I don't mean to mock your care. I'm grateful for it. And for you." Prasutagus's solemnity pains Catia even more than his sharpness. Tears prick at her eyes. "Come along." He smiles. "If you are silent any longer, I will think the spirits swapped you for a shadow wife. Since when did you have nothing to say?"

"Solina did well at the ceremony," she replies, looking away from him.

"Yes," he agrees, easily distracted by praise for his favourite daughter. "Though she would do better if she could only trust her own gifts. I am certain she saw something more in the mirror." There is a pause as both parents contemplate their eldest child. "I have been thinking of sending her to Rome."

"To *Rome*?" Catia draws back, aghast. "Why would you say such a thing?"

"Other leaders in Britain send their children to the capital. To further their education. To win favour and make alliances. The Cantiaci have done it for years."

"They send their *sons*," Catia says, exasperated. "The Romans would never treat a woman with respect. Women are brood mares to them, nothing more."

"Perhaps marriage to a powerful enemy is not such a terrible strategy. It might keep our people safe. And her Latin is flawless."

"No. Never." Catia is horrified at the thought of her child in the clutches of some filthy barbarian. She wants to berate her husband, to tell him it is more honourable to fight your enemies than marry them, but they have argued about the merits of war so many times she doesn't have the stomach for it now. Sometimes she thinks her name is a curse. Catia means *war*, a destiny the gods have denied her, forever distorting the course of her life. Still, this doesn't mean she has to give way on *everything*.

"I suppose Solina is still a little young for marriage," Prasutagus says, deferring their argument without backing down.

"She is older than I was when I married you. You've always been oblivious to women's passions. *I* had to take *you* to bed, before you realised what I wanted."

Prasutagus laughs. "You were certainly the most impatient of brides. But not many women are as ferocious as you. Not many men, either."

"Bellenia has my fire. You should trust her more, the way you do Solina."

"The kingdom will be jointly theirs, as I've always promised." Catia had not meant to bring his death into their conversation, and she opens her mouth to interrupt, but Prasutagus shakes his head to stop her. "You will have to guide them when they succeed. I do not know if both Iceni tribes will accept their authority. I only pray that Rome will."

Catia does not insult her husband with false platitudes about his youth. Instead, she takes his face in her hands, so he must look directly into her dark blue eyes. "I forbid you to leave me. Do you hear? *I forbid you*."

The sadness in his expression makes her want to scream with rage. Or to weep. "My love," he says, tenderly taking her hands from his face and kissing her. "We need to sleep."

Catia leans over to extinguish the lamp. In the total darkness that follows the death of the flame, she reaches for her husband, even though she no longer feels safe when he holds her, only greater fear of losing him. Love, resentment and grief are tangled like a knot in her heart. Prasutagus is many things, not all of them admirable, but above all else, he is *hers*. She lies awake, her head on his chest, aware of the gentle rise and fall of his breathing. Eventually, she lets go and lies beside him, drifting off to the familiar sound of his murmured prayers, as she has on so many nights of their life together.

3

SOLINA

Spring has made little inroad into the woods. Bare branches with their sharp, tapering fingers of twig stretch upwards, hungry for sunlight. Only the blackthorn tree is in bloom, its white blossom a sudden explosion in the drab brown and grey. Underneath thick clusters of petals, I know the tree's talons grow like swords, ready to tear the flesh of any who come too close. Shining white as bone, the blackthorn is unearthly, a doorway to the Otherworld.

Before the tree's dark, twisted trunk, I stand beside my father, studying the remains of a newborn lamb. The air is heavy with the scent of blood and flowers.

"Tell me what you see," he says, pointing to the altar.

The lamb's lifeblood drips from the weathered wooden surface, its entrails spread out like wool carded for spinning. The art of divination is easier than listening for the voices of the gods, but it still requires a leap of faith. I study the shape of the guts, the creature's small heart, then let the colours swim before my eyes into shades of dark red, pink and white, searching for the image behind them. *The mouth of a beast.* A sign which might mean many things, none of them good.

"The wolf," I say. "Is that also what you see?"

My father nods. "The mark of Andraste. She is present."

Andraste the Indestructible, protector of my mother's people, known for her bloodlust. I shudder. "Why is she here?"

My father says nothing. Silence stretches between us and my heart sinks. I know what this means. He wants me to wait, to hear what the gods tell me. I try to empty my mind, to slow my breathing, the way he has taught me, to invoke the trance-like state I have seen him enter when he walks in the Otherworld. The birdsong grows louder, my own noisy thoughts swirl in my head like stones in a pan, and my heartbeat thrums, but no voice comes. My feet remain sunk in the moss of the mortal wood. I glance at my father, his eyes closed, a look of serenity upon his face, and feel a burst of rage towards the gods. *Where are you? Why won't you hear me? I command you to speak!*

There is no answer. I want to cry with frustration, when, to my utter astonishment, I see the top of the blackthorn bend as a crow lands upon it. The creature stamps its clawed feet, settling itself, then looks down upon my father and me, head cocked. Waiting.

"Solina," my father whispers, gripping my arm. "*I did not call her. What does she say to you?*"

I gaze up at the crow, staring into its unblinking black eyes. The creature's appearance has so astounded me I half expect it to open its beak and speak with a human voice. Then, after a moment, it shuffles its wings and flies off. I feel like a fool.

"Nothing," I stammer. "She said nothing."

"Yet you called her?" My father's voice is eager.

"I... I think so."

"What feeling was behind the request? How did you call the spirit to you?"

My cheeks burn with shame. "Rage. I felt rage."

"Then you speak to her through fire. Perhaps you will also hear her through fire."

I have rarely seen my father so pleased, not even when I outdo him in Latin. He clearly believes the crow came from the Otherworld. I do not feel so sure. Perhaps it was just an ordinary bird? Or worse, perhaps it *was* a spirit, but I was unworthy to hear its message. "How do you *know* it's the spirits who speak to you?" I burst out. "How can you be certain you've understood what they say?" My father looks surprised. I have never been this blunt with him before. I wonder if I've made a mistake, but then I think of the tension between him and my mother, the growing threat of Roman violence, and know I cannot stay silent. "How do you know we are not meant to go to war? How can you be sure? Rome is destroying the Druids in the west. What happens when they turn to us?" My father stretches out his hand to take mine, his bones sharp through the thinning skin. We are alone in the sacred grove with nobody to overhear us but our horses and the gods themselves. "Tell me," I insist. "Please. Tell me how you know."

"I first saw the might of Rome twenty years ago, at Camulodunum." My father closes his eyes as if watching the scene unfold. "Their Emperor came with monsters from the Otherworld, the size of which you cannot imagine. The creatures were dressed as engines of war. The men called them elephants, claiming they were ordinary beasts, but some believed our enemy had harnessed the power of the gods." I wait, trying to contain my impatience. None of this is new. "Leaders of the Catuvellauni and Cantiaci were the first to pledge allegiance. Others followed. I prayed to the gods for guidance, and Epona, Goddess of Souls, blessed me with a vision. She revealed that I must pledge allegiance to Rome for a season, but when that season ended, the Iceni will ride to war again. And they will win. That is the revelation which has kept us at peace all these years. The prophecy that allowed me to keep our people's loyalty and prevent Rome from destroying us. In this way, I fulfilled the destiny of my name: Prasutagus."

Prasutagus: *Divine Chief*. I look away from my father, wanting to hide my disappointment. He has not answered my question, only given me a story as well-worn as the stones at our feet. "I am sorry I questioned you," I say. "I will wait for the gods to reveal themselves to me."

"There is something I have not told you before. About the form of the vision." I turn back to my father, surprised. His eyes are open again, and he holds my gaze with an unsettling intensity. "I saw our homes burning, the sacred woods bright with fire, and our fields running red with Iceni blood. It was a prophecy of death. And I knew that *I* held the power to stop this. Tell me, Solina, did this vision come from the gods or my own mind?"

I stare back at him, trying to understand. Is it possible my father *himself* does not know? Is that what he wants to tell me, here in the secrecy of the wood? I think of all the people who have sworn allegiance to their leader, the divine Prasutagus, purely on the strength of his prophecy. "It must have been from the gods."

My father smiles. "I faced a choice between preserving life or fighting for my own pride. And I chose life. What good is a leader who sacrifices the people he is sworn to protect? My reign has been devoted to the gods, Solina, and their will is not only revealed through visions. It is revealed through study, through deep understanding of the forces that bind our mortal lives together and tear them apart. That is where the true power of a Druid lies, in the use we make of our wits. It is that which sets us above others."

I stare at him, wanting to be sure I have truly understood. "You mean I should lie about what I see?"

"No!" He shakes his head. "You give the *truth* to people in a form they will accept. And if you cannot hear the gods, let your own mind be the power you wield. There is no shame in it. Every Druid knows this is how we serve the gods' sacred purpose." His hands clasp my shoulders as he pulls me close and kisses me upon the top of the head. "This is the knowledge my own father, the great Druid Antedrig, once passed on to me. We are destined to rule others, Solina, by whatever means we may."

When we return home, my mother is standing in the courtyard, awaiting our arrival. Seeing her brings up a sick feeling of guilt. My father is the most pious, most devoted follower of the gods. I do not doubt this. And yet he has just confessed to me that he does not always know whether the visions he sees are divine or come from his own mind, that he uses his power to manipulate and command other people, to shape our shared destiny. I wonder if my mother knows this. I tell myself that she does, though in my heart, I know she cannot. She would never have followed her husband's counsel all these years if she thought the prophecies she served came from a man, not a god.

I watch as she holds her hands out to him in greeting, and he kisses her. "Solina summoned a spirit from the Otherworld," he declares. "A crow. It seems she does indeed share her animal-guide with me. Just as I have always foretold."

My guilt deepens when I see the joy on my mother's face, and I wonder if this foretelling about me is also an invention. "Solina! What message did she bring you?"

I know from the hunger in her eyes that my mother hopes the gods spoke to suit her own desires. "I lacked the ability to hear," I murmur, wishing my father had not raised her hopes. "But I saw the mark of the Indestructible on the altar."

"Andraste was present in her wolf form," my father confirms.

His hands are still clasped around my mother's. My parents stare at one another as if some private understanding has passed between them. My mother does not look at me as she speaks. "You must go to your sister now. She is training with Cunominus."

"Is she not weaving?" I ask. I had left Bellenia at the loom and had been looking forward to joining her, to gain some respite from the endless churn of my thoughts. Weaving is hard work, but it also requires deep concentration, and while my fingers are busy, my mind may lie still for a while.

"You saw the mark of Andraste." My mother turns to me. "A sign of war. You must prepare to serve her."

I glance from her to my father, uncertain. There is no trace of the usual tension between them, no indication that he disputes the need to prepare for battle. Perhaps he has finally given in. I think again of his prophesy about Rome, a vision that has kept the peace for twenty years. Has he allowed my mother to take power because of his age, or does he truly believe the divinely allotted season for peace has ended? He holds my gaze, his eyes full of sadness.

"Your mother is right, Solina. You must go where the goddess leads you."

4

CATIA

Catia hears the boy before she sees him. He bursts into the hall where she sits weaving with her daughters, screaming for help. A crowd of servants follow, and the mass of fearful, shouting people blocks the light from the doorway. Catia rises. Behind her, she hears a serving girl's spindle clatter to the floor.

"What's happened?" she demands, crossing swiftly to the child.

The boy clutches her tunic. "My mother… They took her away." He tries to tell her more, but his sobs make it hard to understand what he is saying. Catia places a hand protectively over the child's head, anger gripping her heart.

"Where did he come from?" She looks round the hall for answers.

"The salterns," says a breathless girl. "Roman soldiers are stealing the salt. They are taking people."

Catia stares at the frightened faces before her, cast into shadow from the sunlight behind. She knows it is not *her* they want. They have come to find the king. But Prasutagus is in bed at her insistence, hoping rest will ease the terrible pain in his chest.

"Bellenia!" she calls. Her younger daughter runs forward,

eyes wide with fear. "Fetch Riomanda. And make sure this child is cared for. I will speak to the king."

Prasutagus is pale, his face shining with sweat. His chest rises and falls, but Catia can see from the white knuckles of his clenched hand on the bedclothes that it must hurt to breathe. For a moment she cannot even remember why she came here. He looks so much worse than he did this morning. She touches him gently, feeling a shudder pass through his body as he wakes.

"What is it?" His eyes search hers, sensing her alarm. "What is wrong?"

"Roman invaders have attacked the salterns."

"Are they still there?"

"I don't know."

Prasutagus throws off the bedclothes, struggling to his feet. "Help me dress. I will ride out to them."

"You cannot ride like this." Catia rushes to take his arm, afraid he might fall. "I will go with Cunominus."

Prasutagus gestures impatiently for his cloak. "When have they ever struck so near us before? If they are bold enough to launch an attack this close to the Town of the Wolf, only the presence of the king will repel them."

Catia helps him dress in silence, wiping sweat from his face, even bending to help him with his boots like a servant. She does not want anyone else to see him at his weakest. For some days he has been unable to climb up easily to their loft chamber, sleeping instead in one of the beds at the back of the hall.

"You do not have to go," she says as he stands at the threshold. She reaches to touch his back, then withdraws her hand. "Please."

Prasutagus ignores her and closes his eyes, lips moving with prayer. Then he grips the curtain. He takes a breath before lifting it, and in the moment before he steps away from her, Catia sees him change. Whether it is through the power of the gods or the strength of his own will, Prasutagus sets aside the weight of his years and becomes again the man she needs him to be, striding forward as if every breath does not pain him, as if he feels no weakness at all.

Catia follows him into the clearing outside the hall. Riomanda and Cunominus are mounted on their horses, waiting. She can see the boy who ran for help is seated in front of Riomanda, clutching the corners of the saddle. Riomanda's arms surround him, gripping the reins, and the child is no longer crying, although his face is smeared with dirt where he wiped the tears. He gawps at the king's approach. Catia tries not to look anxious as Prasutagus climbs the mounting block to his horse, but his apparent ease reassures her. When he is safely in the saddle, she swings herself up onto hers.

Prasutagus rides towards Riomanda and the boy. "Guide us," he says, his voice carrying the familiar note of command.

Their ride through town draws people onto the streets, some choosing to follow the king on foot or horseback. Rumours of the raid have clearly spread – many are already armed with scythes, hammers and knives. Some cheer, eager to join, but others look fearful, watching them pass. The sight of their cowardice pains Catia. In her childhood, every street of this town would have been bristling with warriors, ready to kill or die in its defence, but Roman rule has weakened their pride.

They ride out onto the marshland, and the silence makes Catia feel small. She begins to sing, recounting one of the well-known legends of Andraste. At the sound of her voice, others join in, slowly growing bolder, until their song swells towards the vast sky glowing white above them. Behind the clouds, the sun is trapped like the Otherworld on the far side of the mirror. Yet as they draw closer to the salterns, rising smoke stains the heavens.

Catia knows what this means. Iceni homes are on fire. Anger burns in her chest, and she can feel it spread through the crowd too. Their singing tapers off, replaced by shouts and curses. She glances around, wishing they had brought more riders, but the crowd of people from town is bigger than she first thought – perhaps they have been emboldened by the king's presence. Waved and jabbed in anger, the crowd's axes and shovels look more like real weapons.

They are soon engulfed by the stench of burning and the sound of screaming. It is a raid. All Catia's senses are heightened, and she sees everything in fragments, shattered by fear and smoke. Her eyes dart to where fire is raging through blackened homes, where thieves attack any who resist. One Roman waggon is laden with caskets of stolen salt, ready to flee, while another is at the centre of a savage struggle. Armed men are shoving their captives inside, beating back frantic survivors desperate to save their families from slavery. In the crush, people are stumbling over their own dead, trampling bodies into the mud. Catia's eye is drawn to a young girl in a bright green dress. A man is forcing her into the waggon, twisting her dark hair in his hands, and she is screaming, although in the tumult, Catia cannot hear the sound, only see her open mouth. She recoils, as if the violence were happening to her and not the stranger.

Prasutagus stands beside her on the path, his face hard to read.

"Are we enough?" she asks. "What if they attack us too?"

"They will not." The certainty in his voice is infuriating.

Their arrival has not gone unnoticed. The raiders bunch

together around their stolen slaves and salt, watching the king's approach, their weapons raised. With disgust, Catia sees some of the thieves are Britons, most likely from the Catuvellauni tribe, who are forever trailing after their Roman masters like carrion. She murmurs a prayer to Andraste, asking the goddess to strike down her enemies.

Prasutagus does not hurry his pace. Surely the thieves must understand who he is. They have launched an attack on the Iceni king's very doorstep, and now he is here, wearing the golden torc which marks him out as leader, his cloak richer than the salt they have stolen, a shimmering fabric of blue and red. He turns in the saddle and holds up his hand, a gesture for the others to stay back, then rides close to the raiders, Catia beside him. He begins speaking the enemy tongue, and her feeling of powerlessness grows. Only a few phrases are intelligible. "*I am Prasutagus, King of the Iceni, Servant of the Emperor Nero.*" The rest might be the grunting of hogs for all the sense it makes.

Unable to understand the words, she watches her enemies' faces. The Romans seem uneasy, while the Catuvellauni are contemptuous. Prasutagus is speaking with a man who is clearly the ringleader – most likely a former soldier, as most of the worst violence is inflicted by veterans of the invasion. The man is getting heated, but Prasutagus remains calm. He gestures at the waggon of salt, then at the captives, his face impassive, and the exchange seems unending, before the raider finally nods.

Prasutagus turns to his wife. "I have granted the salt as a gift to Rome. The captives will be released."

"They should take *nothing*!" Catia looks furiously between her husband and the thieves. "They deserve to die for what they have done."

"Spoken like an Iceni whore." It is one of the Catuvellauni, obviously angry at losing all the human plunder.

Prasutagus draws his sword, arm outstretched in warning. He speaks first in Latin, for the benefit of the Romans, then addresses the man directly, his voice full of contempt. "My allegiance is only to Rome, not to a tribe of dogs. Insult us again, and I will cut you down."

The man spits on the ground. "You don't frighten me, *old man.*"

The spear which fells the Briton comes so fast, he does not even have time to face it. Catia turns to see Cunominus has ridden forward. Her brother's fist is raised from letting the weapon fly, his face suffused with rage. The crowd behind him are shouting with anger, clearly eager to repay the raiders with blood.

Prasutagus speaks again, his voice loud enough to be heard over the yelling. The king shows no fear, even though the Romans are close enough to strike him down should anyone's nerve fail. He rides back and forth between the raiders and his own people, speaking both languages, so everyone can understand.

"We will grant you the salt as an act of generosity to Rome, and as a mark of the high honour in which the Iceni hold the Emperor. Our people will be released, unharmed. I warn you that our allegiance is only to Rome. Any who have come here from other tribes to steal will be killed, unless they leave immediately under Rome's protection."

Catia watches the Roman leader. The man has a calculating expression as he listens, his gaze flitting from the king to the mass of townspeople, clutching their axes and scythes. Surely he understands that refusal to agree to the king's terms will result in slaughter, not only for the Iceni but for many of his men too. She suspects it is this, rather than her husband's presence, which proves most persuasive. After all, the man has no honour to die for – he only came to steal. After a curt exchange with his followers, Catia watches the thieves set off swiftly with their booty of salt, not even bothering to untie those they have left behind.

With the Romans finally expelled, people surge forward, untying their neighbours and running to rescue the last smouldering house. Among the shouting and confusion, Catia loses sight of the girl in the green dress but is relieved to see the small boy who raised the alarm scrambling into the arms of a woman she hopes is his mother. Catia finds it hard to feel pride, with so many dead and unavenged. She turns to Prasutagus, ready to berate him, but the sight of his face stops her. His pallor is so severe that his skin looks blue, and he seem unable to sheath his sword. Instead, he is staring down at his own arm in confusion, as if it does not belong to him. Catia realises his body is trembling from the weight of holding up the weapon.

"We should return to town." She rides close beside him, her leg pressed against his horse, gripping him by his free arm. "Quickly."

Prasutagus stares at her. "Catia."

For the first time in all the years she has known him, her husband looks afraid. Then the king's sword drops from his hand into the mud.

"No!" Catia cries, unable to believe what she is seeing. Prasutagus sways in the saddle, almost pulling her from her own horse. "No," she repeats, seizing the reins of his horse and desperately trying to hold him upright. "*No.*"

Prasutagus slumps against her, the weight of his body making her own shake with the effort of preventing his fall. Even though he gives her no answer, she keeps begging him to live, holding him tighter as if that might prevent him from leaving. Only when Riomanda and Cunominus come, helping to save the king from the disgrace of falling from his horse, can Catia finally accept that he is dead.

5

SOLINA

It is dusk when we approach my father's birthplace. The City of the Horse looks blue in the distance, crouched like Andraste's wolf, back raised in conical rooftops, body encircled by the river which shines silver in the dying sun. I wonder if the city senses its king's absence, or whether my grief will seep into every stone I touch. A dull ache fills my chest. It feels so wrong that my father is not beside me; I have never been south without him.

He was almost entirely hidden the last time I saw him, his sunken face obscured, with only the bright colours of his robes showing the outline of his body on the tomb's stone slab. I watched as the last strands of willow were woven into his tall, woodland shroud, which lay open to the sky. The grove where we laid him just days ago is familiar to me – he took me to the place once, hidden deep in the forest. I had known then it was where he might one day cross to the Otherworld, that the god Taranis turns his wheel for all mortals, yet this does not comfort me now my father has gone. All I want is to hear his voice again. Not speaking through the spirits as he once promised he would, but through his own lips. Most of all, I want him to comfort me for the pain I feel at his loss.

I tilt my head to look up at the same darkening sky my father now faces but can no longer see. He lies on stone, shielded only by the willow shroud, becoming one with the woods, his eyes taken by the crows who will carry his spirit. And when nothing but his bones remain, then we will bring him back here, to the place of his birth.

The city looms larger as we draw closer. Its banks and ramparts tower over the Ecen Way, the long road which leads south to the Roman colony of Camulodunum and north to the Town of the Wolf. All our kingdom's wealth flows from here, passing through the city's great gates. Fields roll out on either side of us, peaceful in the fading light. We are on the eve of the growing season, and soon the quiet grasslands will be the site of hard labour. I shift on my seat. My joints are sore from the cart jolting over ruts in the road.

I turn to Riomanda, who sits beside me, guiding the two horses with a flick of the reins. I wonder if she misses Cunominus, coming here without him, or if the south brings back bad memories of her brother's killing.

"How long will you stay?" I ask. "Will you go back north after the feast to honour the king?"

"I will stay here as long as you need me," Riomanda replies with one of her rare smiles, before turning back to face the road. In front of us, Bellenia is travelling with our mother. Seen from behind and sat side by side, their blonde heads close together, they could almost be sisters.

"I think Bellenia will return to the north," I say. "And I will stay south, in the City of the Horse. It makes sense for us to be in different places, for the sake of the kingdom."

"The City of the Horse is richer than that of the Wolf," Riomanda says. "But also more dangerous. Rome has a stronger presence here."

"That is why it is better if I stay, as I speak Latin. My father told me it would be impossible to rule without negotiating with Rome's officials."

"You think you can negotiate with Rome? In my experience they only take." I have no reply to this. The creak of the wheels and thud of the horses' hooves fill the silence between us. Then Riomanda speaks again, her voice softer. "I will stay with you, Solina. Forever, if need be. Cunominus has told me he will move south, if we agree that is best for the defence of the kingdom. We would raise our child here. The Horse Tribe are still Iceni."

I know what a sacrifice it would be for Riomanda to leave the north, but I cannot bring myself to tell her I do not want her to move for me, because I do. I feel tears sting my eyes but blink hard, not wishing to look weak. I know Riomanda believes my mother will live in the north with my sister, and she is telling me I will not be abandoned. I wonder if Riomanda will love me as much when she has a child of her own, but I push away the thought as unworthy. "Thank you," I say.

She nods in acknowledgement, her profile blurred by the dim light. My love for her does not need to be spoken – it is understood by us both. It was Riomanda who explained to me what happened during the raid on the salterns, when my mother was too distraught to speak. My father's heart had failed, Riomanda said. That is what people saw, out on the marshland. The king had defied death to defend his people one final time, a soul-bargain with the gods, but when that was done, the gods took him to the Otherworld. I discovered later that my mother blamed herself, believing if she had only let him rest, he would have lived longer, but Riomanda told me it was Prasutagus's destiny to die as a warrior. Even death had not felled the king from his horse. One day, my mother would understand that this was a gift.

"Catia may be regent for some time," Riomanda says,

knowing me well enough to understand my thoughts will have turned, inevitably, to my mother. "She will not leave you and Bellenia to secure the kingdom unaided. Tomorrow's feast is only the first step in winning the tribes' loyalty."

I think of those leaders who will be called to gather at the City of the Horse with my father's kin. I have no stomach for the feast, but know that, as his heirs, Bellenia and I will be expected to hide our grief and win the confidence of the Iceni. The thought of ruling in my father's place is overwhelming. He stood between our people and the might of Rome his whole life, until the weight of that burden broke his heart. Now he has gone, I am not sure there is anyone left alive strong enough to bear it.

We reach a large cluster of new buildings outside the city's ramparts, which sour the air with cooking smells. They are rectangular in the Roman style, daubed red and yellow – the homes and workshops of foreign settlers. I feel uneasy passing through this stretch of road. A shrine to an alien god is painted at the corner of a shop selling colourful glazed pots, and a brace of hare hang outside a butcher's, the animals' blood pooling onto the ground beneath. I shudder. No Briton would ever touch a hare, a creature sacred to the gods. Aggression simmers in this place, as pungent as the stench of roasting meat, and men drinking outside a tavern stop their chat to watch us pass. One makes an obscene gesture at my sister, and Riomanda hisses with anger.

"Don't look at them, Solina. They are lower than vermin."

If they were Britons, my mother would have taken the man's hand for that gesture. But they are Romans, so we are forced to let them be. I look away.

It is close to nightfall when at last we cross the river. The sky glows pink behind the city, the gatehouse casting a long shadow. A metal horse for Epona rides over the arch, her mane flaring in twisted spikes like the last beams of the sun. The Horse's gates are bigger than those of the Wolf, the massive wooden pillars carved with scenes of battle, but for all its grandeur the place does not inspire me with the same sense of safety. The pikes above Epona's horse are bare: no human heads hang here. It would be too dangerous for the Iceni to make such a show of strength in the south where only Rome is permitted to execute criminals. This is my country, yet the drunk settlers we just passed on the road have more rights than I do.

We gather around my father's hearth, and I sit beside my sister, bone-weary from the journey. The roundhouse is bigger than that of our mother's family, used for ceremony and feasting, making our group seem even smaller, like mice huddled around the glowing fire. Scenes from the legends of Epona, goddess of this city, are painted on the walls which surround us, while our family's wealth shines in a display of golden horse harnesses and hanging tapestries. My father was raised in this hall, and he told me it was here that the goddess first blessed him with the sight. Now his chair sits empty by the fire. I turn my face so I do not have to see it. Along with my grief is another darker feeling I can scarcely bear to acknowledge – the fear my father may not have been the man I thought. The fear he may have led the kingdom through lies.

A messenger was already sent ahead to announce his death, but my father's family want to hear the tale of his passing again. My mother relays it all. Flames illuminate her face, lighting up the red of her cloak and the gold shine of her brooch. She gives no sign of her terrible grief that frightened me so much on the day my father died. I watch my cousin Aesu as he listens, worrying he may not understand how much my mother loved the king. Aesu and I were close as children – he learned Latin with me – but as we grew older, I sensed his growing coldness. He is suspicious of the Wolf Tribe. The rot started after the warrior Caratacus came here in his golden cloak, asking my parents to join his rebellion. I was only a child then, but I can still remember how my mother screamed and raged, smashing a glass goblet into the fire when my father refused to fight against Rome. No doubt Aesu remembers this too.

"Why would the king have ridden out to challenge thieves himself?" Aesu asks, his blue eyes narrowed. "Surely it was beneath him?"

"You know how bold the Romans are growing," my mother says. "He felt only the presence of the king would deter them."

"And who will deter them now? The Romans have no respect for women leaders."

"They respect Cartimandua," I say, unable to ignore his provocation.

"The Queen of the Brigantes?" Aesu retorts. "A woman who replaced her husband with his armour-bearer, who is more interested in fulfilling her own desires than the good of her tribe?"

"A woman who holds the northern kingdoms of Britain through birthright." Bellenia's cheeks are flushed with anger. "Cartimandua's first husband was a nobody. She had every right to replace him."

"The Horse Tribe have never respected birthright alone. Prasutagus reigned through the will of the gods and his own unblemished honour."

My mother raises her hand for silence, as if we were nothing more than squabbling children. "Thank you, Aesu, for schooling us in my husband's honour. I am familiar with the quality of the man whose reign I shared. The man who commanded the Wolf Tribe solely through marriage to me."

"We are not in the north now." Aesu glances at Riomanda, standing by my mother's shoulder, knowing as I do that a dagger will be hidden in the folds of her tunic.

"No," my mother responds. "We are in the City of the Horse, where Romans sit at our gates and kill the gods' hares without punishment." Aesu tries to object, but she merely raises her voice to drown out his interruption. "Who does it benefit if we sit here fighting among ourselves? Who was robbing the salterns when Prasutagus died?"

My cousin glares at my mother, as if he might continue his challenge. She gazes back with the cold curiosity of a hawk contemplating its prey. After a pause, Aesu looks down at the floor. "I am merely saddened by the death of the king," he says. "I do not wish to insult you, Catia."

"I know you loved Prasutagus." She reaches over to rest her hand on his shoulder. "Which is why I would ask you to read his will before we deliver it to the Roman legate. The king wrote in Latin, which you know I cannot speak."

Aesu glances at me, eyes sharp. "Solina also knows Latin."

My mother nods. "Still, I would ask you to read it. We have the choice now – either stay united or split the Iceni kingdom. Prasutagus has gone. But I trust you to respect his judgement, even so."

Riomanda hands Aesu the precious roll of vellum on which my father inscribed his will. I stare at the flames while my cousin unwraps it, hoping to hear my father speak through him.

"*To the Emperor Nero, Caesar Augustus, Pontifex Maximus, Pater Patria,*

I, King Prasutagus, son of Antedrig, entrust the kingdoms of the Iceni both to Nero and to my two daughters, Solina and Bellenia, blood of my blood, protectors of the tribes of the Horse and the Wolf. May my enduring loyalty to Rome be the guarantor of my daughters' peaceful succession, and of their undying service to the Emperor. This is the last recorded Will of Prasutagus, divine leader of the Iceni, twice blessed by the gods."

The fire dances red and white, the colours of the Otherworld where my father now walks, unable to impose his will upon the living. I feel Bellenia shift beside me. The weight of the king's request sits even more heavily on her than it does on me. I know she has no real wish to rule, that she does not feel ready. I look up at our mother. Her hands are clasped, knuckles shining. The will does not name her as regent, even though we all know that is what our father wanted. It is certainly what Bellenia and I want. Aesu watches her closely.

"Prasutagus did not mention you," he says.

"He did not believe Rome would look kindly upon me. Better that Bellenia and Solina rule as *his* daughters, rather than as mine."

For a moment I think Aesu might argue, but instead, he nods, his shoulders hunching slightly, as if he too finds the weight of what we all face too heavy to carry. "Will Rome accept my uncle's will?" He sounds more like the child I remember. "Will they leave us in peace?"

"Prasutagus believed so," my mother replies.

Aesu folds up the vellum, placing it in the folds of his tunic, against his breast. "Then in the morning I will ride to London and deliver this to the procurator Catus Decianus myself. May the gods deliver us."

6

CATIA

The light of the rising sun grows stronger, blessing the roundhouse through the open doorway. Catia watches its rays spread across the floor, gold as honey, while shafts of light dance to the rafters. She never slept downstairs here when Prasutagus lived. The king had his own private chamber in the loft above, where her daughters now lie in darkness, granted the honour of the royal bed as his heirs. The rest of the family sleep in the hall below, their small bedchambers ranged at the back of the building, screened by wicker walls and draped in tapestries.

Through a sliver of light in her cocoon, Catia watches the world wake. Servants are raking the hearth, bringing in water, rolling up rugs from the floor to be beaten outside. The shuffle of their feet and murmur of their voices is comforting, like the hum of bees. A little further off from Catia's own chamber, she sees Aesu's mother, Vassura, draw her curtain.

Catia sits up, rolling her shoulders and stretching. She steps into the hall, the tapestry falling shut behind her. The south has never felt like home, and so the drop in status to a bed downstairs has not distressed her. Besides, it's useful to sleep near her husband's kin now that he has gone. The loss of Prasutagus is a curse stretching ahead of her like a road she has no choice but to walk. He infuriated her at times, yet she loved him deeply, and his calm presence was always steadying, as reliable as the beat of her own heart.

Life is even lonelier now she has sent Riomanda home to the north. After several weeks in this place, Catia decided the presence of another warrior from the Wolf Tribe aroused more suspicion than it was worth. The Horse Tribe are traders, well used to strangers, yet they prefer their own to hold all the positions of power.

Vassura begins busying herself at the loom by the doorway, eager to make the most of the morning sunlight. The women of the family are working together on a tapestry to honour the dead king, a record of his deeds in the mortal realm and an image of his new kingdom in the Otherworld. The stone weights sway at the bottom of the loom as Vassura's fingers pull at the threads, and beside her, serving girls spin wool into thread with their reddened fingers. Catia is not sure about all the elements of Vassura's storytelling. Prasutagus's sister has chosen to include the elephants of the Emperor Claudius as a symbol of her brother's status as Rome's client king. Catia understands the reason for the gesture but still feels the less of Rome recorded in her husband's life, the better. She heads to the pool of light in the doorway, catching the arm of a servant girl as she passes, ordering her to wake the girls upstairs.

"Perhaps Aesu will return today," Vassura remarks, the same greeting she has given Catia every morning in the weeks since her son left for London.

Catia smiles, even though she too is growing anxious at the long silence. "I am sure he will, sister."

The two women work silently together, until Catia's daughters descend from the upper floor. Bellenia's dress is as bright as the bluebells carpeting the woods, woven by the town's finest craftswomen. Catia feels affection flood through her. Bellenia is more beautiful than the sunrise, and as her face gradually loses the soft curve of childhood, she looks ever more like Prasutagus when he was young. Solina follows behind her sister, dressed in blood-red, the colour most beloved of her father's family. She looks pale. Catia has the urge to embrace Solina, or to comfort her, but grief has not brought them closer. Instead, Solina has withdrawn even further into herself.

"Do you think father's spirit will be pleased by this?" Bellenia asks, slipping an arm around Catia's waist.

"Of course." Catia glances at Solina, who has said nothing, not even a greeting, but is instead frowning at the border of marching elephants.

"He told me they were monsters of the Otherworld," Solina says, in her usual abrupt manner. "I don't believe he liked them much."

"They tell the story of his life," Vassura retorts, annoyed. "The reasons why he was a great warrior. It can't all be feasting."

Solina shrugs and gathers up some thread, clearly unconvinced. Bellenia lingers by Catia. "Are we not going riding this morning?"

"No," Catia says. "You should help us here. It is better we honour your father."

"I will forget how to use a sword," Bellenia grumbles, going to join her equally surly sister.

Catia feels a sudden blaze of anger at them both. "You are heirs to the kingdom," she snaps. "Not children. We are telling the story of your father's life, so that it can be hung here, in the hall of his ancestors. Nothing is more important than that. And nobody but the women of his family are worthy of undertaking such a sacred task."

"*Catia.*" Vassura's voice is low with warning. "Who is that approaching?"

It takes Catia a moment to focus on where Vassura is pointing. Then she sees them. Roman soldiers, advancing on the roundhouse. In the bright sunlight, their mail shines silver like the dead underbelly of a fish. There are many. Maybe thirty, maybe more. Too many for her to fight off unaided. And they are already too close to make a run for the horses, her daughters would be impaled by spears from behind as they fled. Catia looks back into the house, where the servants are gathering in a terrified huddle by the hearth. "Our weapons," she shouts. "Bring them to me."

"Will that not antagonise them?" Vassura's eyes are wide with fear.

A servant boy runs to Catia, clutching her sword in his hand. She seizes it. "This is all I could find," he gabbles. "Please don't be angry, I don't know where you hide them."

Catia whips round to her daughters, who are both watching the men approach, frozen with shock. "Go upstairs," she commands. "*Now.*"

"No." It is Solina, her face drained of colour. "Mother, you won't know what they are saying."

Catia has no time to argue – the leader of the men is already in the doorway, his sword drawn. His face is in shadow, almost blacked out by the sun behind. He shouts at her in his incomprehensible tongue, pointing the tip of his weapon between her and Vassura. It quivers in the air, and Catia stares at the bright blade, watching its point rather than look at the centurion's face. He handles a sword with ease, like a man used to violence. Catia hears Solina answer him in Latin, her voice low and steady, then Solina speaks to her urgently, in their own language. "He asks us who is the widow of Prasutagus. I have explained that it is you, mother, that I will translate for you."

"Ask him why he comes armed to the house of Rome's most loyal of kings."

Solina speaks to the man, but in answer he merely gestures at another soldier who hands him a stained brown bag. The centurion reaches inside, then draws something out, clasping a fistful of what looks like hair. Before Catia has time to understand what she is seeing, the man has thrown the object at her feet. Instinctively, she looks down. Looking back at her is a battered head, almost unrecognisable, framed by distinctive braids of red hair. Her nephew. Aesu.

Vassura lets out a scream of anguish. The sound slices through Catia, making her gasp, as Vassura prostrates herself on the floor. One of the soldiers knocks the sobbing mother with the butt of his spear, angry when he realises she has seized the remains of her son. Vassura clasps Aesu's head to her chest, cradling it to her body, just as Catia remembers her once holding him as a small child. She steps towards the centurion in anguish and rage, but before she can get any closer, a spear flies into the roundhouse. Catia turns. The weapon is lodged in the ground, a hair's breadth from Bellenia, who is now frozen beside the ladder into the loft. She must have tried to sneak off to retrieve the swords. Behind her, the servants are pressed against the back wall, clutching one another and weeping. Bellenia's face is white with shock, her fingers still gripping the first rung to safety.

Catia wants to go to her, to rip the spear from the ground. But the centurion is shouting again, his hatred clear, even though his words are unintelligible.

"If anyone else tries to escape," Solina says, "he warns that we will be killed where we stand."

"Why are you here?" Catia looks the man in the eyes, even

though she knows he cannot understand her. He begins to speak. She watches his mouth as it moves. His pink lips are wet, spewing evil which takes shape in the soft voice of her daughter.

"He says that our father's will was an insult to Rome. That the kingdom of the Iceni belongs to the Emperor Nero alone. That the kingdom was never in our father's gift. He says…" Solina's voice falters, and Catia turns from the centurion to look at her eldest daughter.

"You are brave," Catia says. "Braver than they will ever be. Tell me."

Solina takes in a shuddering breath, the same way Catia remembers her doing as a child, when she was on the verge of tears. "He says you will be flogged and your daughters raped, so that the Iceni see how rebels are punished. So that we understand we are lower than beasts."

Spoken into the air, the centurion's words seem to expand, like a monster uncoiling. Catia holds Solina's gaze. The fear she sees in her daughter's eyes is searing; it is a pain that burns her soul to ash. Blood roars in her ears, louder than the pounding of the sea, and her heart hammers against the walls of her chest. She steps in front of Solina, hiding her from the soldiers' hated gaze. There is a hiss as Catia draws her blade from its sheath, then silence falls in the hall of the dead king. She stares at the centurion. Her voice, when she speaks, is dark with rage.

"I swear by Andraste, goddess of war, that if you touch my daughters you will pay for it in blood. The bones of your people will rot unmourned in a land that was never theirs, and your mothers will pray you had not been born, rather than endure the suffering I will inflict upon you."

The centurion laughs, and after a quick glance over his shoulder to give a word of command, he steps into the hall.

7

SOLINA

I am falling through darkness, deep under the earth. Above me, a pool of light glows, shimmering like a mirror. I must be in the Otherworld. The thought does not bring fear or hope. My heart is blank. I close my eyes to the light. Time drifts, and the dark is a comfort.

Soft murmurs and dappled sunshine hover at the edge of my senses. Close enough to grasp if I choose, yet I do not open my eyes. I hear my mother's voice, crooning a lullaby, but as the refrain repeats, low and gentle, I realise it is not my mother, it is my aunt Vassura. I cannot imagine why she is here. She is speaking to me, but I do not want to listen. The touch of her hand, stroking my hair, sends ripples of dread down my spine. I turn away.

My sister is crying, over and over. My dread deepens. Bellenia never sounds like that. It cannot be her voice. Perhaps there is a hare, caught in the fields above. The bodies of the animals strung up outside the butcher on the road take shape in my mind, and I see them again, more vivid than memory – their soft fur matted with blood, their slender bodies limp. I want to shut out the sight, but my eyes are already closed.

Feeling begins to come back to me, breaking in waves of

pain. I know where I am. Not in the Otherworld, but in my father's house, lying in the royal bed under the thatch, light filtering through the reeds above. My head hurts so badly, I feel it must have split open. Perhaps I move then, or make some noise, because the bed sinks from the weight of another leaning on it.

"*You are safe, my darling.*"

It is Vassura. I open my eyes. My aunt is leaning over me, so close I can feel the warmth of her breath on my skin. It takes a while to focus on her face. Her eyes are red-rimmed from weeping, and she looks haggard, as if grief has hollowed her out.

I stare at her, unable to form words, my head throbbing with pain.

"You are safe," Vassura repeats.

"Where is my mother? My sister?" The sound of my own voice frightens me, it is so cracked. Vassura leans forward to give me water, but I push the cup away after a mouthful. "Where are they?" I repeat.

"They are... recovering."

"From what? Is there a sickness?"

My questions seem to surprise Vassura. She is clutching the cup, as if at a loss for what to say. "No. You were... injured," she says at last, looking down at her clenched knuckles rather than at my face. "Solina, you were hit very hard on the head."

I touch myself cautiously on my temple where it hurts the most. An injury. This explains my confusion, my time in the Otherworld. I try to remember the moment before the blow, how I came to be here, but my thoughts are still jumbled and hard to grasp. "Did I fall from Tan?"

My aunt makes a choking noise, and I realise she is crying. Her shoulders shake with the effort of containing her grief, and the sight of her weeping sparks something inside. I have seen her cry like this before. Other images cascade through my mind, swift and hard as hail in a storm. The doorway to our home, dark with the figures of men. The bright silver of a Roman sword pointed at my mother. The red of my cousin Aesu's hair on the floor.

My sister's face when they seized her. And my mother, surrounded. Fighting until they swarmed her like ants, devouring her.

I cover my face with my hands. The images are disjointed, as if my memory were a glass vessel, smashed into pieces. I do not want to touch their edges. I do not want to see.

"There, my love, there." Vassura's voice is soft. I realise that I am crying, that she is trying to hold me. It is not comforting. Panic surges through me, and I think I might vomit. I push her away.

"Bellenia! Where is she? I want my sister! I want my mother!" I try to struggle out of bed, but my head is swimming, and I do not have the strength to resist Vassura, who bundles me back in.

"I will go downstairs," she says. "I will see if they are well enough to come see you."

I watch my aunt descend the steps, see her head disappear into the hall of the roundhouse. I want to get up, but I'm exhausted. Even sitting up is too much. *None of this is real*, I tell myself. *It cannot be real.* I close my eyes, listening to the birdsong, willing myself to wake up in my old life.

"Solina!" My mother is pulling herself up into the loft, gasping with the effort. Bruises mark her face, and she does not move like herself. At the edge of the bed, she catches hold of the wood, as if struggling to walk, and shuffles along its side until she is sat close to me. "You are alive," she whispers, gently laying her palm on my cheek. I place my hand over hers. For the first time since I woke, I feel safe. But then I realise there is a tremor in her hand, that she is in pain.

"Are you hurt?" I ask.

"I was flogged." Her tone is dismissive, as if such an act of violence were nothing. "The injuries are healing."

"Why isn't Bellenia here?"

"She is sleeping. She was... more badly hurt than you."

"Please," I say, starting to cry. "Please tell me she isn't dead."

"No, my darling. She is not dead. And you will both get better now. You will take back your honour. I promise."

I stare into my mother's eyes. The intensity of her gaze is no longer soothing. I feel ugly, as if what she sees is not me, her daughter, but my shame. I had wanted to hear her reassurance that nothing has changed, that I am unchanged. That any shame rests only with the men who did this. Instead, I feel myself transformed through the bitterness of her words. I am dishonoured.

"Catia." It is my aunt, hovering behind my mother's shoulder, her head dipping like a moorhen. "She has only just woken. You will distress her."

"Solina is not a child to be soothed by lullabies." My mother winces as she turns too quickly. "She is a warrior of the Wolf Tribe, heir to her father's kingdom. Of course she will want to take back her honour. And she will."

Her words are not a promise *to* me, I realise; they are a promise she wants *from* me. "I had no weapon to defend myself," I say, feeling hollow. "I was unarmed."

My mother nods, her vehemence showing me she has missed my meaning. "Yes. They were cowards. Next time, you will be armed, and you will defeat them. I know it. You are still a warrior, Solina."

There is desperation in her face, and it frightens me. My

eyes fill with tears. I turn away from my mother and my aunt, facing the dark, slanting lines of the roof. "I am tired," I say. "Please leave me."

Days pass, and still Bellenia does not come. Sound and movement from the hall below drifts up to where I lie, the familiar murmur of daily ritual, and I often struggle to stay awake, let alone get up. I allow my aunt to treat me like a child, bringing me bread soaked in honey, stroking my hair when I complain that my head hurts. Sometimes I wonder if this is as much to soothe her own broken heart as it is to heal mine. All the unspent love she has for her dead son needs a home.

At night, the attack returns to me in terrifying, vivid images. I see their faces, and am suffocated by their weight, the overwhelming horror of the rape leaving me drenched in sweat. But when I try to piece together what happened, to become master of my own story, my memories elude me, darting from my grasp like fish in a fast-flowing stream. Vassura tells me this is a blessing and resists my questions. When I press her, she feeds me fragments, dipped in honeyed words like the bread. *Your mother fought bravely, but there were too many men for her to stand a chance. Catia was flogged in the yard, her back so badly injured nobody expected her to survive, yet she recovered, inspired by love for her daughters.*

It is by accident my aunt lets slip that not all the Romans who attacked us have left the city, when she complains about our neighbours' stolen cattle. This is how I learn that the soldiers and their freedmen are still here, drinking and laughing at the inn outside the city walls, stealing from any house they please. It was not enough for them to dishonour us, they came back to ransack our home the day after the rape, seizing the gold and silver harnesses and all the ceremonial bronze which belonged to my family for generations. They even stole my father's sacred tools of divination. I think of him holding his knife shaped like a hare, the one he always used for the most important sacrifices. It seems impossible that the knife is gone. I remember the weight of it in my fingers, the sharpness of the blade, the hare's glinting eyes and the promise it would one day be mine.

More days pass. I grow stronger. My head no longer hurts so much, while nausea and exhaustion lessen their grip. I limp around the small chamber, trying not to think about where I hurt. The knowledge of what was done to my body is like a chasm I do not dare approach, for fear of falling. The world below the loft is frightening too. When I go down that ladder, everything that happened to my sister and me will become real. I cannot face it yet.

Bellenia is the one who finally breaks the silence between us. Her cry wakes me in the night. I open my eyes to darkness, uncertain if her screaming is real, or an echo of my dreams. It takes me a moment to realise that she is calling my name. Terror grips me. *Have the men come back?* I lie rigid at the thought. Then Bellenia screams again. Her anguish startles me into life, and I scramble from the bed, clumsy in the dark, feeling my way to the opening. A red glow from the embers in the hearth glints below. The slats of the ladder are smooth against the soles of my feet, the air cool on my legs. My body remembers the way down without me having to think, and my confidence grows with each step. I jump from the last rung onto the beaten floor.

One of the tapestries lining the wall has been cast aside. I see my mother and aunt standing by the open bedchamber, trying to hold my sister still. I hurry across the hall.

"I'm here, Bellenia!" I cry, startling the others, whose faces shine like pale moons.

My sister is sitting on the edge of the bed. She stretches out her arms to me. "I heard them, Solina! They were coming for you. I had to stop them." I clasp her hands, only noticing the livid mark on her cheek as she pulls me closer.

"Are they here?" I turn to our mother in terror. "Where?"

"I heard them," Bellenia repeats.

"You were dreaming," Vassura says. "It was a dream."

"They never leave me alone." Bellenia is crying now. I can feel her sobs shake my own body as she holds me. "I can't bear it, Solina."

Pain winds tighter and tighter in my chest, my heart consumed by a nameless feeling whose grip strengthens the longer my sister cries. I feel that if I stay like this, helpless while she weeps, I will not be able to breathe. "They will never come near you again," I say. "Not while I am living." I take Bellenia's face in my hands. My sister's skin is blotched from weeping, a dark welt scarring her cheekbone. The tightness in my chest almost makes it too painful to speak. "You are stronger than they are."

"But I'm not." There is a dullness to her contradiction. She is not sparring with me.

"You will be armed next time! You will be stronger!" I am desperate to rouse her, to bring her back to herself, but realise I sound like our mother, repeating words which have not brought me any comfort.

"You don't remember." Bellenia's eyes fill with tears. "One of them hit you so hard, I thought you were dead. You were just lying there on the floor, senseless. I was alone." She looks down, and I see her hands are shaking. "They were not like men."

An image of what my sister must have endured lights up my mind like lightning, then my senses revolt, blotting it out. I lean over to kiss her on the forehead. "I will never leave you alone again."

My sister raises her face to me. "You promise?"

"I promise."

Bellenia lies back down on the bed as if exhausted. I turn to our mother and aunt, whose presence I had almost forgotten. Vassura has her hands over her face, her shoulders hunched. Our mother stands rigid like a figure carved in wood. "I will stay here tonight," I tell them. "I will look after my sister."

8

CATIA

When they were small children, Catia watched her daughters run round the hearth in her husband's ancestral home. It was impossible not to smile at the sight of them, the flash of red and gold hair, the sound of their laughter. There would be Solina, determined to win, followed by Bellenia on her smaller, less sturdy legs, desperate to be loved. And how her mother loved her, the younger child, the braver one, the one who did not possess her father's cleverness but all her mother's fire. The memory is so close she can almost scoop Bellenia up as she runs past, lift her high into the air, laughing with delight. Or she might catch Solina, who will try to dodge her grasp then wriggle for release, annoyed at being prevented from winning this race with no end.

From the day she birthed Solina, Catia knew she would willingly die to protect her children, without a moment's pause, without any regret. And yet she is not dead. She failed to protect them, and she still lives.

In the stale darkness of her bedchamber, Catia lets out a shuddering breath. Even the happiest memories of her daughters now bring pain, because there is no return to a world where Solina and Bellenia have not been violated. The men who came to her husband's home have destroyed everything she held dear, even the memory of Prasutagus himself. Catia is not sure she can ever forgive him for the will he wrote, or his refusal to arm their people for war. Or for dying and leaving her to face this horror alone.

She sits up. It still hurts to lie for too long or put too much pressure on her back. The centurion flogged her so hard the rod broke on her shoulder. She clenches her fists, willing the memory away. It is not her own pain or humiliation that she cannot bear, it is the memory of what she knew was happening in the roundhouse behind her. What the men were doing to her children. Rage grips Catia, a fire that has already burned her heart to dust. She welcomes the release it brings. Better to burn than to grieve. Even love only brings her pain. Nothing can undo her daughters' suffering, but she will take back their honour by force. Rome's violence will be repaid a thousand-fold. Her rage will consume them all.

In the dim morning light, Vassura sits weaving her brother's tapestry. A grey veil of rain falls over the doorway, its patter as steady as the movement of the loom as she works. The elephants have been unwoven, all remembrance of Rome removed. This is Prasutagus's life as his family wished it had been lived. Catia stands watching, not wanting to disturb her. She does not know how Vassura can bear to touch the threads in her hands, or care about the work she does. She had always thought Vassura weak, but since Aesu's death, Catia realises she underestimated her husband's sister. She knows the strength it must take Vassura to face each day, to weave, to care for another's living children.

"You are still determined to go," Vassura speaks without turning around. She has her brother's uncanny ability to sense the movements of those she cannot see.

"Yes. I sent word to Cunominus. It will be easier to prepare for war in the north."

"What about the prisoner? Am I expected to keep him hidden, while you are gone?"

Catia glances over her shoulder. There is no sign of her daughters. Neither of her girls know about the soldier their neighbour wounded on the cattle raid, whose companions left him for dead in the confusion of a blazing building. Still less do they suspect that this man has been nursed back to health in secret, kept bound in the loft of their barn, fed from their own table. "He is vital to the war."

"And you truly believe war is the answer."

"My daughters' honour..."

"Your daughters are *alive*." Vassura has stopped weaving. Catia sees her grip the sides of the stool where she sits. "Why not hide them in the north? The Wolf Tribe has melted into the forests before. Your people still know how. Why drag the girls into more violence?"

"My daughters would never abandon their own people or their kingdom. Neither will I."

"Do you expect me to believe that is why you are doing this, Catia? I know you. I saw your anger at Prasutagus for never giving in to your demands for violence."

Rage flares in Catia. "Anger that was *justified*." She walks around the loom to face Vassura and sees the other woman flinch. Catia realises she is dark with shadow in the doorway, as the centurion had been. A monster blotting out the light. She hesitates. The ripple of pain spreading from Vassura's memory is lodged in her own heart too. "Sister," she says, lowering her voice. "I know you love the girls. But do you really believe there is anywhere they will be safe? Or that Rome has finished with violence? Do you think they will leave us alone?" A steady beat of rain is the only answer to Catia's questions. "War will come, whether we wait like sheep or strike like wolves. Let me avenge Aesu."

"Do not speak of him." Vassura holds up her palm, as if to defend herself from Catia's words. "No amount of blood will bring back my son. He is dead. Violence will never ease my pain, nor will it ease yours. You are a fool to think so."

"Mother?"

Catia looks up, startled. Some distance behind Vassura, Solina is standing by the hearth. Holding her hand, and looking like a ghost beside her, is Bellenia. Both girls are pale, fragile as gossamer. The memory of them as children seems to shimmer where they stand, their laughter in this same hall, their small faces, vividly alive. Doubt hits her. Perhaps Vassura is right. Perhaps she should hide them.

"We are ready," Solina says.

Prasutagus would not recognise the city of his birth. Catia feels a deep sense of shame as she rides through its streets with her daughters, her hood pulled low over her face against the rain. The soldiers have finally headed back to London, back to Catus Decianus the procurator who ordered her family's humiliation, but the stain of their presence remains on everything they touched. She did nothing to protect the people here, instead she lay helpless, too badly injured to fight, while Roman gangs ransacked the place. Everywhere is desolation. The Street of Gold, once the pride of the city, is unrecognisable. Its workshops lie in ruins, their blackened timbers sagging in the rain. Metal-workers and jewellers made their home here for generations, but now they have been plundered so badly, there is barely enough ore left to smelt a hairpin. Worst of all is the fear. It hangs like a foul stench in the air, heavier than the rain, keeping people off the streets. Catia knows they are hiding, terrified of suffering the same fate as their neighbours, afraid they too will be set upon and tied up like animals to be sold as slaves. When they reach the great gates, she is relieved to escape the city's suffocating sadness.

The rain eases off as they head north on the Ecen Way. Catia had believed it safer for them to ride than travel by waggon or chariot; it is easier to evade capture on a horse, and they are less likely to be recognised. Many weeks have passed since she was flogged, but her back is on fire – she is unused to being so long in the saddle. She looks over at her daughters, anxious at how they are faring, but both seem to be coping well with the physical exertion.

As the day lengthens, the number of travellers thins, and villages become more sparsely scattered. Fields are replaced by ragged woodland which creeps up to the edge of the road, sometimes reaching branches overhead to form a rich green tunnel. They come at last to a large oak tree at a crossing, hung with offerings of bleached animal bones. Catia can see an image of the goddess Epona, in her form as a woman with two horses, carved into its trunk. Her heart lightens. They are cutting deeper into the territory of the Wolf Tribe.

At dusk, they camp out of sight from the road, in woodland near a freshwater stream. Catia cannot remember the last time she slept out in the open air with her daughters. They pitch camp where the trees have formed a natural shelter, laying out goat skins to keep off the damp. Bellenia fetches water from the stream, and they sit together, eating the bread and goat's cheese she brought from the city. Her daughters' faces glow in moonlight reflected from the stream, which shines like a silver pathway to the Otherworld.

"Perhaps Esus is here by his river," Bellenia says, the first time she has spoken since they stopped. "These might be the waters where he met Epona."

"Perhaps." Solina smiles.

"Won't you tell us the story of their meeting?"

Catia watches her girls, their figures softened by the failing light. She could almost imagine they were back in the time before, when Prasutagus lived.

Solina clears her throat and begins to sing, her voice soft, telling the story of the gods' meeting – how Esus saw a beautiful woman riding by his river and sent his birds to catch her, but even though her horse never quickened its steps, she was impossible to reach. Twice they chased the strange woman, until on the third attempt, Esus himself flew to meet her, begging her to wait for him. Catia smiles to hear Solina sing Epona's answer. *Why did you not ask me before? I rode this way to claim you as my own.*

"Your father used to sing this tale to me," Catia says in the silence that follows the last verse. She does not add what Prasutagus used to say to her privately, that she had been as impatient for him as Epona was for Esus.

"I remember," Solina says.

The three of them huddle together, and Catia is warmed by her daughters' bodies pressed close to her on either side. She runs her fingers gently through Bellenia's hair, as if her youngest daughter were still a child. "I heard Vassura say we should hide," Bellenia says. "That we might all live in the woods a while. Would that be so terrible?"

Catia feels the fragile sense of peace they have spun together come apart like cobwebs in her hands. She stops stroking

Bellenia's hair. "Vassura is a fool," she says. "There are not woods big enough to hide us, even if we were too weak to fight. Rome would burn every forest in the kingdom, rather than allow us to live freely."

Her daughters stay silent, their resentment palpable, leaving her own harsh words hanging in the air. Grief sits in Catia's heart like a stone. She looks up at the moon, Epona's lantern which guides the dead to the Otherworld. *Why did you leave me?* she says silently to Prasutagus, her anger towards him more painful than sadness could ever be. *Why do I have to face this alone?*

Her only answer is the sighing of the wind.

It is another hard day's riding before they reach the Town of the Wolf. Torches have been lit at the gatehouse, their flames moving over the painted black beast, giving it the illusion of life. The sentries grant Catia entry, recognising her by voice, and she rides with her daughters through the darkened streets to the roundhouse of her childhood.

Her whole body feels stiff and painful as she dismounts before helping her daughters to the ground. Servants move silently from the hall, taking the saddlebags and leading their horses to the stables, while her brother Cunominus stands in the doorway, holding a lamp. It illuminates his face, his red braids, leaving his body in shadow. He looks to Solina and Bellenia, huddled beside her, and his expression softens. "You are home," he says.

Relief floods Catia. She had not realised until this moment how much she feared her brother might hold the shame of the attack against them. They walk into the hall, where a serving girl is piling up the embers in the hearth to bank up the fire. Riomanda hurries forward, her large belly making her movements ungainly. She goes straight to Solina, holding her close, before stretching out an arm to Bellenia, gesturing at her to join them. The three women cling to each other, pressed so close together their sobs are muffled. Catia turns away, afraid she will also cry. She eases herself down onto the long, carved bench whose wooden legs are shaped like those of a wolf, claws splayed at its feet. Her own mother's seat. It is so long now since she saw her mother's face. Catia wishes she were here to hold her, the way Riomanda is now holding Catia's own daughters.

"It is a joy to see you here, home and safe," Cunominus says, drawing up a stool opposite. He studies the girls, still huddled in the arms of his wife, as if choosing his next words with care. "The greatest warriors may be defeated in battle. The shame is not lasting, so long as they repay their enemy."

"We will repay them," Solina says, breaking free from her aunt, and Catia is encouraged to hear the passion in her daughter's voice, even though her face is wet with tears. Catia glances at Bellenia, who simply nods agreement, not meeting her mother's eye.

"You know that in the north we have long believed it would be better to fight the Romans than serve them," Cunominus says. "There will be no difficulty in mustering warriors here. But even if all the Iceni rise, it may not be enough. The enemy have grown stronger since Prasutagus swore allegiance all those years ago."

"I believe many among the Trinovantes will join us," Catia replies. "What more do they have to lose? The Romans have already taken everything from them and still demand more. People are being made to pay for their own enslavement, forced to build that monstrous temple on stolen land at Camulodunum. Rebellion is a chance to take it all back."

Cunominus nudges the edge of the firedog with his boot,

frowning. For all his words about mustering the Iceni earlier, Catia senses he is uneasy at the thought of war. "Whatever little you have, there is always more to lose." He glances over at Riomanda. Catia knows they will have already discussed this. "Rome is an adder, and injuring a snake without killing it can be deadly. Taking Camulodunum will not be enough. We need to drive the serpent from Britain. Caratacus tried to do this once and he was defeated."

Any mention of the great warrior Caratacus is painful to Catia. Her failure to join his rebellion is one of the deepest regrets of her life. "We can learn from the past," she replies. "The Roman legate Suetonius Paulinus is already fighting against the Druids in Caratacus's old stronghold in the west. Paulinus cannot fight on two fronts, so we have the opportunity now to strike while his forces are engaged elsewhere. No campaign is without risk, but I believe Rome has never been more vulnerable."

Riomanda walks towards them, leading Catia's daughters to sit on thebench beside their mother. Then she goes to stand behind her husband, resting her hand on his shoulder. "There is no sacrifice too great that would not be worth the fall of Rome," Riomanda says. "We are prepared to risk everything. But I need to know you understand what it will mean if we fail."

Cunominus lays his own hand over his wife's. "She is right. I did not agree with Prasutagus, but I never believed your husband a coward. I know why he made the choices he did. If it is to be war, all of us need to go into it with our eyes open."

The fire in the hearth has caught now, spitting and crackling, painting the firedogs red. The Town of the Wolf has always seemed immortal to Catia, its existence stretching back beyond living memory, as much a part of the north as the marshes or the sea, as eternal as the gods. Yet she knows that it could be burned to the ground, as so many other cities have been, that perhaps war will reduce this hall to blackened rubble, and the city's name to ash. "I know what we could lose—"

"My father had a choice," Solina interrupts, startling them all. "We do not. The Romans have rejected his will, and they mean to take the whole kingdom. Prasutagus's prophecy only spoke of peace with Rome for a season, before the Iceni rode again in triumph. I will repeat his sacrifice, to ask the gods if that time has now come. But all the signs tell me it has."

Solina is clasping Bellenia's hand, staring at her mother and uncle, as if daring them to contradict her. Catia has not yet heard her daughter speak of her own sacred powers with this much authority. Cunominus, too, seems impressed by Solina's vehemence. "And what of you, Bellenia," he asks. "Is this your choice?"

Bellenia starts at her name, even though Cunominus has spoken gently. "I will fight for my honour," she says, her voice low, "as any warrior of the Iceni would be proud to do." Cunominus smiles, reassured, but Catia thinks of Bellenia's plea in the woods last night. This promise belongs to a past version of her daughter, one who had not been broken by violence. *Fighting will bring Bellenia back*, she tells herself. *She will regain her spirit with her honour.*

"There's no need to speak more of fighting tonight," Cunominus says. "I know you are tired." He picks up the jug of mead the serving girl had left, pouring them all a cup. "Let us drink together, then sleep."

In the days that follow, the Town of the Wolf returns to a semblance of the place Catia remembers from her childhood, with its streets churned to mud by horses and chariots, and its people no longer hiding their knives or hatred of Rome. Cunominus rides out to surrounding towns and villages, urging leaders to gather whatever fighters they can, and his call is answered. A growing stream of men and women arrive at the gatehouse, some armed only with farming tools or axes, though many have long ignored Rome's ban on weapons and bring out hidden swords, javelins and carnyxes, the metal war trumpets fashioned into the heads of wild beasts. They come in waggons and on horseback, whole families arriving, most having to camp in tents outside the city's embankments.

Catia orders some of their most precious livestock to be slaughtered, and hunters bring in wild boar and deer to be served at feasts in the hall of her family's roundhouse. She greets as many of the fighters as she can, understanding the need to make them feel important, though most of her daylight hours are spent training. Out in the fields, in full sight of the city and no longer skulking in the marshes, Catia drills her two daughters and regains her own strength, making Bellenia and Solina practise the fighting skills they will soon need to survive. The death of her children is a fear which has always stalked Catia, but she tries to lessen its grip by pressing them harder, by trying to make them tougher.

Each day, when she returns from training with Bellenia and Solina, Catia stops by the town's old armoury. Iron and bronze are being melted and recast here as swords and spears, the first new weapons to be forged by the Iceni in years, but that is not what Catia comes to see. She brings her daughters to watch the town's most skilled blacksmith work on her chariot. In the sparks of the fire, the three women watch a monstrous form take shape.

The centurion who ordered the rape of her children called the Iceni *lower than beasts*. Now Rome will learn what it means to face a wolf without mercy.

9

SOLINA

The sky above is bright blue with a few tufts of cloud lingering at its edges like Old Man's Beard. Heat beats down on our heads, heavy as a hand. I stand beside Bellenia, looking at the crowd without focusing on their faces, letting them blur into one another. We are in the clearing by the gatehouse, on the verge of leaving the Town of the Wolf, perhaps for the last time.

Our mother is addressing those who have come to see us off, and she speaks not as the widow of Prasutagus but the Iceni's military commander. Watching her is like following a harpist's fingers – her voice rises to a crescendo, inciting the crowd's excitement, then rolls back into calm reassurance. People sway, as if listening to music. She holds complete control over her audience, wielding speech with the same skill as she does a sword, and with the same violent intent.

Before us towers the chariot, a monster of wood and iron. Its wheels show Epona riding in her horse form around the rim. Blades jut out from their centre, making it bristle like a dragon's claw. Anyone who comes too close when the talons move will be cut to pieces. In the press of the crowd, I feel the warmth of another's hand enclosing mine. It is Riomanda. I turn to look at her, and the reality of our imminent parting hits me. We only have a few moments left. My mother's voice is still ringing out, but I can no longer make sense of the words. Riomanda is staring into my eyes, and I know her familiar fierce expression is burning itself into my memory, just as she too is cherishing the image of my face. *Please let this not be the last time I see her.*

People chant *Victory-Bringer! Boudicca!* as our mother climbs into the chariot behind the driver, and the horses toss their heads, excited by the noise. We are leaving. Riomanda embraces Bellenia first, then she throws her arms around me. I do not want to let her go.

"This is not where it ends," she murmurs, speaking the Iceni battle vow into my ear. I want to say the words back to her, but my voice is choked from unshed tears.

Cunominus gently prises me from Riomanda's arms, then helps my sister and me climb up to take our places on the chariot. I cannot watch him say goodbye to Riomanda, his wife, whose pregnancy is too advanced for her to join us. She is now regent of the Town of the Wolf, forced to wait here and birth a child her husband may not live to see. If we fail, the wrath of Rome will fall upon her, alone and unprotected. *We will come back*, I promise myself. *Riomanda will survive.*

I hold on to the chariot's side to steady myself, then reach across to take Bellenia's hand. She grips my fingers so tightly it hurts.

"Don't let go," she whispers, trying to hide her tears with a smile.

I grin back at her, faking a confidence I do not feel. "We are going to destroy Rome," I say loudly, in case any can hear. "We will come home when we have crushed them."

With a blast of the carnyxes, the chariot lurches forward. People part, shouting and cheering, giving as much space as possible to the revolving blades. Tears prick my eyes when we pass the gate. I long to take one last look at Riomanda, in case I never see her again, but resist the urge to turn back.

We travel south, towards the kingdom of the Trinovantes, and our party grows more boisterous the further we ride. Hundreds of warriors follow the chariot, riding two abreast, and behind them rumble all our waggons, stuffed with supplies. Wineskins get passed down the line and Isarninus leads us in a song about the glorious death of the Roman legate, Suetonius Paulinus, caught in his bath with a whore. He makes a meal of the saga, riding as close to the chariot as he dares, trying to catch my sister's eye. He manages to make Bellenia laugh, and I realise it's the first time I have heard the sound since the attack. My spirits rise. Even Diseta, my mother's bad-tempered older cousin, is singing along, riding a piebald stallion, a huge sword strapped across her shoulders and a rusty shield bouncing against her horse's flank.

It is not long before we catch sight of the thatched rooves and coppiced fields of a large settlement. The first target of our campaign.

"We cannot hide what happened," my mother says, turning from my sister to me. "Rome's outrage is what will inspire them to fight."

Bellenia and I nod, any lightness from the journey snuffed out by her tone. We have agreed that our mother will use the rape, and her own flogging, to whip up anger. Transforming our dishonour into a weapon to crush our enemies is a fitting form of revenge, but the prospect of hearing my own violation shouted at strangers still leaves me numb. What if they shun us, rather than coming to our defence? I look back at the line of warriors stretching down the road, reassuring myself of their protection. I know that somewhere, deep inside, my rage burns, waiting for me to claim it, but in this moment, it is too distant, like a boat glimpsed out at sea.

We draw closer to the settlement. A group of children burst suddenly into the road like a flock of sparrows, scattering in all directions. Our mother curses, and the chariot slows to avoid cutting them to pieces. The children hurtle towards their homes, shrieking. All save one. A small girl with bright red hair stands in the centre of the road, watching us. At first, I think she might be rooted there by shock or terror, but then she lifts her hand to her forehead, and I realise she is squinting to get a better look at the chariot.

"Are you Andraste?" She shouts the question at our mother. Her voice has the high, curious lilt of childhood, but none of its fear.

"I am no goddess, little one," my mother says. "Move aside. We don't want to hurt you."

"This is my village," the child replies. "I am not moving." She struggles with her belt, drawing out a dagger which is little more than a knife for whittling twigs. With a flourish, she points the tiny blade at the chariot. "I am the warrior, Senovara. Who are you? What do you want?"

An amused rumble of laughter comes from the warriors behind, and I cannot help but smile. "You are a brave warrior, Senovara," our mother says, without any trace of mockery. "I am Catia of the Wolf Tribe, widow of your king, Prasutagus. These are my daughters, Bellenia and Solina, heirs to the Iceni kingdom. We have come to ask for your help in fighting Rome."

"Ha!" Senovara swishes the knife in the air, her small, ferocious face lit with joy. "Then I will lead you to my house!"

"No, you may ride with us," my mother says. "Come."

Senovara stows her knife into her belt and trots eagerly

to my side of the chariot, giving plenty of space to the giant bladed wheels. "She will hurt herself," I murmur, as the little girl stops to gaze upwards, touching the small foothold where she will have to climb.

"She will not," my mother says.

"No." Senovara gives me a haughty look. "I will not."

The child pulls herself up as fearlessly as if she were climbing a tree. I hold her steady when she reaches the top, my hand big enough to fit across her small body. Senovara pushes to the front, then swivels round to look up at my mother, as if she were gazing at the sun. My mother smiles down, radiating strength and warmth, giving Senovara the full blaze of her attention. I cannot remember when my mother last looked at me like that, and the realisation surprises me for its pain.

"I am ready to fight the Romans," Senovara declares.

My mother gives the command, and our train sets off again. When we arrive at the village, I see the roundhouses lie open to the fields, defenceless, save for the people who have now gathered before their homes. All those shrieking children must have raised the alarm. A flash of silver catches my eye. It is a forbidden sword, a sign that not all here follow Rome's orders. It makes me feel hopeful. The crowd draws back as my mother's chariot rattles closer, except for one boy who runs towards us, his face livid with anger, yelling for Senovara's return. She waves back, her excitement obvious, and the boy hesitates.

"We have not come to fight you," my mother shouts over the clamour. "But to ask you to fight. I am the widow of King Prasutagus, and the mother of his daughters. Will you hear me?"

"The king is dead. Why should we fight for you, or anyone else?" I cannot tell which man has shouted, but his question draws mutterings of approval.

"I do not ask you to fight for me, but for yourselves." My mother pauses, looking out at their upturned faces, pale as blossom in the sun. "Besides, you only have one sword between you. Not much of a challenge to my army. Why don't you have more weapons?"

There is silence, until a woman, clutching a small child to her body with one hand and holding an axe with the other, yells out. "Rome has forbidden them!"

"Yes," my mother says. "You lack swords because Rome made us their slaves. And to our shame, we allowed them to steal everything we have." She bends down and hefts Senovara into her arms, holding her up high, causing some in the crowd to cry out. "This child is a fighter. You should be proud to have such a warrior. She stood alone on the road to stop my chariot, even though it towered above her. She was determined to defend her home. All the others fled." My mother sets Senovara down again, and I can see the girl's eyes are round with amazement, her cheeks flushed. "Your daughter here is surely blessed by Andraste the Indestructible. I do not blame the other children for fleeing – it is natural in the young. But it is not natural for the Iceni to flee, or to allow the Romans to abuse us."

"Nobody here loves Rome," replies the woman with the axe, perhaps the settlement's leader. "But why should we fight now? What's changed?"

"Everything has changed," my mother says, and I can hear the rage vibrating in her voice. "I am the king's widow, and these are my daughters, his heirs. And do you know how Rome treated your dead king's family? What they did to us?" The crowd is quiet, every eye upon her. Sweat starts to prickle my skin. "Fifty Roman soldiers came to terrorise unarmed women. They dragged me outside my husband's house." She pulls the tunic down over her shoulder, twisting so that the people can see the red marks on her back, the scars that cross her spine. "I was flogged. And my two daughters..." My mother breaks off, her voice choked.

At first, I think she is pausing for effect, but when I turn, I realise she is genuinely close to tears. I look round in panic, unsure what to do. Senovara has also noticed. Without speaking, she reaches for my mother's hand, gripping it in her small fingers.

"My daughters were raped," my mother says, her voice strengthening. The words set off a ringing in my ears. *This is not real*, I tell myself. *I am not here.* "My girls were violated in the house of their father. They were not given a chance to take up a sword or fight for their honour. If they had been armed, they would have sent scores of the cowards to their deaths. But the Romans do not fight like men; they are animals. And what does it say about the Iceni, what does it say about *us*, if we allow ourselves to be enslaved by vermin like this?"

People's faces are contorted with rage and disgust, many raising their weapons, shouting their hatred of Rome. Our dishonour has been flung at them like meat to wolves, and they have seized the bait. It feels strange, seeing my pain inflame strangers when my mother's words leave me cold. I glance at my sister. She is clasping her arms around herself, digging her fingers into her skin, a gesture I have seen her use before when trying to quell her panic. Bellenia is reliving the horror of the attack, here in front of all these watching eyes, and I want to warn our mother, but I feel paralysed. She is shouting at the crowd, wholly consumed by rage.

"And if that is how they treated *my* daughters, the heirs of your king, how do you imagine their soldiers will treat *your* children? Do you think any one of them will be spared? They will be enslaved, violated and killed. The men who attacked our home did not stop with my family; they sacked every home in the City of the Horse. Will you wait for them to come here, to steal all you have? *That* is the promise of Rome, *that* is the future they will give us if we do not resist. They have rejected the will of your king and now claim that our land belongs to them alone. That *we* belong to them. That we are lower than beasts." People are shouting and screaming, my mother's anger igniting all their long-held resentment and fear. "I am a woman, and I will fight. My daughters will fight. What of the men among you? Are you brave enough to risk death? Or would you rather live as slaves?"

A savage roar is her answer. Bellenia sways on her feet as if buffeted by the din. Her face is pale, and she is on the verge of fainting, but our mother does not turn round at my scream; it is lost in the shouting. I let go of the chariot, catching Bellenia before she falls onto the spears crafted to kill our enemies.

Bellenia's distress is forgotten in the euphoria of taking that first village. Even our mother makes light of it, perhaps unwilling to sour the glory of the moment. Senovara and several of her family pack up their belongings into a waggon, and the settlement empties, save for their oldest men and a few women and children. The fields and thatched rooves recede into the distance, and I wonder what Senovara feels as her home disappears. Excitement, if her ferocious little face is anything to go by. We press on into Trinovantes territory, riding from town to town, our warriors soon swelling to thousands. My mother's voice grows hoarse from repeating our tale of dishonour, and I watch her, seeing how she transforms the genuine emotion of that first speech into a spectacle. In time, I learn to block out the words, detaching myself from the events she describes, as if the attack did not happen to me. I'm not certain Bellenia ever manages to do the same.

The Trinovantes accept my mother as their leader with an alacrity that surprises me. After suffering so many humiliations at Roman hands, they seem even more eager to fight than our own people, some riding to join us from villages we have never seen, drawn by nothing more than rumours of our gathering. At night we stay at settlements wherever we have mustered fighters, feasting and sleeping in the halls of families who were strangers to us until then, while our followers set up camp in the surrounding fields. We never linger, pressing on from place to place, not wanting to give the Romans time to prepare for our attack. In the Trinovantes kingdom we encounter Roman farms and villas, built by their most aggressive settlers. My mother does not sack these places herself – it would be beneath her – but we watch from the road as our people overwhelm them like flies swarming a carcass, killing any who resist and setting their heads at the gatepost in warning.

I become used to performing. My sister and I meet thousands of people, playing the role of the dead king's wronged daughters with the strength and dignity they expect to see. At night we become ourselves again. We lie together in the dark, telling each other stories from our childhood, laughing at Diseta or remembering our father, finding comfort as well as sadness in bringing him closer. Sometimes I long to share with Bellenia what he told me about his visions, but the secret feels too heavy, and I dread the moments my sister says my name in a particular tone, reaching for my hand in the darkness. I know she wants to talk about the attack we suffered, but I always refuse. It's easier to pretend the violation is only a story our mother spins to win the war. In time, Bellenia learns to hide her distress, even from me. I tell myself it is better this way.

*

Our mother chooses the Festival of Fire as our final council of war. We set up camp near the City of the Horse at a vast sacred grove my father built to honour the gods, where we will now seek divine blessing for the coming fight. Being caught up in this crowd is unlike anything I have ever experienced. This is no longer a muster; it is an army. Whole families are here, piled into waggons with sacks of food and supplies, while herds of cattle graze at the camp's edge, ready for us to kill and eat over the long campaign. Everywhere, children run between larger legs, in danger of being trampled, and I look for Senovara among them but cannot find her. The crush of so many bodies, the stench of sweat and the horde of horses and waggons make it hard to press through to the sacred grove, but the deadly blades of my mother's chariot cause the crowd to ripple outwards, giving us space.

The oaks of the grove are not living trees but giant trunks carved to resemble an army of spirits, replanted in a maze around my father's massive wooden tower. We leave the chariot and make our way through on foot, touching the dead branches as we pass. In the ceremonial clearing at the grove's heart, a bonfire has been lit. Its flames curl upwards, the heat haze making the hall behind tremble as if in fear.

Over the giant doorway, the skulls of our ancestors have been fixed, decorated now for battle with feather and fur. I think of my father, deep in the woods, and feel comforted to know he will return here one day to watch over me again, when birds have stripped his bones of flesh. Inside the hall, I am folded into warm arms. It is my aunt Vassura. She stands back, her hands cupping my face, then she kisses me on both cheeks. Cunominus stands by, grinning, his teeth shining white in the shadow.

"You are both so brave," Vassura says. "Are you sure you are ready?"

I am about to reassure her that we are as ready for war as all the other warriors gathered here, when my mother interrupts. "I have not told them yet."

"Told us what?" Bellenia asks.

"You will regain your honour here tonight," our mother replies. "As a sacrifice before the battle."

I look first to my mother, then Vassura, confused. "How?"

Cunominus steps forward, taking both my and Bellenia's hands. "You will fight one of the soldiers who attacked you. The man has been brought here by Vassura. When you have taken his life, the blood debt is paid."

"No." Bellenia steps back, her voice shrill. "No. Not one of *them*. I can't. Choose any other Roman. Please. I can't do this."

"You were set upon by scores of soldiers when you were both unarmed." Our mother reaches out to Bellenia, but my sister flinches from her touch. "There will be two of you, and one of him. We will allow him a sword, to match yours. That is just, and better odds than you faced in his place. Together, you will easily defeat him."

Bellenia and my mother begin to argue, my sister close to tears. I say nothing. It is as if they are at a vast distance from me. The pain in my chest is so intense I cannot at first name the feeling. Then I understand. It is rage.

"Solina." My aunt touches my arm. "What do you say?"

"I will kill him." My voice is so loud it startles the others into silence. My mother looks from Bellenia to me. There is a flicker of disappointment in her eyes.

I realise then it is not my lost honour that pains her most. It is my sister's.

*

Grey figures slip through the trees of the sacred grove, casting long shadows in the late afternoon sun. Only the most important warriors from the Iceni and Trinovantes kingdoms have been permitted into the sanctuary to watch the heirs of Prasutagus regain their honour. All are dressed for war. It is hard to make out individual faces: the blue sign of Andraste marks every cheek, blending men and women together. Many have their arms or chests bare, displaying the tattoos of their tribes, a rippling company of black-lined boars, wolves, and horses. With the sun behind, their shapes look more bestial than human, distorted by the animal skins, feathers and bones that cover their heads. They do not press right to the centre but leave a wide circle. This space is the arena where Bellenia and I will fight.

My sister and I stand side by side in front of the bonfire to the gods, the heat of its flames burning our backs. Our arms and shoulders are bare, so all can see the Horse and the Wolf tattooed on our skin. Before the waiting crowd, our mother paints our faces. She avoids looking into my eyes until she has finished, then she gives me a tight smile. Cunominus steps forward to dress us in thin mail tunics, then hands each of us our swords. He lingers a moment to kiss us both on the forehead, then goes to stand beside our mother. She looks at us, her daughters, and lays a hand over her heart. "This is not where it ends."

"*This is not where it ends*," Bellenia and I repeat. It is the Iceni promise of survival, made before every battle. I think of Riomanda, whispering the words into my ear, and the vow sends a prickle over my skin. Cunominus and our mother bow their heads, then leave. We are alone. Bellenia's breathing sounds loud and ragged with fear, but I do not dare comfort her in front of so many watching eyes.

Shouts and curses tell us the Roman soldier has arrived.

Warriors jostle, writhing like reeds in a storm, as they manhandle him through their ranks to the arena. I see our enemy thrown onto the dirt. His sword follows, landing with its point quivering in the ground. He seizes it, swinging round, ready to defend himself. A hiss goes through the crowd – the sound of hundreds of blades being drawn. The arena has become a ring of iron. Death is now the only way out.

Then the chanting starts, timed with the stamp of countless feet, an implacable demand for blood. It is deafening. My sword hilt feels hard in my hands, and the heavy blade weighs against my arms, like part of my own body. I step forward. Slowly, I circle the man, watching him twist round, his eyes trained on mine. His face is a blank to me: I do not know him. And yet, some part of me remembers. Perhaps the crowd is still screaming. I no longer know. All I can hear is the roar of my own blood.

"Are you ready to die?"

I speak to him in my own language and see his face contort in confusion. He cannot understand me.

"Are you ready to die?" I repeat, shouting the words this time, not for him but for those watching. "That is the price of my honour. That is the price of my sister's honour. You were brave enough to face us when we were outnumbered and unarmed. Where is your courage now?" He continues to stare at me, uncomprehending, and the sight fills me with contempt. I spit at the ground where he stands. "*Mortuus es.*"

He charges at me then, but I anticipate the blow. My blade catches his near the hilt and I throw him backwards, almost taking his sword. He swiftly rights himself. His face shows surprise, then fear. He had not expected a woman to fight like this. I scream, my face twisted in rage, becoming the savage he believes my people to be.

"*Your blood belongs to me,*" I shout in Latin, making him

leap back as I swing at his head. "*I will cut out your heart and burn it on the altar of Andraste.*"

"Bitch," he yells back, spit flying from his lips. "*I will have you on the floor again, this time with my sword in your guts.*"

My attacker is so focused on me, he does not see my sister until it is almost too late. Bellenia strikes him on the shoulder, sending up a spray of blood. "Die, you bastard!" she screams.

The soldier staggers backwards. He is mortally wounded, his tunic stained red, yet he keeps fighting, sparring with my sister, his injured arm hanging at his side. He cannot match her. All these weeks, Bellenia and I have been training, while he sat bound in my aunt's barn like a pig fattened for slaughter. The chanting of the crowd grows wilder, jubilant at the scent of a kill.

Then something changes. The soldier begins taunting my sister. His voice is low, and I cannot make out what he says at first, but as he continues his tirade, I hear snatches. He is describing the rape to her, and even though my sister surely does not understand it all, the sound of his voice seems to be dredging up the darkness she carries inside. Her face is wet with tears, and her blows begin to swing wild. With horror, I realise he has trapped Bellenia in the past, and she is so distressed he might still manage to kill her.

"*You are weak,*" the man shouts, as she misses again. "*You will never take back your honour; you will die as a whore.*" She falters, almost taking a hit. "*You are afraid of me, aren't you?*" he taunts. "*Even if you kill me, you can never get back what I took.*"

I charge at Bellenia, knocking her out of harm's way, pretending to suffer a fit of jealous passion. "He is *mine*," I scream, striking at the hilt of the man's sword. My blow forces the weapon from his hand. He raises his palm to me, an instinctive gesture of defence, and in answer I swing my sword in a savage arc, slicing off his outstretched hand. He lets out a cry, doubling over in shock and pain.

The crowd falls silent. I wait for the man to recover himself. When he straightens up and faces me, I say nothing. We both know he is dead.

"*I am not afraid of you*," he murmurs, the tremble in his voice betraying the lie. "*I die as a soldier of Rome, and you—*"

He does not get to finish his speech. I plunge my sword into his throat. He stumbles. I grip him by the shoulder to prevent his fall. My rage no longer burns; it is now the merciless chill of winter. The dying man stares into my eyes as I withdraw my weapon, drenching us both in his blood.

"Your debt is paid," I say. Then I let him drop to the ground.

10

CATIA

Dawn at the sacred grove is a pale haze, the trees and fields whitened by mist which rises from the ground. In the cold damp of the morning, Catia watches her eldest daughter reach into the bonfire's remnants, now a grey ring of ash, to light the flame.

Solina is dressed in black, her bright red hair woven with crows' feathers. For the first time, Catia can see her daughter's physical resemblance to Prasutagus. Solina does not have the king's features, but she has his poise, the cold determination of a Druid. The sight ought to fill Catia with pride, and it does, yet she also feels resentment. She cannot forget the way Solina stole Bellenia's kill, shoving her out of the way, casting a shadow over her sister's honour. It reminded Catia of the way her husband once wrested power from *her*, that same gut-punch of betrayal. Solina is becoming Prasutagus's daughter in every sense.

The Roman soldier now hangs from an oak at the edge of the grove, caught in the embrace of the dead tree's branches. He has been cut open, his ribs poking out like the broken bars of a cage. On Andraste's altar below lies his heart. Solina approaches with the torch, handing it to another Druid who stands beside the corpse. Catia cannot risk a bad omen becoming widely known, so only a select few are here to witness Solina repeat her father's prophecy. Her daughter's words have the power to shape the course of the war for good or ill. The dead king's voice comes back to Catia: *I have seen Solina rise above the rooftops of Rome.* Bitterness taints the memory. Perhaps it was his favouritism which emboldened one sister to overshadow the other.

Solina holds up the knife, as if showing it to the man she killed. "May the gods guide my hand and grant me sight." She cuts open her enemy's heart, then takes the torch to set the kindling around it alight. Smoke curls upwards, infused with Roman blood. Solina opens her arms like the wings of the crow she will one day become, throwing back her head to watch the prophecy rise.

In that moment, Catia does not see Solina as her daughter, just as she had not seen Prasutagus as her husband when he took on the mantle of the Otherworld. The black figure by the altar is the channel through which their fate will be known. Catia's heartbeat quickens. She waits, like everyone else, to hear what the gods will decide.

"I see our lands running red with Roman blood, their temples in ash at our feet. It is the mark of death. The promise of peace has ended." Solina lowers her head and turns to Catia. "The war you wanted has come. You will fulfil the destiny of your name."

Hours pass on the march to Camulodunum without the festival atmosphere abating. People laugh and sing, and their gathering grows with each settlement they pass, as the rumour of rebellion spreads. The city is two days away, and the Romans must surely know of their approach, yet they meet no resistance on the road. At night they camp out in the fields, making no effort to hide or draw up defences. Catia and her family set up at the centre, gathering around one of the camp's many fires. Darkness falls, and the stars above glint sharp as spearheads.

Catia calls Bellenia to sit beside her, drawing her close. The fight at the sacred grove has not restored her youngest's spirit. Her daughter's face is blank as an unlit lamp, and her hand moves over the grass, plucking at stems. Catia nudges her to stop, worried people will see. Across from them, Solina sits with Vassura. Firelight softens the shape of her eldest daughter's face, making her look younger, almost childlike. Catia is still resentful at Solina for stealing her sister's kill, but seeing her now, she feels more compassion. Her eldest child has suffered deeply too.

Raucous shouting draws Catia's attention. Cunominus is laughing with her chariot driver, Mandubracius, whose smile reveals the dark hole left by his knocked-out front teeth. She can hear Cunominus joking about her girls behaving like *a pair of wolf pups scrapping over the kill*, promising Bellenia that she will have her chance to spill more Roman blood once they reach Camulodunum. Catia wishes he would stop.

"You cannot fault the pair of them," Cunominus declares, trying to catch Catia's attention and force her to join in the merriment. "Every warrior wants to claim the kill. Bellenia took first blood; it's only natural Solina would fight for the rest."

"He would have died eventually from the injury Bellenia gave him." Solina stares intently at her sister, as if willing her to agree. "The kill was shared."

"Not what you said at the time," Cunominus retorts. "*He is mine!*" His imitation draws laughter, and Catia is annoyed to see Solina smile. Bellenia says nothing but starts to pluck the grass at her feet again. Cunominus watches her, then speaks more softly. "You cannot hold it against Solina. As she said, you also struck a killing blow. The man was dead from the moment you struck him."

"He was the one who hit my sister over the head," Bellenia replies, finally looking up. Her words bring a chill on the company, the cold remembrance of violence and disgrace.

"And now his heart lies in ashes, foretelling the death of his own people," Solina says. The two sisters exchange a long glance, heavy with meaning, then Bellenia nods, her eyes shining with tears.

In that moment, Catia wants to be alone with her daughters, not here under the gaze of thousands of strangers, her every move lit by the glare of a blazing fire. She wants to hold both her girls, to comfort them, to tell them that she would gladly die if that could take back all they suffered.

But she cannot. Catia now commands an army, and that is the only face she can show. "He was merely the first kill," she says, her voice cold. "There will not be a man, woman or child left alive to see the sunrise in Camulodunum, after we have taken the city."

Cunominus inclines his head, no longer smiling. "By the will of Andraste."

The Temple of Claudius shines bone-white on the hill. It rises above the city, bright like the bleached skull of a ram picked clean of flesh. The size of her enemy's offering to their gods is unlike anything Catia has ever seen. It is vast enough to have been set there by giants, with pillars pointing to the sky. Yet *her* army is greater. She feels a rush of exhilaration. Catia has dreamed of this for so long, the moment the Iceni would rise against Rome. Now wooden war-chariots rattle over the road, as swift as they are light, and thousands of spears and scythes bristle, catching the light like a field of sharp-headed reeds. Rising above them sway metal boars, dragons and wolves, their mouths bellowing cries terrifying enough to break even the bravest Roman spirit. It is the call of Death.

Camulodunum was not always hated. Before the Romans cannibalised the city as their capital, it was a beautiful place, but now, squatting in familiar green fields, the colony looks utterly alien, a dragon hoarding stolen land. As they draw closer, the gaudy tombs of foreign soldiers sprout up along the roadside. Iceni men and women pause their march to hack at them, venting their rage on stone figures before their axes meet flesh. This useless army of the dead is Camulodunum's only protection; no legion is stationed here.

Catia looks over her shoulder to where her daughters ride side by side, on the cusp of facing their first battle. Their painted faces make it difficult for her to read their expressions, but both sit tall and formidable in the saddle, their bare arms decorated with tattoos. Pride flares in her heart, shot through with fear. She turns away, not wanting to stare too long, or she will forget they are warriors and only see them as her children.

They come at last to a monumental arch, the gateway to the city. It has been hastily filled with upturned waggons, planks, sacks of grain, even furniture, to form a barricade. No soldiers man it, and even from here, she can see the streets beyond look deserted.

"Fire!" Catia screams, trying to get the attention of any who might hear her in the din of screaming and trumpets. "Fire!"

A group of fighters runs forwards, carrying torches. They look like farmers, with dark trousers and rough tunics – men who would normally be tending their fields, not destroying cities. They hold their flaming pikes against the wooden defences, waiting until the timber catches light, then dart back. Catia watches as the fire climbs, devouring the town's feeble offering, rising into the sky in thick black clouds. The crackle and hiss grow to a roar. Camulodunum's great arch is enveloped in a veil of flame as its defences burn to dust.

11

SOLINA

We pour into the city, smashing into Roman homes with the ferocity of a river that has burst its banks, ripping the place apart. Any who still cower in their houses are dragged out and hacked to pieces in the street. All the horrors which Rome has visited upon us are being returned a thousand-fold, driven by years of pent-up rage. Everywhere is confusion, screaming and smoke, and I am afraid one of our own might kill me, as spears and axes swing wildly in the air, aimed at those desperate to flee but striking any in their path.

My ears ring with the noise, my eyes sting, and I struggle to control Tan's rising terror. He skitters over the blood and gore on the road, nostrils flaring, while I flail with my sword, somehow managing to stay in the saddle. A Roman boy charges at me with a spear, and I strike him down, then watch as he is trampled underfoot by another warrior's horse. My world is shrinking. Nothing exists outside a small circle of survival. Blood beats in my skull, a pounding drumbeat urging me to stay alive, and I thwack at arms and heads, hardly knowing if those who run towards me are fleeing danger or seeking to kill me. We smash into house after house, until we start to realise most are empty, their inhabitants having already fled.

Barricades around the huge temple precinct show where they must be hidden. Our people surge towards it in a bellowing mob.

My sister and I are pressed against the side of a ransacked house, like twigs caught in reeds when a river rushes past. I feel numb, as if watching the unfolding violence through a veil. Bellenia too looks dazed. Her sword is red, and her skin stained with blood.

Our mother has abandoned her chariot in the cramped press of street-fighting, and I see her ride towards us, somehow managing to navigate the chaos on her battle-maddened horse. The sight of her makes me feel the world is not completely unmoored.

"Go to the other public buildings," she shouts, her face lit with passion. "See if more traitors are hiding there."

"I don't know where to look!" I scream back.

She gestures impatiently at a gaggle of men standing bunched at the street corner. One has the distinctive tattoo of the Trinovantes boar across his shoulders. "They know the city. Go with them."

Before we have a chance to say more, she has gone, merging with the human river and riding towards the temple. My sister and I follow the men, weaving our way against the flow, until the crush thins. Bodies lie abandoned on the road, and shop fronts gape, their shutters torn open. I wonder if any of our guides are Trinovantes men whose homes in the city were stolen by settlers, here to punish their former neighbours.

"The baths!" one shouts, a burly man whose face is smeared with blue. "The fuckers have barred the doors against us."

The street is deserted, our people not yet having pressed this far into the city. I have no sense of where the baths might be – all I can see is a high wall, painted red and white, with a giant wooden door. Our companions lay into it with their axes, smashing the wood into splinters, ripping the door from its hinges. The surviving archway is so high, Bellenia and I ride straight between its brick columns into the courtyard, bending low over our horses' necks. In the cocoon of stone walls, the noise of battle is dulled. I turn at the sound of running water. Fountains are set against the walls, with arcs of foam falling from the mouths of carved fish, their blind eyes watching us through the spray. Under Tan's hooves a mosaic spreads in a strange entanglement of sea creatures and monsters. It is beautiful. I catch the look of wonder on Bellenia's face and know mine must look the same.

"Guard the door!" our guide shouts at us. "If any of the rats are hidden inside, they will try to escape this way."

The men run into a darkened corridor which must lead into the complex. I have never seen Roman baths before and am gripped by a sudden childlike wish to follow. My curiosity is cut short by the sound of screaming.

"They have found them," Bellenia whispers, her eyes wide. We bunch together to block the ravaged doorway, just as someone bursts from the corridor into the open space of the courtyard. It is a woman, her face wild with anguish and fear. Instinctively I raise my sword.

"My children!" she screams, not in Latin but in our own language. "They killed my children!"

I have no time to answer or react. One of the Trinovantes warriors strikes her from behind with his spear. She falls forward, collapsing onto the mosaic. Blood pools beneath her, staining the tiles red.

We lay siege to the temple precinct until it grows dark and our mother is forced to pause the assault. I am utterly spent. Cutting through the city had been swift, but here we have hit hard resistance. The stench of blood, excrement and woodsmoke clings to everything, even my hair, making it nauseating to breathe, and in the fading light I can see the streets around the temple are clogged with bodies, thick as autumn leaves. Black stains mark the dead and dying, a blur of shadow and blood. I stare, dumb in the face of so much death, until Cunominus grabs me by the arm. He is almost unrecognisable, his face streaked with ash and sweat. I flinch at his touch, but he grabs my face, forcing me to look into his familiar blue eyes.

"Our dead, Solina. We need to move them, or they will be trampled underfoot."

I look over to where Bellenia is already struggling against the weight of a slaughtered warrior and hurry to help. My fingers slip on the man's cold, damp skin. I grip him more tightly, trying not to look at the mess of his exposed guts, trying not to think about anything other than putting one foot in front of the other. Soon I can think of nothing but the agonising ache in my arms, the strain of so much dead weight, and he ceases to be human at all. We lay him down in an empty alleyway, then return, staggering back and forth, until I lose track of how many bodies we have carried.

The night drags on, our mother also working to honour the fallen, but finally, when I feel I might collapse with exhaustion, Cunominus orders us to rest, promising he will follow. We walk down the dark street to the abandoned house he has chosen for shelter. My arms feel impossibly light, suddenly freed of their dead burden. I glance backwards. Over the barricades, the glow of our enemy's night watch is turning the pillars of their temple orange against the black sky.

I follow Bellenia into the house, holding up a torch to light our way. The place is a mess. Black shadows pool around a half-eaten meal on the table like blood around a carcass. On the bench, a child's game of knucklebones sits as if waiting for the next throw. I stand rigid in the doorway, hating the place, while Bellenia rattles through cupboards, hunting down the family's oil lamps. Once they are lit, the room looks more homely but no less haunted.

"Do you think they are dead?" Bellenia points to the discarded meal. "Or hiding in the temple?"

I shrug, not wanting to think of the people who once lived here. Garlands of flowers and small pink winged boys are painted all over the walls, glowing in the lamplight. I run my finger along the plaster, tracing the shape of one of the figures. They seem so small and pathetic. Nothing like the sacred images on the walls of our roundhouse, which shine with the power of the gods. "We had better find somewhere to sleep," I say.

We creep further into the unfamiliar house. Bellenia's lamp gives off as much smoke as light, as we stumble from room to room. Nothing about the way the Romans build their homes makes sense to me – in place of a roundhouse, they have heaped together a strange warren of small, lonely spaces. We finally find the sleeping quarters upstairs, and clamber into a musty bed. It smells of unfamiliar bodies. Bellenia sets down the lamp and we curl around one another for comfort.

"That mother in the baths, the one who ran towards us," Bellenia whispers. "What do you think they did to her children?"

Her question flummoxes me. What does she expect me to say? *We slaughtered every child we found, did you not see?* Then I realise Bellenia is crying. I grip her more tightly, holding her shaking body close to mine. "They *deserve* it. All of them. None are innocent. If they choose to take from us, then let them die. It's not even as if we have a choice. If we don't destroy them, do you think they will just leave us alone?"

"I cannot bear it, Solina. All this suffering. All this death. Because of us."

I open my mouth to speak but my throat tightens, trapping any words of comfort. I had believed myself ready to face battle, yet the cold certainty I felt in the sacred grove, facing the man who dishonoured me, has been tarnished by the ugliness of slaughter. I know what my sister is feeling, because I feel it too. But if I admit this, I am lost. "It is our destiny to destroy Rome," I say, sounding like our mother. "If we let their children live, they will oppress us one day too."

I wait for my sister to answer, but she does not, and it is a relief not to argue. Her body feels warm in my arms. I close my eyes, shutting out the unfamiliar shadows which creep over strange walls, praying for sleep.

12

CATIA

She has ridden her chariot over the dead, cutting through bodies like a scythe through grass, feeling the bump of bones and armour beneath her wheels. Everywhere she looks, the devastation is gilded by the light of a summer evening. A haze hangs over the smouldering remains of the precinct's barricades, and the Roman soldiers who manned them are now carrion at her feet. Men and women from her army pick over the dead like crows, killing any survivors, rifling through purses, cutting off Roman buckles and belts as talismans of conquest. By the temple steps, a giant mutilated statue of the Emperor Nero lies among his fallen men, his head torn off, ready to be hurled into the river. The ultimate mark of her victory. Yet the golden light of the sun also proves Catia to be a liar. It has set twice on Camulodunum since they began their assault, and still there are Romans here left alive.

In the centre of the carnage, the vast temple stands unconquered, its bronze doors locked against her. Inside, hundreds of people are hiding. It would be easy enough to let them starve – they will run out of food and water within days. All her army must do to ensure their death is wait. But Catia does not want to linger here. Rome will learn what she has done and send their legions to crush her. She needs to press on, to destroy her enemy's cities so completely, they cannot rise again.

Yet still, she hesitates.

It was so easy to promise a massacre. Perhaps Catia even believed her own rhetoric, that it would cost her nothing to kill so many. She knows a Roman general would not hesitate in her place. There is no limit to their barbarity, no end to what they take or what they destroy. She tries to dredge up her darkest memories, to remember the face of the centurion who came to brutalise her daughters. She wants to reignite the hatred she felt that day, the rage which coursed through her when she stormed this city, but all she feels is nausea. The man who flogged her will not be in that temple. It will be full of children, women, the old. To pretend anything else is a lie.

Catia tries again to conjure up the face of the hated centurion, but the face which comes to her is that of her dead husband. Her lips form his name. *Prasutagus*. His hands were not clean of blood, despite his reputation for peace. Any who rebelled against him paid dearly for it, their heads decorating the walls of his cities, their families slaughtered. The Iceni do not spare children in their battles, but after victory, there is always room for mercy. It is expected. A true warrior is just. Prasutagus did not butcher every last child of his enemies, neither did her parents, nor any leader she has known. Taking this many defenceless lives is an act which will forever define her, both in the eyes of mortals and gods.

The image of Prasutagus fades from her memory. In its place she sees herself, taller than any living being. She is a monster with eyes of fire, clothed in robes of blood. The figure is so vivid in Catia's mind, it looks as real as the paintings she has seen hundreds of times in the halls of her ancestors. Then she understands. A massacre only holds its horror for a season, then it fades into legend, a story to be told around the hearth in reverence and fear. This is how she will be remembered. She will no longer be Catia of the Wolf Tribe, a woman with a human heart. She will be the incarnation of Andraste, Goddess of Death, who drove the Roman armies back into the sea from which they spawned. This is what must be.

Catia steps down from her chariot, hitting the paving stones in her battle-worn boots rather than the blood-red robes of her imagination, and makes her way to the temple. Cunominus hurries forward, his face haggard with exhaustion. She waves him aside, her own face a mask. "Call the girls to me."

The temple steps are strewn with the enemy dead. Catia climbs, nudging aside the bodies of the last Roman defenders, until she is standing in front of the bronze doors. They are unimaginably vast, rising tall as oak trees. Above the stone lintel, a series of grills are set high out of reach. A filter for light and air to reach the dark space within where so many are hiding. Catia lays her hand on the metal studs that line the doors, wrought by the enslaved hands of her own people. The surface is gouged with the marks of axes and swords, where her warriors have tried and failed to break in.

Bellenia and Solina walk up the steps to join her, pale and exhausted. Her daughters are all too mortal, their skin and clothes smudged and stained, but they are mercifully uninjured. She smiles, beckoning them to stand either side of her, like the goddess Andraste split into three. Together, they look out over the ruined city. Catia does not have to shout to gain attention. Gradually, people stop to watch, then they move towards the temple, gaining momentum, until a vast gathering is spread below her.

"We have taken Camulodunum," Catia shouts. "You have conquered." She waits, letting the crowd rouse themselves to hysteria through their own shouting. "This building marks Rome's greed, paid for in our people's blood. It cannot be allowed to stand. Those who cower inside believe they have locked us out, but we will devour them. Our gods are greater than their Emperor, the feeble man they demanded we worship." She pauses, drawing strength from the rapt attention of her army, conjuring in her mind the image of herself as a creature of legend. "We will sacrifice their temple to Andraste, in an offering of blood and fire." There is a murmur, a ripple of excitement passing through the crowd, but she sees no trace of horror. None will question her. "Go into the town," Catia commands. "Bring wood, straw, furniture, everything that burns, and stack it against the temple. Once it is destroyed, we will burn the rest of the city, street by street. Camulodunum will become a bonfire whose flames are seen from Rome itself."

It takes time to ransack the city for kindling. The houses have already been thoroughly looted, with stolen valuables heaped into waggons, but by nightfall every building has also been stripped of wood, and the temple bristles like a giant bird's nest. A tangle of beams, bedframes, tables, bales of hay and fabric have been bundled high up the stone walls and lie in a great tottering mound against the doors. If Camulodunum's last survivors tried to open them now, they would have no way of breaking out. They have been sealed into their tomb.

Most of Catia's own people have already left the city. She did not want them to be killed in the chaos of an inferno. Instead, she ordered them to seek safety by the river, where she knows they now stand massed together in the darkness, waiting to see the sky lit by flame. Only a few hundred warriors have remained here with her in the precinct. Their torches illuminate faces bright with hunger and hatred, yet they have still not lit the bonfire. Catia knows they are waiting for their leader's signal.

The crowd parts for her as she walks towards the bronze doors, holding her torch aloft. Her heart beats so hard it is pulsing in her ears, and the people surrounding her feel unreachable, as if she were underwater. At the foot of the ugly tangle of kindling she stops. She has chosen not to think of those inside the temple. They are faceless, nameless, encased in a symbol of Rome; their suffering will be unseen and unacknowledged. Catia closes her eyes to pray, hoping the gods will grant her a vision of glory, but none comes. She is alone in the darkness.

"Andraste, you are the Indestructible One, bearer of death and bringer of war. This sacrifice of blood and fire is our gift. May it please you. In return, we pray you grant us victory."

Catia thrusts the torch into the kindling before her, holding it steady, waiting for it to catch. She cannot focus on the enormity of what she is doing. Instead, she stares straight ahead, keeping her eyes wide open until they sting and swim with tears. She blinks. Her vision clears, and in the jumble before her, one piece stands out, caressed by grey curls of smoke. It is the well-worn back of a chair, the familiar figure of a hare carved across it. The design is not Roman. It is British.

A spark lands on her hand, and she flinches as it burns her skin. The flames have caught. Catia steps back, still mesmerised by the hare, watching it blacken and collapse, lost forever to the red greed of fire. The heat is becoming unbearable, and she retreats, making for the edge of the temple precinct. Other people surge forward to light the kindling, swarming over the temple, shoving their torches into the relics of Camulodunum's sacked homes before running back to safety. The crackle of flames grows, smoke billowing upwards, and then the sound Catia had dreaded begins. The people inside the temple understand what is happening. They are screaming.

A wall of flame rages against the bronze doors, licking its way up to the grill. Catia sees the doors tremble, but they do not open. The metal must be too hot to touch, the bolt perhaps already soldered to its brackets, preventing any escape. Beneath her, the ground begins to shake. A hundred feet are stamping the marble stones, while the butts of spears and axes thump in time to a chant – *Victory-Bringer!* – shouted to drown out the cries of the dying: *Boudicca! Boudicca! Boudicca!*

Flames rise, tall enough to touch the silver moon, which hangs like a shield above the temple. Rome's monument to victory is being devoured; it has become a funeral pyre. The roar of the fire is monstrous – it is an inferno loud enough to drown out the cries of any inside who might still be alive. There is no more chanting either; her people are choked by smoke, and even the air is burning. Catia gives the signal to leave.

Bellenia and Solina walk swiftly before her as they move through the streets of the dead city, the heat of the burning temple at their backs. Every window they pass is dark, every house empty. The place is nothing more than a carcass. In the darkness and the crush, Catia is grateful for the Roman grid of straight roads imposed upon the ancient Trinovantes capital, which now ease their escape. Behind her, Cunominus oversees the retreat, ordering men and women to fan out across the city, torching it street by street.

The giant triumphal arch which crowns Rome's colonial settlement shines pale in the moonlight, its base already blackened by the fire of her army's entry. Catia passes underneath, out along the road into the cooler air of open countryside. She makes for the river, where the mass of her people are gathered, their faces unnaturally bright in the dark, bunched around waggons and horses. She almost stumbles as Solina stops in front of her, turning to look back. The wonder on her daughter's face makes Catia stop too.

Camulodunum has become a beacon to rival the sun. A molten heart burns at its centre, and fire runs across its rooftops, a furious blaze lighting up the city, chasing away the night. Catia is riveted. Even the sky above has been purged of stars, the black fading to a dirty russet brown. The sight must be visible across the country, a flare sent up to give Britons hope and to warn Rome of what is coming.

It is a message for the next city Catia will burn.

13

SOLINA

The camp is squalid, made worse by yesterday's rain, tempers fraying as fires fail to light. People have grown used to days of feasting and dancing, drunk on the realisation that none can resist us, and now the lack of flame feels like a bad omen. If we cannot roast the meat soon, it will spoil, and our dwindling supply of cattle will have been slaughtered in vain. I walk over to check on Tan, who is eating the last threads of hay from his own supper, and rest my forehead against the warmth of his shoulder. It soon becomes uncomfortable. My hair itches from the lice which have spread unchecked through all of us living heaped on top of one another, and my clothes are stiff from days of sweat. I glance over to where Bellenia is standing, our aunt Vassura brushing through her hair, picking out the vermin. A little further away, beside one of our waggons, my mother is speaking to Cunominus, and she is laughing, just as she might have done back in the Town of the Wolf. It gives the brief illusion that our family remains united and unchanged, but I know that is untrue. Behind them, I can see the blackened ruins of a Catuvellauni village we raided yesterday.

I am trying to hold on to the feeling of hope I had after

we destroyed Rome's Ninth Legion in battle. It was a victory which surely proves Adraste is with us, whatever my sister believes. Bellenia and I were fortunate not to have been in the first thick of fighting when the Ninth came upon our army the day after we left Camulodunum. The pair of us were ordered to stay back, only riding down the enemy when they retreated. The terror and exhilaration of that final charge will never leave me. I stroke Tan's mane now, running my fingers along his neck, remembering what it felt like to be at one with him on the field. Death came so close, and yet we lived. Afterwards, when I had ridden through the battle's stinking backwash, picking my way over ground churned up with blood and gore, I had vomited over Tan's neck. Yet nothing, not even the sight of so much horror, could destroy the elation I felt at seeing our enemy flee. Soldiers like those who had attacked me, who had made me feel worthless, had run in terror from my sword and the charge of my horse. I was powerful, and it filled me with joy. I had expected Bellenia to share my excitement, but my sister's loathing of war has only deepened. The more death she sees, the more it distresses her, whereas for me, death is becoming a familiar companion.

Even so, Bellenia is right that something has soured in the camp, although I do not know what. The air thrums with tension, as it does before a storm. I watch Tan's soft nose snuffling the hay and try to understand what has changed. Even though we are winning, somehow the campaign is becoming less hopeful. We no longer try as hard to bring fellow Britons into our rebellion. Instead, every settlement we pass is sacked, plundered for food and supplies, our old grudges against rival tribes like the Catuvellauni fuelling the violence as much as any desire for freedom. My mother still gives speeches about uniting our people and driving the Romans into the sea, but sometimes I feel frightened that her command over so many people is slipping. This army is led by greed, rage and hatred. It is led not by Catia but by Boudicca, a monstrous figure the people conjured into being out of their own anger. Boudicca is not really my mother. She cannot be.

London's rooftops are spread out below us, the thin line of its long wooden bridge shining in the sun, severed at the centre. The place looks peaceful, nestled on the riverbank. I murmur the name of the water's spirit: *Tamessa*, the Dark River, beloved servant of the god Esus. Further down her swift flowing stream, a forest of masts is clustered far out of our reach, safe in the middle of the water. That will annoy my mother. I glance at Bellenia on her horse Kintu. She stares back at me, her face pale, almost hostile. I look away. I know that she does not want to be here.

Our mother's chariot is surrounded by a crowd of Londoners, creeping in as close as they dare, each more eager than the last to bow in the mud and heap her with praise. They are Britons who have been waiting here on the outskirts of their own city, eager to join us and loot their Roman neighbours. I can see my mother is angry to hear both the legate *and* the procurator have fled the city. The news leaves me feeling deflated too. It was the procurator Decianus who ordered our humiliation, who murdered my cousin Aesu, and in my fantasies I had imagined fighting him in single combat on London's streets. Instead, the loathsome man has fled to Gaul, never to show his face here again.

"He may have escaped London, but I will still have the legate's head," my mother is shouting. "Suetonius Paulinus can sit on the spikes of my wheel until his skull has been ground into the mud." People cheer, my uncle Cunominus loudest of all. He rarely leaves my mother's side these days, determined to protect her. It is not only brotherly love. Just as the Romans guard their golden standards from capture, so Cunominus guards our own emblem of rebellion against ambush or assassination. "You are right to have joined us," my mother promises the large gaggle of Londoners. "Camulodunum was built over the bones of an ancient capital, yet this city is nothing but a parasite, founded by Romans, who harnessed themselves to the banks of the Dark River and now use its waters to ship out everything they have stolen. Including our own people, as slaves! We will make them pay."

While she speaks, some of our army is already descending the hill to sack the city, not waiting for my mother's signal, uninterested in anything but stripping London of its wealth. She pretends not to notice. I sit uncertain on Tan, glancing at Bellenia, who does not acknowledge me. I want to know what our mother intends us to do, and look over, anxious for guidance. I catch her eye. For a moment, when she looks back at me, she is my mother Catia again. Her face clouds with concern at the sight of my sister. Cunominus is mounted on his own horse, as close to her chariot as he can get, and I watch her speak to him before she sends him over.

"Your mother does not wish you to take part in the first assault on London," Cunominus announces, as he reins his horse in alongside Bellenia. "You can take part in the second assault, when we burn the city."

"Will we go with you?" I ask, secretly relieved not to be swept up in the first wave of killing and chaos.

"No. I will go with your mother. She wants you to wait there, by that line of trees, and guard the waggons. For now, keep out of the way." He nods briefly, clearly keen to return to his commander.

Bellenia and I do as he has asked, weaving our way through other restless riders. Our position is away from the main mass of the army and there is no sign of anyone else who has been ordered to take part in a second assault – the only people here are children and mothers, sitting on top of their waggons to get a good view of the burning city. From here, I can see our own mother shouting orders from her chariot, as if she were not following the mass of fighters who are already streaming over the fields but leading them. A blast from the carnyxes marks her entry into the assault, and those who had been obedient enough to hold back thunder after her, raising their weapons, screaming with rage. The noise is deafening. Tan tosses his head, pawing the ground, forcing me to turn him in circles until he quietens down. By the time I have him under control, my mother is lost to view.

"You must be glad to wait," I say to Bellenia, who is making little effort to calm Kintu.

"Why?" she asks, clinging to Kintu as he bucks, before finally reining him in. "Because I am too weak to attack?"

"No," I reply, unsure how to speak to her in this mood. "Because the first assault is so ugly."

"Is *that* what is ugly?" My sister nudges her horse closer to mine. Kintu's nostrils are wide, and I'm afraid he will set Tan off again. "Have you ever asked yourself when we will stop sacking cities and build one? When freedom means more than slaughtering and stealing?"

"When we have destroyed every legion like we did the Ninth," I retort. "When all the kingdoms of Britain belong to us again. Or would you rather the Romans stayed as our masters?"

"This isn't about Rome!" my sister shouts. "Half the people we kill are Britons!"

"Then what *is* it about?" My tone is goading, but I'm also afraid. This is a question I have already asked myself.

Bellenia doesn't answer. Instead, she stares at the city

below, its streets already overwhelmed by our army. The dark mass of their bodies casts a shadow across London, the silver of their weapons flashing like lightning in a storm. Without warning, Bellenia suddenly kicks Kintu, and sets off down the hill. For a moment I am too shocked to react, then I scream after her to stop. Bellenia speeds up instead, breaking into a canter. Unsure what else to do, I follow. Tan is excited by the gallop downhill, and soon we are sending up clods of earth, hurtling towards London, unable to stop. Bellenia has cut away from the main thrust of our army's attack, and I am forced to follow, heading straight towards the Dark River.

I am still yelling, but Bellenia only gallops harder, as reckless as she used to be in the green woods at home. I realise that I am crying, that I am both afraid and relieved to see my sister like this, passionate and wilful, as she was in the days before the war. I manage to catch up with her, and try to force my horse against hers, to steer her away from the city.

"How many lives is your honour worth, Solina?" she screams. "*How many?*"

Bellenia's beautiful face is twisted into an expression of unrecognisable anguish. She passes me before I can stop her.

Tan is growing tired, struggling to keep up with Kintu. We should not be galloping like this, using up all our horses' precious energy in a charge, leaving nothing for a retreat. I slow Tan down as much as I can. Ahead of us, Bellenia has joined the road that runs along the river into the city, and eventually Kintu stops, his sides heaving.

"What are you *doing*?" I ask, finally catching her. "You're going to get us killed!"

London is already burning, and we are exposed here, away from our own army, on the very outskirts of town by the water. It looks deserted, but I'm still afraid, wondering what target we might make for those who dared to stay and defend their homes. "Our mother said we should set fire to the streets," Bellenia replies, dismounting Kintu and walking further into London, leading her exhausted horse by the reins. "So that is what we shall do." I am forced to follow, not daring to dismount myself, still begging her to turn back.

"We are in the wrong part of the city," I yell. "We are heading straight for our own line of attack."

"We aren't Romans," Bellenia says. "So why would you be afraid?"

The noise of fighting is getting louder, and smoke hangs in the deserted road. I can hear screaming, the smash of pottery, axe against wood – the sounds of slaughter more terrifying for being out of sight. We pass a side street and a gang of four men smack straight into us. I have no idea if they are our own people, or fleeing Londoners, or which I should fear more. There is a moment's hesitation when they stare, their eyes wild in ash-stained faces, then they attack. The man in front swings a wooden beam and I glimpse the flash of a knife. I raise my sword in answer, but one of the four is already upon me, trying to drag me from my horse.

"I am Boudicca's daughter!" I yell. The man is too drunk on violence to understand, grappling at my waist, and I slit his throat, blood falling hot on my thigh. Tan rears up, and the other men step back, frightened of his flailing hooves. I look around in panic for my sister. She is lying on the ground, where the fourth robber is grappling with her gold torc, trying to steal it. I bend over Tan's neck, swinging my sword, forcing the man to dive out of the way, then I ride at the other robbers, stoving in the head of one, before the rest flee.

I slide from Tan's back and run to Bellenia. She is injured, struggling to rise, blood matted to her hair where she was hit. The relief of seeing her move almost makes me cry, but it's followed swiftly by terror. I have no idea how to get her out of here. Our horses are exhausted, and I will make an easy target with a wounded companion.

"Can you stand up?" I ask. "If I help you?"

"I'm sorry," Bellenia clutches my arm. "This is my fault."

"It's fine," I lie. I can be furious with her later, when we are both safe. I look around for Kintu, but he's nowhere to be seen. Tan is waiting for me, sides heaving, patches of his white coat stained red with blood. He looks more like a horse from the Otherworld than ever. "If you get on Tan, I can lead you," I say, trying to heave my sister up again. Bellenia staggers, too dizzy to stay upright. I'm not sure how I will keep her on a horse without falling off, and I stare round desperately, hoping for inspiration. A large archway on the opposite side of the street leads into the courtyard of what looks like a Roman inn. If we manage to hide inside, we will at least be less of a target than on the main road. "I'm going to carry you in there," I say, nodding towards the inn. "Put your arms round my neck." I half carry, half drag my sister into the courtyard, then run back to fetch Tan.

"Where's Kintu?" Bellenia asks.

"I imagine he went back to the river," I say. "He won't have run into the fighting." There is a mounting block at the corner of the courtyard. I tie Tan up beside it, and am about to help Bellenia climb up, when a door opens onto the courtyard. I freeze. It is a woman in Roman dress, her hair piled up into the strange curls they wear.

"*Is she injured?*" the woman asks in Latin.

I draw my sword, staggering as I try to wield it while holding my sister. "*Don't come any closer!*"

The woman holds her hands up. "*I'm not armed,*" she says. "*Please. I don't mean you harm.*"

"*What do you mean then?*"

"*You're with the rebellion, aren't you?*" she asks, and when I say nothing, she carries on. "*My husband has gone to defend the city. I don't know if he will ever return; all our servants have fled. I didn't want to leave my father – he's bedbound. There's only the two of us here. But perhaps if I shelter you, you will tell the rebels to spare us, when they come?*"

"What's she saying?" Bellenia asks, unable to understand the woman's Latin.

"She's offering to shelter us, if we ask our warriors to spare her."

"Say yes," Bellenia replies. "It's safer for you than going back out there."

"What if it's a trap?" I whisper, but Bellenia only shakes her head, then winces from the pain. "*Very well*," I say to the woman. "*Help me.*"

She hurries over, and we get Bellenia inside. The room is dark, its walls lined with pots and herbs. A large wooden table is strewn with plates, reminding me of the house where my sister and I slept at Camulodunum. We sit Bellenia down on a bench.

"*I will get her some water*," the woman says.

"*No*," I reply. "*Stay here. Where I can see you.*" I am already wondering if this was a sensible idea. What if our army sets fire to this place without even trying to loot it?

"*The water is just there.*" The woman points at a bucket. "*You can see me.*"

I let her bring over the pail. She scoops water into a cup for Bellenia, then wets a cloth to clean the wound on her head. My sister smiles, showing much more warmth than I have, and nods in thanks. I watch the stranger dab carefully at Bellenia's hair, trying not to get in the way as I lean over to see the injury. Thankfully it is not deep, though many have died of infection from such cuts. "*What is your name?*" I ask the woman.

"*I am Lais,*" she replies, tenderly cleaning my sister's wound. Bellenia is grimacing, but silent, not wanting to shame herself by crying out.

"*Are you from Rome?*"

"*I am Greek.*"

Her answer surprises me. I realise Latin cannot be her mother tongue, just as it is not mine. "*Is your husband also Greek?*"

Lais hesitates. "*No. He is Roman. I am his freedwoman.*"

"*Then it is your husband's father in the house?*"

"*Please,*" Lais says, wringing out the cloth. "*He is a good man.*" I realise her hands are shaking.

"*I'm not going to slaughter an old man in his bed,*" I retort. Then I think of the temple at Camulodunum, burned to ash with all its townspeople inside. Lais must have heard what happened.

"*I will get chamomile and rosemary for a poultice.*" Lais points to some of the hanging herbs. "*It will help prevent infection.*"

I watch her prepare them on the table, making sure the herbs are the healing ones she described. "*Why are you doing this?*"

"*Why would I not?*"

I can think of plenty of reasons, but do not say so.

Perhaps Lais guesses this because she adds, "*It gives me something to do, to take my mind off things.*"

"What are you both saying?" Bellenia asks. When I translate, she reaches for Lais's hand. "Solina, please tell Lais how grateful I am."

"*My sister thanks you,*" I tell Lais, who smiles at Bellenia.

The noise of street-fighting is growing louder. I feel uneasy, stuck in this building, and go to the doorway to stand with my back to the frame, my sword drawn, one eye on Lais, the other on the courtyard. Above the rooftops, smoke is rising.

Perhaps the fire is only a few streets away. "*What were you going to do if we hadn't come?*" I ask Lais. "*How were you going to protect your father-in-law? I don't understand why you didn't just run—*"

Lais does not get a chance to answer. A group of our people are charging into the courtyard, led by a warrior on horseback. I see his familiar flash of gold hair, the burnished wolf on his shield, and could almost weep with relief. It is Isarninus.

"Isarninus!" I yell. "This way! My sister is injured."

My sister's almost-lover leaps from his horse and runs to me. I fling my arms around him, never more pleased to see a man. "Quickly," he says. "Let me fetch Bellenia."

Some of his companions follow us into the room, and I suddenly realise I should have mentioned Lais. Before I have time to stop them, one of the men has grabbed her, shoving her against the table, a knife to her throat. Lais shouts at the man in a language I don't understand, trying to fend him off, groping vainly over the table's surface for a weapon.

"No!" I cry. "Stop! She was helping Bellenia – we promised she would be safe!"

Isarninus grabs my arm. "Your mother has been very clear. No Roman is to be left alive."

Before I can answer him, Bellenia has staggered to her feet. She seizes a pot, smashing it over the head of the man holding Lais. He does not see who has hit him, and swings round instinctively with the knife, even as Isarninus yells out in horror.

I see my sister's hands at her throat, covered in blood, and the look of terror on the man's face as he realises what he has done. Then Bellenia collapses. Isarninus lets go of me and I run to her, dropping to my knees.

"Bellenia," I take my sister's face in my hands, as if saying her name might bring her back. She cannot speak, but looks up at me, eyes full of anguish. We both know she is dying. "You are safe," I say, desperate to comfort her. "Epona will guide you, you will be with our father. You will be safe." I keep holding my sister's gaze, clinging to this last thread that ties her to me, the knowledge that her eyes are looking back into mine. Then the thread is broken.

I hold my sister, burying my face in her hair, and howl.

14

BOUDICCA

The flames rise on Bellenia's pyre as London's ruins glow red in the dusk. Catia always knew the risks her daughters faced, always accepted that her love could not be more precious than their honour. But nothing prepared her for this pain. There was no glory in Bellenia's fall. She died at the hands of one of her own, defending a Roman woman. There is nothing for Catia to cling to which might lessen the agony of loss. She stares into the fire, which has already consumed her beautiful daughter. Catia's heart cannot contain her grief. Instead, it flares outwards as rage.

 Solina is standing red-eyed beside Cunominus, and the sight of her surviving child only deepens Catia's anguish. Why did Solina take her sister into that house? What possible reason could she have had to trust such vermin? At least the Roman woman is dead now; Isarninus executed her, along with the man who killed Bellenia. Catia would have executed Isarninus too, but Cunominus prevented her, holding her tight in her grief. Hundreds of warriors would turn against them if she killed a man like Isarninus, he said, and they cannot afford to split the army, not with victory so close. Catia looks out over London, the city where she should have slaughtered

Rome's procurator, but which instead took the life of her youngest daughter. The Dark River shimmers behind the ruined houses on its banks. Tamessa is orange, reflecting the light of the flames, and the water is a traitor, still sheltering a nest of boats Catia cannot reach.

A lone voice begins to sing a lament for the fallen. The melody is picked up by others in the crowd, until it swells to a haunting chorus of voices, louder even than the sound of battle. Tears stream down Catia's face. Thousands have come here to pay honour to the heir of Prasutagus, Boudicca's daughter, but almost none will ever know how she died. It is not a story her family will tell.

Catia does not join the revelry in camp that night to celebrate London's fall. The ground vibrates with music and dancing, the air full of song and laughter, but she sits by a fire with Vassura, close by the trees and waggons. Young children lie fast asleep in many of the carts, tumbled together like puppies under heaps of cloth. The sight of their small, soft bodies fills Catia with longing for her own child. She would do anything to go back in time, to hold Bellenia in her arms again, safe by their hearth.

Catia gazes at the mead in the drinking horn, its golden liquid promising oblivion. She has already drunk so much her head is swimming. "I'm sorry," she says to Vassura. "I did not understand the pain you must have been carrying since Aesu's death. I should have done more to comfort you. Forgive me."

Vassura brushes the hair from Catia's face. "Bellenia is with her father now, the most honoured guest in the halls he was gifted by the gods. She will be feasting there with Aesu." Vassura's kindness bring tears to Catia's eyes. She weeps against her sister-in-law's shoulder, while Vassura holds her. "Where is Solina? You should be together."

"She went storming after Cunominus," Catia says, wiping her eyes. "Shouting at him over some imagined slight." She pauses. "I cannot believe she did this. I cannot believe she took her sister into that house."

"Catia," Vassura says, her voice stern. "This is not Solina's fault."

"Does she blame me?" Both women start. Solina is standing, defiant, by the flames. Looking at her aunt, not her mother.

Vassura rises to her feet. "I will leave you both awhile." She clasps Solina's arm as she passes. A gesture of love, and perhaps a warning.

"Why would I blame you?" Catia says, when Vassura has gone. "Have you done something to earn my anger?"

"You have done enough to earn *mine*." The rage in Solina's voice startles Catia. "Bellenia would not have died if it weren't for you."

For a moment Catia is too shocked to reply. "Was *I* the one who took her into that house—"

"No!" Solina interrupts. "*You* were the one who gave the order that no Romans should be spared. Not even a woman who was trying to save your own daughter. Lais wasn't even Roman – did you know that? She was Greek."

Catia gets to her feet, maddened by grief, her cheeks flaming from the mead. "So, you have more tears for some Greek woman than you do for your sister's dishonourable death?"

"There was more honour in her death than you will ever understand," Solina says, and her coldness hurts Catia more deeply than a display of anger ever would.

"Suddenly you care about your sister's honour," Catia shouts. "But you didn't care when you stole it from her, did you? When you took her kill, in front of every warrior in the tribe. She never recovered from your betrayal. I saw what it did to her. You destroyed the one chance she had to become the woman and the warrior she was supposed to be, before those men attacked her."

"Before they attacked *us*," Solina retorts. "Or does what happened to me not matter to you?" Catia sees the tears in Solina's eyes and instinctively reaches out to her. "No." Solina twists away from her mother's comfort. "You really believe I would steal my sister's honour? I pushed Bellenia aside because I could see he was going to *kill her*, because she was too tormented to defend herself. I killed him to *save* her honour, not steal it. How did you not see?"

The fight comes back to Catia, flickering images like the fire. She remembers what Solina screamed – *He is mine* – but perhaps, if she tries, she can see Bellenia before that. Perhaps she can remember Bellenia weeping, begging Catia not to make her fight the man who raped her. Or Bellenia's growing distress at the war, the nightmares which haunted her, but which Catia could not face or acknowledge. She starts to cry, unable to bear the suffering her youngest child must have endured. "Why did it destroy her and not you?" she asks Solina. "Why did it make *you* so much stronger?"

As soon as she has said the words, spoken in a rush of pain, she understands her question is unforgivable. "Solina, I'm sorry, I did not mean—"

"Because Bellenia was like our father. She had a heart that felt. And I am like you. I have none."

Catia stares at her oldest child. Her face is a mask. She feels then she has lost not one daughter, but two. "Solina," she says again, reaching out her hands, desperate to make amends. But Solina turns, stumbling in her haste to get away, running from her mother into the mass of people dancing and drinking on the edge of a ruined city.

Sunrise brings no hope, only the nauseating remembrance of loss. Bellenia is gone, and Catia may have died with her. But Boudicca has no choice but to live on.

This is what Boudicca realises when she rises to see London's ruins, still smouldering in the pink bruise of dawn. The only way to bear her daughter's death is to fulfil the destiny promised by Andraste. She must destroy Rome.

The camp is quiet, most of the men and women still sleeping off their drinking from the night before. Boudicca walks through the tents to stand on the brow of the hill. She watches the Dark River. Its strong silver line, glinting like a path to the Otherworld, comforts her. Perhaps this is the road Bellenia has taken.

"You should not walk out here by yourself." Cunominus, her ever loyal brother, has followed her, his steps silent in the grass. He looks years older than when the war started.

"We cannot afford to pause our assault on Rome," she says. "The legate has not run away forever – he will be stalking us, gathering more soldiers. If we do not finish him soon, we cannot send people home to gather in the harvest. There will be famine. Some of the London spies say Suetonius Paulinus took the road towards Verulamium. That is where we must now go."

"You can allow yourself a few days to grieve, Catia." Cunominus rests his massive hand on her shoulder, his voice tender. "Nobody would blame you."

"I am not the only mother to have lost a child in this war. Why should I claim more time to mourn than they have?" She shifts away from his touch, not wanting to allow any feeling which might weaken her resolve. "And do not call me Catia. Boudicca is the name the gods have given me."

She sees the flicker of unease on his face. "You should speak to Solina," he says. "She is your child. It is not good for the pair of you to be estranged. Particularly not now."

"I have thousands of children," she replies. "All the Iceni are my children. I must think of them."

"*Solina* is your child," Cunominus says again. "And she is alive. She should be more precious to you than all others. My own child is far in the north. Riomanda will have given birth by now, yet I may never even see my child's face."

"Then maybe you should go to them. I will not stop you." Her voice is so cold, Cunominus sucks in his breath.

"I have been nothing but loyal to you, sister," he says. "Do not do this." She almost wants to say something worse, so that he leaves, and she is left alone with the pain she deserves. But Cunominus is her brother and knows her too well. He takes her firmly by the shoulders. "I will never leave you. Do you hear me? *Never*. So do not do this."

The warmth of his hands, gripping her so tightly, threatens to break the brittle shell surrounding her heart. "Don't be kind to me. Please. I cannot bear it. Go to Solina. I cannot comfort her. You must do it for me."

He looks torn, and his vulnerability makes her think of their parents. Each generation assumes their elders are stronger, and yet with age they learn that nobody ever has the answers. "It's *you* she needs," Cunominus says. "You are her mother."

"I lost the right to call myself her mother the day I failed to protect her and Bellenia from those men."

"Gods! That was not your fault. You cannot—"

But whatever Cunominus wants to forbid her, she does not

want to hear. She shakes herself free. "Go to Solina. Leave me."

She knows he does not want to leave, but since the day he was born, Cunominus has always bowed to his elder sister's judgement. Boudicca watches him weave his way back through the camp, back towards the place his niece is sleeping, his figure soon lost in the blur of canvas and smoke. She turns towards the river, watching the sun climb higher. It is no longer a pink haze but a vast golden disc, burnished like the shields lining the hall of her ancestors. Boudicca has no choice but to carry on, whatever grief she feels. Her army has risen, and like the sun, she cannot now stop until she has claimed back the sky, or the Iceni will be plunged into darkness.

15

SOLINA

The ashes are cold on Bellenia's pyre when I gather her bones. I lead the ritual both as her sister and as a Druid, channelling my grief into this final act of respect. My mind is calm as I handle her precious remains, winding them into a sacred cloth. I do not allow myself to think of how much I miss her or the emptiness in my heart. Instead, I focus on where Bellenia is now. She will be in the glorious halls of the Otherworld, even more beautiful than she was in life, her golden hair shining like the sun. I will not think of how she died. I speak to her spirit with love.

When I say the final words of supplication to the gods, I remember my father, the way he once performed this duty for my mother's mother, how this is the way my family will always be, an unbroken line of Druids stretching back in time. One day I will gather my father's bones from the woods, and one day my own child will gather mine. Even though we are in the middle of a war, and nobody's survival is certain, somehow I know this; I will not allow our line to die.

It is only at the ritual's end, when I give Bellenia's remains to another Druid who will keep them safe until we return home, that I falter. I don't want to let Bellenia go. The man sees my weakness and grips my arm to steady me. I have known him many years; he is the Druid Saenu who advises my aunt Vassura. "You have done well," he murmurs. "Your sister's spirit will thank you."

I nod, blinded by tears, allowing Saenu to take my sister's bones. My mother is waiting for me when I walk from the pyre. I can see in her eyes that she is desperate to hold me, to speak with me, but I swerve away, embracing Vassura instead. The anger I feel is not only about yesterday; I know my mother did not wholly mean what she said. It is worse than that. I should not blame my mother for Bellenia's death, and yet I do. I cannot bear to look at her.

My mother and Cunominus want to muster the warriors immediately to pursue the legate, but they cannot get the army to move. People are too busy drinking, still roaming through London in gangs, ransacking any building that might have escaped our first assault. My own head is throbbing, not from drink, but from grief. It has hollowed me out, leaving me weakened. I keep wanting to find Bellenia, so she can comfort me, before remembering her death is the reason I feel so desperate. There is no Riomanda either, so I seek out Vassura, following my aunt like a shadow, clinging to her in a way that I would have been ashamed to do even as a child. I know she does not approve of me ignoring my mother, but she does not shake me off either. Instead, she gets me to help her prepare our freshly plundered supplies into a meal. I sit beside her in the stink of the camp, husking beans, and the repetitive task is a balm to my misery. At our feet, a battered cauldron rests upon a glowing pile of embers, slowly warming the stew.

"Did you know your mother was younger than you when she married Prasutagus?" my aunt asks, her fingers deftly shelling the beans. It seems she is not going to let the topic of my mother drop.

"Yes."

"I still remember when I first met Catia. Such a wild, wilful creature. The most stubborn person I had ever met. And she was so passionately in love with my brother. You cannot imagine how much she loved him."

"My father loved her too," I reply, uneasy at Vassura's tone.

"In time he did, yes. But he would have accepted her offer regardless. He gained command of the Wolf Tribe through her, uniting the entire Iceni kingdom." Vassura looks at me. "And then she gave him you. The apple of his eye."

I do not know why my aunt would want to speak like this when Bellenia is dead, and I cannot make amends. "It is not my fault that he preferred me," I say, speaking my long-buried guilt aloud.

"No. It was not your fault. Perhaps love is nobody's fault. But his favouritism was always very marked. It left Catia little choice when she had her second child. Your father had already chosen his heir, and it was you."

I stop husking the beans, crushing their skins in my fingers. The pain in my heart is unbearable. "Why are you saying all this?"

"Because your mother loves you, Solina. I know her preference for Bellenia has been hard, but it was not entirely her fault. You were already taken. She was trying to redress the balance."

"But you've always called her a warmonger," I protest. "You always took my father's side against her!"

"On *that*, yes. Prasutagus was right to pursue peace, and I always loathed your mother's enthusiasm for fighting, but that does not mean my brother was right about everything.

However much you loved your father, surely you can also see he had his flaws?"

"You say my mother was very in love with him... Do you think he manipulated her?" It is hard to ask, especially as I already know the answer. But I want to know if Vassura saw it too.

"Prasutagus was a Druid of immense ability," she replies. "He manipulated everybody: Rome, his people, your mother, you. That is what it means, to use the power of the mind to bend others to the gods' will. Or even, at times, to your own."

I think of my father's words in the woods. *We are destined to rule others by whatever means we may.* It is a boast that brings me both shame and pride.

Vassura is watching me, without slowing her shelling. "You are the child of both your parents," is all she says. A remark which sounds obvious yet also manages to be cryptic.

I begin husking the beans again. I think of Bellenia as a child, my sister's reluctance to learn Latin, her lack of interest in every form of study. Was this genuine, or was she simply angry with our father for his favouritism? I cannot ask her now, and the thought brings me intense sadness. "Will you tell me more about what my mother was like when she was young?" I ask Vassura.

"You only have to look inside yourself for the answer."

"What do you mean?"

There is a pause, as my aunt stirs her pile of beans into the pot. I realise there are tears in her eyes. She sighs as she sits back down beside me. "I mean, Solina, that she was like you."

At dinner that night, as we sit around the fire at dusk, I make a point of sitting beside my mother, even though I have still not forgiven her. Vassura and Cunominus are watching, and I can see the relief on their faces. My mother looks a little uncertain – an expression I have not seen from her before – and it softens me. I reach out to take her hand. She clasps her fingers around mine and I rest my head on her shoulder in the way Bellenia often did. The gesture fills me with guilt. I feel as if I am stealing my sister's place, taking the love my mother would rather have given to her other child.

"You were so strong at the ceremony today," she says, stroking my hair. "I felt proud. You reminded me of your father."

"Bellenia will be with him now," I reply, and it is a strange thought, that my sister is with our father while I am with our mother, something that so rarely happened in life. I try to relax, to believe that my mother loves me, that she is not sorry I am the one who survived.

Vassura begins to serve up the stew. All around us, I am conscious of other gatherings doing the same, a scene endlessly repeated in this enormous sprawling family that is not a family but an army. More distant members of our own kin begin to drift towards our fire to join us, Diseta among them. The old woman eases herself onto her haunches, collapsing onto the muddy grass with a grunt.

"There is no greater glory than death in battle," she announces, and although she means well, they are not the words any of us want to hear, especially given the way Bellenia really died. I sit upright, not wanting to be seen curled against my mother like a child. Diseta nods at me. "That's better," she says, straightening her own shoulders in approval. "You carried yourself well today. Excessive mourning does nobody any good."

If Diseta had not lost all three of her own children, I would resent her for saying such a thing in front of two bereaved mothers. But on this campaign, I have come to see that Diseta – who Bellenia and I once called a forest troll – carries her own sorrows, her bravado no more than a mask.

"Have you spoken to your warriors about the urgency of moving on?" Cunominus asks Diseta.

"Yes, but they do not see it. The fools think we have won the war already. Arguments about the harvest will likely sway them more."

"The harvest?" I ask.

"We are going to split the army," my mother answers. "Anyone who is not a warrior needs to return home to bring in the crops. Otherwise, there will be nothing to eat this winter, regardless of when we defeat Rome."

"Families won't agree to being separated," I say, thinking of the waggon-loads of children and women who accompanied their warriors on the road.

"They will not want their children to starve," my mother says sharply. "Sometimes a warrior's duty to family involves leaving those they love behind."

She is looking at me keenly, without any softness in her eyes, as if challenging me to disagree. It gives me a sinking feeling. "When are you going to split the army?"

"When we reach Verulamium," she says. Then she turns to speak to Diseta, urging her to convince her people of the plan. It feels as if my mother is slipping away from me again. I see Vassura watching across the flames, the orange glow softening the lines of her face. Her eyes are full of sadness.

It takes days to muster the army to set off for Verulamium, and I suspect it is only the promise of more looting which finally persuades people to move. Every town has fallen to us so easily, it is hard for anyone to take my mother's sense of urgency at defeating Paulinus, the Roman legate, seriously.

I ride beside Cunominus, staring straight ahead at my mother's chariot so that I do not focus on Bellenia's absence on my other side. I wonder if Tan misses Kintu the way I miss my sister. Nobody could find her horse, even though we searched for him, which is yet another loss. Kintu was not only a horse – he was also Bellenia's brother-in-arms. We raised Tan and Kintu together as foals, breaking them in under the watchful eyes of Riomanda and our mother when we were little more than children ourselves. I almost hope Kintu is dead, and my sister rode his spirit over the Dark River to the Otherworld, following the light of Epona's moon.

"I am glad to see you and your mother have reconciled," Cunominus says, breaking the silence between us.

I glance over at my uncle, my mother's most loyal companion. I feel a stab of jealousy that he still has a sister to love, when I have lost mine. Then I remember he has been forced to leave Riomanda and his unborn child behind. The war has ripped through so many peoples' lives. "Do you really think we will have to split the army?" I ask.

"Rome is fighting on many fronts and so must we," Cunominus replies. "Just look around you, see what they've done."

I do not need to follow his pointing finger. Ruined, blackened stalks stretch out for miles, where a short time ago there were ripening crops. Everything has been burned. If the legate cannot defeat my mother in battle, it seems he will try starvation. I wonder what sort of commander he is to have abandoned London to its fate, then obliterate everything in his path. At first, I thought he was a coward, but seeing all this destruction, I am not so sure. "Do you think Suetonius Paulinus is drawing us into a trap?"

My uncle is silent, his expression grim. "Whether he is or not, we have to pursue him."

"That means yes, then."

"Whatever Paulinus has planned, our army is still many times the size of his. He will be no match for Boudicca."

I glance over my shoulder. Our army is vast, it is true, and every warrior will fight to the death for their freedom, but our wildness in battle could also be a liability if the enemy is highly organised. In my mind, I try to visualise who this man, Paulinus, might be. It is possible to piece together traces of his thinking from what we found in London. Ships packed with survivors, moored out of our reach in the river. Warehouses burned before our arrival so we could not stock up on food. The sole bridge broken so we could not pass the river. And now these blackened fields, leading us to his army. "How did the legate campaign against the Druids in the west? Was he vicious like the procurator?" I ask.

"There was no campaign of corruption against the people, like the Iceni suffered in the east." My uncle glances at me, as if nervous to have raised the ghost of the attack at my father's house. "But he is ruthless. Any place Paulinus met resistance, he simply destroyed it, without leaving any survivors."

A figure starts to take shape in my mind, like smoke rising from the altar after sacrifice. I see a shadow warrior, black as the burned fields, wielding a sword of flame, and his heart is cold as death.

"Whatever this legate is like, we need not fear," I say, as if no vision had come to me. "Boudicca is destined to defeat Rome."

"By the will of Andraste," Cunominus replies. I glance at him, but he is staring straight ahead, impossible to read.

After a bitter trudge north through so much desolation, the hope of reviving our army's ebbing spirits through looting is dashed. Verulamium is almost bare. The legate has been here before us, destroying supplies we might have stolen, emptying the place of almost all its people, hastily boarding up buildings. We rip apart what we can, burning the main street, but it is a half-hearted sacking after the glory of Camulodunum.

When we have subdued what remains of the town, Cunominus takes over Verulamium's richest house as a mark of our family's status. I walk through the strange villa. It does not have the beauty of a roundhouse – even its largest rooms are small when set against my father's hall – but I am drawn to the images which dance across their floors. Bending down, I run my finger over the ridges of tiny tiles. The pictures show Roman gods, but many are drawn with symbols I recognise – Epona's sheaves of wheat, the horns of Cernunnos. I think of the mosaic at the baths of Camulodunum, and the British woman's blood running red across it.

I am still studying the floor when my mother walks in. I straighten up, not wanting to be caught off guard.

"Solina," she says, and there is so much love and grief in the word I am fearful of what she is going to tell me.

"Are Cunominus and Vassura safe?"

"Yes."

"Then what is it?"

My mother takes both my hands. "I want you to lead the company back to bring in the harvest."

"What? No!"

"Listen to me," she says, raising her voice. "I believe the

legate is camped nearby. All we must do is follow the trail of burned fields, then we will find him. You know I will crush his army. But there are too many families here who cannot fight, and the harvest is dying in the fields. What will people eat after our victory? What will it mean to drive out Rome if we starve?"

"But there are so many *other* warriors you could send! Why me?"

"Because you are the last remaining heir of Prasutagus. People will follow you."

The words feel like a knife-wound of rejection after my sister's death. I am my father's child, not hers. "You don't want me to fight alongside you," I say, shoving her away from me. "You don't want me there with you when you finally crush Rome."

The pain in my mother's eyes instantly makes me regret my words. I am about to apologise, but then she speaks, and her voice is cold. "If that is what you want to believe, so be it." She hesitates, as if waiting for me to contradict her, but when I am silent, she turns, leaving me alone.

16

BOUDICCA

She has transcended her name, but in doing so she has destroyed all that it meant to be Catia. That is the price the gods demand in war. Boudicca closes her eyes. *She sees herself taller than any living being. She is a monster with eyes of fire, clothed in robes of blood.*

When she opens her eyes again, she looks out at the assembled Iceni, filling the fields outside Verulamium. They are here to watch a sacred ceremony. The decision to separate families has not been popular, so Boudicca is having to call upon the gods to make the decision for her, allowing Andraste's hare to run towards the chosen path. Solina is not the Druid who is helping her with this ceremony, it is Saenu, Vassura's advisor. The old man approaches her now, holding Andraste's sacred hare, wincing as it kicks. Boudicca takes the struggling animal, pressing it against her robes so that it cannot scratch her. The drum of its heart beats frantically under her fingers.

"I call upon you, Andraste the Indestructible, Goddess of War," she shouts. "May you guide your people with your wisdom, and may you lead us on your chosen path to victory."

She lowers the hare to the grass, its fur brushing her skin as it springs from her hands. The creature hesitates, overwhelmed by freedom, then sprints for the left-hand side of the assembly, where the women and children are gathered – representing the harvest – not the right where the warriors stand, representing battle. There is a cry of excitement, and Boudicca sees the hare leap straight into the arms of a child. There could be no surer sign of Andraste's will.

"The Goddess has spoken," she cries. "We will split our company and gather the harvest. Release the hare and come forward, child."

There is a scramble as people part to let the hare run free, then a little girl is trotting over the grass. When she gets closer, Boudicca realises she has seen this child before. It is Senovara, who stood in the road to stop her chariot, at the very first muster. This must surely be a good omen. Boudicca squats down so she is at the child's eye level and holds out her hands.

"Senovara," she says, clasping the girl's small fingers. "You are a true child of the Wolf Tribe, chosen by the gods." Senovara looks at her, eyes shining, her face lit by ferocious pride. Boudicca lifts the girl into her arms, holding her up for the whole assembly to see.

"This child is sacred," she cries. "Chosen by Andraste as the saviour of her people. Behold, the warrior Senovara."

A roar goes up, an acclamation for the will of the goddess. Even if people dislike the idea of separating families, Andraste's decision could not have been clearer. The hare's path was true. Boudicca lowers Senovara but does not set her down – instead, she gives in to a sudden, protective impulse and cradles the small, warm child in her arms. For one moment she allows herself to be a mother, not a commander, and remembers how it felt to hold her own precious children like this, when they too were small. Tears spring to her eyes. It hurts so much.

"You will go with my own daughter, Solina," she whispers. "You will return with her to the Town of the Wolf and help gather in the harvest. It is the task the gods have chosen for you. And one day, when you are older, you will be a great warrior." She lays a hand upon the child's wild red hair, in blessing. "May fear always be an enemy that passes you on the other side of the road. Greet him, but do not stop." Boudicca sets the girl down. "Go now to your family." She smiles so the little one will not notice her face is wet with tears.

Boudicca watches Senovara run across the field, swift as the hare, and thinks of Solina. It is unbearable that her own child does not understand why she is sending her away, when the reason is so clear. She does not want to deny Solina battle. She wants her daughter to survive.

The final gathering of her family before Solina leaves for the north is held outside, untainted by the Roman villa. Bellenia's absence is unspeakably painful, and Solina's face is blotched from crying – whether over her sister or at being sent away, Boudicca is not sure. Perhaps both. They eat a meal together around the fire, another one of Vassura's atrocious stews, and even Cunominus cannot bring himself to tell his obligatory bad jokes.

"I am jealous you will see Riomanda before me," he says to Solina. "But she will be so glad to have you home. Tell her I think of her always and long to meet our child."

"I will," Solina says. "And you will see them both soon." She turns to Vassura. "Are you very sure you will not come with me?"

"I am staying for Aesu," Vassura says. "My son's spirit will stand beside me in battle."

Cunominus shoots Boudicca a look at this, one sibling to another. They both know Vassura is hopeless with a sword.

"Perhaps you might keep Solina company," Boudicca says. "Aesu would understand."

Vassura slurps her stew. "You think I will disgrace myself on the field, Catia. I will not."

"You could never disgrace yourself." Solina rests a hand on her aunt's arm, her voice warm with affection.

"Except with the stew," Cunominus says, trying to lighten the mood. Vassura doesn't smile.

Solina meets her mother's eyes. "Will you chase the legate down, or make him chase you?" Her face is anxious, and Boudicca understands this is her daughter's attempt to make amends. She smiles at Solina, not wanting her child to carry the pain of parting on bad terms.

"I am a wolf. We will chase him."

"Do you think, maybe, that's what he wants? That he might be trying to set a trap?" Solina's fear is unmistakable.

"Our army is many times the size of his, as I've told you before," Cunominus interrupts. "We will all be returning home, niece. Do not distress yourself."

Solina gets to her feet, silently crossing to sit beside her mother, as close as she can get without clambering onto her knee. Her mother wraps an arm around her. "Why don't you sing for us, Solina?" she says. "One of the songs of the gods your father taught you."

Her daughter sits in silence a while. Then she starts to sing, a tale of fire and hope, the power of Esus as the rising sun. It takes Boudicca back to the time she was Catia, when her husband would sing this prayer to greet the spring, standing in the light of the dawn outside the roundhouse where he was raised. She closes her eyes, allowing herself to step back in time, taken home by Solina's voice.

When the song ends, she stays for a moment in darkness,

not wanting to pick up the weight of the present. Then her daughter speaks, and she opens her eyes.

"That song has always made me think of you, mother," Solina says. "Because of your fire."

Boudicca cannot speak, only kisses her daughter on the head, holding her closer.

It is late afternoon. The waggons are beginning to leave. All around her, families are saying their goodbyes; there is the sound of weeping, people calling out farewells from the road. But Boudicca cannot think of anyone's child but her own.

"Solina," she says, cupping her daughter's face in her hands. "I am not sending you away because I don't want you to fight beside me. I am sending you because I—"

"I know," Solina blurts out. "I know why." Then she bursts into tears and flings her arms around her mother's neck. "Please don't die."

"My love," Boudicca says, stroking her daughter's hair, unwilling to make a promise she cannot keep. "I swear to you we will be together again, if not at the Town of the Wolf, then in the halls of the Otherworld." Solina sobs even harder, and it cuts like a knife through her heart. "You must be stronger," Boudicca says, sounding harsher than she intends because she does not want to start crying herself. "You are a warrior of the Wolf Tribe. Never forget this."

Solina suppresses her grief, regaining control of herself. She breaks free of her mother's embrace. Then she lays a hand over her heart. "This is not where it ends," Solina says, her voice steady.

In that moment, Solina's tear-stained face looks just as ferocious, and almost as childlike, as Senovara's. Boudicca gazes at her daughter, mirroring the vow. "This is not where it ends," she repeats. Then before she can tell Solina she loves her, before she has a chance to say anything more, her daughter has turned, striding towards Tan.

Solina swings herself into the saddle, tall and strong. She nods to her mother, and then to Cunominus and Vassura, who have come to stand beside their commander. "May the gods be with you. And may you crush Rome."

"May the gods be with you," Cunominus calls, as his niece digs her heels into Tan's flanks, cantering to join the waggons already rumbling north. Boudicca watches Solina until her daughter's form finally vanishes, merging into the shimmering lines of the horizon.

They follow the black trail of scorched fields left by the legate. His army's tracks become fresher, the fields he torched red and smouldering the closer they get. And now, after three day's march, they have finally hunted him down.

The Roman army is at the top of a narrow field, a forest at their back. Trees snake around the sides, encircling the plain like a claw, preventing escape. It is a position which gives Paulinus every strategic advantage, removing the possibility of her army surrounding his men, and yet his numbers are still dwarfed by the Iceni. The Romans look puny on the hilltop, their mail glinting in the sun, a small band of soldiers compared to the vast horde she has assembled. Retreat now is unthinkable.

All around Boudicca is excitement. Warriors are yelling insults at the enemy, the carnyxes are bellowing, and she can even hear the shriek of children. Many of the waggons stayed with the army to carry supplies, and not everyone could be persuaded to bring in the harvest, even by the will of Andraste. Now those that remain are lined up at the back of the field, with families perched on top of bags of grain to watch the afternoon's entertainment. When this battle is won, Rome's presence in Britain will be over. It will be time to celebrate.

Boudicca glances out across the cavalry, searching for Cunominus, then Vassura, hoping to see where they are. Once she has spied them, she turns away, not wanting to be distracted by love. She is glad Solina is not here. Her daughter's absence makes it easier to focus on the battle, and has even helped her pretend that Bellenia is alive: she can imagine that both girls are with Riomanda, that she left them behind in safety, just as Vassura once told her to do.

The sound of the Roman trumpets rings out, and she knows she cannot allow them to be the first to strike a blow. Andraste demands boldness. Boudicca rides her chariot along the ranks, her sword raised. She is unable to speak over the noise, but at the sight of their commander, the Iceni smash their weapons against their shields, screaming for her victory. *Boudicca, Boudicca, Boudicca.*

Her foot soldiers surge forwards to take up the front, the cavalry and chariots staying at the rear. Across the field, the enemy seem unnaturally still. She knows their commander will have ridden his own horse behind their ranks just as she did, inspiring his men to kill, but now they are a solid wall of shields, immobile and inhuman. With a sudden blast of the carnyxes, Boudicca's army surges forward, not even waiting for her signal. The Iceni stream over the field, ready to swarm and overwhelm their enemy, but the Romans respond with a hail of spears, darkening the sky with black rain. Warriors fall, and the wall of shields advances. Only, now she sees it is no longer a wall; it is a wedge, pointed like a spear. Boudicca realises too late that this is not like facing the Ninth. There is no room for her people to move from the line of fire – they are trapped in a head-on collision in a narrow space, hemmed in from retreat by their own waggons behind. Numbers will not matter now, only the brute force of the first assault.

"Do not break the line!" she screams. "Do not let them break through!"

Panic ripples through the army as Roman shields smash into Iceni bodies. Boudicca does not have time to shout another command – the line is already broken, unable to withstand the attack. She tries to surge forward, to strike back, but she is trapped by the bulk of her own people, unable even to fight. To her horror, she sees Cunominus pulled from his horse, and then her brother disappears into a seething mass of iron and blood. He is gone. With a shout of anguish, Boudicca abandons her chariot, clambering over her own dead in her desperation to reach her enemy, her grief drowned by the madness of battle. The Iceni line is utterly broken. Romans swarm everywhere like rats, slaughtering oxen to prevent the Britons' waggons from moving, trapping everyone in this pool of death.

Boudicca finally reaches the enemy. She cuts down a legionary who swings at her neck, and then she is lost to thought or feeling, hacking and thrusting, unable to move with the swiftness for which she is famed, yet still determined to die as she lived, resisting Rome.

The screaming, the stench of blood, and the horror is overwhelming, but still she keeps killing, until she is inexorably driven back, nearly skewered by the talons of her own chariot. She fights pressed against its side, the carved legend of Epona digging into her hip, her chariot driver and her horses already dead at her feet.

Then a single savage blow, struck from behind, brings oblivion.

*

When Boudicca wakes, it is not to the Otherworld. It takes her a moment to realise where she is, what the scene of devastation means. Then she understands. Her army is defeated. Roman soldiers are crossing the field before her, clambering over the Iceni dead, running through any survivors with their swords, even those who cry out for mercy. Smoke rises where waggons have been set alight, and everywhere there is the sound of the enemy's shouts and laughter. Boudicca tries to pull herself upright, to die fighting, but she has been too badly injured to stand, not only from the blow to her head but a deep wound in her thigh. She slumps back against her shattered chariot. Through the haze of the field, she sees a man on a black horse, riding through the carnage like a dark shadow. His armour is black and gold, the crest of his helmet is scarlet, and he stops whenever the men near him turn over the bodies of dead or dying Iceni. It must be Suetonius Paulinus. The enemy commander is looking for her.

Boudicca knows he cannot find her alive. She will not be brought to Rome in chains, to suffer and die as a slave for the pleasure of their cursed Emperor. Mud slides through her fingers as she feels for her sword, finally grasping its hilt. She holds it tight, unafraid of death, but still overwhelmed by the enormity of what she must do. The grief she feels for those who have died on this field, and the horror that the Iceni will soon face, are too vast for her to comprehend. Instead, her world shrinks until it is filled by just one person. Solina.

The last commander of the Iceni lifts her sword, staring at the blade. She will go now to Bellenia, to Prasutagus, to Cunominus, to her ancestors. Yet she is leaving Solina behind. And for this, her last act in the mortal world, she is no longer Boudicca, she is Catia. Solina's mother. Any pain she feels at dying is not for herself, but desperation for her daughter. Nothing matters except Solina's survival.

Across the field she hears a shout. The Roman legate has seen her chariot, he is advancing quickly, and she has no more time. She grips her sword and prays to Esus, the god most beloved by her daughter. *Let Solina live, I beg you. Let her not be harmed.* Catia closes her eyes. Then she lifts the blade to her throat.

17

SOLINA

We have been travelling north for days when we see the soldiers. At first people think the riders in the distance are our own people, come to share news of our victory, and wild cheering breaks out. Only Senovara, clasped in my arms, spies the Roman standards shining gold in the sun. Dread has lain in my stomach since we left my mother, yet still I struggle to accept what I am seeing. *She cannot have been defeated.*

"Off the road!" I scream, yanking Tan around, riding him along the verge back the way we have come, shouting at those I am supposed to protect. "Abandon the waggons, get off the road!"

People gape at me, unable to comprehend that death is riding towards us. Waggons stop and families clamber on top of sacks of grain and looted goods to get a better view of the Roman advance, trying to convince themselves that what they see is not true. Then, just as I despair of anyone doing what I ask, there is panic. Mothers and children scramble onto the road, abandoning everything, hurtling towards the shelter of the trees.

I hold back, trying to make sure the last stragglers leave their carts, but some fools have begun to loot their neighbours, snatching bags from one another, trying to take as much treasure as they can into hiding.

"Leave them!" Senovara screams, beating her small fists against my thigh, before reaching over to yank Tan's reins in the direction of the woods. I obey her, cantering over the rough ground towards the forest. My heart is painful in my chest, my thoughts jumbled. *Where is my mother?* I picture her as I last saw her before the battle, impossibly brave, as strong as Andraste herself. I tell myself that perhaps the soldiers we spied are merely a small band of survivors, that she crushed the rest as we did the Ninth. But the dark cloud on the road behind looked too huge to be the shattered remnants of a defeated army.

We reach the trees, pressing into the forest. As a single warrior, there is little I can offer as protection. If the Romans come to find us here, our best chance of survival is to spread out as thinly as possible and hope the soldiers are more interested in taking the waggons than scouring the woods. *Even if only a few escape, I won't have failed completely.*

I have always felt safest in woodland. Forests are sacred to the gods, their trees reaching for the heavens, sheltering the world below in soft, green sunlight. I canter through narrow twisting pathways, past the thick gnarled trunks of oaks, every now and then passing the white flash of a frightened face. People are scattering through the trees and ragged undergrowth, hiding until the danger has passed.

"I will take us as far as I can," I say to Senovara as if she were my equal and not a child of seven. "We are going to the Town of the Wolf, where my aunt Riomanda will be waiting. But if the Romans come too close, you will be safer hiding in the woods without me. Can you find your way back to your own village from here? Then you could take a horse and ride to Riomanda yourself."

Senovara does not whine or cry at the thought of being abandoned. "My youngest brother is back home," she says. "And my mother. I will find them." Then she presses closer, the first hint of fear she has shown. "But you will outrun the Romans – you will take us to your aunt." Her voice wavers. "Then your mother will come back to find us."

My mother. I am trying not to think of her. "Of course."

Very few of our party were on horseback, and we soon lose sight of those who fled with us. I feel intense guilt at leaving them behind, but I cannot afford to give up; I must reach Riomanda. If I do not manage to warn her that the Romans are coming, nobody in the Town of the Wolf will stand any chance of escape.

The woods are silent apart from the thud of Tan's steady canter, and I have started to hope we might make it through, when I hear the cold cry of Roman trumpets. I press Tan faster, but the crashing and shouting is growing louder. A horse is a hard target to hide. If I do not act quickly, Senovara will have no hope of escape. We reach a clearing by a shallow stream, and I bring Tan to a halt.

"Take this." I fumble with the brooch on my cloak, a curve of silver with a carved wolf's face, and give it to Senovara, then I urge Tan into the water, following the stream to hide our tracks, shouting to the child over the splash. "My aunt Riomanda will recognise the brooch. She gave it to me when I came of age. Tell her that I sent you as a warning. She must take our people out of the city immediately and prepare to live in hiding. It's only a matter of time before Rome attacks the Town of the Wolf. Tell her I am sorry not to have news of Cunominus, but she must not wait for him." Senovara is clinging to Tan with her knees as she attaches the brooch to her tunic, hiding it so that the precious wolf is against her skin. "I will follow you, but Riomanda must not wait for me either. Tell her to leave the brooch on the embers of the hearth if she makes for the marshes, or in the pot hanging above if she chooses the woods." I stop Tan, as close as possible to the opposite side of the bank. "Promise me you will do this, Senovara."

She turns to me with the same look of ferocious determination as when she stopped my mother's chariot. "I promise."

Senovara slides from Tan's back, missing the water and landing almost noiselessly on the forest floor. She bends down, rubbing her cheeks with dirt so they will not catch the light.

"Here," I say, suddenly realising she has no food. "You'll need this!" I throw a full saddlebag at her, and she catches it, then runs swiftly into the trees. She is lost to sight almost immediately. I do not linger but gallop off in the opposite direction.

I sense my hunter before I see him. So does Tan. His ears flatten back against his skull, and he puts on an extra burst of speed. With a sick feeling, I realise that the other rider is not behind me but alongside, a blur of black and gold through the trees. My pursuer is playing the same trick my sister used to love; he is planning to cut me off in front. I look desperately for a turning on the opposite side, but the trees are thick and the path narrow. There is no way for me to force Tan through all the brambles; we will become snarled up in the undergrowth and taken prisoner. Then before I have any chance to change course, the man on the black horse bursts out onto the path in front, even faster than I was anticipating. Tan rears up in fright, almost throwing me from the saddle. My horse thumps back down onto all fours, jarring my spine, and I draw my sword.

The man before me is unmistakably Roman. The snaked golden head of Medusa is set on his black breastplate, and a wolf's pelt covers his shoulders. He draws his own sword, not hastily like I did, but with cold deliberation. I realise from the flick of his eyes over my shoulder and the thud of further hoof-fall that I am surrounded. My body is on fire with the threat of battle, and I send up a prayer to the gods: *May I die bravely.*

"I am the daughter of Prasutagus, King of the Iceni, twice blessed by the gods. Who are you that dares challenge me in my own kingdom?"

I watch the man's face closely, trying to judge the effect of my words, but his eyes are steady, giving nothing away. The black of his horse recalls the shadow warrior of my vision. "If you are truly the daughter of Boudicca," he says. "Then you should know that she now lies dead on the field, along with the entirety of her army. We took none alive."

Even though I had realised we must have been defeated, it is still agony to hear the loss spoken aloud. My mother, Cunominus, Vassura. All of them gone. "I do not believe you."

"Believe me or not, you will put down your sword."

"No. I challenge you to fight me."

He raises his eyebrows. "You are surrounded. It is not your place to issue challenges to the victor. You will surrender to me now, as a captive of war, or I will leave you to my men to punish as they see fit."

I hesitate, memories of the attack in my father's house returning to me in a dark flood. I cannot die that way, dishonoured by scores of soldiers then murdered in the woods. Not after everything my mother sacrificed. "How do I know you will not give me to your men if I surrender?"

"You have my word." There is no compassion in his expression, but his gaze remains steady. He looks like a person who does not lie – not because he is virtuous, but because he has no need.

"Who are you, that I should believe your promise?"

"I am Gaius Suetonius Paulinus," the man answers. "Legate of Britannia. This kingdom does not belong to you, Boudicca's daughter, it belongs to the Emperor Nero. You are on Roman land. The Iceni kingdom has been destroyed. Now put down your sword."

We stare at each other. I do not have to look behind me to see his men; I can hear the snort of their horses, the shiver of their mail. If I ride towards the legate now, a spear will swiftly land between my shoulder blades. I am not so afraid of death, more of being mortally injured, unable to protect myself from what would follow. Yet if I am taken captive, I might live to escape. I look at the blade in my hand, forged the day of my birth on the Street of Gold, blessed by my father at the altar of Epona. It cannot protect my people now.

"*Forgive me*," I say in my own language. Then I stretch out my arm, holding the legate's gaze, and let my weapon fall to the ground.

PART TWO
CAPTIVA

"For victory will not bring more joy... The final cast of lots for everything will bring all evils on the vanquished. All guilt upon the victor."

Lucan, *Pharsalia*

"Suetonius Paulinus, a conscientious and circumspect commander"

Tacitus, *Agricola*

18

PAULINUS

Verulamium is gilded by the dying sun when Paulinus rides through its shattered streets. The newly liberated town is his base for the night. Some refugees are already returning to their looted homes; he can see them scurrying past, removing their dead and clearing debris, reassured by massed legions on the fields outside. It was difficult to set up camp here, building over the filth and churned-up mud left by the rebels, but Paulinus knows it is important to show the town is back under Roman control.

Relief at the thought courses through his veins. Boudicca is defeated. After weeks of retreat, when he was forced to abandon London to its fate, when he felt as if the entire province might be lost, the Goddess of Fate finally granted Rome victory. He knows the aftermath of the rebellion is going to be gruelling, but for one night, he will allow himself to feel the satisfaction of winning. Shouting from a nearby street makes him glance over, alert to danger, and his stallion Viribus pricks up his ears. Paulinus runs his hand over the animal's mane in reassurance. "Not for us," he says.

Paulinus has valued every horse that carried him into battle, across many campaigns, but Viribus has proved an especially resilient companion, showing immense courage in their last fight. The battle's aftermath had been brutal too. Paulinus placed no check on the men, allowing them to slaughter everyone left on the field, venting all the rage and resentment they felt at being humiliated by a woman for so many months. He took captives later, when they found a rump of rebels returning to bring in the harvest, and the bitter taste left by Boudicca's suicide was sweetened by the discovery of the daughter. An Iceni princess will be a fitting gift for Nero when Paulinus returns to Rome.

He glances down at his wife Fulvia's *lunula*, the silver necklace looped twice around his wrist, its small moon hanging like a charm. If he can find a shrine in the house where he is a guest tonight, he must light some incense, so her spirit knows he remembers her. The image of his wife is vivid in Paulinus's mind – her shy smile and the curls of her dark hair. It would have been a joy to write to Fulvia this evening, the only person in Rome more impatient to hear news of his survival than his victory. Fulvia used to weep when he left on campaign, desperate for his safety, and Paulinus still cannot comprehend that death did not stay with him on the battlefield where it belonged but instead came to his house as a common fever and took his wife. He had not understood, until Fulvia died, how precious it is to be the centre of another human being's world.

The villa's atrium is small, even though it is the grandest Verulamium has to offer. Flags of the two legions who now control the town cover half the walls. The Boar of the Tenth and Capricorn of the Fourteenth shine gold against the red, their huge expanse of fabric almost hiding a blue Iceni wolf the rebels daubed upon the plaster just a few days earlier.

Their host is one of many refugees who fled Verulamium to trail after the Roman army; Paulinus remembers his face, though not his name. The man is working the room, ingratiating himself with senior members of Paulinus's staff, clearly eager to reassert his identity as a person of importance. There will be time enough to suffer his host at dinner, for now, Paulinus would like to escape.

He spies his tribune Agricola, and gestures to catch the boy's attention. "Is there somewhere to discuss the day's intelligence?"

Agricola nods. "There is a study, general."

They walk together down a corridor off the atrium, another soldier striding ahead with a torch, its light dancing across the walls. The plaster has been gouged with spears, mutilating a fresco of poorly drawn songbirds. A strange symbol is etched repeatedly over the painting, perhaps a curse left by the Britons or a prayer to their savage gods. Paulinus pauses to look, and his two companions are forced to stop.

"What do you think this is?" He points at the symbol.

Agricola looks uncertain, although he is used to his commander's peculiar interests. "Could it perhaps be a face?"

"I think so." Paulinus gestures impatiently for the torch to be brought closer, then squints at the plaster. The face – if that is what it is – is a series of swirls, a strange, magical version of reality. "I saw similar marks to this in Mona. On a few of the trees. It must have some meaning." Agricola waits, patient and polite, but with nothing more to add. Paulinus will have to write to Pliny if he wants a companion who is interested in his observations on barbarian culture. They walk the rest of the way in silence.

His own desk and chairs have been brought over from the camp, and another flag is propped up in the study, the room lit by braziers. Agricola never fails to think of the theatre of each moment; he is meticulous in his duties, as Paulinus once was as a tribune. At nineteen, the boy is young. Paulinus took him on purely as a favour to Agricola's widowed mother, but he has proven exceptionally useful.

If Fulvia had given him a son, would the boy have grown to be like this – honest, hard-working and keen to please his father?

Paulinus sits, gesturing at Agricola to do the same, leaving the auxiliary standing guard at the door. "What more have the British captives told you?"

"Flogging them made little difference. The main intelligence, that Boudicca's daughter had fled into the woods, is still the most useful information we gleaned. Our scouts have found no trace of reinforcements or abandoned campsites. It seems the queen had indeed sent them all home to work on the harvest. I do not believe we will face another battle."

Paulinus nods. "Good. With their leader dead, morale among the Iceni should collapse. But we must continue the campaign eastwards, to destroy any town that supplied warriors for the rebels. I will leave a detachment from the Tenth here, to protect the town and help with the rebuilding, and send another to London. Then we must press on. Reinforcements are being sent to us from Gaul."

"Will you execute the daughter? To prevent her from becoming a figurehead?"

"No," Paulinus says. "She is more valuable alive. I intend to make a gift of her to the Emperor. And in the meantime, if she is known to have surrendered to live as the legate's concubine that should be enough to dishonour her in the eyes of her people." He relays this plan as if it has no personal implications. Perhaps it does not. What matters is the public appearance of conquest – Paulinus is not going to pander to the opinion of others by stooping to behaviour that he considers beneath him.

"She is being held in one of the rooms here," Agricola says. "I didn't want to risk leaving her in the camp. I thought you would wish to interview her yourself."

Paulinus thinks back to the girl in the woods. Though Boudicca is dead, much can still be learned from the daughter. "You did well. I will go question her." He gets to his feet. "And I shall see you again at dinner."

The girl is already standing, waiting for him, when Paulinus enters the room. She has the stance of a soldier, and his eyes flick down to her hands, still securely tied. Around her neck is a golden torc, familiar to him even before he found her in the woods. It is a close match for the one he now holds in his hand.

"You may go," he says to the two men who have been standing guard. Paulinus watches her watch them leave.

"I am grateful you kept your word, legate."

Her Latin is heavily accented, as he remembers from the woods, but her tone surprises him. She speaks softly, like one expecting to be treated with courtesy. He assesses her for the first time as a woman rather than a potential threat. Dirt smears her skin, but her face is clear of the Britons' ugly warpaint. He realises that she is beautiful, which he had not noticed before – an asset which increases her value significantly for one as vain as Nero.

"You are Boudicca's daughter." He walks towards her. She does not flinch at his approach. "You seemed in some doubt over your mother's death earlier." Paulinus holds out the torc, still stained with blood. "I took this from her body. Perhaps you recognise it?"

The girl stares at the gold circle, then looks back up at him. "I do not believe *you* killed her."

"No," he says, keeping his face impassive, although her perception unnerves him. "She took her own life." Boudicca's daughter says nothing, though her blank eyes shine, perhaps with tears. "Why were you not beside your mother in battle?"

"She commanded me to leave."

"Why would she do such a thing? Were you sent to gather reinforcements?"

"There were no reinforcements."

"Why send *you*, of all her warriors, to oversee the harvest? Did she wish to ensure your survival? Is that why?"

The girl shrugs. "If she were not dead, then you could ask her. I was not in the habit of questioning my mother's commands."

Paulinus raises his eyebrows at her rudeness. He could have the girl flogged for insolence, but suspects violence will not break her. Besides, he is more curious than offended. "What do you think I should do now with the child of my enemy?"

She smiles slightly, as if there were no menace in his question. "I am the heir of Prasutagus, rightful King of the Iceni, loyal servant of Rome."

Her claim is so outrageous, he laughs. "You are no more a loyal servant of Rome than I am a Druid. And you did not answer. What should I do with the daughter of my enemy? What would your mother have done with me?" The Iceni girl remains silent, staring past him as if he hadn't spoken.

Paulinus knows he is a physically imposing man. There are few who would stand much chance against him in a fistfight, and his mere presence in a room has often been enough to prompt male prisoners to speak. This girl's self-possession is unusual, and he is forced to ask his question again. "What would Boudicca have done with the Legate of Britannia?"

Her eyes, when she looks up at him, are startlingly dark in the white skin. "My mother would have killed you."

"And no doubt stuck my head on a pike. Then we would never have had the pleasure of speaking. But you still haven't answered. What should *I* do with *you*?"

"Perhaps you should challenge me to single combat. To prove you are not a coward."

Paulinus feels a flicker of amusement. She has guts, at least. "There is no honour for a man in fighting a woman, and commanders do not fight their captives. You are already defeated, so it would serve no purpose. What is your name?"

There is a long pause, and he thinks she might refuse to answer. "I am Solina."

"Solina," he repeats. "You may keep your name. That is my first act of generosity. My second is that I will allow you to live, though you may not keep your life. That now belongs to me. You are a captive, a symbol of Rome's victory. All who see you will know from your enslavement that your mother is dead, the rebellion destroyed, and your people conquered. Your humiliation is also theirs."

Solina's face flushes with rage. "You are a fool if you think that is all they will see. The shame is *yours*, a Roman thief, cursed by the gods."

Paulinus is unmoved. "A Roman thief," he remarks, as if mulling the insult. "Interesting. Yet I thought you were your father's daughter, a loyal servant to Rome?"

Solina springs at him so swiftly he almost doesn't have time to brace for impact. She bowls into him, shoulder first, and even though her hands are tied behind her back, she brings her knee up hard. She has good aim, but he is quick, so she only hits his hip. Then she tries to smash her head into his, to knock him out, but he is too tall for her. There is a scuffle, longer and far more undignified than should be the case, given she is a girl… and a tied-up girl, at that.

"Don't be a fool!" Paulinus shouts, wrestling her into a

crushing bear hug which ought to incapacitate her. Somehow, she continues to thrash around. He slams her against the wall, hard enough to knock the breath out of her, granting a pause in hostilities. "What are you fucking doing?"

The Iceni girl's eyes are wide with rage. "Don't touch me!" she screams.

Some of his own anger dissipates at the absurdity of her demand. "It would be smarter not to launch yourself at people if the aim is to avoid contact."

To his exasperation, she continues to struggle. He remembers a chair somewhere behind him, over to the right, pushed next to the bed. Perhaps he can loop her arms over the back of it. Paulinus bundles the kicking, struggling woman across the room, an experience about as pleasant as carrying a sack of fighting cats. When she sees where they are headed, her desperation increases to a point of hysteria. At this rate, he will have to punch her.

"Are you going to surrender or do I have to knock you out?" he asks.

Her struggling subsides while she considers this. "You will not force me if I stop?"

"That's generally the point of surrendering."

"Among honourable men, it is," she says bitterly. "But Romans are not honourable."

Paulinus is now thoroughly irritated. He doesn't have any rope, so reaches for her belt, yanking it free to tie her up more securely. Solina cries out in terror, the first sign of fear she has shown. Suddenly he understands. She thinks he is going to force himself on her. They stare at one another.

"Please," she begs. "Can you give me a moment?"

The words sting worse than a slap. Through some cruel joke of the gods, Solina has repeated Fulvia's words to him on their wedding night. His two worlds collide, throwing him off balance. Grief, then anger, hits him, and Paulinus does not know whether his sudden rage is meant for the British girl or himself. He tilts up her chin, intending to insult her, but the sight of her desperate face makes him feel worse. Yet he knows he cannot afford compassion. She is not his wife, she is a savage, and unlike Fulvia, he owes her no kindness or consideration.

He thumps her down on the chair, yanking her arms over its back so that she will have difficulty disentangling herself. In silence, he ties the Iceni girl's hands to the chair legs with her own belt while she sobs. Boudicca's torc lies on the floor, dropped in the scuffle. Paulinus crosses to pick it up without looking back at the daughter. Then he leaves her locked in the room, alone.

19

SOLINA

All my grief, all my fear, humiliation and pain will find their solace in one source. The death of Suetonius Paulinus. I will not even grant this man the humanity of a name. He is *the legate*. I imagine killing him, cutting out his heart on the altar of Andraste. I imagine watching him die.

For now, he is very much alive. He rides his black horse directly ahead of me, without any fear I might strike him from behind. My hands are trussed up behind my back, chafing my wrists and making my shoulders ache. The horse they have tied me to is nothing like my beloved Tan, who I have not seen since they captured us both. His loss adds to the burden of grief I carry, which has grown so huge I am numb.

Riding beside me, leading my horse, is another soldier. I will not look at him, even though I understand the insults he shouts in Latin. They have made me wear the clothes of one of their camp followers, a cheap green shift and a string of bells to mark me out as a whore, so that my people know I am disgraced. My mother's torc sits around my neck over my own, and the weight of so much gold is painful, but I refuse to be shamed by the legate's attempt to turn my family's pride into a mark of slavery. I tell myself that if Senovara reaches

Riomanda and saves the Town of the Wolf, none of this humiliation will matter.

We have been two days on the road since leaving Verulamium. The Romans have their own method of marching, seemingly organised by status, which I have yet to understand. They do not move in a mass, but in strict formations, each section of the army in their own place. Some of the men speak unfamiliar languages and carry strange weapons, and much of the cavalry seems to be from Gaul. All those close to the legate are Italian, save his translator Matu, who is from the Catuvellauni tribe, the Iceni's ancient enemy. Matu is a sly weasel of a man who seemed disappointed to discover I speak Latin, denying him the chance to translate my words for the legate. Matu is the only Briton I have seen.

Around midday, the march slows. The legate does not ride at its head, but I can see the front of the column has stopped to surround a small town. I recognise this place. We are on Trinovantes land – I stayed here with Bellenia and my mother when we mustered the army. I think back on the feast the people held in our honour, remembering the singing and dancing, the bard telling a tale from the legends of Epona especially for Bellenia and me. Fear twists in my stomach. All the warriors left this place to fight. Anyone who remained will be completely defenceless.

At the legate's order, I am obliged to ride with him to the roundhouses ahead. The whore's bells draped over me jangle to my horse's hoof-fall, and my face burns. Soldiers have already rounded everyone up, forcing them to stand in the town square. There is only a handful of men; most are elderly, the rest are women with children. I do not know their names, but I recognise the face of a pretty serving girl who waited on my family at the feast. She stares at me in horror. I cannot bear to meet her eye.

The legate speaks, with Matu translating. "You sent your men to fight in Boudicca's rebellion," he says to the huddled villagers. "They are dead, along with the queen they fought for. Now you will pay for your treachery." I watch, helpless, as some begin to cry. A mother holds her small son to her chest, shielding her child's face from the soldiers, and I jerk my chained arm, instinctively reaching for the sword I no longer possess. The legate turns to his waiting men. "Gather all the grain, any supplies we can use, then burn the houses and the crops. After that, execute the traitors."

"No!" I scream, unable to restrain myself. "Please! Please have mercy."

The legate turns to me. It is a shock to meet his gaze. We have not spoken since the night of my capture. "Did your mother show any mercy for the children of London when she burned their city?"

"*Please*," I beg him, overwhelmed by my own powerlessness. "Please don't kill them."

He stops as if considering my request. I am too desperate even to feel hatred, I just want him to agree. After an agonising pause, he speaks to Matu. "Tell the traitors that, at the request of his concubine, Boudicca's daughter, the Legate of Britannia has agreed to spare their lives. Every other command remains the same. The settlement will be sacked and burned, along with the crops."

"But they will starve!" I burst out. "How will they survive with no food, no shelter?"

"I have shown far greater mercy than your mother," the legate replies. "I did not slaughter their children." He turns his back on me, and I understand what he has done. He is not granting the townspeople mercy as a favour: he guessed I would beg for their lives, speaking to him in Latin like a Roman whore. He has made me seem complicit in his violence.

I watch Matu translate his message to the huddle of Trinovantes. The serving girl turns sharply towards me when she hears that the princess she once waited on has become the legate's concubine. I force myself to return her gaze, expecting to see disgust in her eyes, but there is only anguish. We stare at one another, and with a sick feeling, I realise she must see her own fate in me. The soldiers will not spare her. My mother fought this war to avenge Rome's violence against her daughters, but now she is dead, and there are no warriors left to resist.

The legate's army marches east, leaving fields of fire in its wake. The harvest my mother sent me to oversee is burning, and smoke hangs over the land in a dark veil. Famine will follow. Every village my mother visited, and many she did not, is sacked. With each settlement that burns, my shame grows heavier. The legate makes me beg for every captive's life, using my pleas to dishonour me, destroying any lingering loyalty to Boudicca. I cannot refuse the part he makes me play, fearing more people will die if I do.

The road we travel is still churned up by the waggons, feet and hooves of my mother's army. We are retracing the rebellion's path. If Tan is still alive, I wonder if he recognises the landscape we rode through together. I try to shift in the saddle to which I am tied. The pain of being unable to move freely is intense – my shoulders ache as if they are being pulled from their sockets – but I feel guilt for caring about my own discomfort when so many are dead. I think of my mother, wondering why I did not also turn the blade on myself when the legate demanded my surrender. I feel ashamed to admit that the thought of suicide never even occurred to me. It seems my will to survive is an animal thing, stronger than my honour or my grief.

As evening approaches, I see a black shape growing larger against the pink sky. Camulodunum. The site of my mother's first victory. I stare at the former colony, marvelling at how her rage has forever transformed the landscape. The temple which once dominated the surrounding fields is gone, and all that remains are a few blackened pillars, reaching for the sky like an outstretched claw. Lying in rubble around this shattered symbol of Roman conquest are heaps of burnt-out houses, and beyond the city are fields of ash. Even this far down the road, the stench of decay lingers. Soldiers who had been entertaining themselves with marching songs grow quieter. I remember what it felt like to watch Camulodunum burn, the horror and the wonder of it. My sense of powerlessness lifts. Boudicca is dead, but the Romans will never forget what she did.

The legate orders a halt, riding with a small number of men towards the city. To my surprise, I am taken too and wonder if he means to kill me here. My heart races at the thought, and I pray to the gods for courage. We reach the giant arch, blackened beyond repair, stopping at the threshold of the ruins. The smell is nauseating, but my hands are not free to cover my face the way the men around me are doing. We sit upon our horses in silence. Away from the mass of the army, I can hear a strange noise. A low hum, like the angry murmur of voices. It takes me a moment to realise it is the buzzing of thousands of flies. I look through the archway. The charred and rotting bodies of those we killed still lie on Camulodunum's streets. I think of the boy who came at me with a pike and was trampled underfoot, the mother and her children killed in the baths, and I remember all those I loved who fought here – my mother, my sister, Cunominus, Vassura – who also now lie dead.

The scene of horror swims before me, and I realise I am weeping. The grief I feel is endless, enough to drown a burned city.

20

PAULINUS

A light hoar frost is on the ground, and he can smell woodsmoke as he kneels at the unknown children's grave. Paulinus could not leave Camulodunum without making this last private act of devotion. A small flame flickers before him. It is an offering of grain, sweetened with honey, burning on the stone slab that has been laid as a temporary tomb.

The grief which hit him upon first seeing the ruins of Camulodunum was shattering. He had expected to feel rage and the need for vengeance, but instead a wave of emptiness swallowed him whole. *All those thousands of Roman lives.* After long years in the army, he had thought himself impervious to the sight of death, but this place was unlike the gruesome aftermath of battle. It had made him feel ashamed. He failed to protect the people here, he failed to save London, and the suffering which followed his failure was unspeakable.

The rebuilding of Camulodunum will take years. This past week, all they could do was try to honour the fallen. At the temple, his men have spent long, black days digging through the ruins to recover whatever human remains they can, but most were reduced to ashes by the intense heat. All except for a huddle of children, whose small bodies were partially preserved by a collapsing wall. The sight of them had finally ignited his rage. Paulinus does not know who these children were, they had been too badly burned, but he knows at least one was a boy. The child had been wearing a silver *bulla*, the sacred necklace all free Roman parents give their sons shortly after birth. It is a counterpart to a girl's *lunula*, like the one Paulinus now wears looped around his wrist, a memento of his wife Fulvia's girlhood. There are few objects in a Roman family that speak more strongly of love than these first gifts to a child.

In his fingers, Paulinus turns a coin round and round, feeling the cold press of the metal. The little boy had been carrying a purse full of money, perhaps a desperate attempt by his parents to ensure his safety, alone in the temple. There cannot have been room for all the townspeople inside; Paulinus supposes many gave up the space to their children. He has buried the coins with the boy, all save one, which he replaced with a more valuable silver piece of his own. Perhaps the boy will give this coin to Charon in the underworld, so that the gods know there is someone in the mortal world who will avenge the child's fate.

Paulinus becomes aware of Agricola, shifting on his feet behind him, and realises he must have been kneeling for longer than he thought. He rises, turning to face the men who accompanied him. Agricola looks stricken. It had been the young tribune's idea to add honey as an offering to the spirits instead of wine: *children like sweet things*. Agricola only gave up wearing his own *bulla* a couple of years ago, and Paulinus feels some regret, thinking of how little innocence will be left to Agricola by the end of this campaign. He grasps his junior officer by the arm. "We will avenge their suffering," he says. "By the will of the gods."

*

They take the Ecen Way towards the City of the Horse, the city ruled by the Iceni's last king, but that is not where Paulinus intends to set up camp. His slave Matu has told him no place holds greater power for the Iceni, or is considered more holy, than the sacred grove Prasutagus built a short ride from his capital. Paulinus does not trust his translator, but neither does he doubt Matu's deep hatred of an old tribal enemy. Transforming this Iceni stronghold into a Roman garrison will be a clear sign to every barbarian in the east that their kingdom has fallen.

When they come to the place Matu described, it has long since been deserted by Druids. Paulinus stands at the edge of the dead oaks. The place is eerier than any of the groves he burned in the west of Britannia. Offerings are tied to the leafless branches – small animal skulls, carved figures, even feathers. Beyond the dead trees, and looming over them, is a huge tower made from wood. He turns to Boudicca's daughter, who stands beside him in her cheap shift. He has decided to use her as a guide. "Is that a temple?"

"No. We do not have temples. Our gods do not need them."

"What is it?"

"It is a sacred house, where our leaders can meet and speak with the gods. The grove is used for sacrifice."

A temple, then, Paulinus thinks but does not say. "You will show me the place."

She looks at him coldly, not taking a step forward. "If you pass the maze, you will be cursed. It is beyond my skill to lift the Druids' magic, even if I wished it. The enchantment protects the trees from any who mean them harm. My father laid the curse himself, and he was the most powerful Druid in our kingdom."

"I have earned a thousand Druids' curses," Paulinus says drily. "I think I can risk adding one more to the tally."

"Then if you enter, understand it is not by my invitation."

"No," he says. "It is *you* who enter by *my* command. Now take me to the temple."

The girl walks through the dead oaks, dipping her head reverently as she passes. Fifty of Paulinus's men follow, several making the sign of the evil eye. Paulinus refrains from doing the same. He was not lying about the weight of all the Druids' curses he carries; it is too late to worry about that now.

Inside the enclosure he sees several altars set up against the inner ring of trees, with the faces of Iceni gods carved into the wood. Above one, hangs what he imagines to be tattered strips of fabric. Paulinus ignores it and strides towards the tower, gesturing impatiently at the men who came here as torch bearers. He stops to look up. Set over the vast doorway are a series of bleached white human skulls, marked with tattoos. He points. "Who are they?"

Boudicca's daughter stares at the skulls, almost as if she expects them to answer on her behalf. "Our enemies taken in battle," she says at last. "Set here as a warning."

Paulinus shakes his head in disgust, then lays his hand against the doors. Locked, of course. Intricate carvings of the writhing bodies of animals and human faces cover the wood, perhaps telling legends of the Iceni's dark gods. He traces his finger over one, a man sprouting the horns of a stag, and resolves to write a letter describing the savage scenes for Pliny. His friend has an interest in barbarian curiosities.

"What do they show?" he asks.

"The creation of the world," the girl replies.

Paulinus summons one of the men, who has come prepared with an axe. "Cut out the lock but try to leave the carvings intact."

Before the soldier can obey his command, the centurion Paulinus left in charge of the grove hurries over. "General, we have found evidence of human sacrifice in the grove."

Paulinus rounds on Solina. "Is this true?"

She says nothing, so he seizes her arm, dragging her after the centurion. They head to the tree Paulinus noticed earlier, draped in strips of fabric. When he draws closer, he finally understands what he is seeing. Human remains. He shoves the girl to stand before the altar. The corpse is almost entirely decomposed, showing white flashes of bone picked clean by carrion, its body caught in the arms of the barbarous tree. A wolf is carved onto its bark.

"Are you not ashamed?" he shouts at the girl. "What sort of savages are your people that your gods demand human sacrifice?"

"There is no greater power of divination than that which lies within the human heart."

Her voice, which sounds completely unmoved, makes him even angrier. "Did you see the victim die? Were you part of this?"

"He was a criminal."

Paulinus seizes her by the shoulders, forcing her to face him. "Who performed the rites?"

"A Druid," she says, staring into his eyes. "My father's chosen successor in his art."

"Then the man is as dead as the corpse before you." He releases her in disgust. "We were sure to kill every Druid on the battlefield." Paulinus turns from the altar, furious to see his soldiers are in a pathetic huddle, keeping well away from the corpse. "Don't just stand there like fucking sheep," he shouts. "Take the body down and bury it! And you," he says to Solina. "Take a good look at this place. It is the last time you will see it. Your grove will not be burned; I will have it uprooted, every tree pulled from the ground, as if such an abomination never even existed." He turns back to the centurion. "When you have breached the doors, take the prisoner into the hall. If the place has rooms, lock her up, and see she is guarded."

Paulinus does not watch as Boudicca's daughter is led away. Instead, he turns back to the sacrifice. The skull looks down on him, as the men start to cut the body free.

21

SOLINA

I am blind in this room. A small gap under the eaves tells me day from night, but it is a lightwell, not a window, and I cannot see out. My father once kept this upstairs bedchamber for his guests; now it is my prison. I pace the length of it, walking to the Town of the Wolf and back, without ever leaving the room. I have no weapon, but that is no reason to let my body grow soft and useless. A refusal to curl up and rot feels like an act of resistance. I do whatever exercise I can against the walls and floors, repeating the thrusts and parries I once made with a sword, moving myself for hours upon hours. I will need all my strength to escape.

Each day, the legate sends out his soldiers to seize weapons and sack villages, determined to track down every surviving rebel. Or so Matu tells me. The Catuvellauni translator takes greater pleasure in giving me bad news than he does in bringing food or water. I can see the greed in his eyes when he stares, but I don't believe it is my body he is hungry for – it is my grief. He would feast on it if he could. It is through Matu that I learn the City of the Horse has been destroyed, burned to ash like Camulodunum. He tells me famine is coming for the Iceni, that any of my people left alive will soon die from starvation. His words bring me immeasurable pain, but I refuse to give him the pleasure of seeing me cry.

I long to ask about the fate of the Town of the Wolf but know, if I do, Matu will alert the legate to the place's significance. It seems they believe my family only lived in the capital, not understanding my mother came from the north. At night I pray to the gods, asking them to keep Riomanda and her child safe, and I conjure visions of Senovara reaching my home. Lying in the darkness of my father's tower, I listen for the fall of Senovara's footsteps as she walks to my mother's hearth, imagining her as the saviour of the Iceni's last remaining rebels. If only I can escape, I will join them.

The legate never visits, even though he sleeps in my parents' room, a few paces away. It is a relief, yet also a strange disappointment to be so completely forgotten. I have spent my life surrounded by people, and isolation is as tormenting as my inability to act. I often talk to the dead, speaking to my beloved family, hoping their shades might come close enough to hear me. In my mind, I see my father, tall and strong, lit by flames at the Feast of Darkness. I see my mother's smile and feel her warmth. I watch Vassura weaving, the gentle dance of her fingers. I see the flash of Cunominus's red braids and hear the deep sound of his laugh. Most of all, I see my sister, imagine riding with her again through the woods, too fast for any living being to catch. Thinking of my family makes me cry, yet their love also gives me the strength to keep living. I am all that remains of them now.

Dreaming of escape is not enough. I must plot. As the weeks pass, I force myself to pay attention to every detail in my mind-numbing routine, trying to discover chinks in my Roman prison. I act as docile as possible, even snivelling a little, so

Matu imagines he has broken me. He starts to grow more careless, turning his back from time to time, even leaving the door propped open with a bucket to spare himself the trouble of the rusty lock. The guards too become less diligent. I sit with my ear pressed to the door until the whorls in the wood indent into my cheek, and listen to their gossip, trying to learn of any festivals, or times when they might be drunk. I begin to recognise the profound silence that means there is no guard outside, testing this theory by throwing my weight at the door, feeling elated when nobody shouts at me to be quiet.

The day I plan for my escape is a late autumn festival for the Roman's warrior god Mars. The legate will be outside, inspecting his men, all of them showing off their precious armour and swords, which I hope means fewer will linger inside. With any luck, I will be able to sneak out through the camp and swiftly lose myself in the marshes. Let arrogance be their undoing.

At dawn I hear the men rise; I even hear the legate's voice as he heads down the stairs directly outside. Then there is quiet. I wait a while then kick the door, yelling insults. Nothing. The first hurdle is cleared. Now all I need is Matu. My plan is to lure him further into the room, pretending to be sick, then attack when he leans over the bed.

The sound of his key, scraping ineptly at the door, sets my heart racing. I let out a moan, as if in pain.

"What is it, bitch?" he snaps, dumping the bucket down in the doorway, just as I hoped.

"I fell and hit my head on the bedframe," I whimper. "I'm injured."

"Are you faking?"

I do not answer, only whimper more. Slowly Matu creeps across the floor towards me. He is getting closer, thinking I cannot see him, as I have partly pulled the blanket over my face. I wail again for good measure, then to my horror, watch the sneaky bastard fish a knife out of his tunic, a lecherous look in his eye. This was not part of the plan. He holds out the weapon, ready to threaten what he assumes is a defenceless girl, and I am obliged to act much sooner than I wanted. I spring out of the covers, aiming a kick at his wrist, forcing him to drop the weapon which skitters under the bed. Matu lets out a bloodcurdling scream. There is no point hanging around trying to incapacitate him; he will have alerted every Roman in the building.

I leap over the bucket in the doorway, hurtling down the stairs, while the weasel scrambles after me, shrieking.

"*Boudicca's daughter has escaped! She says she means to kill the legate!*"

I do not waste my breath calling Matu a liar but make a dash for the doorway. It is too late. Soldiers have already scrambled to block it. I veer off, running to the wall where my family's ceremonial swords are kept, and wrench one from the carved wolf claws holding it in place. The blade is heavy, made of bronze, and I have no idea if it has even been sharpened in the past hundred years, but I still feel a rush of euphoria as I swing round with a weapon in my hands.

Fifteen armed men are before me, their own swords drawn. I will be no match for them all; my only hope is to shame one of them into fighting me. If I survive long enough, perhaps I will have my vengeance upon the legate. "You!" I shout, pointing my blade at the biggest man. "I challenge you to single combat."

The man stares, incredulous, then all the soldiers laugh. I realise I must look ridiculous – a girl in a camp follower's dress, clutching an ancient sword. Matu sidles up to his masters. "The legate said she was to be given for his men's use as a whore, if she defied him." He shoots me a venomous look. "No need to accept her vain demands."

I ignore Matu, looking straight at the man I challenged. "Are you so afraid of me you do not dare fight a woman?" I demand. "Does Boudicca still hold such power here?"

At the mention of my mother, the man's face darkens. "I will fight you, little whore," he says. "And when you are defeated, you will beg me to kill you."

The others draw back, but I only have eyes for my opponent. My best hope is to evade the man's blows until he exhausts himself, then strike. A memory comes to me of training on the marshes, and I hear again my mother's voice: *You fight like a coward, Solina, without striking a blow.*

Watch me, I think.

The soldier and I circle each other. He is smirking, imagining this will soon be over, and no wonder. He is even more enormous than I first realised, broad as an ox and tall as a tree, and I am hemmed in. Suddenly he rushes me. The move is a gift. I dodge, sprinting past him into the hall, then turn just in time to catch his blow on my sword. The force jars my entire body, and I break contact before he can wrest the blade from my hands, jumping out of his way when he swings again. We circle each other. He is eyeing me more warily now, surprised I am not already skewered.

He aims another blow, but I elude him, light on my feet after so many hours of ceaseless movement. In my hands, the weight of the bronze sword is becoming more familiar, and for the first time since my capture, I do not feel helpless. Even if these are my last moments alive, I will own them all. The ox strikes, coming closer this time, then follows up swiftly with another thrust, this one aimed at my face. He slices through the end of my braid as I jump clear. Then he comes at me with a flurry of blows, each more violent than the last. It is like a dance. I only have eyes for his weapon, following the cues of his body, learning the jolt of his feints, and the true movement before he strikes.

He pauses, breathing hard. "You are no warrior," he shouts. "You run from the sword like a woman!"

"I *am* a woman." I tilt my head and smile at him, enjoying his fury. More soldiers are watching us now. I can sense their presence, but do not dare look away from my opponent. Any slip and he will have me.

The ox swings at me again, and this time I return his taunting. "You fight like an animal," I shout. "Without thought, only force." He roars in anger, thudding into the table as he misses again. I laugh. Perhaps I am about to die, but in this moment, I feel completely alive. "What does it mean if you cannot defeat a *woman*? What sort of man does that make you?" This time, when he charges, I do not dodge his blow but block it, testing his force, then return his violence with a strike of my own. My father's hall briefly rings with the sound of iron on bronze, then I break away. I need to exhaust him further to be sure of a hit.

The ox, however, is determined not to give me the chance. He rushes towards me, managing to catch the hilt of his sword against mine, flinging me backwards. Then he swings, bringing his weapon down full force on the table, missing me by a hair. For one brief, precious moment, he is unbalanced, tugging his sword free. I do not have time to get close enough to strike but grab a silver pot from the table and hurl it under his feet as he steps backwards. It is a thief's trick to trip a man over, but it works. The ox is down and before he can rise, I have stamped on his wrist, forcing him to release his weapon. Our eyes meet. We both know he has lost, even if it is me who will die. His companions are upon me before I can strike. I feel the press of a blade at my back, and more are pointed at my face. My disgraced opponent pulls himself upright, grabbing his sword from the ground, then he lifts it, ready to smite me in rage.

"Do not kill her." It is the legate's voice, ringing out across the hall. I look over to where he must be, and one of the soldiers uses my distraction to knock the sword from my hand. I lunge for it, but I am too late – another man has seized it. My exhilaration at winning is snuffed out. Now, when it truly matters, I am unarmed. There is silence as the legate walks towards us. "What did you possibly hope to achieve by trying to escape?" he asks. "Or did you simply wish to die?"

"I made no attempt to escape," I lie, breathing hard from exertion. "I wish I had. Matu came at me with a knife. I was trying to get away from him; I thought he was going to murder me." I shrug, as if there were not fifteen swords pointing at my face. "Having been granted my freedom unexpectedly, I decided to use it. Who wouldn't?"

"She is lying!" Matu shouts.

"The knife will still be under the bed where I kicked it, you little shit," I snarl back. "So save your breath."

"You could have told my men this, rather than issuing a challenge. Why didn't you?"

The legate asks the question almost as Cunominus would have done, as if he expects my answer will be worth hearing. The resemblance might only be my imagination, but it is worth a last roll of the dice. "You already know why," I say. "It is what any warrior would do, given the chance of holding a sword once more before they die. It is what *you* would have done. I defeated a soldier twice my size. You all watched me. And I can take that small honour to the Otherworld now, to counter the shame of ever having surrendered to you."

The legate does not reply. He stares, and I cannot tell if the intensity of his gaze is understanding, or anger, or something else entirely. Then he looks away.

"Take her back upstairs," he says to one of his men, his tone dismissive.

I am too depressed to resist as the soldier twists my arm behind my back and shoves me towards the steps. It was madness to imagine a Roman had any honour. The fight meant nothing, as did my attempt to escape. I am to be shut up again in the darkness, with even less hope of vengeance than before.

22

SOLINA

In the long hours I spend in the darkened room after the fight, I both dread and long for the door to be opened to put an end to my uncertainty. When it finally does, nothing prepares me for the surprise of who is standing in the lamplight. It is a slave girl. The first woman I have seen since my capture.

I squint at her, my eyes becoming accustomed to the light, then I struggle out of bed, not wanting to be caught unawares if an attacker is behind her – Matu rattled me with that knife. The girl has a lamp in one hand, a wooden stool in the other, and she sets both down inside the doorway. Then she turns to pick up a bag and a bucket of water from one of the guards standing watch outside. I'm too surprised to say anything.

The girl leaves the door ajar and beckons me over. "Who are you?" I ask, saying the words first in my own language – although she does not look like a Briton – then in Latin. She shakes her head, and I remember Lais. "Are you Greek?" I suspect she understands me, as she gives me a sharp look, but still says nothing.

"Get undressed, please," she says in Latin. Then she points to the bucket. "You must wash."

I do as she asks, grateful to be able to wash in front of a

woman rather than Matu. When I have finished, she undoes my braids with soft, swift fingers and tips the bucket over my hair to wash that too. I dry myself with the cloth she hands me, then put on a long wool tunic she gets out of the bag. It is a servant's dress, not unlike the one the girl is wearing, but it is warm and smells clean, unlike the rank green shift I have been forced to wear.

"Sit down." She points at the stool.

I do as she asks. It is hard to think beyond the present moment. The failure of my long-planned escape is crushing. I should be in the marshes now, on my way to Riomanda. I don't want to guess whatever horror might be waiting next, and after the exhaustion of the fight, my relief at being in another woman's company is overwhelming. She begins to brush out my hair, the way Vassura once did. The memory is so intense, and the girl's fingers are so gentle, my eyes fill with tears, and soon I am crying in silence. I had not realised until the Romans took me that, in captivity, loneliness can be even more crushing than fear.

The girl has finished dressing my hair. Some is braided and some left loose, a style I do not recognise. I wipe my face hard with my hands, not wanting to leave any trace of weakness. I am alive. This attempt to escape failed, but I will never give up.

"Come," she says, gesturing for me to stand. "You must come with me."

"Where are we going?" I know she will not answer but cannot stop myself from asking. The girl simply shakes her head, but her eyes are not unkind. Then she turns and I am obliged to follow. The guard outside watches us pass. My palms are sweating, so I clench them. We walk to the door of my parents' chamber. Dragons are painted on it in red and white, and I want to lay my hand on one, to draw strength from the creature, but the girl has already knocked. "You will go in," she says, part encouragement and part command.

I don't want to leave her, or perhaps I don't want her to leave me. "Thank you," I say. Then I walk into the room.

The legate is standing facing the door, the way I do when I don't want to be taken unawares. We stare at one another. My entire body is braced for him to make a sudden move, unsure what I will do if he does. He stays where he is.

"You used his strength against him. To tire him out." It takes me some time to understand that he is talking about the fight in the hall. I nod, unsure if he is making an accusation. "An obvious strategy."

There is silence. The thought I might have been summoned to listen to a lecture on flaws in my swordsmanship is so absurd a bubble of hysteria rises in my throat, threatening to break out as a laugh. I cough to stifle it. "You may be right," I concede.

"How did you manage to move like that, after so much time in captivity?"

This is a more dangerous question. I have no desire to spend my remaining days in chains. "Perhaps I am a natural."

"*Nobody* is a natural. That is a story for children who imagine some men are uniquely blessed by the gods to become heroes. The only skill or strength a man has in battle comes from what he earned himself, through hard training."

"Maybe women are different."

The legate raises his eyebrows. "I rather doubt it." It feels as if he is teasing me, yet he cannot be, so I do not smile. The moment passes. "Do you stand by your story about Matu?"

"Yes."

"He denies it. He says the knife was yours."

The legate's face gives away very little, but I cannot believe he is unaware of how slippery his translator can be. "If I had a knife, he would be dead," I say bluntly. "And Matu is a liar. He told your men that they could use me as a whore, that these were your orders if I escaped. Is it true that is what you commanded?"

He does not reply, but a flicker of surprise in his eyes tells me that, no, he did not. And now the legate knows Matu lied, if not about my escape, then about this. He points at one of my arms. "What do those mean?"

His question confuses me, before I realise he must mean the tattoos. "The mark of the wolf, for my mother's people on the left. And the mark of the horse, for my father's, on the right."

"May I see?"

Clearly, I cannot refuse him, but I am surprised that he would even phrase his demand as a question. "If you wish," I reply, hoping he can read the unspoken words in my answer: *Yet I do not wish it.*

He walks over and carefully examines my right arm, not seizing it as he has done before. It takes all my willpower not to snatch it back. "I have seen this design in the hall downstairs," he says, running a finger over the black curve of a horse's neck. His touch is gentle, not unlike the girl who just dressed my hair. "It is for Epona, isn't it?" He looks up. I nod. My stomach is churning at being so close to him while my mind darts over all the ways I might use this encounter to my advantage. If he is intending to take me as a concubine, it will at least be a means of getting closer to my enemy and learning how to manipulate him. Better that than rotting alone in a room. I brace myself, waiting for the inevitable moment of seduction, telling myself I can endure it, that I am strong enough. He releases my arm. "Interesting," he remarks.

I realise he is going to walk away again. "This is the wolf, for Andraste," I blurt out, offering my other arm. He takes it warily, almost with an air of obligation.

"Interesting," he says again, though this time he does not sound interested.

"You prefer Epona?"

"A friend of mine has a particular interest in the horse goddess. He served in Germania, where her worship is also widespread. There she is often portrayed in the shape of a moon."

I point at the crescent hanging from the silver bracelet on his wrist, grazing his skin with the tip of my finger. "Do you also worship her?"

This was the wrong thing to say. He bats my hand away, annoyed. "That is not for Epona."

I fumble, trying to make amends. "Forgive me, I..."

"It belonged to my wife."

Belonged. She is dead, then. "Loss is hard," I say, trying to think how I might use this new information to manipulate him, but instead of lighting upon a ploy, my own losses loom so large in my mind that grief makes me lose my train of thought. Loss is not only hard, it is unbearable.

"Yes, it is," the legate replies. He is looking at me, if not with sympathy, at least with less hostility. I realise then that I cannot return to my prison alone: I will never escape that way. I must find some means of fixing my captor's attention. There might never be another chance like this.

Slowly, so he has ample time to see my every movement, I reach my hand towards his, then take his fingers in mine. His eyes remain locked on my face, not with desire, but the way I might watch an adder, poised to strike me. His hand is warm, and I clasp it more tightly. He runs a thumb over my palm, then smiles to himself. "That is the first time I have known a woman's hand calloused from training with a sword," he says.

I expect him to pull me closer. He does not. But neither does he release me. I reach out to lay my free hand on the fabric of his tunic over his heart, then, when he does not push me away, I kiss him on the lips. At first, he does not respond, then he kisses me back with a surprising amount of passion, caressing my face and running his hands through my hair, as though he is desperate to hold me closer.

I am exultant at catching him so quickly – men really are easily fooled – but then he stops. With shock I realise from his cold expression that I was not the only one pretending. "And why, I wonder," he says calmly. "Would you have had a sudden urge to do that?"

I am too flummoxed to think of a sensible reply. "You are a very attractive man," I protest.

He looks incredulous, then laughs. "Clearly, I must be *extraordinarily* attractive, for you to overlook the fact I have conquered your kingdom and taken all you have. Or was my being a Roman thief forgotten in the heat of the moment?" His amusement angers me, which makes him laugh even more. "I am not a complete fool, Solina. Tell me the real reason."

The legate is, in fact, a very attractive man. If he were Iceni, I would have kissed him for this alone. Somehow that makes me even more furious. I think of my father by the blackthorn tree, when he told me the most powerful manipulation comes not from lies, but the truth. "Because I am alone," I burst out. "Because I was loved, and now I am nothing. Because I cannot bear you to lock me up again to rot."

This is not the answer he was expecting. The legate stares into my eyes, which are now full of tears. "You cannot expect me to believe that is the *only* reason."

"No," I reply. "But does that matter?"

He contemplates me, and my heart quickens as I realise his desire was not wholly pretence. "Maybe not."

Still, he does not move. Perhaps he means to test me, believing it is easier for a woman to allow herself to be seduced than to choose a man, if she does not want him. Perhaps he thinks I will lose my nerve. Instead, his stillness helps me. I crush down my fear of getting close to him, telling myself this is nothing like the attack at my father's house. He is not like those men. I have chosen this.

"*You will be mine*," I say, speaking my own language, knowing he cannot understand. Then I lean forward to kiss him again, confident that this time he will not stop me.

23

SOLINA

My father's hall has been set up as a court. Prasutagus was always the ultimate judge on disputes brought by his people – I would often join him when he heard cases with his most learned Druids – but his sacred role has been usurped by the legate. Paulinus is not only the commander of the army, he has sole authority to enforce capital punishment in Britannia. Now he sits at my father's table, his own sword placed in front of him, as a symbol of power, and armed soldiers line the hall. In the City of the Horse, there was no need to overawe with force like this: everyone knew my father's rule derived from the gods.

The legate has not looked at me since I was brought in. If I had imagined that lying with him last night would bring me any special favours, his demeanour now tells me otherwise. I watch him listen to one of his men, his face intent as they discuss some point of Roman law. His expression is familiar: a few hours ago, I held the whole focus of his attention, not only as a woman but as an opponent. I had to draw upon memories of my former lover Vatiaucus to get through the experience, remembering what it felt like to enjoy a man's body without much liking the man. Or, in this case, hating him.

One of the legate's tribunes has begun reading a statement on the greatness of Rome, and the murmuring voices fall silent. Nobody has told me why I am here, but I can guess. Either Matu or I will be tried for my escape. The thought does not frighten me. For now, I cannot take vengeance against Rome, but I am determined to punish the weasel of a translator.

A shaft of light reflects off a golden standard, making the sword upon the table blaze. I am called to stand before the legate, as are Matu, the ox and the other men who I challenged yesterday. I had not noticed Matu before this – he must have been standing behind me – and I feel some satisfaction at seeing his dishevelled appearance, knowing *he* has spent the night locked up for a change.

The legate asks for Matu's account first. The Catuvellauni snivels through his tale, claiming I came at him with a knife, then threatened to gouge his eye out with a spoon after he kicked my weapon under the bed.

"She is a savage." Matu points a shaking finger at me. "The Iceni are little better than beasts. They live in the bogs and marshlands, breathing underwater like toads."

I snort, shaking my head.

"You dispute this?" the legate asks.

"Clearly, I am not a toad," I say. "I never tried to escape; he chased me from the room. And *he* is the one who brought the knife. If he had not been armed, I would have knocked him out with a single punch."

"That is quite a boast," the legate says. "Prove it."

"You want me to knock him out *now*?"

"If you are genuinely capable of such a thing. Otherwise, I will think you a liar."

Matu begins to protest, but the legate holds up his hand for silence. I face my opponent. There's no need to spend much time sizing him up – I have spent days doing that already. The translator dodges and weaves, not like a warrior, but like a thief. I wait until he drops his guard, then throw my entire weight behind the punch, catching him under the chin on the left side, the way Riomanda taught me. Matu's head jerks and he crumples, falling to the ground. I nudge him with my toe, to be sure he is not going rise, then turn to the legate.

"That is what I would have done," I say. "No need for a spoon."

"It seems not," he replies. The legate turns to the ox and his other men. "I understand Matu told you that you might take the Iceni concubine as your own if she escaped. Is that correct?"

The ox looks at his companions for confirmation. "Yes," he says.

"For the avoidance of doubt, that is not my order. If Boudicca's daughter were ever to escape, she would be brought to me, and I would execute justice myself." He turns his attention back to me. "I accept your story that you did not plan to escape, as I know you cannot have had a knife. But neither did you hand yourself in. If you show such reckless defiance again, or take up arms against any of my men, Rome will not be merciful. Not only will you be killed, a hundred Iceni will be killed with you. And should you ever manage to escape, I swear by the gods, you will be found, and any settlement which shelters you will be destroyed. You will not be anyone's liberator, Solina. You will be their death. Do you understand?"

I nod, unsure how to reply.

Two guards have picked up Matu, ready to carry him off.

"When he comes round, execute him," the legate says, then he gestures at a guard to take me aside. "I wish her to remain to hear the next case."

The guard's hand grips my arm, and my heart beats faster. There is no opportunity to feel vindicated at Matu's punishment; I cannot imagine any pleasant reason why the legate wishes me to stay. We wait while another prisoner is brought into my father's hall. I strain to see who it is, but the prisoner is filthy and hunched over so it is difficult to see their face. Then as they come closer, I gasp.

My mother's cousin no longer looks like a warrior. She moves stiffly, her clothes are stained, and old blood is caked on her cheek. "Diseta!" I shout, unable to stay silent.

Diseta raises her head. "Solina?" There is amazement in her voice, and she reaches out a hand towards me, but the guard slaps it away.

"She is just an old woman!" I exclaim, rounding on the legate. "You must spare her. What possible threat can she be to Rome?"

"Her age was already known to me," he replies. "And it seems the woman herself is known to you." I say nothing, fearing I may already have put Diseta in mortal danger by recognising her. "She was found in the woods near the battlefield with a stash of weapons, and she will be executed. But since I currently lack a translator, I thought *you* might give me the old woman's story."

Diseta is going to die. I can read her sentence in the legate's face. Unless I find some way to change his mind. "Very well," I say, blinking to stop myself from betraying my distress.

The legate nods. "Ask her who she is and why she had the weapons."

I step forward eagerly. "Diseta, the legate has me captive here, to translate for him. The Romans want to know your name and why you had the weapons." I speak in our own language, gabbling as fast as I can, to try and disguise the length of my question. "Shall I say you are a beggar woman I once knew? We can tell them you found the weapons, that you were going to sell them for scrap."

The old woman looks at me in outrage, more like the forest troll I remember. "Have you completely forgotten yourself, Solina? Why would you threaten to disgrace us both? You will tell them I am Diseta, warrior of the Wolf Tribe, cousin to Boudicca." She turns to face the legate, shouting the rest of her answer even though he will not understand her. "Tell him the weapons were to kill any Romans I found, like the fucking dogs they are."

"I cannot say this!" I hiss at her. "Please. They will murder you." I am aware of the soldiers watching this exchange, so much longer than the question I was told to ask, and do not dare look at Paulinus.

"Slavery is worse than death," Diseta says fiercely. "Or have you already abandoned everything your mother taught you? You will tell them exactly what I said, cousin, or I will curse you from the Otherworld."

My eyes fill with tears at the sight of Diseta's face, but I turn back to our captor. "I tried to persuade her to beg for your mercy. She refused." I pause and raise my voice to deliver my cousin's final message to Rome, so every man in the hall may hear. "She asked me to tell you that she is Diseta, warrior of the Wolf Tribe, cousin to Boudicca, and that the weapons were to kill any Romans she found, like the dogs you are."

There is a murmur at this, and I see one of the guards behind Paulinus twist his face in disgust. The legate merely nods, unmoved by Diseta's defiance. "Then you must tell the prisoner the sentence is death."

Any hatred I felt for him before is dwarfed by the rage that burns in me now. I turn back to Diseta. The sight of her, so proud while physically crushed, hurts my heart. I want to beg for her forgiveness, but I am too ashamed, knowing I do not deserve it. "I cannot save you."

She nods. "I wish you to carry out the sentence, Solina. Then I have chosen my death, and I will not die a slave."

"I cannot!" I exclaim, appalled.

"You will do this for me," Diseta insists, showing more of her old fire. "And you will do it for yourself as the daughter of Prasutagus, last King of the Iceni. He held the only power I recognise to execute justice in this kingdom, and you are his blood."

We stare at each other, then I nod. "It will be as you ask, cousin." I hesitate, desperate to go to her, but when I take a step forward, the guard prevents me. "My mother," I say, almost choking on the word. "Cunominus. Vassura. Did any of them escape?"

Diseta shakes her head. "I will go to them now. As I should have done, then."

I turn to face Paulinus, blinking back tears, determined not to shame Diseta by crying, then I lower myself to my knees before him. "I ask that I be allowed to carry out the sentence. As a sign of my own remorse and as a pledge of my loyalty to Rome," I look up, so I can see into his eyes. "And above all, as a pledge of my personal loyalty to you."

Even though the legate is skilled at hiding his emotions, I know from his pause before answering that he is surprised. "If this is a ruse to try and escape, or to take your own life, or to free the prisoner, the full weight of punishment will fall on *her*, not you. I will have her crucified. Do you understand?"

"I understand. I will not fail you."

The legate turns to the tribune standing beside him, a boy

about my age. "Agricola, give Solina your sword. Mine will be too heavy."

The boy does not look delighted by this request. He walks over and lays it on the ground so I have to crouch down to take it, by which time he is safely out of reach. I pick up the weapon, shooting him a look of contempt.

I turn to Diseta, whose eyes shine with tears. The sight makes my throat tighten, but I cannot weaken. This is the death she has demanded, and the death I owe her. I expect to be led outside into the open air, but instead we are only brought to the threshold of the hall, armed men blocking the doorway. The light makes me blink, it is so long since I have seen the sun.

"Please," I say to one of the guards. "Let me practice wielding the sword. It is unfamiliar to me, and I wish to give her a clean death."

The man looks over towards the legate, now some distance away, waiting for a signal of agreement. "Very well. But only for a moment."

I grip the Roman blade and let my mind go blank. I do not think of Diseta or what I must do. Instead, I balance my weight against the weapon, testing the strength I will need to wield it at speed and with force.

"That is enough," the legate calls, his voice ringing down the hall. "You will pass sentence."

Diseta does not look at me as she kneels – her focus is already on the Otherworld, and I do not wish to distract her, or keep her spirit tethered to the mortal realm. I stand behind her, sweeping the hair from her neck so that it will not obstruct the blow, then I rest my hand gently on top of her matted head. *This is where it ends. I send you now to the halls of your ancestors, by your own will and as the gods demand."*

There is silence. Time seems to hang suspended, and in that one appalling moment, I am conscious of Diseta as my last living relative. I can feel the warmth of her where my hand touches her hair, and I know I cannot be the one to bring about her death. It is impossible. But then Diseta's own voice rings out, loud and fearless.

"*May I go to the gods undefeated.*"

My heart breaks, but still, I lift my sword.

24

PAULINUS

Horses are engraved into the bronze, galloping along the edge of the sword. The hilt is twisted around with gold filigree, ending in a peculiar design of three prongs. It is surprisingly heavy. Paulinus turns the weapon over in his hand, inspecting the blade in the lamplight, before setting it down on the desk.

The Britons seem as attached to the horse goddess Epona as the Celts in Gaul, he writes. *I have seen the horse motif carved into trees at crossroads; it decorates innumerable weapons and even marks the skin of some of the people.* He stops, thinking of the tattoo below Solina's collarbone, where he has kissed her. Not a detail to include in his letter to Pliny this evening.

He picks up the sword again, examining its hilt, squinting at the filigree. Lit by flame, the gold glows. It is the weapon she used against his men in the hall. He should not have allowed that fight to play out, but the sight of her sparring had been so startling it had taken him a moment to react, and then curiosity won over. He wanted to see what she did. It was not an impressive fight – she barely touched swords with her opponent, but it was an intelligent one, and he learned more of her character from watching the way she moved than he had from anything she said.

The moment before she threw the pot to unbalance her opponent, Paulinus knew that was what she would do. He felt a rush of satisfaction when she seized it, the vindication of having understood his enemy. Afterwards, when she had made a transparent attempt at seduction, it was another pot she had thrown, this time hoping to see him fall. Paulinus smiles. She has guts. It had been difficult not to laugh when she knocked out Matu, her strike as swift and lethal as a goat.

He leans back from the desk, twisting the sword, feeling its weight, and thinks about the way Solina executed justice against the old woman. That had been genuinely surprising; he still isn't sure what to make of it.

Her claim she wanted to pledge allegiance to him was undoubtedly false. Far more likely she had formed a suicide pact with the old woman, not unlike relatives agree in Rome to avoid execution. Even so, Paulinus had not believed the Iceni girl would be capable of carrying out such an act. The old woman was her cousin, someone she must have known from childhood. And Solina is only young. He has seen traces of her vulnerability. The strength of will it takes to kill one of your own is simply beyond most people, even hardened men with a lifetime in the military.

When he saw her lift the sword, when he understood she was going to do it, he had wanted to stop her. He still cannot fully understand his impulse in that moment, or why he wished to spare her pain.

Paulinus sets the sword down on his desk, covering it with a cloth, wanting to blot the Iceni girl from his mind too. He picks up the pen to finish his letter to Pliny. "*One of the most important roles Epona plays for the Britons is as the guardian of souls, guiding the dead to Hades, which they call the Otherworld...*"

*

It is daybreak in the camp. Mist obscures much of the landscape, sitting like damp wool in the dips of the valley, stretching like a veil across the trees. Most of the Druids' sacred grove has now been uprooted, save a small section which is used for target practice; some joker has even dressed one of the dead oaks in women's clothes as a mocked-up Boudicca. All around Paulinus are the familiar sounds of life under canvas: shouting, the ring of metal, laughter, the thud of training. He has been out here since dawn, and after disarming Agricola for the third time, it is difficult not to lose his temper.

"You have to block me," he shouts. "Don't freeze, for fuck's sake. Block me!"

"I'm trying," Agricola replies, red-faced with exertion. They go at it again, and again Paulinus wrests the heavy weighted wooden blade from the boy's hands. It's true, Agricola *is* trying. He just doesn't have the strength.

"Then tire me out," Paulinus says, remembering the way Solina fought in the hall. "If you cannot overwhelm a larger opponent, you must exhaust them. Until they weaken or make a mistake."

Agricola fares better this time, forcing his commander to move, then darting out of reach. Paulinus breaks out in a sweat and starts to feel hopeful of a breakthrough for his tribune. But Agricola is not as quick as the Iceni girl, who made evasion look easy, and the boy only succeeds in tiring himself out rather than exhausting his opponent. There is no kindness in granting Agricola a win he has not earned. Paulinus disarms him again.

"That was better," he says. "But you need some more time practising against the stake." Agricola's face falls. It is a demotion to go from paired to solitary training. "Cheer up,"

Paulinus says, amused. "I'm trying to keep you alive. When you next face a Briton, they're not going to give a fuck what drills you've been doing. They're just going to try and kill you."

"How long did it take you to get here," Agricola says, wiping the sweat off his face. "To be as good as you are?"

"You never get there," Paulinus replies, uncomfortable at the compliment. "That's the point. You're only as good as the fight you're about to face. Which means drilling every day and never being complacent. It takes months to build your strength, and only days to lose it." He thinks again of Solina, and the willpower she must have to keep training, locked alone in a room. It is impressive. "You should train for an hour or so on the stake now," Paulinus says, dismissing Agricola. "I will drill with you again in a couple of weeks to see how you've got on."

Paulinus watches him go, then heads off to find the centurion Scaeva, the best fighter in the Tenth, always his preferred partner in drills. Scaeva is an even better swordsman than Paulinus, and more importantly, he thinks nothing of landing a commander on his arse if he deserves it. When it comes to fighting, flattery will only get you killed.

The sun limps higher on its course, lighting a sky the colour of curdled milk, and Paulinus trudges through the camp, making his weekly inspection. No aspect of their campaign, however menial, can be ignored. He visits the men digging trenches and building walls, sees those cleaning armour, and visits the soldiers still recovering from injury. Even a complaint about the latrines demands his attention.

The afternoon darkens early, and the men who left a few days ago to scour settlements return, bringing back seized weapons and goods. It is the usual tale of swords thrust into thatch and dangled down wells, along with a wealthy Druid found harbouring a large stockpile of spears. After executing all the criminals, the centurion in charge loaded up the Druid's treasure. Paulinus has it all brought into the hall. Clattering heaps of bronze lie on the old king's table, twisted into sinister shapes. There is a helmet with antlers, a savage collection of knives and other objects he cannot even identify.

Taking dinner with his senior staff, his eye is continually drawn to the Druid's hoard glowing in the torchlight. It looks like the carcass of a fantastical beast, picked clean to the bones. He thinks of the fresco of Hercules in his childhood home, remembering an image of the hero defeating the Hydra which he used to gaze at for hours. Real monsters can be less easy to identify.

Paulinus is not a heavy drinker, and has no desire to linger all night, casting a shadow over the others with his sobriety. This is the time of the evening he most misses Fulvia; it is when he used to write to her. He retires upstairs, taking a few of the objects from the table. Solina will be able to tell him what they mean. It is not disloyal to seek out another woman's company, and entirely reasonable he should ask for her explanations of barbarian ritual. Paulinus ignores the fact that throughout his meal he has been intensely conscious of the Iceni girl sitting upstairs above him, perhaps cold and cross-legged on the floor, eating her own portion of the same stew.

If Solina possessed the bunched-up aggression of a goat when she knocked out Matu, now she is wary as a fox. She pads over to him, a flinty expression on her face. Her cheeks are flushed, and he realises she must have been crying.

"I had the old woman buried," he says, even though that is not the greeting he had planned. Solina says nothing, her hostility palpable. "The old woman you executed," he repeats, in case she has not understood. "I assumed you knew her. She has been buried out of respect."

The girl takes a long shuddering breath. Paulinus waits for her thanks, before realising there won't be any. "She had a name," Solina says at last. "Diseta. *I* should have been the one to carry out the rites."

"I thought only Druids could perform sacred rituals?"

Solina narrows her eyes. "I was her kin. That also gives me the right."

"In Rome we have a custom when a close relative is condemned to death." Paulinus sits and gestures for her to do the same. Solina obeys him, lowering herself onto the chair as enthusiastically as if it were made of knives. "Rather than allow a stranger to kill a beloved, either they commit suicide, or they are killed by family. It is a means for the condemned to retain their honour." Solina stares at him, her lips a tight line. "I believe this is what you did. Isn't it?"

Her eyes flick away from his. "I did not know Romans had this custom," is all she says. Solina's attention drifts to the desk, now piled with the Druid's treasures. She rises from the chair without warning or permission, swiftly crossing to take up the nearest object. "How did you get this?" she demands.

Paulinus also rises, annoyed by the girl's absolute refusal to understand her position. "That does not matter," he says, his voice cold. "You will explain to me what these curiosities mean."

Solina reverently circles the bronze disc in her hands, engraved with two crescent moons. "You should not have touched this. It is a mirror to the Otherworld."

Paulinus is not such a sceptic as his friend Pliny, but still, he is unimpressed by this idea. "How is it used?"

"To ask the gods for their guidance. Those who are truly gifted, like my father, would be able to look into the mirror and see visions of the future through its surface." She sets it down. "I am not touching that one." She points at a hunched, goblin-like figurine with a spout for a mouth. "It is used to divine demons and harness their power. Whoever owned this creature understood the dark rites. My father told me such rituals are still practiced, but I have never seen them done." Solina hesitates. "Would you cover it, please? If it can see, it brings bad luck."

"I'm surprised to discover there is anything that frightens you," Paulinus says, but he obliges her by covering the bronze creature with a cloth.

The Iceni girl gazes at him, surprisingly wide-eyed and earnest. "Only a fool would not fear the gods," she says. "Do you not fear them?"

"I respect the gods," he replies. "That is different. And I do not believe in magic." Solina has picked up the mirror again, clearly in awe of the precious object. She looks quite different from the wily creature of the other night. She is clearly naïve enough to believe everything the Druids have taught her from childhood. He finds her innocence reassuring, more in keeping with what he would expect from a savage.

"Why did you cover the demon-catcher when I asked you," Solina says quietly, still looking down at the mirror. "Yet you did not spare my cousin?"

Paulinus hesitates, the way he might pause at a fork in the road. Solina has no right to ask him such questions – she is a captive. If he keeps granting her requests like this, or overlooking her impudence, it will shift the balance, granting her a humanity he ought to deny. Yet he remembers her standing in the hall, lifting the sword, and understands he has already chosen how to treat her. "One is a courtesy, the other is justice," he says at last.

"Justice," she repeats, her voice bitter.

"The execution was not personal," he says calmly, as if speaking to a child. "I do whatever is necessary to establish Rome's authority. That is justice. Sometimes it is brutal, even cruel. The aim is not to hurt you, even though I understand it will. But if a matter only concerns the pair of us, I will always treat you with courtesy. I hope, even with kindness."

"You did not send for me last night," she says, setting down the mirror and looking up at him. To his shock, her eyes are bright with tears. "*That* is personal. And it was not kind or courteous. I was alone."

Paulinus does not know what to say. He profoundly distrusts the girl, yet at this moment she is gazing at him with an air of wounded disappointment that reminds him of his wife. Fulvia would look at him exactly like that, eyes full of reproach, whenever he blundered and hurt her feelings without realising. Then he would have to spend days begging, apologising and trying to make amends. For Solina to make such an assumption about his obligations towards her is absurd. He ought to rebuff the girl. And yet, he finds he cannot. Encouraged by his silence, she walks over, until she is standing so close he can feel the warmth of her body. It makes him remember the intimacy of the night before. "Solina," he says, resisting the temptation to touch her, even though that is what he has wanted to do from the moment she walked into the room. "Nothing will change the conditions of your captivity. If you defy me, I will still execute you. And nothing you do is going to win you favours, either. You don't have to lie with me."

"Do I look like a woman who does anything she does not

wish to do?" She rests her hands on his waist, before sliding them round to the small of his back, digging in her nails. "And I do not believe you called me here only to explain the uses of ritual objects."

Her switch from innocent to knowing is so abrupt he laughs. "No," he admits. "Perhaps not." He rests his hands on her shoulders, running them gently down her arms, which are so much stronger than he is used to seeing in a woman, then bends to kiss her. He breaks off before taking things further, wanting to be certain she is willing. To his surprise, she grips him by the shoulders, running her calloused hands down his arms in a more forceful echo of the way he just touched her, lingering to feel the muscle, almost as if he were a horse she is examining. There is a look of satisfaction on her face, which might be desire, or perhaps aggression.

Then, before his suspicion has a chance to reassert itself, Solina is kissing him, pulling him closer, and Paulinus no longer cares why she seems to want him so badly, only that she does.

25

SOLINA

In my prison, the air whistling through the eaves grows colder, and I know the Feast of Darkness is approaching. For the first time in my life, I feel afraid of who might step through the veil. Diseta is dead, yet her words haunt me. *Slavery is worse than death. Or have you already abandoned everything your mother taught you?*

At night I see Diseta in my dreams, I see myself lifting the Roman sword. And in the day I can no longer fantasise about redemption through escape. Even if I manage to reach Riomanda, the legate has sworn to track me down, bringing death to any who shelter me. I would not only have Diseta's blood on my hands, but Riomanda's too. The thought makes me despair. I hurl punches and kicks at nothing, venting my rage on the air, then I walk back and forth, conjuring the Town of the Wolf in my mind, imagining that I am not only heading north but walking back in time. I close my eyes. When I arrive home, all will be as it once was; I will find my family at the hearth, Cunominus and Riomanda laughing together, my parents arguing, my sister eager to ride with me. I try to blot out the sounds of the Roman camp outside, to make the vision clearer, to bring my family closer. It is no good. I know they are gone. I open my eyes, pressing my fist against my mouth to prevent myself from crying.

The room swims. It no longer feels as if this building belongs to my life before. Sometimes I forget this place was founded by my father. Red curves repeat on the walls – the wings of Esus's birds – and white lines represent his river. A swelling row of scratch marks is spreading out along the base of the waves: the stain of all my days here. I have been Paulinus's concubine for many weeks now, yet I am still so far from manipulating him into dropping his campaign against the Iceni that it is making me feel desperate. I am confident he is becoming attached to me, and yet the man spends his days destroying my kingdom with as much determination as he did before I lay with him. Sometimes I think of my mother, how she spent her whole life trying to convince my father of the need to resist Rome and how he steadfastly ignored her. I am amazed now she did not kill him out of frustration.

Murdering Paulinus remains a possibility. He is a supremely cautious opponent and never falls asleep in my presence, but in time I suspect an opportunity may present itself. Yet I cannot shake the sense that killing him would be an empty act of vengeance. He is only one man. His death would achieve nothing, save mine. Rome will not pack up and leave Britain because he is gone. I am not sure his death would even restore my honour – slaughtering a sleeping man in his bed is the act of a coward.

At the thought of it, I start to pace again, faster and faster, as if I might outrun my own thoughts. There are other, less noble reasons I am reluctant to murder him. I still hate the legate with all my heart, but it is becoming harder to think of *Paulinus* as the legate. He has split into two men in my mind. Paulinus is still my enemy, but occasionally I almost like him. Captivity is unrelentingly lonely, and it is hard not to look forward to the only moments in the day when I have company, whoever that company might be. And it's even harder to resist the comfort of physical affection. Nothing about Paulinus's behaviour towards me recalls the horror of the attack, his 'courtesy' is always apparent. At first this was a relief, but now I find his gentleness, whether real or manipulative, makes it harder to shut him out.

I stop pacing, resting my forehead against the cold wooden wall, closing my eyes. It is mortifying that thinking of Paulinus makes me want to see him. Sometimes it feels as if trying to manipulate my enemy is like dismantling a bonfire – every flaming branch I grasp only burns my own hands, leaving the fire untouched. I knew all the worst aspects of his character before I lay with him. It is no surprise that he is brutal, ruthless and Roman – there is nothing new to discover on that score. Instead, I have learned the man is grieving his wife, that he is lonely, and I cannot see how this knowledge serves me. I try to imagine how my mother might have handled this situation, how she might have manipulated such a man, but the thought of her only makes me want to curl up with shame. How she would hate what I have become.

I sit down heavily on the bed, shivering in the cold. A memory of Bellenia comes to my mind from the last Feast of Darkness; I see her face bright in the flames, encouraging me. It is almost as if her spirit were close by, offering comfort, but I feel ashamed to accept. I cannot believe I have survived, even though my beloved family is dead. I suppose the gods must have saved my life for a purpose, but if so, I am yet to discover it. I turn away from my sister, even though I know the more I abandon the memory of those I love, the more it is Paulinus who will slowly, insidiously take their place.

*

The serving girl comes to me earlier than usual. The Greek girl has not become more talkative, despite all my efforts. Today she is carrying a heap of fabric over one arm, a distinctive green, with hares embroidered in gold thread. The sight of it brings a lurch to my stomach.

"What is that?" I say, my voice sharp.

"From your house in The City of the Horse. You are to wear it."

"Matu said the house was burned down."

"Yes, but first they took everything."

My own belongings have been looted from me, and now I am being given something back as if it were a gift. I imagine someone – perhaps this girl – rifling through a heap of precious tapestries, jewels and fabric, then landing on this dress because it was the smallest. But although it did belong to one of Boudicca's daughters, this is not my dress.

"That is my sister's dress," I say, speaking once I can trust myself not to cry. "I cannot wear it."

"You must. The legate wishes you to wait on him in the hall at dinner."

"Wait on him? How?"

"At dinner," she repeats, as if I am stupid.

I am too surprised to speak. I know at once this is not a gesture of affection. It is one of dominance. My mind goes to the bronze ceremonial swords on the wall, wondering if they are still there. Might I now be able to do what my mother would surely demand of me? Is this a chance to kill him? "I do not know what service the legate wants," I say, folding my arms. "My mother never waited on a man." Memories of the last days of my father's life, when I suspect my mother helped him to dress, make me a liar. *But never because she had to*, I think.

"You will sit beside the legate and serve him his wine. If he asks, you will sing for him."

"I cannot sing."

"He knows you have a beautiful voice. I have heard you sing your own language here, many times, when you are alone."

It is painful to know the girl is a spy, although I have long suspected it. There is a slight air of defiance in her face as she looks at me, and I realise this is the most she has ever said. I always assumed she refused to speak because she was commanded to be silent, but perhaps not. Perhaps the Greeks despise the Britons, as much as the Romans do.

We do not say anything more. She hands me the gown, helping me with the fastenings. It is too short, but I find it unexpectedly comforting to wear Bellenia's clothes. It almost feels as if my sister were a third protective presence in the room. Perhaps this is why I sensed her come to me earlier. The Greek girl's fingers are as gentle as always when she styles my hair, but I no longer trust her touch. Captivity is teaching me that sometimes a person can be so starved of kindness, they see it when it isn't there.

Roman flags line my father's hall. It feels like the worst form of mockery that the fabric is scarlet, the colour of the Otherworld, in this hall that was built to serve the gods. Nothing remains of the rich decoration made over hundreds of years by Iceni craftsmen; there are no swords, harnesses or tapestries. Everything has been taken from the walls, and ugly holes mark the wood where the gold embossing has been ripped out. While I have been locked upstairs, the soldiers have been busy dismantling the building.

There are not many here – perhaps the legate only eats with his most trusted circle. I am conscious of the men's eyes as they watch me walk along the line of the table, but I do not lower my own, nor do I deign to look at anyone. None of Boudicca's enemies will see her daughter look ashamed. I carry a heavy jug of blood-red wine, stopping to serve each man in turn. It is almost amusing the way they fall silent as I approach, as if expecting me to crack the pitcher over someone's head. I do nothing but pour, filling my family's silver cups for these men, as if they were not thieves but honoured guests. The Greek girl lied when she said I was expected to serve the legate his wine; it turns out I am expected to serve them all. I make Paulinus wait until last, then sit beside him.

He smiles warmly, no doubt pleased my obedience has made him look powerful. I do not smile back. Then he takes my hand, and the warmth of his skin on mine is a shock. "You did well, Solina," he says. He is staring at me, and the kindness in his eyes makes him look like Paulinus, not the legate. Pain and confusion must show on my face, because he leans forward to kiss me, then turns away to speak to the young man on his other side. I am left staring at the food on my plate, any appetite I had now gone.

All around me is the murmur of voices, the sound of laughter. The soldiers are eating their meal, their plates heaped with bones and fat, while outside they have left the Iceni and Trinovantes to starve. Before me sits a meat I do not recognise, congealing in an evil-smelling fish sauce. With a sick feeling, I wonder if it might be hare.

The legate's voice is louder than the others because he is closer. I listen to him speaking to his young companion. "I have told Alpinus to leave well alone," he is saying. "The man is from Gaul. Who knows where his sympathies lie. And in any case, he has no idea of what is necessary to crush a rebellion." I look up sharply, wondering what this might mean, and the boy notices my interest. He nods anxiously at the legate.

"General, the British girl, your...." He trails off, unable to find a polite word to describe me to his commander. Paulinus turns swiftly, and I am startled by the coldness of his expression – though perhaps it is more surprising I ever forget he is Roman, and I am his enemy.

"I was told you wished me to sing," I say loudly, and the boy beside the legate looks down in embarrassment.

Paulinus looks uncertain, as if trying to weigh up my intentions. I think of all the times he has kissed me, when he killed my suspicions with an onslaught of affection. "It is an honour I wish to give you," I lie.

"Of course," he says, softening. "If you wish, Solina." I hear someone snort with amusement, but I ignore the fool, standing up abruptly from the table, and am gratified by the hush that falls. For the first time, I choose to look at the faces of the men here. Their eyes are wary. Perhaps some of them saw me fight before.

"You are in the house of Prasutagus, son of Antedrig," I say, my voice low and harsh like my mother's. "Were he alive, I have no doubt my father would have made you welcome, as he was a loyal servant of Rome, and unfailingly generous to his guests." I do not look at Paulinus to see how he responds to this barb couched in flattery. Let him guess what I mean. "My father's people are from the City of the Horse, blessed by the goddess Epona." I pause, knowing that every man here had a hand in destroying the city, that its only existence now is in my memory and my words. I turn to Paulinus then, even though it is painful to see his face. "I believe you are interested in the goddess of the moon, so I have chosen to sing of her for you."

I lift my arms as I used to do at the altar for sacrifice, the way my father taught me to reach for the gods, and close my eyes, to shut out the sight of the barbarians desecrating his hall. Then, for the first time since I was captured, I direct the power of my voice at Paulinus.

The Romans do not sing as we do – the Iceni call upon our gods from the throat. It is a wild and haunting sound, and every Druid is trained to conjure the spirits with the skill of their song. I sing the legend of Esus and Epona, the love story I recounted for my mother and sister when we camped in the woods on the eve of war. I have chosen this song to call them closer to me, in the hope their spirits also remember that night. I understand now that, even if they cannot forgive me for what I have become, I would rather have my family's hatred than nothing at all. When I have finished singing, I open my eyes and look straight at Paulinus, as if there were only two of us in the hall. "I have told you the story of how the god Esus won the love of Epona; he believed he was in pursuit, but he only caught her when she permitted it."

I ignore the other men's laughter, only looking at the legate. Paulinus smiles, pleased to have his authority over me burnished so publicly. Yet he does not understand what I have told him. Epona always held more power than Esus. Everything her lover thought he had, was an illusion.

26

PAULINUS

The landscape is a wasteland. He has ridden past fields of burned crops, the blackened ruins of villages, and the rotting carcasses of oxen, dead of starvation by the roadside. It is a scene of relentless destruction. Rome has repaid a thousand-fold the massacres at London and Camulodunum, and the Iceni kingdom is now in the grip of famine, its people so broken they will never again find the will to rebel. He tries to find satisfaction in the sight, and yet this victory does not bring joy. It feels hollow.

Paulinus sits upon Viribus. He is chilled to the bone. The wind here is ferocious, tearing across the open plains of the salt marshes, flaying every scrap of exposed skin. In his gloved hand, numb with cold, he holds the coin he kept from Camulodunum, in memory of a murdered child. The boy has often been in his thoughts on this campaign. Any time he wavered at inflicting such destruction, or his affection for Solina made him question his actions, he thought of those small, burned bodies, huddled together in the temple. Children slaughtered by Boudicca. The newly appointed procurator, Alpinus, has warned Paulinus against destroying the north of the kingdom, saying the Iceni have suffered enough. But Alpinus is a Celt, his own brother a rebel in Germania. The man would never understand what it felt like to bury those children, to see the *bulla* around the boy's neck.

Paulinus watches his men burn the salterns, trying to remember how the smoke rose from the honeyed offering on the children's grave. The huts here are already deserted, the trenches silting up, but he has still ordered everything to be set on fire. Flames rise, shimmering across the desolation of the marshlands, blotting out the grey sea behind. It will be years before salt is gathered here again. He tells himself this is justice.

Lukodunon. The Town of the Wolf, the Iceni's most northerly settlement, lies before him. No smoke rises from its rooftops, and Paulinus knows before they enter the town that it has been abandoned. He waited too long to sack this place, caught up in destroying the more populous lands to the south. The revelation of the north's significance had only come to him one night when he lay with Solina, running his hand over the curving lines which shine black against her pale skin: *the mark of the wolf for my mother's people.* Paulinus had thought at first Solina was describing the dark god her mother served, but now he understands. Boudicca did not come from the Iceni capital; the queen had had her own seat of power. He did not ask Solina to tell him where to find her mother's city – he knows she would never reveal it – but he used the British word for wolf, *luko*, to help him track it down. His hunch was confirmed when Solina made a particularly obnoxious effort to wheedle him out of his campaign, as she so often does, and he lied, telling her it was too late, the north had already been destroyed. Her distress had been so great it left him in little doubt this was once her home. Though her weeping also left him with a queasy sensation. *Guilt.*

They have reached the gatehouse of *Lukodunon*, and Paulinus reins Viribus to a halt. The wooden doors yawn outwards and the streets within are deserted, with no sign of recent tracks or footfall on the road. He looks up at the painted symbol above the doors. It is a wolf, its back painted with spikes, a close copy of Solina's tattoos. Tattered skulls are set above it, and the sight makes him grimace in distaste.

Armed scouts go on ahead, breaking into the buildings, street by street, making sure no fugitives are lurking. It is the empty grain stores which convince Paulinus the place is truly abandoned. He rides down the central path, casting a long shadow on the road, making for the enormous roundhouse at the settlement's heart. The building looks ancient, as much a part of the landscape as the woods or the marshes. He dismounts, handing over Viribus's reins, then walks over the beaten earth of the town square, wondering if this is where Boudicca mustered her first warriors. A memory of Solina comes to him, the sweep of her arm as she drew her sword to challenge him in the woods, and he feels an unwelcome rush of emotion. Not disgust, but *affection*. Months ago, he told Solina he would execute her if she ever defied him. Yet he now knows, whatever the girl did, he could never kill her.

He stands at the threshold, under the shadow of the thatch. Two giant wolves are carved onto the doors, painted black, their fur glittering with inlaid silver, some pointing outwards in curling spikes. The beasts stand on their hind legs, snarling jaws meeting at the central arch, but what strikes Paulinus is not the savagery of the design, but its beauty. Again, he thinks of Solina, imagines her standing here as a child, her hair shining red, eyes full of laughter, and he feels reluctance to harm something that must be precious to her. It is hard to think of this as Boudicca's home – he can only see her daughter. His weakness is followed swiftly by anger, both towards Solina and himself.

Breaking into a roundhouse is beneath a commander – it is a job better suited to any of the men standing beside him – yet Paulinus still asks for the axe. He told Solina once that the only strength a man has, he earns himself. It is why, after so many years in the army, he never misses a day's training. And it is why he knows the only way to overcome the unworthy guilt he feels at destroying something sacred to Solina is to do it himself.

The old oak is tough, and Paulinus is soon pouring with sweat, his muscles burning. He does not slow his pace, but smashes into the doors' centre, cutting out the lock at its heart. It is a type of redemption, knowing that even though he could never bring himself to inflict violence on Solina's body, he is still capable of inflicting it here. Eventually, the doors surrender, relinquishing their age-old protection of the house. Daylight floods into the darkness as Paulinus steps into the hall, and stale air greets him. The walls inside have been stripped bare, the bedchambers at the back naked of the tapestries which must once have shielded them. Nobody has lived here in some time.

All that remains is the wooden furniture, too heavy to move, and an ancient firedog guarding the dead hearth. A battered cauldron rests on the grey embers. This is the only object left in the room, a striking enough detail to draw Paulinus over to examine it. He looks inside and sees a flash of silver. Retrieving the small object from the pot, he turns it over in his fingers. It is a woman's silver brooch, shaped with the face of a wolf. Perhaps a talisman left to protect the house. He suspects Solina might understand its meaning but also knows he can never ask her. Instead, he slips it into the small leather bag he always carries, the one which holds the boy's coin from Camulodunum.

"Search upstairs," Paulinus commands. "And when you are certain the place is empty, we will set fire to the town."

They leave the north in flames. *Lukodunon*, Boudicca's birthplace, has been destroyed. Paulinus felt relieved watching the fire climb to the summit of the gatehouse, engulfing the painted wolf. Let that signal the rebellion's end. He pretended to consider pressing into the wild green woods, to hunt down any survivors from the abandoned city, but the vast scale of the forests covering the north was enough excuse to refrain.

Paulinus is almost certain he caught a glimpse of pale faces, watching from between the trees, but he kept this to himself. The fugitives will largely be women and children, not worth the expense of energy and time it would take to track them all down. He cannot admit to himself the real reason he left the woods alone: he is beginning to feel uneasy at how much he has destroyed.

It is night when he arrives back at the camp, and its torchlight marks the only sign of life he has seen in miles. Orderly rows of tents cover the uprooted sacred grove, and the tower at its heart looks increasingly like a regular part of the garrison, rather than a savage temple. When he leaves Britannia, this too will be dismantled, but walking now into the hall, he almost feels he has returned home.

Paulinus does not seek out Solina the moment he arrives. He does not wish to admit to himself he feels that much affection, even though he has been absent for over three weeks. Instead, he spends some time answering a letter to his steward Cosmus in Rome about the state of his house, before he sends for her. His smile at the sound of her footsteps evaporates at the sight of her face. She is obviously in pain.

"Are you sick?" He goes to take Solina's arm and guides her to the bed. Her skin is clammy, a sheen of sweat on her pale cheeks and she presses a hand to her lower abdomen as she sits.

"I was pregnant. And now I am not."

Whatever he expected to hear, it was not this. Paulinus feels winded by shock. He stares at her without speaking.

"It is not so surprising," she says, in her usual abrupt manner. "This is what happens when a man lies with a woman. Did you think my people were different this way?"

"No. I just had not thought—" He stops, not wanting to betray too much. He was married to Fulvia for over ten years, and before that he had kept a long-term mistress, Thais, who already had two children by other men. Yet there was never a hint of a pregnancy with either woman. Or with *any* woman who shared his bed long enough for him to know. Men are rarely blamed for a lack of children, but that does not mean Paulinus has not always secretly feared the fault lay with him. "Are you certain?" In his urgency to know, he does not sound very sympathetic.

"I would not say such a thing otherwise. Ask the slave girl, if you do not believe me. She brought in the camp doctor."

The sense of loss Paulinus feels is one that carries the weight of years of disappointment. "Then I am very sad," he says. The words are wholly inadequate, but he is unsure how to share his feelings with Solina, or to know what she wants from him.

"Are you sad? I thought you might be relieved by the loss. That you might not want—"

"No. Please, stop. Of course this makes me sad." He wonders what sort of monster Solina imagines him to be for her to assume he could be pleased by the loss of his own child, or her suffering. Then he thinks of what he has done to her people, her kingdom, and again Paulinus feels a sting of guilt. "Are you—" His question is cut off by the realisation that she is crying, her body shaking with suppressed sobs. He takes her into his arms, stroking her hair as she weeps into his shoulder, unable to stop himself from imagining her locked up while he was gone, alone and in pain, losing the child he has spent his whole life wanting. It is unbearable. "My darling," he says, unthinkingly using the endearment he once reserved for Fulvia. "I'm so sorry."

After a while, her crying subsides, and she is calm again. Solina disentangles herself, looking up at him, as if seeking his reassurance.

He lays his hand gently on her stomach. "Perhaps next time, you will not suffer a loss," he says, unable to stop himself from speaking his own hope aloud.

She stares at him, her lips slightly parted. Then she lays her hand over his. "I have been afraid to tell you something, because I know you do not believe in our gods. But it's important you should know."

"What of your gods?"

"I am destined to give you a son. I saw this in a dream, brought by Epona, the goddess who carries souls between worlds."

Solina's words are so outrageous Paulinus hardly knows what to say. He looks at her sharply, searching her face for any trace of deceit. It is not as if his mistress is a stranger to lying. She is still trembling, her face blotched with tears that are surely impossible to fake, and her distress is painful to see. Solina is only young, and he knows she is deeply religious.

Perhaps she really does believe this nonsense, even if he does not wish to hear it. He opens his mouth, but she speaks before him.

"What were you doing while you were away from me?"

The image of the great roundhouse at *Lukodunon* appears vividly in Paulinus's mind. His axe sinking into the wood. The crack as the ancient carvings splintered, the shame he felt about being unable to inflict such violence on Solina's body, and the fleeting, hateful wish that he could. "I have already ordered you never to ask me about Rome's campaign," he says sharply.

She looks on the verge of weeping again. Guilt grips him and he pulls her back into his arms. "I forgive you. Don't think any more of it." Solina clings to him, and Paulinus closes his eyes, unable to shut out the image of the wolf, burning above the gatehouse, its body devoured by flame.

27

SOLINA

I lie in the dark, staring at the soft shadows of the moonlit eaves above me, wondering what I have done. Beside me, Paulinus is asleep. It has taken half a year and the end of a pregnancy, but my captor has finally allowed me to sleep in his room. My body hurts, my heart worst of all. I do not know what possessed me to tell the man such a lie.

It had been a relief to miscarry. I had only become certain I was pregnant shortly before Paulinus left, and the fear was already intolerable. What sort of life would my child endure in captivity, born to me by a man who would hate the baby's bloodline? The loss was very early, but still painful, alone in that room. I told myself it was better this way, that my child's spirit would remain safe in the Otherworld with the rest of my family. I had not expected the legate to care. Nothing had prepared me for Paulinus's grief, the realisation that he *wanted* a child from me. It forced me to imagine a life where he loved me, one where I did not have to despise him for everything he has done, and the pain of it had been too much. Then I had seen the greed in his eyes, the hunger he had for this child, and I understood. His sadness had nothing to do with me.

Paulinus had believed he could not have children. Like every Roman man, he wants a son.

What made me promise him one?

I tell myself I did it to manipulate him. That I had seen a way to lessen his campaign of violence, that I knew the promise of a child would give me even more influence, because I do believe I have sometimes forced Paulinus to doubt himself. And I have lied to him to protect my family before, telling him the skulls above the door belonged to our enemies rather than my ancestors, in the hope he would not desecrate their remains. It is also true that deceiving him has become a habit. Sometimes I lie about trivial things – the name of a god or the meaning of a symbol – simply to try and place some distance between us. I lie to Paulinus for the same reason I push him away when I want to hold him close.

But this lie is darker. I invoked the gods from the most unworthy impulse, not only to protect what remains of the Iceni, but because I want Paulinus to love me. I want to hold the same power over him that he holds over me. He has taken everything I have, even my last hope of finding Riomanda alive, and now I might make him responsible for my mother's line living on. If there is truly no way back home for me, if I cannot escape or save the Iceni, at least I might ensure my family does not die out. Perhaps this is why the gods allowed me to survive. I think of my father's prophecy: *I have seen Solina rise above the rooftops of Rome.*

My tossing about on the bed wakes Paulinus. He reaches over to take my hand, and the feel of his fingers, warm and strong around mine, is calming. "Are you in pain?"

"No," I lie, unable to admit any weakness to him.

Paulinus leans over to kiss me. "You so rarely let me hold you. It might be comforting." I wonder who he means it would be comforting for, him or me. He pulls me closer, sighing with contentment when I do not extricate myself. His heartbeat is loud in my ear, faster than I might have expected, as my cheek rests on his chest. "I care for you," he says, gently, as if I were indeed precious to him. He waits for my answer, but I give him silence. "Perhaps you might also grow to care for me."

I already care for you, I do not say. *But you are an unworthy bastard.*

"Were you lying to me earlier?"

There is an edge to his voice which I pretend not to understand. "No. I was pregnant."

"That's not what I meant. Were you lying about your vision of giving me a child? Please be honest, Solina."

With my cheek snug against his chest, I can hear his heart beating more quickly. Perhaps Paulinus is not as free from fear of my gods as he claims. I push myself upright, so that I can look down into his face. "I am the daughter of the Druid Prasutagus," I say. "His successor by blood and prophecy. My name holds its own promise: *Solina* means 'sight' in my language. My father taught me to interpret dreams. I would never be mistaken."

The words are a travesty of my own gifts, but even my father once gave a fateful prophecy without knowing if the vision was true. In the end, his words did not save lives, as he hoped, only delayed the kingdom's loss. My own lie is small in comparison.

Paulinus reaches up to cup my cheek in his hand and I tilt my head to rest upon it. "I find it difficult when you speak like this."

"Why?"

He sighs as if the answer should be obvious. "How can I be happy to know you are descended from Druids? Your name reminds me of the sun god Sol." He threads my hair in his fingers. "Bright as your beautiful hair."

"Why should I be named for a Roman god?" I fling his hand from my face, angered by his disgust at who I am. "And the sun is not red."

For a moment Paulinus looks angry too, then his face changes, and he laughs. "I don't mean to mock you," he says quickly, trying to gather me into his arms again when I move away. "Truly. I like how you are..." He hesitates. "And your strength means our son will not be a coward."

Paulinus looks vulnerable, and I do not know what to think. If I am to make this man my family, it is hard to imagine how that might feel. I lay my hand against his face, and he tilts his head to rest against it, mirroring my gesture from earlier, which makes me smile. He smiles back.

"You should try to sleep," he says. "To recover."

I allow him to draw me close, and for once I do not pull away when he curls his body around mine. The warmth of him, and the tenderness, makes it impossible to hold on to my hatred. I tell myself that I will pick up the weight of it tomorrow, that I will hate him again tomorrow, and pretend he is a different man while we sleep.

28

PAULINUS

The streets are a riot of noise and movement, packed with carts of masonry which lurch alarmingly on the uneven roads, everyone yelling or hammering or trying to sell something, even if it's just a few mud-coloured clay pots by the roadside. London does not act like a city that was recently burned to the ground: already it is struggling to rise again, aggressively digging its elbows into the earth, forcing itself upright. Paulinus had dreaded returning to this place and the people he abandoned, wondering if the same streets which welcomed him with such desperate hope when Boudicca was poised to attack would greet him with hatred for his betrayal. He had not been prepared for the sheer indifference his presence provokes. London seems to move on as swiftly as the vast river at its heart, largely ignoring the presence of Britannia's legate riding through its streets. He supposes they are used to soldiers here; he sent a large contingent to help rebuild the place, and perhaps people cannot tell one rank from another.

Paulinus heads for the banks of the river where the new procurator, Alpinus Classicianus, has set up his headquarters. Tall wooden warehouses are springing up along the waterside on the ashes of the old, and through their half-built forms he can see a mass of heaving boats and trading vessels, a shifting, creaking forest of hulls and masts. London's ships largely survived Boudicca's attack – Paulinus himself instructed them to take cover downstream – and from the looks of it, they continue to shelter many of the city's residents, no doubt charging an exorbitant sum for the privilege. This shabby outpost on the edge of the known world could not be more removed from the grandeur of Rome, but in one sense it reminds him of the Empire's capital: it is a magnet for fortune hunters.

The legionaries guiding him to the procurator's house bring Paulinus to a building in a more finished state than its neighbours. He rides Viribus into the courtyard and dismounts, handing the reins to a waiting slave, before Alpinus's steward approaches him. The man is a shifty-looking Briton, who places his hand to his heart in greeting.

"The procurator is honoured by your visit," he says.

Paulinus nods politely in response to the lie and follows the steward through the hallway and ramshackle atrium to the procurator's unpainted study. Alpinus rises to greet Paulinus. He is tall, like so many of his people, and his formal Roman dress does not wholly hide his origins; the man is not cleanshaven but has a long moustache in the German or British fashion. He looks more like foreign fighters Paulinus has faced than a high-ranking Roman official. A woman with elaborately dressed blonde hair is standing beside him, her hand resting on the desk in a gesture that looks far too proprietorial for a slave.

"You are most welcome here, general," Alpinus says, in an accent as thick as Solina's. "Forgive me that the building is not fit to host the legate of the province. Julia Pacata and I are honoured by your visit."

The woman is Alpinus's wife, then. Paulinus nods politely

to them both. "The honour is mine," he says, as insincere as his host. He expects Julia to leave the men to their business after the introduction, but she does not, merely taking a step back to watch from a dimly lit corner. It is an act of boldness which would have been unimaginable in Fulvia.

Alpinus smiles and gestures for them both to sit. As the man lowers himself into his chair, Paulinus sees the flash of silver from the brooch the procurator wears. It is an ornate rendering of Epona, the most beloved goddess in Gaul. "I am glad to learn your campaign of terror has ended," Alpinus says.

"The rebellion has been crushed."

"And now not a crow remains alive to pick the bones that lie in the fields." Alpinus's tone is light, almost pleasant, but his animosity is obvious. "The rebels are dead, and so it seems is everyone else in the east, meaning the Iceni cannot produce so much as a block of salt or a bag of grain for the rest of the province. Since Britannia's financial affairs are *my* affair, it is hard for me to rejoice at so much destruction."

"Nobody is rejoicing in it," Paulinus says, not allowing himself to be goaded. "The campaign was necessary to prevent the Iceni from rising again. Otherwise, there would be no province remaining here to raise revenue of any sort for Rome. The whole of Britannia rested on a knife-edge and now it is back under control."

Julia has been standing like a guard dog throughout this exchange, her eyes flicking between the men, and now she makes a remark to her husband in German, which Paulinus feels certain cannot be complimentary.

"Julia asks if your men have acted with proper respect towards the women. She has been concerned by rumours of outrages committed by Rome's soldiers."

Paulinus feels a flare of annoyance. "Please assure your wife she need not concern herself."

Alpinus folds his long pale fingers into a steeple. "Yet that is how the rebellion started, is it not? Through the rape of the late king's daughters."

"That was on the orders of your predecessor, the procurator Catus Decianus, who abandoned his post rather than fight Boudicca. He will face prosecution on both counts. Nobody questions the assault was an outrage. I was unaware Decianus had made such a rash command, or I would have intervened." Paulinus stops. He does not want to think of what happened to Solina. He knows she was brutalised.

There is an expression of unwelcome curiosity on Alpinus's face. "I understand you have taken one of the daughters as a concubine," he says.

"That is hardly unusual treatment of women captured in war. Even if your wife does not approve."

"You are aware the girl is a Druid?"

"Her *father* was a Druid," Paulinus corrects him, irritated.

"Women may also be Druids. And the elder daughter was the chosen successor of Prasutagus, or so I have heard." Alpinus looks amused. "You did not know this?"

"I do not believe you asked me to London to discuss the daughters of Prasutagus. Perhaps you would like to enlighten me as to why I am here."

For the first time, Alpinus looks uncomfortable, confirming Paulinus's suspicions of what is coming. "Gaius Suentonius Paulinus," Alpinus says, addressing him formally. "You are a general of the most distinguished service. You have achieved a glorious victory in bringing the province to heel, to the great glory of Rome, but now is the time to conciliate the east, to forestall the possibility of further unrest. It is a measure of your immense military success that this will be more easily achieved by a new legate."

"I am to be recalled for successfully crushing a rebellion," Paulinus says drily.

"This is not a recall with any implications upon your honour. You have served Rome well, and Caesar—"

"You may spare us both," Paulinus interrupts. "I am well aware that you have briefed Caesar's officials against me."

"You are not my enemy, Paulinus. You crushed the rebellion and now it is in Rome's interests to rebuild our relationship with the Britons, which another commander will be better placed to do. Although you may not believe it, I have only done what I thought best for the province and its people."

"For *its people*," Paulinus says with contempt. "You mean the rebels who slaughtered every child in Camulodunum and burned this city to the ground? We are speaking of savages, not citizens."

"Savages may become citizens in time." Alpinus gestures at himself, his pale fingers glancing off the brooch of Epona. "Or do you think me less Roman than you are?"

From the corner of the room, Paulinus is conscious of Julia Pacata's eyes glinting in the shadows. "I respect you as a citizen of Rome, and as the Procurator of Britannia," he replies, rising to his feet. "I believe we have nothing further to discuss."

Alpinus remains seated. "What will you do with her?"

Paulinus is perplexed, unsure if this is a peculiar German way of referring to the province. "I will hand over my responsibilities to my successor in the usual fashion, once the man has been appointed. It is unworthy of you to cast aspersions on my loyalty."

"Forgive me, of course I do not doubt your integrity... I

meant the Iceni girl. The daughter of the late king. What will you do with her when you return to Rome?"

"As a captive of war, she is the rightful property of the Emperor," Paulinus says, aware that this does not answer Alpinus's question.

Julia Pacata says something in German, and Alpinus answers her in the same incomprehensible language, much to Paulinus's annoyance. "Forgive my wife's sentimentality," Alpinus says, his tone ingratiating. "She hoped to hear you would marry the Iceni girl, given her lineage. Prasutagus was well known by reputation to Julia's own father. The late king's abilities as a Druid commanded great respect in Germania."

Julia Pacata is glowering while her husband speaks, the least sentimental looking woman Paulinus has ever seen. He is offended to be asked such a question, but masks this with a smile. "Your wife is indeed extraordinarily sentimental," he says. Then he inclines his head to the procurator. "Be well."

"May the gods guide you," Alpinus replies. But Paulinus is already striding from the room.

29

SOLINA

The moon is vast, a giant crescent shining with the light of Epona. I gaze up at her curved face, and drink in the night air, only slightly soiled by the fetid smells of the camp. Even though I am a captive, it is impossible to feel hemmed in by the stars. Their bright faces watch me, vivid against the black. Paulinus allows me much greater freedom now – so long as I am watched – and I have longed for his return from London, knowing as soon as he was back, I would be granted the pleasure of leaving the tower. He is beside me, and he is talking, but I do not hear him. It is such a joy to be outside.

"Solina! You are not listening!" His voice is a bark, making me want to shove him.

"What?"

"I am trying to tell you something important."

"Can it not wait until we are inside?" I fling my arms out and tilt back my head, as if I might embrace the night sky.

"No." I lower my arms, gritting my teeth. Paulinus rests a heavy hand on my shoulder. "Solina, *please*."

The man never begs me for anything. I squint at his face, the dark sea of tents behind, and am suddenly nervous. "What is it?"

"I have been recalled as Legate of Britannia. I will take you to Rome in a few weeks."

All my happiness at being outside disintegrates. I stare at him, appalled. "A few weeks?"

"You always knew this would happen. I'm not sure what difference the timing makes. You will like Italy." He takes my hand. "And I will be able to offer you a better life there, than here."

His calloused palm is warm, holding me tightly. I stare at his fingers and imagine wresting him off, sprinting through the camp in a wild bid for freedom, before plunging into the dark marshes. I know it is only a fantasy. Even if I got away, I could never go home. I failed to protect the Iceni, and the north has been razed, its destruction spelling the death of all my hopes. Riomanda is not waiting for my return. My whole family is dead. Escape would only make me a fugitive, bringing misery upon any who dared shelter me. Yet the thought of leaving Britain is still unbearable. "Can you not leave me behind?" I say at last. "Please. I don't want to go."

"I cannot leave you here," he says, and the kindness in his voice is enraging, given *he* is the one doing this to me. "I promise I will always care for you. And the gods themselves have promised you a child."

His words almost make me regret my lie about the son; it has worked so effectively. Yet I told Paulinus that lie for a reason. If I am to wield any power over my life now, I know it will have to be through him. He takes my other hand, wanting to see my face, perhaps uncomfortable at my silence. "I swear I will always care for you," he says again.

I do not look at him. Instead, I gaze at the sky. The moon looks back at me, vast and cold, yet also holding the promise of light in the darkness. Her face must still turn towards Rome, even as she watches me here. I remember my mother, unconquered, even in death. I remember Riomanda, the last words she murmured in my ear, her promise life would continue. I was once brave enough to ride into battle, to trample my enemies underfoot, and I can be brave enough for this. I turn to Paulinus. He holds so much power over me, yet in this moment it is him who looks afraid.

"May the gods hold you to your promise," I say.

My mother's rebellion started in earnest here, at the sacred grove built by my father, and now it marks the point of my departure for Rome. I glance over my shoulder to watch the building recede into the distance. It looks entirely like a prison to me now, the place my relationship with Paulinus was forged, and it is impossible to reimagine the hope the desecrated grove once inspired, or believe it was founded by Prasutagus, last King of the Iceni. Even the Druids' curses are nothing but dust on the wind.

We head south with a military escort, not to London, but to the port of Noviomagus Reginorum. My body aches from being on a horse, but even with my hands tied behind my back, it still feels natural to be in the saddle again. Riding is the sole consolation of this journey. My heart breaks seeing what has been done to the Iceni kingdom. Deserted settlements creak in the wind, and any surviving crops have rotted in the fields. I knew this was what the Romans had done, *what Paulinus had done*, yet seeing it for myself is worse than anything I could have imagined. When we pass the borders of the kingdom, and the fields turn green, marking a return of life, it feels like a gut-punch. The Iceni paid an unspeakable price for wanting our freedom.

It takes over a week to reach the villa of the client Atrebates king, my final post in Britain. We arrive as dusk is falling.

Honeysuckle is planted on the approach and its sweet scent mingles with the salt tang of the sea. This far to the south, the spring evening is surprisingly warm. King Togidubnus is a stranger to me, but I know my mother called upon the Atrebates for support during the rebellion. The king denied her aid, and the huge building now sprouting up on his land is Rome's reward for that choice.

Servants of Togidubnus greet us at the door and we walk through to the hall, built in the square Roman style. Torches are set against the walls, their light rippling across a mosaic floor. Strange goat-fishes – which I have also seen on the legions' flags – are picked out in small black tiles. It seems odd to me that the Romans walk over the same beasts that they bear into battle.

"May the gods bless your stay by my hearth."

The loud, sonorous welcome is made in Latin, but it is a British phrase. The King of the Atrebates stands before us, dressed in a sweeping scarlet robe, a golden torc around his neck. He and Paulinus kiss in the Roman greeting. Even allowing for Paulinus's formidable build which makes most men seem slight in comparison, Togidubnus looks feeble. My mother would have felled him with a single blow.

"I am honoured to be the one who hosts your last night on this island," Togidubnus says. "You have our profound gratitude for bringing Britannia safely from civil war to peace." He glances over Paulinus's shoulder at me, and I see the shock of recognition on his face. I know he met my parents many years before, when he and my father pledged their allegiance to Rome. Perhaps he sees my mother's features in me.

"I am grateful for your hospitality, and for your loyalty," Paulinus says, as the king leads us further into the villa.

I walk behind them, together with the more senior members of the military escort. We enter a room containing three large couches, set beside small spindly tables covered in plates of food. Togidubnus's idea of a feast is poor. The man has no hearth, no hall, no great table set with silver, and no bard to sing of the gods. He is as much a concubine to Rome as I am, yet he has managed to keep his people safe, where I failed. The thought makes me feel ashamed.

The men recline on their couches and Paulinus gestures at me to join him. I find it stressful to eat this way, and tonight I cannot bring myself to lie down. I perch at the foot of the couch, sitting upright, my body rigid. Togidubnus laughs.

"I did not imagine Catia's child would be such a fearful creature."

Catia. It is the first time I have heard my mother's real name spoken aloud since her death. I look at the Atrebates king, this man who knew my family, and his eyes are cold. "Your mother disgraced your father's sacred memory with her monstrous war. Perhaps you will learn the humility she lacked."

Before Togidubnus has finished speaking, I am aware of Paulinus moving to sit upright beside me. I tense, wondering if I am going to be forced to lie down. "Solina is unused to our customs," Paulinus says. "There is rarely a chance to enjoy the luxury of reclining at camp." His tone is impeccably polite as he addresses his host. "Not that I should ever wish to compare your magnificent home to a military base. Perhaps we might all sit with her to enjoy the generous meal you have offered."

I watch Togidubnus struggle into an upright position, his cheeks flushed. "You are very generous to the girl. I hope she understands how extraordinarily fortunate she is."

Paulinus smiles as he accepts a glass from a slave. "I am sure she does."

His complacency chills the affection which had begun to warm me. I want to tell Paulinus that whatever courtesy he shows me can never atone for the horror of what he has done to the Iceni. But I do not say it.

I sit in silence for the rest of the meal, listening to the men speak, and the meek image I must present feels like a being utterly unlike myself. It is not a good omen for my life in Rome.

The bedchamber Togidubnus has prepared for Paulinus is the finest in the house. In this custom of hospitality, Romans and Britons are alike. It is a vast room, hung with garlands of oak leaves and flowers, as if this were not a villa but a roundhouse. I change into my shift, knowing I must wait for Paulinus while he spends time relaxing in the baths with the other men. A huge wooden bed, carved with scenes of Esus and Epona, sits in the centre of the room, and I thump myself down on it, still angry with the client king who refused my mother aid. The bed is a relic of the past, surrounded by the Roman present. Black-and-white tiles form a meaningless pattern of lines on the floor, and slight, pink figures dance across the red walls. I stare at them. It is the same design of painted dancers I once saw in Camulodunum, when my sister and I slept in the abandoned house. Grief is entwined with the memory, so I get up, padding back and forth, the way I have tried to soothe myself so many times over so many months in captivity.

I walk to the shutters, opening them slightly to reveal a dark sliver of sky, speckled with stars. Outside, an owl is calling. I hold myself still at the sound, listening. My father once told me that the bird is a messenger of Epona, that its voice carries word from the dead. I wonder if my family want to speak with me, and if I still possess the ability to hear.

The click of the latch makes me turn. Paulinus is standing in the doorway, dressed only in a plain tunic, his dark hair still wet from the baths. I am taken aback by how attractive he looks. The way he appears now, he might not be Roman at all, he might be a man I chose for myself.

"I'm sorry I had to leave you," he says, crossing over to me. He is so close I can feel the heat of the baths from his skin. Lying with him now would help me find oblivion, the way another might seek it in wine. But I do not want my last night in Britain to be spent giving myself to a Roman man, however much I desire him.

"My sister was calling to me," I say, kissing him on the cheek, a familiar signal between us that I do not want anything more than affection. "But now I cannot hear the owl."

Paulinus is bemused. "Your sister?"

"I believe the owl was my sister." In truth I have no idea if it was Bellenia speaking to me, but I can hardly tell Paulinus that on my last night in Britain, the voice I want to hear above all others is Boudicca's. Or that *because of him* I will spend my whole life longing for my mother's forgiveness, while fearing it will never come.

"It is natural that you loved your sister," he says, sounding as if he is reassuring himself rather than comforting me. "And it is natural you feel sad to leave your home. I understand this is hard for you." He traces his finger over the horse by my collar bone, slowly following the pattern down my arm. I wonder if he would like to erase the marks, if he wishes I were not Iceni, just as I wish he were not Roman.

"What will happen in Rome?"

"As long as I live, I will try to protect you." He kisses me on the forehead, so I cannot see his face.

Paulinus has started evading my questions about our lives

together, unlike his earlier fulsome promises, so I try to be more direct. "Will I live at your house?"

"That is what I would like." He holds my face in his hands, to gaze at me. "You know I care deeply for you, Solina, don't you?"

"You tell me you do," I say. "Why would you lie?" I stare at Paulinus, who has a strange, intense expression on his face. He looks uneasy, as if I have not given him the answer he wants. I cannot bear to tell him I love him, if that's what he is after. Not because I have suddenly developed scruples about lying, but because he does not deserve it. "I want to live in your house," I say, trying a different tack. He looks at me stupidly, so I am forced to explain further. "With you," I add, taking his hand and laying it over my heart, so that he can take a deeper meaning from the gesture, if he wishes.

Paulinus's embrace is fierce, crushing me against his chest. I listen out for the owl. I hope that even if my mother cannot bless my choice, she will still understand why I made it.

30

PAULINUS

The forests of southern Gaul are not like those in Britain. On the world's most northerly island, damp mists creep through woodland, trees twist into unearthly shapes, and paths glow green from the moss, but here, Paulinus can breathe the familiar dry scent of pine again, riding between their tall, straight trunks. A brilliant blue flashes through the canopy above, so much brighter than the grey washed-out wool which the Britons call a sky. The sight of it lifts his spirits like a blessing from the gods.

They are halfway to Rome, the guests of the governor of Gallia Aquitania, a childhood friend of Paulinus, who has arranged a boar hunt in the semi-tame woodland on the edge of Gaul's capital city. It is a welcome diversion on their long journey south, and Paulinus has decided to bring Solina. Her eagerness for the hunt delights him, even as he knows the others are perplexed. Paulinus no longer cares. The further they have travelled from Britannia, the more freedoms he has allowed Solina, until she has blossomed, not like a flower, but like the blackthorn tree, whose strength is inseparable from its beauty. It is impossible not to be swept up in the sheer passion she seems to feel at being alive, now her captivity is ended. There is a certain cruelty in giving her freedoms she cannot keep, and he knows it, but the exhilaration of seeing her excitement has made it hard for him to stop.

Anger drives Paulinus's recklessness too. He sees no reason why he should be a slave to propriety on this journey, not after he has been so gracelessly removed from his post. Alpinus did not even stab him in the back, rather straight in the front. Even thinking about it makes him furious. He tilts his head up to look at the blazing sky. The recall is a painful blow to his ego, but if he sets that aside, he supposes that moving from the role of general to jurist will not be entirely disagreeable. In some ways he prefers legal practice to military life. His first public role had been as praetor, one of Rome's chief magistrates, and he took a prosecutor's zeal into his military career, seeing the work of legate as another branch of justice. Building up his legal practice again should be rewarding, as well as arduous.

Paulinus smiles. At least he knows where he will begin. The prosecution of Catus Decianus, Britannia's disgraced former procurator. The scandal it would cause for him to lead this himself would be counterproductive to the case, and besides, he is not an orator, but he has already briefed Pliny. Paulinus has gathered more than enough evidence of corruption, given half the taxes raised under Decianus seem to have gone straight into the man's own pockets, and then there is the obscenity he committed against Solina and her sister. The procurator should pay for it. Paulinus has never discussed the rape with Solina, but he is aware of ways it has made her vulnerable, despite her skill at hiding her fear.

She is riding ahead of him now, sitting astride like all Celtic women, a spear gripped in her right hand, her body at one with the movement of the horse. He had known she would be a good rider, but the first time he permitted Solina to take to the saddle with her wrists and legs untied, he had been unprepared for how impressive her control of an unfamiliar animal would be. She has more skill than half his cavalry. Today he has permitted her the use of a weapon, much to the disquiet of his men. Even Agricola had looked on the verge of objecting. Long and cruel, the javelin would be lethal if Solina chose to hurl it at the wrong target. Paulinus did not have to teach her how to hold the spear while she rode – her grasp of the weapon has the ease of long familiarity – yet he is not afraid she will turn it against any of them. Solina has had many opportunities to harm him, and he still lives.

A bray from the dogs in front, piercing as trumpets in battle, signals they are close to the boar's burrow. Solina looks back at him, her face lit with excitement, as the hunters on foot fan out through the trees with their nets and spears. The animals in this section of the woods are not truly wild – they are bred for sport – but Paulinus still feels a pang seeing Solina charge towards danger. He has ordered her to remain on horseback, rather than try to corner the animal on the ground.

The burrow is in a semi-open glade, and the dogs splash across a shallow pond to reach it, barking loud enough to wake the dead, though not it seems the boar. Paulinus dismounts, tying Viribus to a tree, and advances on foot with the other men. Solina is obliged to stay back with a couple of other mounted hunters, her spear arm raised, the weapon ready to throw. One of the men from the governor's household is poised above the burrow with a rock, while another flings stones into the opening, to provoke the beast to move.

With a bellow, the boar charges out. The man with the rock misses, knocked aside by one of the dogs which have leaped upon their prey, snarling and tearing at its thick hide. The boar is massive, and it flings itself towards Agricola with its tusks lowered, two of the dogs still clinging to its back. Paulinus rushes forward to help his tribune, whose spear thrust is not strong enough pierce the boar's thick skin. Maddened and bellowing, the boar turns, charging not towards Paulinus, but the gap he has left. The net bearer darts aside, too frightened to try and catch an uninjured animal.

With horror, Paulinus realises Viribus is blocking the boar's path, but before he can hurl his spear, Solina has dismounted, running to stand between the boar and his horse, her spear raised. She takes the full brunt of the beast's charge, and Paulinus cries out in horror as he sees her knocked backwards onto the ground. He rushes over to where she is lying. For one terrible moment he thinks the blood splatter on her tunic is a mortal injury, until he sees the point of a spear protruding from the back of the boar's head. The animal is lifeless, and Solina is struggling to her feet. She must have managed to skewer the boar by braving the charge and driving the spear straight into its head. Behind her, Viribus is bucking and rearing, trying to pull loose from the tree.

Paulinus grips Solina by the shoulders, unsure if he wants to embrace her or shout at her. "Why would you risk your life for a horse? What were you *thinking*?"

She shakes him off. "He is not only a horse! He is your brother, as loyal to you as any of the men here."

Solina turns and walks to Viribus, catching his bridle to stop him from rearing up. Paulinus watches as she quietens his horse, speaking calmly to the stallion in her own language, as if she had not just been moments from death. Her bravery staggers him. Seeing Solina with Viribus, he feels a pain in his chest, remembering when she begged him to let her see her own stallion, whose name he cannot even remember. It had been shortly after he first took her as his mistress, and he had been so irritated by her pestering he had lied, telling her the animal was dead. The memory makes him feel sick with shame.

Near his feet, local hunters are trussing up the boar, winding it in nets to carry back to the capital. His own men are standing back, discontented. It was a poor hunt, tarnished by the kill going to a woman.

"Agricola!" Paulinus calls out. "We will name the hunt as yours, as you struck the beast first." The boy has the grace to look ashamed, knowing as well as his commander that he did not manage to pierce the boar's hide, but nobody objects. They will not want the embarrassment of naming Solina at the feast.

Paulinus walks over to her, bracing himself for an argument over the unfairness of being denied her dues, but her attention is solely on Viribus. She is running her hand firmly along the stallion's neck to soothe him, talking to the animal as if he could understand her. The words make no sense to Paulinus, but her voice is full of kindness. In that moment he decides to stop pretending he does not understand what he has come to feel for Solina. He loves her.

"Your horse didn't die," he says, laying his hand gently on her shoulder. "I gave him to my cavalry. I don't know what happened to him after that, but he will have been well treated."

Solina turns to him, her lips parted in shock. "Tan is alive? You lied to me?"

"As far as I know. Forgive me. I should never have told you something so cruel."

She does not answer but turns back to Viribus, laying her check against the horse's neck. Paulinus is afraid she might cry. Somehow the fact Solina is not furious makes him feel worse.

"You should ride Viribus back into the city," he says. "You earned it by saving his life."

Paulinus has never allowed anyone else to ride his horse,

the animal he trusts to lead him into battle. It is an honour a hundred times greater than being named master of the hunt. Solina turns to him, and her expression tells him that he is unforgiven. "Yes," she says. "I have earned it."

Lugdunum is Rome's finest colony in Gaul, the centre of every trade and military route to Rome, and the birthplace of the Emperor Claudius, conqueror of Britannia. Paulinus knows the governor's palace in the Gallic capital is more luxurious than anything Solina has ever experienced. Before the hunt, she had been excited to explore the gardens, and he had looked forward to basking in her affection, but now he is obliged to spend hours winning her around.

He leads her through the orchards and colonnades, describing the legends and stories behind every fresco and fountain, until his voice is hoarse. It is dispiriting to know that riding back on Viribus barely thawed her coldness, despite managing to earn him even more disapproval from everyone else. Eventually Solina slips her hand into his, squeezing his fingers, and he wants to laugh, both with relief but also at himself for caring so much for a woman's opinion. He is a fool.

"That is not Roman," Solina says, pointing at a large Gallic carving of a god. It has been set in an ornamental grotto, dedicated to Mercury.

"It is Lugus," Paulinus replies. "The Gauls named this city for him. Is he also worshipped in Britannia?"

Solina lays a hand reverently on the stone figure. "As Esus. These are his birds, you see?"

"We know him as Mercury."

"I cannot believe they are the same god."

"Why is that?"

She shakes her head, refusing to answer. "When I live in your house, will we hunt together, like today?"

Paulinus knows he should tell Solina the truth. He has lied to her for too long about what will happen in Rome. But her face looks so hopeful, and he has only just won back her affection. "It might not be considered proper, no." He hesitates. "You will tell me, won't you, if you even suspect you might be…"

"Is that the only reason you want me? For the son?" There is no accusation in her question, though she holds his hand more tightly, perhaps with fear.

"No, I will always care for you. It would just mean—" He stops himself, unable to tell her the rest. *It would mean I had a greater claim to retain ownership of you.*

"You promise me this is not another lie?"

"I promise you, Solina, it is not a lie. I will always care for you."

She smiles, and lays her hand over his heart, murmuring something in her own language, then she kisses him on the lips.

"What did that mean?" he asks, a little unnerved.

"The phrase has no translation in Latin," she replies, then laughs when she sees his doubtful expression. "So, you will have to trust me that it is not a curse."

Solina has never told him she cares for him, but looking into her eyes, he knows without question that this is what she feels. He almost wishes she had cursed him instead.

31

SOLINA

If my mother had known the true reach of Rome's power, I wonder if she would have ever dared to rebel. Its Empire seems unending. On the journey south, through Gaul and then northern Italy, we stay at progressively larger cities, the colours and landscape changing until nothing looks familiar. Paulinus basks in the sun's intense heat, his skin turning darker, while I find it saps me of energy. The blue of the sky is startling but relentless, and I miss the subtle shades of white and grey, the mists and the rain. Everything here feels exposed, brighter and more garish. Everything that is, except the clothes. Nobody in my family would deign to wear such drab outfits as the people we pass, and the women seem pitiful creatures, swathed in fabric, their hair often hidden as if they were ashamed to have anyone look upon them.

I do not tan, but my face is soon freckled and Paulinus is dismayed, obliging me to stay locked in a carriage rather than ruin my exotic skin. I had not considered myself a rarity before – I looked no different from anyone else – and it is unnerving the way he sometimes peers at my face, reassuring himself the freckles will fade. My hair has not been cut since I was captured, and has grown uncomfortably heavy, falling in waves to my waist, but he does not want me to cut that either, saying Roman women pay a fortune to have wigs made this colour, shearing the heads of their Gallic or British slaves.

Paulinus has never made any secret of enjoying my appearance, but I dislike his new interest in my body. It does not feel flattering. My tattoos, which used to fascinate him, must now be completely covered, and by the time we are close to Rome, I am swathed in long, shapeless robes, my movement severely restricted. I am not sure this new look of mine pleases him any more than it pleases me, so I cannot understand why he insists upon it. When we are alone, he alternates between intense, overwhelming affection, and a strange, restless anxiety. At times he barely seems to hear what I say. All of this makes me uneasy. In Gaul I had started to hope that I might eventually be able to accept Paulinus, without spending my whole life hating him. He had seemed a different man from the one I knew in Britain – freer, more loving and less like a captor. In a moment of madness, I even told him I cared for him, though fortunately not in Latin. Now he has become another, third man, who I am yet to understand.

Our final night before we reach Rome, we stay at Volsinii, a city set beside a lake. Evening is the most beautiful time in this sweltering land, and it is especially lovely here, with the scent of pine on a soft breeze, and the vast mirror glowing pink and gold as the sun dips lower towards the water. Paulinus insists I accompany him to make an offering at the Temple of Nortia, a famous site which means nothing to me.

We walk through the town, painted red and yellow like so many Roman settlements, and Paulinus grips my hand, pulling me along the narrow pavement as I cannot walk quickly in these cumbersome clothes. A veil has been set over my hair as if we were married, and the fabric keeps slipping over one eye. I resent the way Paulinus is yanking my arm, but am also frightened of him letting go, not only because this would strand me in a strange city. He has destroyed my family and the world I knew, but he also keeps me connected to my past. If I lose him, there will be nobody left who remembers who I once was.

A towering stone roundhouse rises out of the buildings before us, set in the centre of a paved square. Paulinus slows, and I try not to trip over my robes.

"That's the temple." He looks back, starting in surprise at how much my veil has slipped. He carefully adjusts the fabric to make me appear more matronly, his face softening as he sees me looking up at him. "Nortia is an ancient goddess," he says. "She was worshipped by the Etrusci, a people Rome conquered in northern Italy, hundreds of years ago. Nortia has power over fate and fortune. We need to make an offering to ensure our two fates are bound together, yours and mine."

"Why would this goddess listen to the prayers of a people who enslaved her own?"

"The Etrusci were not *enslaved*," Paulinus says sharply. "They joined with Rome. It is different." I know that I have frustrated him but do not know what to say. To me it seems unlikely this goddess will wish to grant a Roman general any favours. He takes my hand, stroking his thumb over mine, an intimate gesture which makes me feel closer to him again. "Please, my darling. I want you to ask this of the goddess with me. Perhaps she will hear both of us."

"As you wish," I say, giving his hand a squeeze.

We walk between the columns that encircle the stone roundhouse, and my heart quickens as we approach the bronze doors. I cannot see a Roman temple without thinking of Camulodunum, or the people who my mother burned.

It is dim inside as we cross the threshold, the air thick with incense smoking from bronze bowls. People are clustered around a giant painted statue set against the far wall. It is a woman, standing with her arms outstretched, her hair falling in two thick braids over each shoulder. She is smiling and horns sprout from her head as if she were Taranis, God of the Sky. Behind her is a rippling bed of nails, hammered into the plaster, their sharp heads protruding like the spiked spine of Andraste's wolf. Even if Paulinus had not told me Nortia belonged to another people, I would know this goddess is not Roman.

At a table, people are scratching prayers onto small squares of wax, then rolling them up like tiny scrolls to place in a bronze bowl at Nortia's feet. The words must be burned as an offering, only to be cooled and reused again, in an endless cycle of prayer. Paulinus leads me to the table and takes out his stylus from the leather satchel he carries, scratching a message into the wax. I cannot think what to say. My written Latin is poor, and besides, I do not know that Nortia will hear my words. I catch hold of Paulinus's arm, to stop him rolling up the wax when he has finished.

"I will add my message to yours," I murmur. "It is better, if our fates are to be joined together."

Paulinus hands me his prayer. I do not read what he has written but jab the metal point of the stylus into my thumb. I hear his intake of breath as I smear blood over his words, rolling up the wax before he has a chance to stop me. We stare at each other.

"Nortia is a goddess of blood," I say, my voice so low it is barely a whisper. "That is the offering which will please her, and that is what will tie your fate to mine."

I hold out the prayer to him. All the authority I once possessed as a Druid lies in the gesture, as I will him to obey me. He takes the wax scroll.

"As you wish." He turns and walks to the goddess, his

figure taller and more powerful than any man present, other worshippers naturally giving way to let him pass. Paulinus bends to add our prayer to the heap of wax in the bronze bowl, then bows deeply to Nortia.

We leave the temple without speaking. He clasps my hand as we step onto the pavement, but I no longer mind the force of his grip. Paulinus has acknowledged the power I hold as a Druid, willingly taking part in a blood rite, and although he may not understand, I know it is his complicity, as much as the offering, which will bind him to me.

I can remember the sight of the white temple of Camulodunum as my mother's army advanced over the fields; the image is forever emblazoned onto my mind. It had looked unimaginably vast. Now I see it was only a tiny puddle set against the ocean that is Rome. This city is so enormous it seems to have no beginning and no end, sprawling over hills like a forest, its temples and towers piercing the sky in all their wild, gaudy magnificence. It is breathtaking and terrifying.

Paulinus stops on the approach, allowing me to step outside the carriage, perhaps greedy for my amazement, and he laughs when the sight of his city renders me speechless. But before I can ask him to point out or explain any of the palaces and temples, he makes me go back inside, ordering me to sit at the back where I cannot readily be seen. We are not travelling to his house, we will go straight to the Imperial Palace, so that Caesar knows Paulinus has no higher call than his sense of duty.

It is hot and stuffy inside the wooden box. I cannot see Rome, but I can hear and smell it, the yell of street-sellers and the waft of cooking, incense, and horse dung from the road. We jounce on through the streets and I start to lose all sense of time and space. The thought of being in the presence of the Emperor seems unimaginable, and Paulinus has told me so little of what to expect. The only instruction I have from him is to remain silent, whatever happens. Paulinus says he will present Nero with gold and treasures, belongings he has looted from my family and other Iceni warriors, while I am to stand silently beside him as the symbol of his conquest. Then he will formally lay claim to me as payment for his service. There was a time when such a prospect would have filled me with overwhelming rage, but captivity has blunted my pride. I have been forced to endure so much that I tell myself this is only one more day of humiliation. Then I can build whatever life I might lead with Paulinus, here in his city.

We come to a stop, and during the long wait I am desperate to stick my head out of the window to see what is happening, but I remain obedient. Then the carriage climbs another hill, the noise of the streets dying away. I realise we must be in private grounds, and scramble forwards to get a glimpse through the small window. We are on an avenue, lined with trees and gilded statues, rising steeply upwards, the horses slowing from the strain. Then the carriage turns, and I realise from the sudden darkness and echo of hooves that we have been swallowed by a building. We emerge into a massive stone courtyard, and I am helped outside, feeling stiff and sore from the journey. The second carriage, full of chests of Iceni treasure, is being unloaded by slaves.

I gaze up at the palace. It is not one grand building as I expected, but several, a strange mixture of ages and styles, though all of them grand and painted in bright colours. People are milling about in the courtyard, clutching pieces of paper, kept back from the entrance by a massive armed guard of fifty or more men. Paulinus does not take my hand or make any sign of affection, only gestures for me to follow, without meeting my eye. At least I don't have to stumble after him like a fool, wrapped in a ridiculous robe. I am dressed in my own clothes, wearing one of the richest tunics his men stole from my family's home, and a patterned cloak that once belonged to my mother. A torc is heavy around my neck.

Paulinus announces himself to the chief guardsman, and then we are required to wait for admittance. It is late morning, the sun climbing towards its noonday position, but I am already exhausted from a journey that began well before dawn. After a long wait, a man in scarlet and silver passes through the guards to greet us, and I am about to bow, thinking he is Nero, but swiftly realise my mistake.

"Paulinus! Caesar will be overjoyed to see you," the man cries. "We have awaited your return from Britannia with great impatience."

Paulinus politely returns a kiss, but I know him well enough to sense this man is not a friend. "Tigellinus," he says. "My gratitude and loyalty to Caesar is, as always, my life's greatest honour."

Paulinus's face is left lightly dusted in powder from their greeting and I realise the man, Tigellinus, is plastered in make-up, his eyes widened by kohl. My own face is unpainted, and I feel suddenly naked in comparison. He peers at me. "And who is this?"

"The daughter of Boudicca, conquered leader of the Iceni. Here to beg forgiveness of Rome on behalf of her wretched people."

"How curious!" Tigellinus exclaims, his eyes running up and down my body in a knowing manner that makes me want to slap him.

Tigellinus has brought his own armed guard, and we follow, wandering through an ants' nest of bewildering, winding corridors, their vaulted ceilings impossibly high, before we come to a vast marble hall. Like the courtyard outside, it is full of men, either milling around or sitting on benches.

"Could we not wait somewhere more private?" Paulinus asks.

"You are Caesar's most honoured guest," Tigellinus says, his voice obsequious but his eyes cold. "There is great distinction in the wait, I can assure you, as he will wish you to join him for dinner as a friend, not call on him as a petitioner." With a bow, the man strides off.

I know that Paulinus is annoyed, even though his face is impassive. He strides over to a bench. "You will sit there, Solina."

"I am not a dog," I say, disliking his tone.

He widens his eyes at me. "You will sit there, and you will stay there, and you will not make a scene."

Paulinus stands, partially screening me, while I obey. The chamber is a huge echoing space, every surface made of marble, with windows set around the high ceiling to let in the light. Several of the other waiting men approach Paulinus, eager to greet him and curious about his companion, but he is clipped with them all. In time we are left alone. Hours pass, the windows onto the sky above growing darker, the vast hall emptying. Eventually, Paulinus sits beside me.

"What is happening?" I whisper. He does not reply. "Paulinus, *please*. Speak to me. I feel afraid."

He takes my hand for the briefest of moments, squeezing my fingers. "Trust me."

By the time we are called, I have almost nodded off, leaning painfully against the cold marble wall at my back. There is no apology for our excruciating wait, and I sway when I get to my feet, needing a moment to allow the blood to flow back into my limbs.

I understand from Paulinus's curt nod that the man who

has come to fetch us must be a slave. We set off down another warren of corridors, punctuated by armed guards or people in clothes so luxurious I cannot tell if they are high-ranking servants or guests. I am soon disorientated. At the end of one particularly long corridor, we descend a flight of steps, the sound of flowing water, music and laughter growing louder, before we enter a spectacular room. Water cascades down the wall on our right, shimmering with brilliant blue gems set into the rock over which it flows. It is the centrepiece of a tiny marble theatre, whose design I recognise from one Paulinus took me to see in Gaul, and on the stage are women flute players, dressed in silver. But there is no seated audience. Instead, we are in a dining room, open to a garden at the far end and sheltered above by a pavilion whose purple columns are topped with gold. Tigellinus greets us at the foot of the stairs.

"Caesar is thrilled you could join him." He takes both Paulinus's hands as if they were old friends. "He is longing to speak with you after dinner."

We follow Tigellinus into one of several small rooms off the main dining area, which are filling up with guests. Even though I know very little about Roman hierarchy, I suspect the three empty couches at the centre of the open pavilion must be the positions of honour where the Emperor will dine. They are ranged around a glittering pool, lit with floating lamps sculpted as swans, and I stop, mesmerised by their movement, until Paulinus touches me lightly on the back. Tigellinus gestures at the couch with a view of the stage for Paulinus, before throwing himself onto the less favourable one opposite. As he does so, I see the glint of a sword beneath his cloak.

I have learned enough to know I am expected to recline behind Paulinus, not in front, and climb onto the couch as he does, so my awkward movements are hidden. A waterfall pours down the back wall in this room too, its spray sprinkling my skin, and we are surrounded by inlaid marble, gems and pearls, with a painted ceiling above. I stare up at it. I am starting to recognise the heroes of Roman history and believe this is Hercules. Later, I will ask Paulinus if I am right. I notice Tigellinus watching me with an amused air. He must have guessed what relationship the former Legate of Britannia has formed with his captive.

He nods at me. "Does she speak any Latin?"

"Not much," Paulinus lies.

"But enough for your purposes, I imagine." Tigellinus smirks. "You must be relieved to leave the barbarians behind in Britannia and return to Rome."

"I would also have been content to serve out my duties as legate," Paulinus replies. "But of course I am bound to serve Caesar, however he requires."

"You are fortunate to return at such a happy time, shortly after the wedding." Tigellinus gestures at the chests of my family's treasure being carried into the room by slaves. "Our Empress will be delighted to receive the gifts you have brought to celebrate her union with Caesar."

While he speaks, the murmuring and laughter which had filled the room begins to die down, before a total hush falls. The flute players have been replaced by a harpist, who strums a lilting tune, as a male singer strolls down the steps at the side of the stage. A floral tunic wafts around his legs from the breeze cast by the waterfall, a silk scarf is flung around his neck, and auburn curls are piled on his head. I feel Paulinus's entire body stiffen. The singer's voice is high and reedy, and I cannot understand why everyone is paying this mediocre performance such rapt attention. A pregnant woman, in a lavish golden robe, approaches the singer, clasping her face as if awestruck by the sound. The musician is serenading her.

I shift, bored and restless, until I feel Paulinus lean against me in warning. The singer's warbling finally ends, rounded off by a kiss to the woman in gold, who I have now realised is astonishingly pretty. Rapturous applause follows, as if every guest had already downed ten cups of wine. Then the singer and his partner make their way to the room's only remaining empty couch. With every step they take towards the position of honour, the truth creeps closer.

Could *this* be the Emperor Nero?

Tigellinus is still applauding. "Delightful, *delightful*." He beams at Paulinus. "The most touching song."

I do not need to see Paulinus's face to know that he is neither touched nor delighted. "Caesar has certainly found his voice," he says. "I had not expected to be treated to such a performance."

Servants in white tunics arrive bearing platters of sea urchins piled in glistening heaps, alongside silver fishes, green olives and stuffed eggs. I find it hard to eat lying at this angle, and take a small plate despite my hunger, not wanting to spill it on the couch. My eyes are continually drawn to Nero and his new bride. I think of my uncle Cunominus, or even Paulinus, men who are capable of commanding armies into battle, whose physical strength is apparent in their every movement. Men whose very presence demands respect. This Emperor is no weakling, but he looks absurd, bashfully tossing his hair, as if he were shy of all the praise being heaped upon his singing. The woman in gold beside him looks a much more formidable figure. Perhaps she is the one in charge.

"Poppaea Sabina looks radiant, does she not?" Tigellinus says, and from the warm look in his eyes, I suspect that he must have genuine fondness for the Empress.

"She has always been a most impressive-looking woman," Paulinus says.

"You knew her before?"

"I met her when she..." Paulinus hesitates and Tigellinus laughs.

"When she was married to Otho?" Tigellinus says, in a mock whisper. "You're so discreet. Which *of course* does you credit."

The meal continues with the two men talking about people I have never met, whose names are unfamiliar. Largely hidden from sight by Paulinus's broad shoulders, I watch a troop of dwarves who dance from room to room, leaping and tumbling for the guests' amusement. It is more uncomfortable to remain silent when Tigellinus finally asks about the state of my homeland, praising Paulinus for crushing the rebels to save Britannia for Rome. But even this is a grief now so familiar, I am almost numb to it.

Platters continue to circulate in a never-ending stream, sweet pastries replacing the meat, the light fading until it is fully night, everything glowing in the light of lamps which float in the dining room's many pools or hang from the ceiling. I begin to wonder when Paulinus will be granted his audience. Even Tigellinus looks a little embarrassed, glancing over at his master, who has not yet seemed to notice the presence of the returned legate. Eventually Tigellinus rises, excusing himself, and goes to speak to Nero, bending to whisper into his ear.

"Paulinus!" The Emperor shouts, lurching round to see where he is, then beckoning him over with a wildly over-affected look of joy. "My dear friend!"

The other guests' voices subside to a murmur as Paulinus crosses to the central couch. Nero leaps to his feet, kissing him loudly on the cheek, introducing him to Poppaea, who smiles prettily but without obvious enthusiasm. I cannot hear what the two men are saying. Tigellinus has returned and is sipping his wine, watching me from the couch opposite with his dark fox eyes. I say nothing, not wanting to expose Paulinus's lie that I speak little Latin.

Slaves arrive, picking up the chests of treasure to take them to Nero, and Paulinus turns, making eye contact with me. He nods and I understand he wishes me to step forward. Both Nero and Poppaea are staring at me, curious.

"Mind how you go, little warrior," Tigellinus whispers, but I ignore him as if I have not understood.

The chests are being stacked up in a pile, and a slave opens the one on top to reveal a wealth of gold necklaces and ornaments. I can see the headdress Vassura used to wear at the festival of Epona, and in that moment I miss my aunt so much it is a physical pain.

"I have brought you and your beloved Empress some of the Iceni's most sacred treasures as a small gift from Britannia," Paulinus says.

Poppaea is looking curiously at the gold, as the slaves holds up pieces one by one for her to see. "What funny looking things," she exclaims. "I should look quite the barbarian in that. It's very generous of you, of course. Perhaps we will have it melted down to make something prettier."

After so much loss, I had believed myself capable of enduring any humiliation, but the thought of the last precious relics of my family being destroyed makes me start forward in distress. Paulinus lays a restraining hand on my arm.

"And that's the Iceni girl," Nero says, pointing at me. "How curious."

"This is the daughter of the defeated warrior queen, Boudicca. She is called Solina and is here as a symbol of her peoples' obedience to Rome. I believe her to be deeply remorseful for her mother's treachery."

"Boudicca's daughter!" The Empress is finally interested enough to sit up, one hand resting protectively on her belly. "Is she tame? Does she speak?"

"She is perfectly tame," Paulinus says, a remark which in any other setting might have made me laugh.

"My darling, she looks *so* like that girl Cartimandua sent you as a gift. The same bright red hair! I haven't known what to do with the other one. But together, they will make a perfect pair." She rises from the couch, and heads for the open chest of gold, fishing out a torc to show Nero. "Look! I can make them match!"

The Emperor smiles, pleased to see his wife's obvious delight, and turns to Paulinus. "You have done well with your gifts," he says. I wait for Paulinus to explain that I am not a gift, that I belong to him, but he says nothing. "You must tell us what you would like as a token of thanks for keeping our Imperial province safe from the rebels. I would not have you imagine you will not be rewarded. We are most grateful to you."

"I would humbly ask to keep the girl, Boudicca's daughter," Paulinus says. "As a memento of my campaign."

Nero waves a hand, as if swatting away a fly. "Choose something else," he says, irritated. "You can see that's not possible."

There is a long silence, and I can feel the pulse of my heart pounding in my ears. "Then there is nothing," Paulinus says at last. "Your thanks are reward enough, Caesar. I live only to serve Rome."

Nero smiles, his good humour returning at the compliment. "Since you are too modest, we will think of something more fitting at a later date."

Throughout this exchange I have been trying to control my rising panic, holding on to Paulinus's command to trust him.

I tell myself that *now* must be the moment he will argue I am his, *now* is when he will explain that the gods themselves have tied our fates together, but he is not even looking at me. The chests are being moved, then one of the slaves begins tugging at my sleeve as if I am an animal which will not understand speech. I realise I am to be led away.

"Paulinus!" I shout, unable to keep the anguish from my voice. I am desperate for him to look at me. There is a further lull in the noise, people's interest caught by the prospect of a scene. Nero laughs, eyes sparkling with amusement.

"Well, Paulinus," he drawls. "It seems you made *many* conquests in Britannia."

The other guests laugh, much more loudly than the joke deserves. Paulinus is obliged to smile.

"I hope you don't begrudge me your little gift," Poppaea says to him, with a pout.

"He doesn't begrudge you anything!" Nero exclaims. "Do you?"

Paulinus is a taller, more physically powerful man than Nero – he would beat the Emperor in any fight, with any weapon. And yet it is clear where the true power lies between these two men. "Of course not," Paulinus says, sounding wholly unconcerned. "I'm delighted my gift found favour with the incomparable Venus Sabina."

The Emperor waves airily to dismiss me along with the chests, turning his back on his British plunder to talk to Paulinus, and the slave begins tugging at my arm again, more insistently this time, obviously fearful of a struggle. Paulinus is listening to Nero, his face one of studied attention, but I will not move until he acknowledges me. Finally, his eyes flick to mine. It is not a lover's goodbye but a cold glare of warning. Then he deliberately drops his gaze. The brutality is as shocking as if he just ran me through with a sword.

Yet Paulinus was always the same man as the legate. I just couldn't bear to see it.

The familiar lines of his face swim, blurred by my tears. I turn my back on him, allowing the slave to lead me away.

PART 3

SERVA

"But Octavia, young though she was, had learned to hide sorrow, affection, every feeling."
    Tacitus, on Nero's abuse of his first wife, *Annals*

"I have seen people put perfume on the soles of their feet, a trick that Otho taught the Emperor Nero. How, pray, could this be noticed, or how could there be any pleasure from that part of the body?"
    Pliny the Elder, on Nero's extravagances, *Natural History*

32

SOLINA

If I felt disorientated on my journey through the Imperial Palace before, it is nothing compared to the bewilderment I experience now, blinded by grief and rage, walking through this warren towards a wholly unknown future. I follow the slaves carrying the chests of my family's gold, the thought of attempting to run away no more than a fleeting madness. Where would I go? How would I even find my way out?

The shock of Paulinus's betrayal is so profound I struggle to believe it is real. At every corner I expect to see him. Every noise I hear I imagine is his footsteps, or his voice calling me, begging my forgiveness. I can still feel the warmth of his skin on mine, and my body remembers his. It was only last night that we lay together, and he held me afterwards, promising not only that he cared for me, but that he *loved* me. Why would he have made a vow to the Goddess of Fate, only to break it?

The slaves carrying the chests of my family's gold turn off down a corridor, and I am left alone with the boy who tugged my sleeve. Somewhere on our journey he must have picked up an oil lamp. He leads me silently through a plain door into a narrower passage, with small chambers set on either side. There are no torches or hanging lamps here, and we are obliged to make our way with nothing more than the light of his lamp. It flickers up the walls showing simple paintings of flowers, unlike the vast, gaudy scenes in the main palace. We must be in the servants' quarters. He ushers me into a tiny, darkened room on the right.

"Who's there?"

It is a woman's voice. The slave raises his lamp to illuminate a small bed. A girl is on it, lifting her hand to shade her eyes from the sudden light.

"It's another Briton," the slave says, and it is startling to hear him speak, to remember he is human like me. "The Empress means to make a pair of you."

"Are you from High Town?" The girl leaps from the bed in excitement, addressing me in our own language. Her dialect is unfamiliar, and the accent strange, but I can still understand. She clasps both my hands as if we were sisters.

"I am Iceni. From the Town of the Wolf."

"Oh." She looks slightly disappointed. "I thought you might be Briganti. I am Ressona."

"I am Solina."

"You are a Druid." She understands the meaning of my name, her smile brightening again. Then her face suddenly lurches into darkness, and we both realise the boy is about to leave, taking the light with him. "For fuck's sake!" Ressona yells in Latin. "You might let us find our way to the bed at least. It's pitch-black in here."

"Since you ask so *nicely*." The boy holds up the lamp again. He is grinning and does not seem at all offended.

Ressona leads me over to the bed, which is little more than a pallet. "There's not much room, but you can lie near the wall, so you don't fall off."

The boy watches us scramble under the covers. "Right, I'm going to bed myself now," he says. "Goodnight!" The room vanishes from view the moment he's left the doorway. I manage to jab Ressona somewhere soft and exclaim in apology.

"Oh, don't worry," she says. "The bed's shit." There is a pause as we lie squashed together, two strangers in total darkness. "I know you are sad to be here," she says. "It does get easier."

My eyes well with tears. I cannot imagine how to tell this girl my story, or how to ask for hers. Whatever else, I don't want to admit that I am not only crying for my family, but for the Roman soldier who captured me. My stupidity at ever having cared for Paulinus makes me want to claw off my own skin with shame. "It's so far away from home," I say, my voice choked.

"I know," she replies, putting an arm around me. In the darkness, she could almost be Bellenia. The memory of my sister makes me cry even harder. "It's shit." She gives me a squeeze. "But it's not the worst place, once you get used to it. Not like we're going to starve, is it? And the men should leave you alone. Poppaea Sabina is an absolute bitch, but she also doesn't like anyone using her maids. She's quite fierce about the idea, which puts off most chancers."

I had not considered the likelihood of rape, and the thought chills me. "How long have you been here?"

"Queen Cartimandua of the Brigantes sent me as a gift to Octavia, the true Empress. I'm not sure how long ago that was now. Nero divorced Octavia a while back, and she had to give up most of her servants for his new wife. I loved Octavia, but Nero was so violent to her, and then his mistress Poppaea nagged and *nagged* him to divorce her. When Poppaea got pregnant, he finally did. Perhaps Octavia will be safer in exile.

I hope so." She pauses and I wonder if it is deliberate evasion that Ressona has told me so little of her own life, and so much of her mistress instead. "So that's my story. How about you?"

I stare into the darkness, wondering how to set down the weight of my life. "I was the daughter of King Prasutagus and fought with my mother in the Iceni rebellion against Rome. The Legate of Britannia captured me after our defeat. This evening, he gave me to the Empress."

"You fought in the rebellion?" There is awe in Ressona's voice. "I did wonder, when you said you were Iceni." We both lie in silence while she ponders my story. "Cartimandua spoke of your father Prasutagus once or twice. She said he was wise, but that his wife was some sort of wild warmonger."

Her blunt speech should offend me, but instead it makes me snort. "I suppose that's fair enough."

"Well, I'm sorry for you but happy for me that you're here," she says. "I've not spoken to another Briton in... I'm not even sure. And it must be a relief to get away from the soldier who captured you." Ressona shudders at the thought.

"Yes," I lie. "It is."

"Goodnight, then," Ressona says. "Best to get some sleep now."

"Goodnight. Thank you for making me welcome."

"Of course," Ressona yawns. "We'll have to stick together."

She lapses into silence and soon I can hear her breathing deepen. I close my eyes, willing myself not to think of Paulinus, still less to cry for him. Instead, I think of my mother, the *wild warmonger*, the woman who destroyed the Ninth legion, who burned down three cities and almost took back Britain from Rome. Paulinus made me forget what it meant to be Boudicca's daughter. Now I will have to remember.

*

In the daylight, it becomes clear that Ressona and I look nothing alike. We both have red hair and are a similar height, but there the similarity ends. My face is angular, my dark eyes fringed with pale lashes and my mouth too large, all features I inherited from my mother. Ressona was chosen by Cartimandua as a gift for Rome purely for her beauty. She is even prettier than Bellenia, with a soft, round face, eyes like a doe, and a tiny rosebud mouth. And then there are the tattoos. Ressona is not a warrior, so her arms are completely unmarked.

None of this seems to deter the Empress, Poppaea Sabina. We are brought to her private chambers, and she spends the morning decorating Ressona and me as if we were a pair of dolls, rifling through the chests Paulinus gave her to find us matching "barbarian jewels", and dressing us in my old clothes from home until she can have "suitably savage" outfits designed by a witless dressmaker who hovers at her elbow. I soon realise there is a strict hierarchy among the Empress's maids – some she almost seems to treat as friends, laughing and gossiping with them, while others, like Ressona and me, are barely human. This distinction is difficult to understand; it is hard enough to see myself as a slave at all. Ressona has warned me several times to remain silent, but when Poppaea muses aloud on the possible uses of my aunt's headdress, I ignore Ressona's advice and leap to tell her what the symbols represent. I make myself as charming as possible, hoping I may be able to find a way to manipulate my new captor. If I become a favourite, perhaps she will free me.

Poppaea sets down Vasurra's jewellery. I think she will ask me further questions, perhaps curious about what I have said, but instead she slaps me lightly across the face.

"You will not speak uninvited," she says.

We stare at one another. She is the most beautiful woman

I have ever seen, but this is not what holds my attention. I am assessing her strength. Poppaea is slender, her arms soft, unmarred by muscle. I have little doubt that if I took hold of this woman's head, I could take break her neck in a single twist, the way Riomanda trained me to do, should every weapon but my hands fail me. Perhaps the Empress reads something of my thoughts in my eyes.

"You are not a princess here," she says. "You are a slave. Your people are slaves. You will not forget this."

I lower my gaze in a false show of humility, but in that moment, I determine to destroy her. I will not make the same mistake I made with Paulinus. The Empress represents the power of Rome and for this alone she deserves to die – a lesson my mother tried so hard to teach me.

One of Poppaea's maids ushers me aside to cut my hair to the same length as Ressona's, and the Empress watches, taking the arm of a woman who seems to be a visiting friend rather than a servant.

"I might try something similar with the Armenian girls," Poppaea says. "I've been wondering what to do with them – Corbulo sent Caesar so many. But we could choose the prettiest two and have another matching pair. Oh! Perhaps we might represent all of Rome's provinces! How that would please Nero! Two blondes from Germania, two girls from Egypt and so on. We could show him the reach of his entire Empire through my women."

"Wonderful!" the other woman trills. "Perhaps you could have them put on a special performance?"

"Yes, yes, let us plan it!" Poppaea sweeps off, trailed by her women. I think of my mother's hall at The Town of the Wolf, the Iceni warriors who trained long years to defend their people, and I cannot believe the world is ruled by such children as this.

"Come *along*," Ressona hisses in our own language, obliging me to join the vast gaggle pursuing Poppaea.

"Where are we going?" I whisper back, hurrying to keep up.

"Who knows. Probably the gardens."

We pass through a dizzying array of rooms, somewhere along the way picking up the troop of dwarves I saw last night, before spilling down a gilded staircase into the gardens. A huge pond, set with fountains, glitters in the sunlight. Peacocks strut around the water, birds I had only ever seen before in paintings Paulinus showed me, and the air is heavy with the scent of roses. Poppaea goes to sit in the shade with her friends and I realise the rest of us are expected to mill around like the peacocks.

"See." Ressona takes my arm. "I told you it could be worse. Not the toughest work, is it?"

We stand together in a patch of shade. "What will she want us to do?" I ask.

Ressona shrugs. "Nothing, probably. We're just here to wait on any whim she has."

I look across the gardens. The dwarves are tumbling by the pond, looking sweaty in the sun, and other servants and slaves are grouped around chatting, all of us keeping an eye on the Empress, ready to enact any demand she might make. "Was it like this serving Cartimandua?"

"No!" Ressona laughs. "Cartimandua never had half these many maids. Can you imagine this lot in a roundhouse? I was one of the queen's favourites – she used to have me dress her. I waited on her after the death of her daughter, little Brigantia, when she hardly saw anyone else at all."

Poppaea seems in no mood to move from the garden, and after a while, refreshments are brought to her, though not for her slaves. Neither are we allowed to sit. In this strange dream-like world I have stumbled into, Ressona feels like an anchor. We share memories of home, bringing the wild woods and grey skies of Britain to life in this ornamental Roman garden. Whenever I think of Paulinus I feel a surge of anxiety. My world has revolved around him for so long it is hard to believe he has gone, along with the rest of my past. My future feels wholly uncertain. I suspect this palace may prove as hard to escape as my father's tower; it will take me time to plot a way out.

The Empress is still enjoying her pastries when a messenger hurries over. Whatever the man says makes Poppaea start to her feet, then she is crossing the gardens back to the palace. "Stay!" She calls out, her voice as commanding as my mother's.

When she has gone, everyone else's voices rise like scales on a harp, and I realise how tame we must all have been in her presence. "I wonder what *that* was about?" Ressona says.

With no mistress in sight, we head to a bench to take the weight off our feet. The dwarves sprawl on the grass like basking lizards, seizing the chance to rest after all their tumbling, and some of the younger slaves, who are no more than children, run between the rose bushes, chasing one another and shrieking. I am listening to Ressona's account of her family, the sisters she left behind in High Town, when a man's voice rings out.

"*Where is the British girl?*"

Ressona and I freeze, gawping at each other, then she jumps to her feet. "We're here!" she cries.

"Get moving, then!" The bellow comes from a servant standing at the entrance of the palace, gesturing at us to join him.

"Which of us do you want?" I ask, trying to stay calm, squashing down the hope that this is a summons from Paulinus.

The man looks between us. "She didn't tell me. Better you both come."

"What is it?"

"I'm not to say."

"But why?"

The man ignores me and Ressona takes my hand. I am not reassured by the look of fear on her face. We scale the stairs and plunge into the rabbit warren, eventually reaching a green octagonal room, covered in golden stucco. A soldier stands in the centre, his back to us.

"There are *two* British girls," our guide says to him. "Which one was it she wanted?"

The soldier turns and I see he is holding a platter. It takes me a moment to recognise what rests on it. A human head. Ressona screams and falls to her knees, weeping hysterically. I stare at the head, unmoved. I wonder if Cartimandua of the Brigantes did not stake her dead enemies to the gates of High Town for Ressona to react this way.

I walk over to the soldier and peer at the remains. It is a young girl, her face already sunken with decay. I look up at the man, angry at this cheap attempt to frighten us. "What trick is this?"

"It is the head of Octavia, the adulteress killed for her treachery to Nero," the soldier says. "The Empress particularly asked for the British girl to bring it to her."

At this Ressona cries out in agony, and her hysteria finally makes sense to me. She loved the girl whose head now rots in a soldier's hands. That is why Poppaea sent for her: to punish Ressona for her past loyalty to a hated rival.

"Yes, I see that it is Octavia," I lie. "It will be *me* that the Empress intended for this task."

"You are certain?" He looks doubtfully at the sobbing heap on the floor.

I snatch the platter from him, and the fool gasps. I rest my hand gently on Octavia's hair, holding her steady, sorry to see a woman Ressona loved treated with such disrespect. "The Empress will not care for this delay. Take me to her at once."

The man looks completely unnerved, staring at me as if I were a monster. I stare back, willing some part of him to understand the words I dare not say. *If I held a sword, it would be your head on this plate.*

"Very well," he says, the apple on his neck bobbing as he swallows. "The Empress and Emperor are waiting for you."

The soldier turns and knocks on the gilded doors; they are opened by yet more armed guards. I do not look back at Ressona but follow the men into a huge room. Gilt and gemstones are encrusted on the walls, as if I am walking into a treasure chest. Poppaea, Nero and Tigellinus are reclining together, drinking wine and laughing, as excited as small children expecting a gift.

I hold out Octavia's head and walk slowly towards them. At the sight of his former wife, Nero grips the couch he is sitting on and leans forward, both eager and fearful. Poppaea is smiling, an expression of triumph on her face, as if she were the one brave enough to have wielded the sword. Only Tigellinus is not looking at Octavia; he is watching me, one hand clasped around his glass of wine.

"Bring it closer," Poppaea demands. In the excitement of seeing her rival, she has entirely forgotten which British maid brought the trophy, as I suspected she might. "Can you believe *that* led people to riot in Rome and pull down my statue?" she asks Tigellinus, who laughs, then she rests a hand affectionately on Nero's knee. "The nasty little bitch can't harm you now, my darling."

Nero pokes Octavia's cheek with his finger. "She always did look sour. Look at that horrible, scowling face!" He picks the girl's head up by the hair. "*Oh no, Nero! Stop, Nero! Don't hurt me!*" he shrieks, imitating a woman's terrified voice. Then he chucks the head back on the platter, splattering blood on my clothes, and he and Poppaea fall about laughing. Tigellinus is still staring at me, his gaze so brazen I stare back. It is dangerous as a slave to acknowledge I am a thinking, feeling being, but I cannot help myself. I know the contempt that burns in my heart must show in my eyes.

"You seem calm," he says to me. "I suppose death is no stranger to you."

Nero squints up at me, and recognition crosses his face. "The Boudicca girl. A shame Paulinus did not bring her mother's head back for me. But I think he was too busy fucking the daughter." He turns to Poppaea. "You quite ruined the man's night, my darling. Taking his lover away."

"Oh, is it that one?" Poppaea finally notices I am the wrong maid. "I wanted the other. The one that served the little bitch." She sticks her tongue out at Octavia, making Nero laugh.

"What are you thinking?" Tigellinus asks me again, but I say nothing, only stare back at him.

"It doesn't speak Latin." Nero is irritated by him showing so much attention to a slave.

"Oh, but I think she does." Tigellinus smiles. "What have you learned today, Solina?"

All three of them are staring at me now, Poppaea and Nero with some annoyance, as if it were me, not Tigellinus, who is distracting them from their entertainment. "Thus perish all enemies of Rome," I say, my voice ringing out loud and harsh like my mother's.

Nero rolls his eyes. "Happy now?" he says to Tigellinus, gesturing at me to give Poppaea the platter. "Leave us." He waves a hand.

I bow deeply and turn, walking towards the guards at the

door. Behind me, I can hear the most powerful people in the world laughing over a young woman's broken remains.

33

PAULINUS

He wakes suddenly in the night, blinking into the darkness, confused for a moment about where he is. A sliver of moonlight stretches out over the mosaic on the floor, picking out a lion's dark eye. It is his own room. He is home.

Paulinus tries to settle back into the warmth, to go to sleep, but he is painfully alert. His wife used to lie beside him in this bed, her body soft and warm, her dark hair spread out on the pillow. How little he had understood of love then, how easily he had taken Fulvia's devotion for granted. Yesterday he visited her grave on the Appian Way, trying to find the right words, pouring a cup of her favourite wine into the tomb, laying his hand on the cold stone so that she knows she is not forgotten. Instinctively he runs his fingers over her *lunula*, looped around his wrist. He misses Fulvia, he will always miss her, but he has grown used to his grief, the weight of it familiar, like a heavy cloak. The woman who has caused him to wake, full of anxiety, is alive.

Even if he closes his eyes, Paulinus cannot shut out the sight of Solina's face. Her look of pain and disbelief. He sits up in bed, swinging his legs out from under the covers, padding over the cool tiles to the shutters, pulling them open, breathing in the autumn air. Rome is not silent at night. This window looks out onto his garden, but he can hear the distant rumble of carts, the call of voices, and see the terracotta rooftops rising and falling like waves of the sea. The Imperial Palace on the Palatine is not visible from here.

He cannot regret what he did. There was no other choice. If he had made a fuss about handing Solina over, Nero would have thought little of killing a war captive simply to spite him. But he bitterly regrets not explaining to Solina that he might not be able to keep her. At the time he had told himself he was doing it to protect her from needless worry. After all, if Poppaea had not taken a sudden fancy to the girl, Solina would be safe with him now. Paulinus turns from the window, still restless. His guilt lies in knowing there were less forgivable reasons he hid the truth. He had wanted to enjoy Solina's affection on the journey, and if their time together was only going to be brief, all the less reason to ruin it. He now sees how utterly selfish this was. Solina must hate him.

He sits on the edge of the bed, heels pressed down onto the tiles. Not only can he not protect Solina as he promised, he has no idea what is happening to her. It is tormenting to imagine his blunt-speaking woman in such a pit of snakes. The Caesar now in Rome is different from the boy Paulinus left four years ago, when he took up his post in Britannia. Since then, Nero murdered his own mother and has now killed his first wife. Paulinus can remember meeting Octavia. She had been a gentle girl, undeserving of the violent and prolonged death she endured. He only hopes Solina has the sense to stay out of the Emperor's way. With a sigh he stands up, weary at the churn of his thoughts. Perhaps that faint glow in the distance is the coming dawn. No point now in trying to go back to sleep.

*

Paulinus watches Pliny pore over one of the wax tablets which sit in a tottering pile before him. His friend is squinting with concentration, tunic askew where he has absent-mindedly yanked it over one shoulder, while a slave hovers behind, ready to do his exacting master's bidding. Daylight streams into Pliny's large library, catching the dance of dust motes in the air, and the place has the soothing smell of wax and parchment, something Paulinus has missed on campaign.

"We have ample proof of bribery and theft," Pliny says. "The man was rapacious, which will help our prosecution, and the desertion of his post is damning. But I would have liked a little more debauchery. Juries love that sort of thing. It's much more enjoyable for them to hear a scandal than to sit through a long lecture on how the Procurator of Britannia fiddled the books or charged too much interest."

"Surely financial corruption is quite enough," Paulinus replies, irritated. "I don't care who the man fucked. It's not the point."

"Not the point for *you*," Pliny says. "But other peoples' sense of justice is less easily outraged. Most of the jury will have taken a few bribes themselves. You need to bear these things in mind. It's not only about justice. I doubt Cicero would have finished Verres so spectacularly if it weren't for the orgies."

Paulinus huffs, sitting back in his chair. Pliny's library is meticulously laid out, the walls covered in shelves full of tablets, scrolls and maps, which his long-suffering slaves tend with all the care they might give a firstborn child. Anything Pliny himself touches, however, swiftly becomes a mess, spread out over the desk in abandon, left for others to tidy, as his mind leaps nimbly from one topic to another. Right now, his desk is covered with evidence of the crimes of the former Procurator of Britannia, Catus Decianus, along with a heap of Iceni curiosities Paulinus brought him as a gift.

"Well, I didn't think of orgies," Paulinus says. "I've no idea who or what the man took to bed."

"If he seduced a few Roman matrons, that would be ideal."

"He ordered an appalling attack on three British women in the east, which sparked a rebellion and nearly cost us a province. *That's* your scandal."

"No," Pliny says firmly. "I've explained this. The assault is too politically sensitive. I will touch on it, yes, but I cannot hang a case on a crime against rebels." Pliny picks up another tablet. "Besides, I would have thought you, of all people, would hardly ask a jury to have sympathy for Boudicca."

"A crime is a crime and should be treated as such. It's not about sympathy."

"You have been in the army too long." Pliny squints at his tablet, marking up one of the notes, then gestures impatiently at his slave to set it aside. "If you want to practice law again in Rome, you need to persuade your audience, not simply bludgeon them with facts."

"That would be true, if I were intending to make my name as an orator," Paulinus says. "But the bulk of my legal work has always been advisory. I can leave the speeches to you."

Pliny snorts. "Well, I'm sure you will be in demand. Though do you truly want to leave the military after building such a distinguished career? The recall was not a dishonourable one."

Paulinus glances at Pliny's two slaves. One is a scribe he does not know, the other is Secundus, his friend's longstanding steward. Both are likely loyal, but any slave can break under torture if their master is accused of treason. Unless Paulinus is alone with Pliny he cannot speak the truth: that he was willing to serve as a general when Claudius was Caesar, but not Nero. "I think now is not an opportune moment," he says. Pliny looks up, his gaze sharp, and the two men stare at one another, communicating without words.

"I understand." Pliny closes the wax tablet. "And I think that might be as much of the procurator's bribes as I can stomach for today. Let's take another look at this." Pliny waves at his scribe to lift the heavy fragment of Iceni door which Paulinus brought him onto his desk. "Much more interesting." Pliny runs his fingers over the carving, like a lover's caress. "Explain this to me again."

"It shows the creation of the world," Paulinus says, remembering what Solina told him. "This is the mother goddess, split into three. I suppose she is like Gaia. And this"—he points to the horned god, riding a stag—"is Cernunnos, the horned one, who can grant rebirth through his cauldron, which is carved over there. I was told many legends about this object – sometimes it is their goddess Epona who controls the cauldron, sometimes Cernunnos. The stories are ancient, but the door was made relatively recently, on the instruction of Prasutagus, the Iceni's last king."

"His symbol was the horse." Pliny traces the outline of one, galloping along the wood.

"Yes." Paulinus experiences an unwelcome jolt as he remembers the marks on Solina's skin. It is impossible to believe he will never hold her again. He pauses, torn between the desire to speak of her and the knowledge this might not be wise. "I think I mentioned the king's daughter to you before, the one I gave to Nero."

"She was the Briton who explained these doors to you?" Pliny is not looking at him; he is sketching an outline of Cernunnos into a wax notepad.

"She was. I'm profoundly sorry I had to give her away."

"Well, yes, clearly her knowledge would have been very useful to us now. But it can't be helped." Pliny waves at his scribe to lift the door to the light so he can see it better.

Paulinus feels frustration at his companion's inability to take a hint. Pliny is his dearest friend, whose intelligence he admires, but Pliny has never been married and seems entirely unmoved by women. Or men either. Outside of proving a point in court, sexual passion has never had any bearing on Pliny's own life. "The king's daughter is called Solina," Paulinus says. "I took her to the Temple of Nortia to ask the goddess to bind our fates together."

"Why ever would you do that?" Pliny's incredulity at his friend's odd remark briefly distracts him from his sketch. "She cannot have been *that* knowledgeable, surely."

"I was fond of her. I hoped to keep her with me in Rome."

"Don't be ridiculous." Pliny sounds irritated. "She is a Briton. A savage. Hardly even a woman at all."

Paulinus is used to this view of the Britons, perhaps at times he has even felt the same, but coming from Pliny about Solina, it annoys him. "She is very much a woman and, despite being a Briton, has many qualities I value."

Pliny finally puts down his wax booklet. "I do hope that infatuation for this girl is not the reason you want me to prosecute Decianus. I would find that *most* disappointing."

"Solina has no idea about the prosecution," Paulinus says, rattled by his friend's shrewdness. "Of course, I believe she suffered greatly from the atrocity he ordered. But that is irrelevant to my interest in the case, which I would have launched regardless."

Pliny looks unconvinced. "That had better be true," he says. "I don't want the defence to be claiming debauchery as *your* motive for bringing the action. A fine tale they could spin about the Legate of Britannia being ruled by Boudicca's daughter. Although now the girl is firmly in the hands of Nero, we should be safe on that score."

Paulinus says nothing, and watches as Pliny is again absorbed in sketching the Iceni gods, humming to himself as he studies the cauldron. It is as well his old friend's attention is elsewhere, or Pliny might have guessed what Paulinus is plotting from the expression on his face. Solina is in the hands of Nero *for now*. But that doesn't mean Paulinus intends to leave her there.

34

SOLINA

If I had not understood the dangers of the Imperial Court before, the murder of Octavia is a swift lesson. For all his singing, parties and gold, this Caesar is a killer. In my father's house warriors would openly carry their weapons, speaking their minds without fear, settling scores with the sword. For the Iceni, Death is a king who announces himself, not a thief who lurks in the shadows. In Rome, all the knives are hidden, and Death is spun on a web of smiles, cocooning the victim before the lethal sting.

I learn to wear a mask, to hide every emotion. Here, I am a slave, often as still as one of the statues decorating the gardens, and always as silent. It is easy enough to escape Nero's notice, yet nothing I do deters Tigellinus, who is forever trying to trick me into speech. The man is a venomous spider, and as head of the Praetorian Guard, never far from Nero or Poppaea. Ressona warns me he is also a notorious whore, and although I do not believe this is what Tigellinus wants from me, I have no desire to be proved wrong. I strive to avoid him.

Without Ressona, my life would be one of profound emptiness. Our natures are very different, but in this alien country, loneliness and loyalty bind us together. We rise in the semi-dark, taking our bread with the other servants on our corridor, then after dressing one another in some Roman fantasy version of British clothes, we spend our days wafting after Poppaea. The Empress names us both maids of the yellow linen, which means on the days she wants to wear yellow, one of the night slaves will fetch us to dress her.

Even when we are not serving Poppaea, none of her maids can escape her shadow. Ressona is in love with another slave, a Greek boy called Alexios, but the pair of them never fulfil their desires, for fear of punishment, as pregnancy is forbidden. It seems Ressona has resigned herself to a life which others will waste. I cannot. It is impossible to forget what it felt like to race my sister through the woods, to study the heavens with my father, to spar with my mother, or even to argue with Paulinus. My past feels solid and real, while my present is as insubstantial as a shadow on a wall.

Poppaea Sabina persists in her idea of making women from all the Imperial provinces perform for Nero. She decides to stage this on the Feast of Jove, when the Romans invite their gods to dinner. We spend the day of the feast rehearsing on the dining-room stage, directed by one of Poppaea's stewards. Half the guests are already here, although they cannot see. Brightly painted statues of the gods lie rigid on golden couches, ready to be served by priests who will eat on their divine counterparts' behalf at the feast later. My eye is most drawn to Minerva, a warrior goddess whose bare wooden arms are as muscular as my mother's. Jove, the Roman's divine king, is an ugly figure with glaring onyx eyes and a beard of solid gold. He reclines close to where Nero will lie.

While we wait our turn on the stage, Ressona and I spar with lightweight wooden swords. My friend is no warrior, and even trying to teach her the simplest block is impossible – she only winces or drops her weapon in fright. Physical aggression is a language she cannot learn. I think of my sister, how swiftly she moved, the fire in her blade, and it hurts my heart. None of the other serving girls are expected to fight in the performance, most will sing or dance, apart from the two blonde Germans, who have been asked to wrestle while wearing almost nothing. It is a man's fantasy of women at war, with shrieking and hair-pulling, and I pity the pair of them.

From the corner of my eye, and partly screened by dancing Armenian girls, I watch Poppaea recline on the same couch where she once took me from Paulinus. She lies there, swathed in furs and gold, receiving an endless procession of priests and astrologers to foretell her unborn child's future. I have never hated a woman more. Even though I feel anger at Paulinus for his betrayal, I do not believe he intended to abandon me. Without Poppaea's interference, I would have had some hope of rebuilding the shattered remains of my life.

An astrologer, whose robes shimmer with images of the constellations, is taking his leave of the Empress when I hear her next visitor announced as the *Druid of the Deified Claudius*. I turn, curious as to who this might be. The man descending the steps is tall, with greying red hair, dressed in white British robes. The shock of recognition is so great I forget what I am doing, and Ressona scores her first hit, whacking my arm. I ignore my friend's yelp of triumph, riveted by the figure now sweeping across the room. It is the man in the golden cloak, the glorious warrior I once saw visit my parents' hearth, asking them to join his rebellion against Rome, all those years ago. *Caratacus*.

Without thinking of the consequences, only knowing I must

speak with him, I run to block his path. He stops, startled. When he sees my face, he gasps.

"Catia?"

"Her daughter," I answer in our own language.

For a moment, he simply stands there, speechless, then he recovers himself, and his look of wonder is replaced by one of calculation. "Incomparable Empress," he cries out in Latin. "It is a blessed day. I have before me the daughter of the great Druid Prasutagus. I will harness the power of her line, strengthening my vision for your child." He turns his devious blue eyes upon me. "*Trust me*," he says, speaking our own tongue.

The last man to say those words was Paulinus, and that hardly ended well, but I am too curious to know what Caratacus will do to refuse him. I follow the sweep of his cloak, walking alongside the two attendants he has brought, feeling reassured that at least he lied to Poppaea. There is no means for one Druid to harness the power of another.

We stop at the feet of the Empress. The Druid ignores me, focusing the full beam of his attention on Poppaea, who preens under his gaze. I last saw Caratacus through a child's eyes, but as a woman I realise he is exceptionally handsome. I wonder how my father felt, seeing his much younger wife captivated by an attractive man her own age who promised the military glory her own husband denied her. "I will pray with the girl," Caratacus is saying. "Together we will harness the power to lift the veil to the Otherworld, to see what is promised."

He is speaking nonsense. There is no such ritual. I watch as he takes out an incense burner, beckoning for one of his attendants to light it. The burner is British, but it is not sacred, rather the sort of object that might be filled with sweet-smelling herbs to reduce the smelly fug of a roundhouse in winter. Caratacus is enough of a Druid not to mock the gods, only his Roman masters. I like him more for this.

The attendant sets up a bronze tripod, placing the burner upon it. Caratacus kneels before it, gesturing for me to do likewise. I take up my position opposite him and copy his gestures, turning my palms upwards, easily falling into the rhythm of his deception. Smoke rises between us.

"Do you trust the other Briton here?" he murmurs in our language.

"Completely," I reply.

To my surprise, Caratacus's next words are sung as an incantation. "I trust your father taught you how to chant. That is what we will do now, so this sounds like prayer."

"It will be as you say," I sing back.

"I wept to hear of your mother's defeat, and I grieve now for your enslavement. Catia was one of the greatest warriors I ever met. If you have any favour to ask of me, I will grant it, if I can. Your mother sent me aid in my darkest hour."

I am so surprised I almost answer in speech rather than song, and Caratacus widens his eyes in warning. "What did my mother do for you?"

"She sent me chests of gold in secret from the Wolf Tribe. To atone for the warriors your father refused. It bought me many weapons and secured the loyalty of many men."

I am hungry to know more of his story and my mother's part in it. "How did you come to live as a free man in Rome after your defeat?"

"That is a tale for another time. Ask me your favour now, though you must understand I do not have the power to free you."

"Let me think a moment."

Caratacus closes his eyes and bows his head. I do the same,

my mind racing, trying to think of what I might ask. There is only one person in Rome I can seek out for help. Paulinus. The thought of begging him for anything is absolutely galling, and besides, I am not sure Paulinus would listen to pleading. Instead, I must send a message that might move him to fight for me.

"I have my favour." I chant.

"I am listening."

"You will give a message to the man who defeated my mother, the man who brought me here," I sing, knowing I cannot give Paulinus's name which will be recognisable even in another language. "Do you know who this man is?"

"I know."

"Do not let him know you have seen me. Tell him you have had a vision from the goddess Nortia, spoken in anger, and it is this. *The Goddess of Fate asks, where is the wife she gave him, and why has he rejected the child she promised him?*"

Caratacus's eyes are intent on my face as I speak. He repeats the message back to me, to show he has understood, then he bends his head. I do the same.

"It will be as you ask," he chants. Then he begins to sing in earnest, his voice shifting to one of true prayer. "*Great Taranis, God of the Sky, forgive this mockery, made to deceive your enemies. Understand we serve you, now and always.*" He presses his thumb to his forehead, a gesture of devotion I saw my father make many times, and I do likewise. Then he picks up a sieve one of the attendants placed beside him, holding it over the smoke, pretending to study the pattern it makes. "The veil to the Otherworld has parted," he says in Latin. "I see a daughter, glorious as her mother, followed by many sons. They will be gods among men, and the whole world will be their kingdom."

Caratacus is the first soothsayer today to promise a girl.

It interests me that he would make this choice – perhaps he means to impress Poppaea with his boldness. The Empress is gazing at him, lips slightly parted, her hand resting protectively on her belly. "Nobody else has seen a daughter."

"The glory surrounding her was so great, I may have been blinded," Caratacus says smoothly. "But son or daughter, I saw nothing less than a god."

Poppaea nods, pleased. "You will be rewarded." She looks at me with less fondness. "The girl was useful to you?"

Caratacus hesitates. If he praises me too highly Poppaea will be less likely to let me go, and he must have guessed from my message that this is what I want. "She was most useful," he says. "How wise you were to place her in my path."

"I have always found her arrogant," Poppaea replies, as if I were not there. "The girl still thinks herself a princess. You can see it in the way she moves. She does not understand it is her destiny to be a slave."

"Then would you grant me permission to dismiss her?" Caratacus says. "Before I discuss the vision with you further."

Poppaea nods, no doubt glad to be the sole focus of a man's attention. Caratacus turns to me, switching to our own language. "*I have prayed for your mother every day of my life. May the gods guide you, daughter of Catia.*" He gives a dismissive wave, at odds with the warmth of his words, and I know better than to reply.

I walk back to Ressona, who is staring at me, slack-jawed. She is the only other person in the room who will have understood what was said. "You have a lot of explaining to do," she whispers.

"Later," I reply, picking up the sword, gesturing for her to do likewise. I can tell she is frustrated, but she pulls a face and obeys me.

We spar again, and I force myself not to watch Caratacus

leave. I hear him bid farewell to Poppaea, catch the flash of his cloak from the corner of my eye, then he is gone. His words sound in my head. *I have prayed for your mother every day of my life.* Grief makes me hit Ressona's sword harder than I intend, sending her blade spinning across the floor. She shoots me a dirty look and trudges to pick it up.

I will never know if my mother regretted her marriage to my father, or if she wished her life had taken a different path. All I know is that I have sent Caratacus to Paulinus, my own fateful choice. I can only pray this was the right favour to ask.

35

SOLINA

The lake is lit by a thousand floating lamps, bright as the stars reflected on its dark surface. Men and women seem to float upon the water too, perching on stepping stones and bridges which link one part of the villa to another, while the air is soft with music and laughter. This place is called Sublaquem, and it does truly appear to be a world that rises from the water, with rivers flowing into rooms in gem-lined canals, or cascading down walls into pools that ripple with colourful mosaics. For one night, I am determined to lose myself in the enchantment. It is the eve of the Saturnalia, the Roman festival which replaces our Feast of Darkness, and although it lacks the sacred rites of the winter solstice, like every slave, this celebration is precious to me. For a few days, we are allowed to speak, or sit, or laugh, or dance, almost as if we were free.

I know Ressona is unable to enjoy the festival fully, even though she has looked forward to it for months. She finally abandoned caution to lie with her beloved Alexios, and imagined they would share this time together. But Nero is holding a more sedate celebration than usual, as Poppaea is close to her time of giving birth, so the court is here at his lakeside resort, east of Rome. Alexios has been left behind in the capital. In the darkness of our room, Ressona cried bitterly for her lover, just as I have suffered the torment of wondering if Caratacus ever delivered my message. It is many weeks now since I spoke to the Druid, and although I have not given up all hope of Paulinus acting, the wait is hard. To be a slave is to watch your own life slip through your fingers like sand, unable to stem the flow.

Ressona and I sit together now at the edge of the lake, where it is damp despite the blankets spread on the grass. Poppaea has retired, leaving us in peace, and Nero is discussing poetry and philosophy some distance away under the shelter of a pavilion, surrounded by a group of admiring men. Among them is Lucan, a poet whose wife Polla is sitting with us. Ever since she learned I am the daughter of Boudicca, Polla has not left me alone. I enjoy her curiosity; it reminds me I am not wholly erased, even if my past is now no more than a party trick to entertain Rome's elite.

"Did you not see the rebellion as a form of civil war?" Polla asks me. "Your mother must have killed many Britons too."

"Only those who had collaborated with the invader," I say, pushing away the memory of Lais, the woman at the baths, the children in the temple. I do not want Polla to judge my mother. She has not earned the right.

"Yet it achieved nothing except further bloodshed." Polla picks up one of the lamps as it drifts past her. The lamp is shaped like a ship, and she holds it up to examine the design, before setting it back down on the water to glide away. "So many lives lost, and for what? I do not see *any* glory in war. It corrupts men and ruins women, bringing guilt to the victor and misery to the vanquished."

"This is why Cartimandua of the Brigantes is a loyal queen to Rome," Ressona interrupts, keen to distance herself from any talk of rebellion. "She acts to protect her people."

And to line her own pockets, I think, but do not say. I have grown to love Ressona and feel no desire to insult her queen. "My father took the path of Cartimandua for many years," I say. "But my mother was granted fewer choices."

"I cannot believe you come from a land of queens," Polla says, and even though we are slaves, I can hear the envy in her voice. "Women who rule kingdoms and command men. It is unimaginable to me. As impossible as riding Pegasus or meeting a dragon."

Polla is gazing at us both, as if we too were mythical creatures. She is a strange woman. Sometimes her curiosity reminds me of Paulinus, but she lacks his urge to destroy what he cannot understand. I lean forward to touch her arm, in an impulsive gesture of friendship. "If you were Iceni, I believe you might be a Druid."

She draws back. "A Druid?"

I am offended by her rejection but know that even on the Saturnalia I cannot afford to show my true feelings. "Druids are deep thinkers, who study the mortal and immortal realms," I say. "My father was a great Druid. I intended to compliment you."

There is an awkward pause. "I did not know your father was a Druid. I thought him to have been a warrior, like your mother."

"He was both."

"Prasutagus, son of Antedrig, twice blessed by the gods," Ressona recites, loyally coming to my defence. "*Twice blessed* means a leader is both warrior and Druid. Not many hold the title." Ressona knows, but does not say, that I am also twice blessed.

"Did your father ever kill men or women on the altar?" Polla's eyes hold a strange greed as she asks me this question, as if the darkness of human sacrifice both fascinates and repels her.

"No. The human heart holds great power. To use it in divination, a warrior must defeat the sacrifice in combat, or the blood will not surrender its secrets." I pause, thinking of the soldier I killed on the eve of war, whose remains Paulinus found on Andraste's altar. He never did guess that I was the one behind the man's death. "But really," I say to Polla, "how is this so different from the way you kill men and women for entertainment in your arenas? What is *that* if not a form of human sacrifice?"

"I had never thought of it like that." Polla runs her fingers along the surface of the water as she turns my words over in her mind. "I suppose you are right." She smiles, delighted to see the world in a new way. "How interesting."

"What is interesting?" Her husband Lucan has come striding over, his cloak thrown over one shoulder, giving him an arrogant air. I have met the man before and do not like him.

"Boudicca's daughter just suggested that gladiatorial shows are a form of human sacrifice," Polla says, kissing Lucan as he bends to sit beside her. "Don't you think that's fascinating?"

"What nonsense!" Lucan exclaims, laughing at his wife. Polla looks crestfallen, and I dislike him as much for belittling her, as I do for his insult to me. Ressona tenses as he continues to laugh, long after he should have stopped.

"But don't you think that—"

"Which gods do you people use for human sacrifice?" Lucan cuts across Polla before she can finish her thought. He is addressing Ressona and me as one person, because I suspect he cannot remember which of us is Boudicca's daughter.

"Only three are gods of blood," I answer. "Taranis, Esus and the god of the tribe. For the Iceni that is Andraste."

"Teutates." Lucan turns to Polla. "That's what they call him in Gaul. That's the name for the god of the tribe."

"Andraste is a goddess," I say. "A *woman*." Lucan ignores me.

"It is as I have written," he continues, speaking to his wife, who gazes at him with adoration. "The blood savages spill at their shrines is an evil akin to civil war." Lucan does not wait for Polla to reply but pulls her to her feet. "I am tired now, my love. We should go in."

Polla has the grace to glance back at Ressona and me, but she does not say goodbye. Instead, she trots obediently after her husband.

"He's a bit of a prick," Ressona says, switching to our own language.

"He's ridiculous." I tear up a fistful of grass and fling it at the lake. I was enjoying Polla's company and now Lucan has ruined the evening. "How does he imagine it is clever to compare a Druid's blood sacrifice to civil war, but not to all the slaughter in the arena? Using the human heart in divination shows respect. Sending hundreds of people to die in a beast hunt is grotesque."

"No point getting angry about it, is there though," Ressona says, with a yawn. "Let them think whatever they like. We can't change anything."

My friend has a slave's lifelong fatalism which I am yet to learn. Even though it is the Saturnalia, I suddenly feel depressed. I stare out at the bobbing lamps on the lake, sending ripples across the reflection of the moon on the water, shattering it into fragments. Ressona is a Briton, but she is not Iceni; she is not my family. Even beside her, I am alone.

*

Pink light glows upon the water as the sun rises, turning the lake into a red mirror to the Otherworld, and the grass looks sharp, edged by frost. Nobody else is out in the gardens at this hour, and I do not want to waste one precious moment of freedom. I cross the stepping stones on the crimson lake, thinking of my beloved family who lie on the other side of the veil. As it thins, I pray their spirits come closer to me.

The frozen grass crunches underfoot as I walk further into the gardens. They are semi-wild, or as wild as the Romans ever choose to be, with their false groves and man-made grottos. I press deeper into the trees. Even though this is not a real wood, the place still brings me peace, and I walk until the path opens onto an artificial grove. A painted shrine to Diana stands in the centre. Her altar is heaped with offerings, and the trees surrounding it are hung with prayers, all made on behalf of Poppaea to help her safely through childbirth. I touch one, curious. Paulinus used to tell me stories of the hunter goddess. I wonder if Diana would hear a Briton's call to strike down my enemies.

"How delightful to find you so devoted to the wellbeing of your mistress."

I resist the urge to whip round. Instead, I turn slowly. Tigellinus is standing behind me, in the shadow of the trees. I cannot see the sword he always carries as prefect of the Praetorian Guard, but I know it is there, hidden beneath his cloak.

"What do you want?"

"Such charming manners." He laughs. "But I suppose it *is* the Saturnalia, so I forgive you."

"Did you follow me?" I demand, masking my fear with aggression.

Tigellinus sighs. "Please don't be tiresome. The former

Legate of Britannia might enjoy fucking Amazons, but I can assure you, it is not a taste I share."

"Then why are you here?"

"This might astound you, but my position means I keep very long hours. I simply happened to see you, Solina."

His use of my name makes me even more uneasy. Why does the man even remember it? "That still doesn't explain why you followed me."

"I have good wishes to pass on to you from a friend, but after your rudeness, I'm not sure you deserve it."

"What friend?"

"You made such a scene when he handed you over. What did Paulinus promise you, I wonder? Did you think you would be his wife?"

I say nothing. Tigellinus has been watching me long before I met Caratacus, and I do not dare to hope his promise of a message from Paulinus is genuine. "Why would I wish to marry a Roman general?"

"He's very rich," Tigellinus says, looking amused.

"I am the daughter of a king." The words should sound hollow, given I am now a slave, yet they do not. This Roman schemer will never destroy who I am.

"What happened between you?"

"Why do you even care?"

Tigellinus rolls his eyes. "Because it *amuses* me. Paulinus is an extraordinarily predictable man. I cannot think of anyone duller or less likely to be embroiled in a scandal. And now he seems to have completely lost his head over some barbarian woman he picked up on campaign. The daughter of Boudicca, no less. I want to know why."

Whatever else may be true, I know for certain that Paulinus won't have lost his head. It is not in his nature. "What has he said to you?"

"Suetonius Paulinus declared his undying love, begging you to forgive him. Comparing your beauty to the radiance of the sun."

Now I know for certain Tigellinus is lying. I look at him with contempt. "If the general thinks *that* is enough to earn my forgiveness, then he never knew me."

The prefect is blocking my path, but I no longer feel afraid. I am full of rage. My fury is not only for Tigellinus, but Paulinus too, for abandoning me to such fools as this. I shoulder my way past, and stalk down the path without looking back. Behind me I hear the bastard laugh.

36

PAULINUS

It has been so long since he spent time outside Rome, Paulinus had almost forgotten the sense of peace the countryside brings. Visiting his own estates at Pisaurum is never this restful – there is always too much to do. But here at Vespasian's villa in Cosa, he has no obligations other than those of a guest. Vineyards stretch out from the house, and the rhythmic song of crickets makes the spring evening even more soothing, as he walks through the orchards on a carpet of apple blossom petals.

He had been reluctant to leave his siege of Tigellinus, who he has been petitioning constantly for Solina's release, but the Imperial Court is currently in Campania, meaning there is nothing more he can currently do. He hopes to put Solina from his mind for a while. This is not easy. Paulinus will never forget the moment a ragged soothsayer accosted him in the Forum, speaking a message from the goddess Nortia. It had been an immense shock. He had already been determined to get Solina back, but now he knows he cannot fail. *This is the wife, and the child, the gods themselves intend for him.* Even though he has had little success with Tigellinus so far, the soothsayer spoke to the desire of his heart, which gives him hope. Paulinus has always believed he was meant to be a father.

He stops under the oldest tree in the orchard, remembering standing in the same spot as a boy. The others have yet to join him – as always, Paulinus is early. His afternoon was spent hunting with Pliny and Vespasian, both of whom are predictably late for dinner. One is still soaking in the bath, the other poring over a scroll. The three men's friendship stretches back thirty years, and although not exact contemporaries in age, they have shared many of one another's triumphs and losses. When he is with them, Paulinus feels both old and young, remembering who they were as boys but also more conscious of the passing years, seeing age mark his friends. All have served in the military, moving up the ranks from the Equestrian class, and they share similar attitudes to public service; Paulinus is as sure of Pliny or Vespasian's honesty as he is of his own. When it comes to character, they are less alike. Vespasian is blunt-speaking and affable, rarely without a lover, and never without friends. Pliny is bookish and peculiar, but even so, Paulinus privately loves him the most.

He wanders back to the house, stopping to admire a statue of Vespasian's grandmother, Tertulla, who guards the steps to the ornamental gardens. It makes him smile to see the indefatigable old woman, her features so like those of the grandson she raised in this house. Vespasian has several likenesses of Tertulla dotted over the villa, including a household shrine dedicated solely to his grandmother's spirit.

"He still asks her advice before every campaign, you know."

Paulinus turns to see Antonia Caenis, Vespasian's lover, watching him from the top of the steps. He smiles. "She was a formidable woman. Vespasian has kept the entire house to her taste. It still looks exactly as it did when I visited as a boy."

Antonia laughs. "I think he is afraid she might return to

scold him otherwise." There is no malice in her joke, only affection.

Paulinus follows Antonia to the outdoor dining room, feeling envious of his friend. After the death of his wife, Vespasian has lived openly with Antonia without any thought to his reputation. She is the woman Vespasian wants, and he simply expects everyone else to accept her. For the most part they do. Antonia is highly intelligent, she worked as a secretary to the Emperor Claudius's mother, and she has replaced Vespasian's grandmother as his most trusted advisor. Paulinus had hoped to lead a similar life with Solina, before Poppaea took her, though he must admit Antonia is a less scandalous choice for an unofficial wife. If he were to leave Solina alone to make small talk with his friends while he took a bath, who knows what blood feud might have been ignited by the time he returned.

Antonia and Paulinus are politely discussing the day's hunt when Vespasian strolls in. He kisses his mistress in greeting and stretches out comfortably on the couch beside her. "Pliny still studying?" he asks, although it's not a question that needs answering. "We'd better start dinner without him – he could be hours yet and I'm hungry."

His remark is heard by one of the waiting slaves, who immediately pads off to execute his master's wish, returning moments later with wine, stuffed eggs and cheese. Vespasian tucks in.

"When are you expecting Titus home?" Paulinus asks, enquiring after his host's son. "His wedding must be fairly soon."

"He's on the way back from Britannia now," Vespasian replies. "I'm not sure he rated the man who replaced you there. A shame the boy couldn't have served under your command instead."

Paulinus has little doubt this is flattery, but appreciates his friend's effort, nonetheless. "I'm sorry not to have served with Titus, too. And I hope his wedding won't be delayed by the mourning in Rome. The death of Poppaea's baby has hit Nero extremely hard."

"Absurd behaviour over a four-month-old girl," Vespasian exclaims, with the confidence of a man who has three living children. Paulinus remembers his own sadness over the loss of Solina's pregnancy and feels a rare glimmer of sympathy for Nero. "I had to sit through an extraordinarily tedious harp recital Caesar gave on the topic of grief," Vespasian continues. "It was so dull I managed to annoy him by nodding off."

"I'm not surprised he was annoyed," Antonia says. "You snore."

"It hasn't done too much harm," Vespasian replies. "I'm mercifully banned from sitting through any more recitals, and Tigellinus is sending me to Carthage." Antonia sighs and Vespasian pats her arm. "It will be warm, darling. And think how much more of me you'll see."

"It was Tigellinus who offered you the governorship?" Paulinus asks in surprise.

"Is there anything he's *not* doing, these days?" Vespasian says. "Nero is too busy singing to do anything so dreary as rule an Empire. Apparently, he's determined to go on stage in Neapolis while he's visiting Campania. So, our dear friend Tigellinus is busier than ever."

"You shouldn't just blurt out these things," Antonia says, exasperated.

"I hardly think *Paulinus* is going to report me." Vespasian laughs. "If a man cannot trust his oldest friends, that's a sad state of affairs." He takes a swig of wine. "I did look out for your Briton when I was at the palace, like you asked," he says. "But Poppaea has two. One is very pretty, the other looks like she would sooner stab a man in the eye than grant him a private conversation."

"I've never seen the other Briton," Paulinus replies. "But Solina could be either of the two women you've described."

Vespasian laughs. "Then I hope you manage to buy her back. She sounds priceless."

"Who is priceless?" Pliny has arrived, managing to get his tunic entangled with one of the slaves bringing out the main course. They are setting out large plates of moray eel, roasted with honey and quince. Pliny makes his way to the empty couch, managing, as ever, to look extremely unrelaxed while relaxing.

"We were talking about the British girl Paulinus is pursuing," Vespasian says.

"Are you still pursuing her?" Pliny sounds displeased and Paulinus reaches for the eel without answering, feeling annoyed with both his friends. "Has he told you the ridiculous tale about the soothsayer?" Pliny persists.

"I wouldn't say it's ridiculous," says Vespasian, who has inherited his grandmother's deeply superstitious nature. "But I might feel rather peeved if it were me, to think Fate found me a Briton, of all things." Paulinus is aware that Vespasian had several British lovers himself, when he served in Britannia years ago, but he does not want to hurt Antonia's feelings by saying so.

"I'm sorry that you miss her," Antonia says to Paulinus. "And *you* shouldn't scoff." She turns to Vespasian. "Think how upset you would feel if it were me." Antonia's intervention comes from a place of kindness, but Paulinus is more mortified by it than the men's mockery.

"Do you actually *love* her?" Vespasian asks, as if this had not occurred to him before.

"Yes," Paulinus replies.

"I hadn't realised." Vespasian puts his arm around his own mistress, drawing her closer. "In that case, ignore Pliny. Don't give up on the girl."

"You cannot compare Antonia to a Briton!" Pliny snaps. "I don't think you should encourage him with this nonsense."

"Why not?" Vespasian asks. "Why shouldn't he have the woman he wants? Life is too short as it is, without bothering what people think. Who cares about a few raised eyebrows. I don't."

"Speaking of which, did Pliny tell you about his recent prosecution?" Paulinus says, wanting to move away from the topic of Solina. "People have been quoting the more scandalous parts of the speech, calling him a second Cicero."

"Mere flattery," Pliny says. "*Nobody* is a second Cicero. But it was good work of yours to dig out some debauchery attached to Decianus; it helped us win."

"I don't know how the pair of you can stand practicing law after life in the army," Vespasian says, wolfing down his food.

Paulinus is not offended. There was a time he would have envied Vespasian's new military post. He had many ambitions when he went to Britannia, imagining it was the province which would make him famous. In some sense it did, although his defeat of Boudicca will always be inextricably linked to the shame she brought on Rome, and his own recall that followed. But his time in Britannia was also when Fulvia died, and two years later, when he found Solina and finally discovered he might become a father, only to have this taken from him too. Nothing puts a career in perspective so profoundly as personal loss. "I think I prefer the law," he says. "A sign of getting old."

"The pair of you are both ten years younger than I am," Vespasian says. "So less of the old, or you will offend me. Not to mention Antonia! She just turned forty-five."

"Thank you so much for sharing that, my darling," Antonia says wryly.

"Why should you care about your age when I love you?" Vespasian asks, as if the only consideration Antonia could possibly have in life is for his regard.

"May we all live to as glorious an old age as dear Tertulla," Paulinus says, knowing that a mention of Vespasian's late grandmother will be sure to turn the conversation.

They all raise their glasses to Tertulla's memory. Paulinus tries to imagine what it might be like, if he were to bring Solina here to meet Vespasian and Antonia. *Why shouldn't he have the woman he wants?* He drains his glass, thinking of a new tactic to win over Tigellinus, in the way he once planned for the siege of cities.

37

SOLINA

Ressona is pregnant. She and Alexios are beside themselves with grief, knowing full well this is not a prelude to a happy family life. At first, I try to reassure her with the story of my own early loss; I only carried my baby a few weeks at most. Perhaps she will also have a miscarriage. But now Ressona is beginning to show, and she is sick and exhausted. If it were not for the absurd floating robes we wear, and Poppaea's own grief, the Empress might have realised her condition by now.

Even though disaster is looming in the servants' corridor, we are forced to follow the rhythm of our masters' stories, rather than our own. Everything revolves around the grief of the Imperial couple. Poppaea gave birth to a girl, as Caratacus predicted, and the celebrations were more spectacular than anything I could have imagined, but then shortly afterwards, the baby died, and the mourning too has been excessive beyond measure. Nero declares his child, Claudia Augusta, to have been a god, deifying her, vowing to build the baby a temple.

Seeking to rouse Nero from his misery, Tigellinus plans a spectacular entertainment for the Roman's summer solstice, which they call Fors Fortuna. It is to be a banquet on a giant raft, held on a lake in the centre of Rome. Poppaea will not be attending, which means neither will her maids, as the whole purpose of the spectacle is to put women up for sale. Tigellinus is having gilded brothels and booths built all around the banks of the water, and for one night, no woman at the party, whether slave or free, is allowed to refuse a man. I think little of such a grotesque spectacle, which is no more than gossip in the servants' corridor, until one of Tigellinus's slaves sends for me on the afternoon of the banquet.

I leave Ressona and the two German girls, Henna and Frida, in the gardens where Poppaea had draped us around a fountain, and hurry after the man. "What does Tigellinus want?" I demand. The prefect still takes any opportunity he can to tease me, but he has never *summoned* me. It feels ominous.

"Tigellinus isn't here," the slave replies.

"Then why did he send for me?"

We are inside the palace, climbing the steps, and the slave is taking the turning that leads to the courtyard where I first arrived at this place with Paulinus, a whole lifetime ago. "You have a buyer at the banquet for Fors Fortuna."

I grab the man's arm, forcing him to stop. "No," I say, furious. "I refuse."

"My master said you might object." He shakes me off. "Unless I told you the buyer." The slave is savouring my reaction, perhaps enjoying holding power over someone else for a change, rather than being crushed himself.

"Who is it?"

"I'm not allowed to tell you." The man smirks. "The prefect says you will guess."

His words make me pause, torn between anger and hope. This might be a trick, a means of ensuring I am violated in the most public, revolting way possible. Or it might be a chance to see Paulinus again. That is clearly what Tigellinus *wants* me to believe. But do I dare trust such a liar?

The slave is getting impatient. "Well?" he demands. "Are you coming?"

I think of the monotony of my life here, the slow suffocation of everything that burns within me. Fors Fortuna is a goddess of Fate, like Nortia. Perhaps this is a sign from the gods that I should be bold. I turn to my tormentor and stare, until he grows uncomfortable and blinks.

"I will go."

A golden raft floats upon the lake like a giant platter, as if rather than feasting, Nero and his companions will be feasted upon by the god of this place. I imagine Esus, rising from the water, his mouth wide, swallowing the mortals who dare to disturb his sanctuary. The solstice is when Esus is at his most powerful; he can be seen in all sources of energy, from rivers to the rising sun, and it is Esus who I used to worship on this day with my family.

The afternoon here in Rome is sweltering hot, and there is nothing sacred about our gathering. Women have been brought in ahead of the party, left to wander around among the exotic birds and animals which Tigellinus shipped from abroad. On the opposite side of the lake to me, there are prostitutes who have been given open, curtain-less booths. They sit on the shore, laughing and chatting together, naked but keeping warm in the sun. On my side, there are not booths, but small painted wooden houses with outdoor dining rooms and private chambers above. These are for the 'ordinary' women who have agreed – or been forced – to take part. It is where I am left by Tigellinus's slave, along with instructions to go to a specific house, where a room has been assigned to me.

It is a small, cramped space under the eaves, with a window. Once I am inside, the door is locked.

As dusk approaches I can feel the tension build, the way it does before battle. I drag the bed across the floor to block the doorway, so that anyone who enters will only do so by my permission. I feel increasingly afraid Tigellinus has lured me here as a trick. Perhaps he will even be the one to knock on my door. A sharp stick I picked up from the shore is my sole weapon, only effective if stabbed into an eye at close quarters, but better than nothing.

Music begins to play. I walk to the window and look out. There are flautists on the giant raft, along with couches and tables heaped with food, and it is being towed over the water by naked men in small golden rowing boats, inlaid with ivory. When the strange, floating dining room is secured against the banks, I realise Nero is approaching. His chestnut curls mark him out to me from above, and I watch as he makes his way onto the raft. When all his guests are on board, it is pushed from the shore, gliding over to the opposite side, to collect some of the prostitutes.

I grow tired of watching but also feel too tense to sit on the bed and wait, blind to whatever is happening outside. Darkness falls, and the trees and booths around the lake sparkle with lights. My room is dark. Through the floorboards, glimmers leak through the cracks, and I can hear laughter from the men dining below. I suppose they will bring their lamps when they seek out the women, so that they can see their prey hiding in the dark. It is not a comforting thought.

At last I hear the creak of footsteps and raucous laughter on the stairs, and am torn between wanting to keep as far away from the door as possible, and knowing my weight on the bed will make it harder to force open.

"Solina. Are you there?"

His voice is loud and instantly recognisable.

"Yes, but I barricaded the door, let me move it," I call, sounding much steadier than my thumping heart. I drag the bed away with a loud crunch and scrape, then Paulinus unlocks the door, and squeezes through the narrow space, holding out a lamp that brings the dark room to life.

I have imagined being with him again so often that this moment feels unreal, as if I have conjured an illusion. Paulinus looks older than I remember. I walk up to him and place my hand on his cheek, to make sure he is solid. He smiles, mistaking it for a gesture of tenderness, and lays his hand over mine. Instantly, I am flooded with rage.

I withdraw my hand, smacking him hard in the face. His reflexes kick in and he catches my wrist before I can thump him a second time. "Do that again, and I might drop the light." He nods at the burning lamp in his free hand. His calm practicality takes me aback, startling me out of my fury. "You have every right to be angry," he says. "But please, listen to me."

"You abandoned me, you shit," I snarl, furious that my eyes are smarting with tears. "I trusted you."

"It was unforgivable," he says, still restraining me from hitting him again. "I know that. But I never expected Poppaea to demand to keep you. If I had made a scene, it would have placed you in even greater danger. You must have lived at court long enough to know that now."

"I didn't know it at the time, though," I say, finally wresting my hand back to wipe my face, furious that the sight of him is making me cry. "You should have said something."

"I know. Please, Solina. I don't deserve your forgiveness, but I am begging you to believe me that I did not mean to hurt you."

I say nothing, still too angry to allow him any grace.

Paulinus however, takes it as a victory that I am not still trying to punch him. Cautiously, he reaches out to take my hand. Then he sets down the lamp.

"I thought Tigellinus was lying," he says, his fingers warm around mine. "Until I heard your voice just now, I didn't believe you would really be here."

The relief of being close to him again is overwhelming. I am still furious but also exhausted, so I say nothing and rest my head on his chest, closing my eyes. Paulinus holds me, also saying nothing. Slowly my heartbeat starts to even out, as if my body has been waiting all this time to feel safe. I hate that this is the man I have chosen, but I also accept it, the way I accept that the sun rises and sets, and grief follows loss.

"I tried to get you back, the morning after I was forced to leave you there," he says, his hand caressing my back. "I promise there has not been a day I have not thought of you. And then I was given an oracle from the goddess Nortia herself." He disentangles himself from my embrace, clearly keen to see my reaction. I try to muster an appropriate amount of awe.

"An oracle?"

"Yes, delivered by a soothsayer in the Forum, a man totally unknown to me."

"What did he say?"

"He told me you are the woman that the Fates have chosen for me, the destined mother of my child."

I'm curious that he does not tell me Nortia was angry with him for his abandonment. I wonder if Caratacus's soothsayer softened my message, or whether Paulinus has decided it would be prudent to keep that part to himself. It is almost touching if he is trying to manipulate me over a prophecy which was mine. "Then it is Nortia who brought you to me," I say. "You cannot trick the Goddess of Fate."

"Solina, I confess I did not wholly believe the vision you told me about our child in Britannia. I didn't question your sincerity, but I thought grief might have made you imagine things. I should never have doubted you. To be singled out by Nortia this way is a blessing beyond any I could have imagined." He kisses me then, as if I were infinitely precious to him, and my desire is mingled with intense satisfaction at the power I now hold. Paulinus pulls me closer, and I hold him tightly. It is so long since we have lain together I had forgotten how much I enjoy his touch. "I went back to Volsinii," he says, tenderly taking my face in his hands. "I paid the priests to make a blood sacrifice to Nortia at the turn of the new year, when her power is at its height. I promised the Goddess of Fate I would marry you when she returns you to me."

He is gazing into my eyes, expectant for a reply, as if he has just laid a great gift at my feet. I would be offended at him doing this without asking my permission, except that I have never told Paulinus we are already married. For the Iceni it is enough that a woman chooses a man, and he agrees to lie with her. Only disarming him in a fight can dissolve the union. I squeeze his fingers, so he knows I am pleased about the sacrifice to Nortia.

"That was wise," I say. Paulinus looks bemused, then he laughs. "What?" I demand.

"When a man tells a woman he wishes to marry her, she doesn't usually respond by solemnly congratulating him on his good sense."

"I meant the sacrifice was wise," I say, but at that he laughs even more, unable to stop himself. "*Of course*, I wish to marry you, Paulinus. That should be obvious."

He realises my irritation and tries to recover himself. "I wasn't mocking you," he says, kissing me. "I enjoy the way you speak. It is unlike anyone else. And I have missed you very much."

His words make me feel a sudden terror of the morning. "You can't leave me again," I say, gripping hold of his hand.

"I will get you back," he says calmly. Perhaps it should annoy me that he does not look distressed, but instead his detachment is comforting. It helps me believe him. "I'm sorry that it is taking longer than it should." He hesitates. "Have you been harmed there?"

I understand what he means. "No."

He looks relieved, and I do not know if it is because he loves me or feels jealous. Perhaps it is both. "Tigellinus told me you lay with him the same night I left you." He holds up a hand to stop me protesting in outrage. "I never thought you would have done so by choice, and I always suspected it was a lie, especially since he denied it soon after. But I still worried he might have hurt you."

"Nobody has hurt me, and Tigellinus would be dead if he had tried. Why does he dislike you so much?"

"I don't know that he does," Paulinus says, with an easy confidence I would not feel in his place. "But he likes to humiliate people. Tigellinus made his fortune in chariot racing, it's how he became friendly with Nero. When I was younger, I think he believed that I snubbed him, because I was never interested in the life he offered. So, it amuses him now, that I would chase after a British woman. I imagine it's why he arranged for me to see you here, at the sort of party I once refused."

I become aware of the growing noise outside and walk to the window. On the shore opposite, men have started fighting over the women and their booths. Paulinus joins me, and I hear him huff in annoyance. "Here, take this." He hands me a knife. "In case anyone breaks in." I am about to ask why I am the one with the knife, then realise he has one too. "Better we're both armed," he explains, seeing my face. "I don't intend to die in a brawl, but I would rather know you could still defend yourself if I did."

"Are you not afraid I will use it on you?"

My question is not a serious one, but I can see it still annoys him. "I think we're past all that. Given you're going to marry me."

I used to find it difficult, sometimes, to talk to Paulinus. He can be insufferably Roman. But I have been so starved of his company, I never want our conversation to end. I tell him about my life serving Poppaea, and ask a hundred questions about his days, trying to store up as much knowledge as possible to guard against whatever lies Tigellinus will tell, and to build a sense of what he is doing when I cannot see him. For the first time since I have known him, Paulinus speaks with respect about my knowledge as a Druid, asking me to describe the vision I had of our son. Telling him about this imaginary child, I feel such longing, I almost forget the whole thing is invention. I can see the strength he draws from my words, and how convinced he is that I am the woman he wants. I do not feel guilty for deceiving him. My father was right – sometimes a lie can be the way to convince others of the truth. This is the future Paulinus owes me, after stealing my past.

We are among the very last to leave. Paulinus stays with me until the same slave who brought me here returns to take me back. The man is much more polite in the presence of an army general, waiting respectfully out of earshot on the now ravaged shore of the lake. I am so distressed at having to go back to enslavement I cannot think of anything to say.

Paulinus takes my hand, and lays it over his heart, mirroring the gesture of affection I have often used towards him.

"*Dearer than oak,*" he says. I stare at him, too astonished to reply. It is not Latin, but my own language he has spoken, and he has repeated back to me the words I said to him in Gaul, the day I saved his horse. My eyes fill with tears. Paulinus swiftly drops my hand and walks away.

38

SOLINA

After Tigellinus's banquet, the entire court moves to Nero's seaside villa in Antium, to escape the heat of summer in Rome. I find it painful to leave behind Paulinus and the possibility of freedom, but I do not like to show my sadness when Ressona's anxiety grows ever more acute. The swell of her stomach now stretches against some of her clothes, and discovery cannot be far off. We sit together on the edge of the roof terrace, basking in the breeze from a sparkling blue sea, while Nero, Poppaea and their favourites party just below. Music and laughter drift up on the warm evening air, much pleasanter at a distance. We will have to accompany the Empress to bed later, as she is wearing yellow, but for now we are stealing a moment for ourselves. I keep my eyes trained on Poppaea, as if she were a target I meant to hit with a spear, waiting for any sign she might be tiring.

"I'm not sure how she bears it," Ressona says, as Nero exchanges kisses between his wife and new mistress, Messalina, who sit either side of him. "I should hate to share a man like that."

"I don't suppose she loves it either," I reply. "But she's smart enough to accept other lovers, so long as she has his ear when it matters." I loathe Poppaea, but for this at least I do not judge her.

"Did you have to do that?" Ressona is endlessly curious about my relationship with Paulinus after the meeting by the lake.

"No," I retort. "He isn't that type of man."

Ressona rolls her eyes. "He's *Roman*. They're all like it. Their men don't know the meaning of loyalty." The thought of Paulinus enjoying other women had not even crossed my mind. I realise that not only do I dislike the idea, but it makes me furious. Ressona sees my expression. "Maybe your one is different," she says hastily. "I mean, I'm sure he is."

"Well, I don't care," I lie.

Ressona wrinkles her nose. "Gods, that's such a disgusting smell," she says. "What are they eating down there?"

"I can't smell anything," I say, before realising I should have played along. It is the pregnancy that has made her so sensitive, everything nauseates her. Fear crosses her face as she realises.

"Do you think there's *any* chance she will let me keep it?"

Ressona has asked this so many times. No, is the answer. I reach over to take her hand. "I don't know."

"She won't," Ressona says dully. "Alexios has been here longer than me. They never let personal attendants keep their children past a year, sometimes not even that."

I squeeze her fingers. We look down on the party below, at the swirls of colour, the shimmer of glass mosaics and the graceful yellow form of our mistress, who laughs as she dances, giving no sign of the cruelty in her heart.

Silver is rippling across the black sea from the light of the moon, and Ressona is asleep against my shoulder when the party begins to break up. I shove her in the ribs, and she jumps awake with a snort, then we are hurtling down the marble stairs. We are swept up in the mass of attendants accompanying Poppaea and Nero to bed, following them along the torchlit colonnade that looks out over the waves. The Imperial bedroom sits at the end, and it is exquisite – inlaid marble dolphins leap across the walls and floor, and a window is angled to give the appearance that we are floating on the sea. The room is full of slaves, some like Ressona and me are here to undress Poppaea, others to undress Nero, still more to bring refreshments. We keep total silence as we work, maintaining the illusion that we have neither eyes nor ears.

Poppaea is terrified of ageing, and when she is not lying with Nero, I have had to slather her in creams before bed, or bring jugs of asses milk for her to bathe in, all to preserve her skin. Tonight, however, maids redo her make-up, rather than remove it, so that her husband never has to see her with an unpainted face. Poppaea's expression is blank while red paste is smeared on her lips, and I wonder what she really feels about the man she married. I saw Nero strike her once. Ressona tells me his violence is nothing compared to what Octavia suffered, but still, if Poppaea were not so cruel herself, I might pity her for that.

They fall naked into bed together and some of the slaves retire, but Ressona and I creep into a corner, our service not over until the lights are out, when we will have to sleep on the floor. I stare out at the sea, not disgusted, but having no desire to watch Nero and Poppaea either. My attention is caught when I realise Nero is shouting, and not with pleasure. With dismay I see that he is pointing a finger at Ressona and me.

"You!" he yells.

I gawp at him, frozen with horror. The man has never asked us to join them before.

"Fetch Fabius!"

I cannot scramble from the room fast enough. Before I shoot through the door, one of Nero's attendants grabs my elbow. "He's in the gardens," he whispers. "He wanted to keep out of sight."

I run back along the colonnade, and down the sweeping steps. The gardens are lit by torches, never lost to the darkness even at midnight, but it's still harder to find someone than in the day. "Fabius!" I yell, stomping between the fountains and the sweet-smelling lavender. "Caesar needs you!" I see a shadow moving, someone trying to hide behind a statue of Adonis. I creep closer, sneaking around the monument, then pounce, grabbing him by the scruff of the tunic. "What are you doing?" I hiss.

"Can't you just say you couldn't find me?" he pleads. Fabius is still a boy. He must be the age Bellenia was when she died, but it is not his youth that startles me whenever I see him. He looks so like Poppaea he could be her younger, masculine twin.

"I can't," I say. "Sorry, but I'm not taking a beating for you."

Fabius nods wearily. We walk together up the steps and along the corridor. I glance out at the moon, hating myself, hating Nero and Poppaea more.

Ressona and I are asleep, bunched up together on cushions on the floor, when a messenger disturbs us in the hour before dawn. I listen in the darkness, as the man tells the Emperor that the city of Rome is burning, a fire raging uncontrollably between the Celian and Palatine hills. Hundreds will have already died, whole neighbourhoods razed. With a sick feeling I realise that I never asked Paulinus where he lives in the city.

I sit up in the darkness, stiff from the cold marble, straining to hear more.

"We will return if it reaches the palace," Nero says. "I am sure the Night Watch will soon have the blaze under control. Rome has suffered fires before."

To my amazement, the man goes back to sleep, almost as soon as the messenger has left. I lie awake, listening to his snores, thinking of my father. King Prasutagus rode to his death when a mere saltern was set alight. This Caesar cannot get out of bed for his capital city. I try to visualise Paulinus running to safety, but cannot, because whatever else I know of the man, he is not a coward, and he will be running towards the flames, not away from them. I tell myself the anxiety I feel is only for myself, and for my own future if he dies, but this cannot fully explain why the thought of his death brings me such distress.

"He will be alright," Ressona whispers, instantly guessing why I am tossing restlessly beside her. "You said he's a big brute of a man, tall as Taranis – for sure a few flames aren't going to finish him off."

I accept Ressona's hug, willing myself not to cry, embarrassed to have shown such emotion. *Tall as Taranis.* I had forgotten I once described Paulinus that way, and realise it betrays so much more than my sense of his height. If you tell enough lies, it seems you can even lie to yourself.

39

PAULINUS

The heat from the fire is unbearable, even several streets away. He is soaked in sweat, his eyes sting, and it feels as if his lungs will never be clear of smoke. Rome has been burning for four days. His own house will soon be devoured, one of many sacrificed to try and stop the spread; the only way to save the city now is to destroy great swathes of it, in the hope of containing the inferno. A line of catapults confronts the largest warehouses of the Esquiline, as if they were an enemy citadel. Paulinus gives the order to launch a volley of stone at a granary that towers above him. The missile hits with explosive force, rocking the wall. He helps the men reload, then they fire again, this time knocking a hole in the brickwork, and the wall above sags.

Behind him, Paulinus can hear the screams and curses of the merchant whose livelihood he is destroying. The man is being restrained by the Night Watch, who are wrestling him away from the catapults. Paulinus ignores the yelling, scanning the building, looking for its weakest points. "Aim there," he says to the retired soldier beside him, pointing at a crack fanning out from an arch. The man obliges, turning the deadly contraption in the direction Paulinus commands. Stone smashes into brick. The crack spreads into dark channels, like a river bursting its banks, and more of the wall crumples. It is not enough. They need to level the whole street to rubble, and fast. "Keep going," Paulinus says, moving on to the next machine, staggering slightly from lack of sleep.

The fire is bad enough at night, lighting up the sky with its unearthly orange glow, but now in the blazing heat of the day it is monstrous, the sweltering July weather accelerating the flames' spread. And then there is the animosity of his fellow citizens, like the hysterical merchant behind him, or worse, the looters who come to steal whatever the flames have missed. At least he knows Solina must be safely away from here, in Antium with Poppaea.

Paulinus has destroyed countless towns and cities, but never imagined he would turn against his own. If he thinks about what he is doing too deeply, it will affect his judgement. Already so much of the sacred city has been obliterated – centuries-old temples, streets he has walked his whole life, and his own home sits empty and waiting to be devoured. The fire is spreading too quickly; they have had to abandon whole neighbourhoods, hoping to create a buffer before the flames reach them. Paulinus knows he is fortunate his household escaped with their lives, that he had a chance to move his wealth and most precious possessions to safety, but the thought of his family home being consumed is still appalling. The house is one of his last links to Fulvia. And he had to leave so much behind. The bed where they slept, all the flowers she planted in the garden, the fresco of Victory she commissioned after he returned from Mauretania.

"You should take some rest, general." It is one of the men from the Night Watch.

"When this street is down," he rasps, his own voice unrecognisable from the smoke. Paulinus turns back to the warehouses. "Aim for the crossbeam," he orders the soldier at the catapult, yet another veteran volunteer, like himself. The explosion is loud, even over the roaring of the fire, and this time the building surrenders, each floor collapsing down upon the next, until the warehouse is defeated by its own weight. When the dust clears, Paulinus sees his companions are coated in grey powder, their eyes wild and red. He realises he must look the same.

In the distance, the fire continues to rumble, like the rattling breath of a leviathan, and the air is thick with screams and explosions. Paulinus watches his city through the haze of smoke and dust, remembering how the Iceni town of *Lukodunon* burned, destroyed on his orders. All the pain he feels now, Solina has already felt. He turns back to the catapult, to help move it to the next building. When this is over, the ash will wash from his skin, but guilt is a stain he is only just beginning to comprehend.

40

SOLINA

Flames dance in the Imperial gardens, glowing red against the dusk. Nothing like as vast as the great fire of Rome, which has long since been extinguished; these are human torches, hundreds of men and women tied to stakes and set alight. They are people from a strange Jewish sect, called Christians, who have been blamed for plotting the blaze, even though everyone knows it started in a cook shop near the Circus Maximus. But now that Nero has begun a land grab on the streets razed by the fire, some have accused him of starting it, so it was convenient to find a scapegoat.

I watch the victims burn from a window in the old Palace of Augustus, the only part of the Imperial residence to escape destruction. A huge tent city also stands in the gardens, sending up a stench of smoke and human filth, reminding me of the camp Paulinus built over my father's sacred grove. The homeless have been given shelter on Caesar's own land to try and blunt the rage that simmers in the city. Thousands have lost everything, and although the building work is relentless, carrying on through the night, none of it is busier than on the Palatine, where Nero's monumental new palace is taking shape.

Ressona stands opposite me, so that we make a matching pair flanking the window. I know her feet must be hurting from staying still so long, and I worry about the chill autumn air, the smell of burning flesh which even the incense in here cannot dispel. My friend's pregnancy is obvious now – Poppaea must have guessed, yet she has said nothing. I like to think this means Ressona will be spared, but our mistress's character gives me little cause for hope. Her silence is almost more ominous than rage.

The Empress is reclining while a boy reads poetry aloud, and a harpist trills an accompaniment. Some of her women friends are draped around her, also listening. One of them is Messalina, Nero's mistress, whose company Poppaea seems to enjoy. Or at least she pretends that she does. I watch the two women. Both are pretty, with similar soft, dark curls and pouting lips, though Poppaea is noticeably more beautiful. Messalina seems to have accepted rather than sought her position as mistress, and if she harbours any ambitions of supplanting her friend as Caesar's wife, she hides it well.

I try to listen to some of the poetry, but it is so dull my mind wanders. Lucan is no longer read in the Imperial Palace. He mocked Nero's own verses one too many times, and now the man's work cannot be performed in public, ending his career. I miss Polla's visits, even if I do not mourn her arrogant husband. Theirs is not the only recent banishment. The atmosphere at court has changed after the fire. Partly it might be that we are all crammed on top of each other in a reduced space, partly it is Nero's new obsession, his Golden House, which neither Poppaea nor Tigellinus think he can afford. I have heard Nero and Poppaea argue over the new palace – perhaps her influence over him is slipping.

I glance back outside the window. Some of the human torches are guttering into charred shapes, and as the dusk darkens into night, huge pools of the city turn a deeper shade of black. I know these are the scorched areas of ash, rubble and bones where no lamp burns, or mortal walks. I pray to the gods that Paulinus is not buried there, and all my hopes of freedom with him.

When Poppaea finally sweeps off to watch a harp recital given by her husband, Ressona sags with relief.

"If I had to stand there another moment, I swear I was going to pass out," she grumbles, speaking our own language.

Henna and Frida, the German women, are laughing together, shaking out their arms which must be stiff from holding plates of fruit. The four of us sleep crammed into a tiny room together now that the old palace is gone.

"We should all head to bed," I call to them both in Latin. "Before she comes back and decides she needs us for something else."

At this, one of the guards step forward. "The pregnant one cannot go with you."

Henna and Frida abruptly stop laughing. I stare at the man. "What do you mean?"

"She has been sold. I need to take her now."

Ressona lets out a cry, and I stand in front of her. "No," I shout. "Get away!"

"Don't make this difficult," the man says, squaring up to me.

"Where are you taking her?" I clutch my friend's hand, determined not to let her go. I cannot believe Poppaea has done this, that she did not even tell Ressona herself. Nothing prepared me for such a sudden separation.

"Get out of the way," the guard snaps, grabbing me by the arm. I swing for him, but he ducks.

"You little..." He raises his fist, ready to punch me, but Ressona rips her hand from mine, stepping between us.

"Don't," she says to me, blinking as her tears fall. "Solina, please. It won't make a difference. I don't want to say goodbye like this." I stare at her, unable to find any words. Ressona embraces me. "Perhaps it will be better this way," she whispers into my ear. "Perhaps, wherever I am going, I can keep the baby."

I hold her tightly. "You are right." I force down my tears. "That's what will happen. It will be better for you than here."

"Enough now," the guard says. "Come along."

I see him reaching out to grab hold of Ressona again, so I let go, not wanting him to hurt her. I raise my voice as they take her from me. "May the gods be with you."

Ressona says nothing, her face white with shock, and then the guards hustle her through the door, and she is gone. I am left standing alone, no longer in this Roman palace, but on the fields outside Verulamium, seeing my mother, Cunominus and Vassura for the last time. "May the gods be with you," I repeat, as much for my lost family as for my friend.

"Solina." I feel a timid touch on my arm. It is Frida. "We go now. Before man comes back to punish you."

I look at the two friends huddled together, close as Ressona and I were close, with their own secret language I will never learn, and their broken Latin. My troubles are not theirs.

"Yes," I nod. "We will go."

In the morning, while the foul stench of burned flesh still lingers, the whole court is taken to walk along the Oppian hill to admire the progress of Nero's new palace, his Golden House. I have barely slept. I keep trying to picture my friend somewhere safe and cared for. I tell myself the new owner will allow her to keep her child, that she will suffer less than if she had remained here. I remember Ressona's kindness when I first came to this place, and imagine her finding another friend to welcome her, just as kind as she once was to me. Yet I know all these wishes are as empty as the wind. I will never know what has happened to Ressona. She is lost to me.

I stare at the building works, the house which will become my new prison. We are walking along a narrow path on the very edge of the half-finished gardens, which grant a vast panorama over Rome. At this moment, the view only exposes the suffering of the city beneath us, much of which is being swallowed by the new palace. Far below, a huge pleasure lake is being built where there were once shops and houses, and space is being created for a colossal golden statue of Nero himself. In the cold autumn sunshine, the men at work on the ground look as small and sharp as etchings on stone.

As slaves, we are left to linger at the back of the company, only present to make the entourage look more impressive. Up ahead, Tigellinus is close to Poppaea. The prefect of the Praetorian Guard has not spoken to me for weeks. I watched him during the endless harp recitals Nero gave at the time of the fire, singing of the fall of Troy, but Tigellinus rarely acknowledged me in return. At first, I took comfort from his silence, considering how much pleasure Tigellinus would get from bringing me distressing news. Now, however, so much time has passed, I am increasingly afraid Paulinus is dead, and my nemesis has lost interest in me altogether.

I watch as Tigellinus wanders slightly apart to look down at his own mansion, which was damaged in the fire, but miraculously escaped complete destruction. He stands alone on the very edge of the terrace, as the rest of the party walks on ahead. It would be reckless to go to him now, yet caution brings me nothing. I think of Ressona, snatched from her own life. If I remain enslaved, this will also be my fate. To disappear. To hold no control over my future. To be separated from my friends without warning. To lose everything I have – even the will to resist.

I break off from the company, picking my way over the uneven ground towards him. Tigellinus is aware of my approach before he turns; I can see it in the way he stiffens. "Is Paulinus alive?" I ask, not bothering to introduce myself.

Tigellinus's face looks shuttered, as if he is no longer even relishing the chance to tease. "He saved my house," he says, his voice flat. The man's blank unconcern enrages me. The arrogance he has, to toy with *my* life. I grab his arm, aware as I do, how very close he is to the edge. One shove would be all it took to topple him onto the building works below. Tigellinus sees it too, and a flicker of interest returns to his face as he looks at me. "That would be most unwise."

"You have turned me into a shadow. Why shouldn't I die with you now?"

He removes my hand from my arm with a look of disdain. "No man is worth dying for. Neither for love, nor vengeance."

"If Paulinus really did save your house, and that is not another lie, then why won't you do what he asks?"

"Because I cannot," he snaps. "I would not *choose* to spite a former general who has done me such an immense favour. What purpose would that serve?"

"I don't believe you."

"Then don't believe me. But I am telling you, you should forget him. I cannot grant the favour he asks; it is not in my gift." He glares at me. "And if you wish to stay alive, you would be wise never to lay hands upon me again."

Tigellinus stalks off, leaving me by the sheer drop of the hill. I watch him rejoin the company, seeking out Poppaea's bright blue dress, which is shot through with silver thread, ensuring she is the only woman who glitters in the sunlight, the only princess present.

If it really is not Tigellinus who refuses to release me, that leaves one other possibility. I think of the way the Empress once spoke of me to Caratacus: *She does not understand it is her destiny to be a slave.*

It must be Poppaea.

This knowledge does not fill me with despair but a rush of hope, the first I have felt since Ressona was taken. When I was captive in Britain, an entire army stood in the way of my freedom, making it impossible to kill my way out. But here, it is not a legion, only one woman who stands in my way.

41

PAULINUS

The Temple of Saturn gleams in the early evening light, touches of gold shining on the marble. Paulinus sees the building most days. It stands beside the Basilica Julia where he gives legal advice on civil cases, and for many years he felt pained to look at it. The temple houses the state archives, and every day new fathers climb its steps to register the birth of their children, some proudly carrying tiny babies to mark the occasion. It was also outside Saturn's temple that the soothsayer accosted Paulinus with the prophecy from Nortia, almost stopping his heart. The immense hope he felt that day is slowly being crushed.

All the weeks of effort he put into infiltrating the Imperial slave network, trying to find a means of contacting Solina, have been destroyed by Calpurnius Piso's attempted coup against Nero. Sending secret messages now would put Solina in lethal danger. Paulinus sighs, looking up at the canopy of leaves above him. He is standing in the shade of the Forum's sacred Fig Tree, in front of the Basilica Julia, waiting for Pliny to finish his case. His surroundings show no hint of the tumult currently engulfing Rome's elite. It is early evening, and the murmur of voices, laughter and street-sellers give the impression of raucous good humour, while the brilliant white marble magnifies the light. Paulinus watches lawyers descend the steps of the basilica, some despondent, others congratulating one another, and thinks of how often he saw Piso himself here, celebrating a win in court. Now the man is dead, along with so many others, and everyone is paranoid about who might be next.

Piso had not been a friend – the man was vain and bombastic – but Paulinus was aware of Piso's discontent with Nero, which is shared by so many others. Discovering that this had moved beyond disgruntled lawyers' gossip to a full-blown assassination attempt was a shock. The conspiracy seems to have reached every corner of the Imperial Court, and now Nero is using it as an excuse to get rid of all those he dislikes. Which might be anyone.

Across the square, he sees the distinctive, rumpled figure of his friend descending the basilica steps. Pliny weaves his way through the crowd to the Fig Tree, a symbol of Romulus and Remus who once sheltered under its shade.

"That took longer than expected, but at least it's settled now," Pliny says by way of apology for the wait. "How did it go with Vestinus?"

"He was so pleased by my advice on the case, he has asked me to dinner."

"You've not accepted?" Pliny says, his voice sharp.

"He's the consul. I hardly felt it polite to refuse." Paulinus thinks of the show Vestinus made on the square earlier, marching to preside over the senate, led by his twelve lictors. His own time as consul had been brief – Paulinus was brought in only because the appointed consul died – but he still remembers the immense pride and majesty of the office.

"I still don't think it's wise," Pliny mutters, and Paulinus does not need to ask why. Tigellinus has already been sniffing around Vestinus, trying to implicate him in the Piso plot, but the consul's only crime is being married to Messalina, Nero's mistress.

"A man who is ruled by fear dies a thousand times before his death," Paulinus says as they stroll back towards the Palatine, thick with scaffolding and building work. "If I live that way, where does it stop?"

Pliny raises his eyebrows. "That's quite the closing argument, but we are not in court now. And I'm not sure a *dinner invitation* is worth such a stand." They pass the house of the Vestal Virgins, which is being repaired for fire damage. "I suppose you will stop here, rather than return home with me?"

Paulinus looks fondly at his old friend. For the past few months, Pliny has been his host while his own house is rebuilt, and he is aware of how trying it must be for such a fastidious man to put up with all the clutter Paulinus saved from the fire, which now lies piled across several rooms. "I think so. Vestinus's house is only a short walk away."

"I will wait up for you," Pliny says, and Paulinus realises then that his friend must truly be anxious.

"Really, there's no need—"

Pliny waves a hand in dismissal. "There's that text on the habitat of dragons you gave me, which I'm eager to read. So I will be awake anyway."

Paulinus watches Pliny cross the square, soon lost to sight in the crowd, aware his friend is more of a brother than his own will ever be.

It does not take long for Paulinus to regret accepting the invitation. He is stuck on a couch with Vitellius, a vain former consul who he has never liked, and the man spends the entire evening berating him for not drinking enough, while getting completely smashed himself. To make things even less pleasant, Vestinus and Messalina appear to have had a row before their guests' arrival, and several people do not turn up.

Vestinus is only a slight acquaintance, and this is the first time Paulinus has been to his house. The meal itself is luxurious, as he would expect a consul to offer, and the solid silver dining ware is covered in erotic images, which makes for a dependable – if wearisome – source of jokes. Paulinus finds it hard not to stare at Messalina, curious about the woman who caught Nero's eye. She is pretty, but also ordinary, not striking like Solina, who remains the most astonishing woman Paulinus has ever seen. He suspects Vestinus's lack of concern at his wife's fidelity may be connected to the attractive slave boys with bare, oiled torsos who lurk in every corner of the room.

One of the boys is warbling a closing song to entertain the guests, and Paulinus is hopeful his escape home is near, when the sound of shouting drifts in from the atrium. The boy's singing stutters to a halt as armed soldiers from the Praetorian Guard burst into the dining room.

"Marcus Julius Vestinus," one declares, turning to the host with the aggression of a bull. "You are wanted by the commander."

Vestinus sets down his glass. "For what cause?"

"For building an army in full view of the Forum, turning your very home into a citadel to rival Caesar."

"An army?" Messalina exclaims, jumping to her feet. "But that's absurd! Where are the soldiers?"

"All around us," the guard says, sweeping his hand towards the gaggle of terrified, half-naked boys.

Beside him, Paulinus hears Vitellius give a drunken snort. "I'd like to see any of *them* take on a legion."

"This is not a laughing matter," the soldier bellows, making the drunken Vitellius lurch in surprise. "Or are you amused by a plot against Caesar? Perhaps you are part of it." He looks round at the rest of the room. "Perhaps you *all* are."

The silence which falls is cold as the tomb. Vestinus stands, pushing in front of his wife. "There is no need to take me to the commander. I will make the necessary arrangements here."

Paulinus feels obliged to intervene. "The consul has the right to due process," he begins. "If there is an accusation of—"

"No," Vestinus says, raising a hand to stop him. "I do not wish any of you to be involved." He turns to the soldiers. "My guests have done nothing wrong beyond accepting an innocent invitation to dinner. I would ask that they all be released to go home now."

"You no longer have the authority to make such demands," the soldier retorts. "My orders are that the guests stay."

Vestinus is visibly sweating, even though he is trying to appear calm. "Very well," he says curtly. He beckons one of the quivering slave boys over. "You will fetch the doctor. Tell him to bring his tools for blood-letting."

At this Messalina can no longer contain her distress. She flings herself at the soldier, clutching his arm. "Let me go to Caesar! Please! There is a mistake, let me go to him! He cannot want this! Let me speak to him!"

For the first time, the man looks uncomfortable. He must know her position in Nero's life. "My orders are that nobody leaves. Even you, mistress."

She collapses onto the floor, sobbing. "This is my fault," she wails. "If I had not—"

Her husband kneels beside her, cutting her off before she can say anything incriminating. "Hush, my love. Enough. We have a son. Whatever you must do, I forgive you. Do you understand?"

Messalina's sobbing grows wilder, and Paulinus's heart begins to race, not with fear but with rage. If he had not despised Nero before, this scene would be enough to earn his eternal loathing. Vestinus attempts to comfort his wife a little longer, helping her over to a couch to sit beside his sister. Eventually he lets go of both women, moving towards the door. Messalina becomes completely hysterical, understanding what this means.

"I must leave you to set my affairs in order," Vestinus says to his guests. "Please forgive my absence." He walks from the room, flanked by two of Nero's guards.

All the guests are now sitting upright, nobody having the stomach either to eat or recline, knowing that upstairs their host will shortly enact his own execution. Paulinus looks between their frightened faces, hating them and himself for such enforced cowardice. "Could you not allow the women some privacy in their grief?" he asks the soldiers, gesturing at Vestinus's weeping wife and sister. "This is unnecessarily cruel. And there is a child in the house."

The soldier in charge does not look at him. "My orders are that nobody leaves the room."

"For how long?" one of the other guests pipes up.

The soldier says nothing.

"Well," Vitellius drawls, helping himself to more wine. "We may as well drink. If not to our host's health, then to his swift and painless exit."

At this, Messalina jumps to her feet, rushing towards the guards, trying to wrestle her way past. "You tactless fool," Paulinus hisses at Vitellius. Then seeing nobody else is standing to help Vestinus' wife, he walks over, laying his hand on her shoulder. "Mistress, your husband would not want this. You must think of your son, as he asked you to do."

"But he's alone up there," she cries. "I can't bear it."

"Perhaps it is easier for him that way. He has made his decision, and it is an honourable one. You must trust him."

Messalina returns to the couch, lying face down, so that she does not have to look at any of the guests. Paulinus sits back beside Vitellius, wondering how Messalina will cope when Nero next calls for her, knowing her lover killed her husband, and she cannot even reproach him for it. He wonders too, if all the guests will now be killed like their host. The thought of his own death is not frightening, but it fills him with impotent rage. It would be the most senseless way to die, on the whim of a despot, with his own life so desperately unfulfilled. He would leave no child, no legacy save the grief of his friends, and the total abandonment of the woman Nortia chose for him. His entire existence would be for nothing. For a *dinner party*, just as Pliny said. It makes him want to punch the wall in anger. Being held captive against his will, even for an evening, is so completely maddening. Paulinus cannot imagine how Solina ever endured it, or how she endures it still.

He stares up at the ceiling, painted with scenes of Zeus and Ganymede. Above the frolicking gods, Vestinus is ending his own life rather than suffer the humiliation of torture and execution. Perhaps he is already gone.

Nero clearly enjoys dangling the threat of death after dinner, as Vestinus's guests are held captive for the entire night. Despite the tension, some manage to nod off as the hours drag on, and Vitellius snores loudly, knocked out by the wine. Paulinus stays awake, wanting to show respect for the shade of their dead host. When they are finally released, Messalina rushes from the room, desperate to reach her husband, perhaps vainly hoping he is still alive. The sound of her screams, echoing down the stairs, reverberates in Paulinus's ears as he steps from the house into the light of dawn.

The air, cool on his face, is a relief. He stands on the threshold of the dead consul's house, still steeped in horror. Below him stretches one of the finest views in Rome – a panorama of the Forum, already filling with people, the rising sun turning the marble pink, and beyond it the glorious temples of the Capitol climbing the hill, shining white and gold. Vestinus passed through this sacred place in the full majesty of his office, only yesterday. How little any of it meant. Paulinus begins his descent, walking back to Pliny's house, already looking forward to embracing his friend.

42

SOLINA

The flurry of deaths that follow a foiled plot to kill Nero feels endless. Paranoia consumes the court. Nero seems genuinely shaken anyone would wish to depose him, despite the cruelty he has so liberally inflicted on others, and where before he was oblivious, now he sees assassins everywhere. Guilt is not always required for the sword to fall; sometimes envy or spite is enough, with Poppaea and Tigellinus behind the most malicious false accusations.

Still, Caesar's murderous mood may serve my purposes, given how swiftly he is turning on former favourites. The man has already rid himself of one wife. All I need to do is ensure he divorces another.

I have neither the ear of Nero nor Poppaea, and no hope of gaining either. My poison must come from another source. When I stand for hours in service, I no longer daydream but listen, the same way I once pressed my face to the door of my prison, with the same determination I once felt in training with Riomanda. Anything which might bring discord between Nero and Poppaea is valuable.

I discover that he has become anxious about her fidelity, and knowing he divorced Octavia on a false charge of adultery, I wait days for an opportunity to add to this fear. When one of the men at the court forgets to replace a ring he removed at dinner, I plant it in Poppaea's rooms where Nero will find it. They have a furious row, but their relationship has always been volatile, and they soon make up again.

Poppaea's temper remains as fiery as her husband's, and so I sow discord in the other direction too, repeating gossip I have heard of Nero spending money at the races, all within earshot of favoured maids who I suspect will report this to their mistress. Sometimes the things I drip feed are not even true, adding to Nero's sense he has married a shrew.

But then Poppaea falls pregnant again, and I despair of his ever divorcing her. The only way I might be rid of her now is if she is guilty of treason, and hard as I look, I see little sign of that.

The Golden House is taking shape. As the weather brightens, Poppaea leads her maids to the gardens, to watch the green being planted with spring flowers. The scent of narcissi is sweet; they are sprinkled over the grounds, white as stars. Ordinary Romans are invited to attend too, as part of Tigellinus's scheme to endear the people to the Emperor's vastly expanded palace by making it a public park. I am with Henna and Frida, since we now form a trio of foreign fair-haired attendants, and together we loiter, watching desperate people trying to press their petitions into the hands of the Empress – or at the very least her maids.

One woman looks especially distraught; her face is scratched, perhaps by her own nails, and her hair is wild where she has torn it loose. With a jolt, I realise I know her. It is Polla. Her husband Lucan was recently ordered to kill himself, one of many implicated in Piso's plot against Nero. I slow down, leaving Henna and Frida behind, allowing Polla to press close enough to reach me.

"Solina," she exclaims, clasping my hand. I can feel the crackle of papyrus against my palm. "I want you to take my husband's last verses to Caesar and tell him *I* sent them. You must do this for me."

Polla looks almost deranged with grief. I know what these last verses contain: a character assassination of Nero. They are famously one of the reasons Lucan is dead. I swiftly stuff the scrap of papyrus down my front, as if smoothing down my tunic. "There are quicker ways to kill yourself," I say.

"I want it to be through the words of my beloved," she replies, her tears starting to fall.

I embrace Polla tightly, so that my lips are pressed against her ear. "Listen to me," I say. "You must live. Who else will ensure your husband's immortality, if not you? Who else will finish his great poem on the nature of war? Only *you*, Polla." I think of Tigellinus's words, *no man is worth dying for*, but I do not repeat them, knowing she will not listen. "Promise me you will not harm yourself."

Polla steps back from me. "I am not worthy of completing his work."

I gaze at her, remembering my father, and the absolute authority with which he delivered his visions, instilling belief into all who heard him speak. "I have seen it," I say. "Through the black eye of the crow. Your husband's words, etched into the heavens, yours the hand to set them there."

She looks at me in wonder, then a flicker of fear crosses her face. "And the verses—"

"Will be destroyed," I reply before she can finish. I nod to her as a gesture of farewell, wanting to move away before we attract attention. In the mill of people, we are easily lost, but not if I linger too long. I walk back to join the other maids, some of whom are proudly clutching the petitions they have been given for Poppaea. When one asks if I were given one too, I say that no, I was merely accosted by a madwoman.

If any words spell the end of Poppaea, they are those written on the papyrus roll I now carry against my skin. Nero would surely never forgive his wife for owning such a poem. I need to take great care in choosing the moment when I plant the bait. This is a blade so deadly it might cut any who touch it; the words of a dead traitor, written in his own hand.

I pay even greater attention to the bedtime routine of Nero and Poppaea, noting which belongings of hers he tends to rifle through when a fit of jealousy is upon him. He is often moved to do this after she has accused him of something, as a form of retaliation. If possible, I need to plant this poem at a time when they are already bickering.

Then there are the practicalities. I am never alone in the Imperial bedrooms, but the times when it is only Henna and Frida with me are the safest. Neither are very observant, and I would be surprised if either woman wishes me harm. This means my best chance is in the morning, when we clear up, and when there is some excuse to handle Poppaea's belongings.

Above all, my scheming can only come to pass through the Empress's own command. I am obliged to wait until she decides to wear yellow, the colour she once assigned to me. The colour of good luck.

The evening we are next called to sleep on Poppaea's floor, Henna and Frida grumble about the uncomfortable night ahead. I join in their complaints to avoid suspicion, as we wander along the winding corridors to the Imperial bedroom.

The feel of the papyrus rolled into my tunic has become so familiar, and I have guarded it so closely, it is almost a wrench to let it go. Such a fragile object could easily be lost without ever drawing Nero's attention. And even if it fulfils the task I intend, I must still rely on Paulinus to keep his word to free me. So much could go wrong.

Poppaea is already in bed when we arrive, and her husband is not yet present. Perhaps he is lying with Messalina or Fabius tonight. This is a potential obstacle. I need it to be Nero, not Poppaea, who finds the verses. I glance over at her. The Empress is resting against the white covers, her face glowing in the soft light of an oil lamp, her hand caressing her stomach. It unsettles me to see her so vulnerable. I try to remember how little pity Poppaea had for Ressona, the way she mocked the dead Octavia, and how my own chances of freedom or family will die if I remain here. I have been cornered like a wild animal; there is no place for compassion in a cage.

I settle down into a corner with Frida and Henna. We are not so favoured to sleep like dogs at the foot of Poppaea's soft bed – another maid has been given that privilege, one of her favourites. I hope the girl leaves early tomorrow, or I will have to hide the scroll another day.

We all wait for Nero, but he does not come. Eventually, Poppaea has the light put out. I can hear her crying in the dark, but nobody comforts her, since even those who might pity the Empress will be afraid of earning a slap for their impertinence. After a while, she falls silent. I watch the shadows creep across the gilded ceiling, chasing pale slivers of moonlight. The breathing of all the women in the room gradually shifts, until I am the only one awake. Stress combines with the hard floor to rob me of sleep, yet I suppose I must finally drift off, because Henna wakes me at dawn.

The three of us rise silently, not wishing to disturb Poppaea, but needing to look ready to serve her whenever she opens her eyes. It is punishable for slaves to sleep past their masters. Exhaustion makes me lightheaded, but I stand with the others at the windows, poised to open them the moment Poppaea stirs, as if the sun rose only for her. We do not have to wait long. The pregnancy wakes her early to pee.

The moments that follow have the outward appearance of calm routine, yet inside I am a seething mass of suppressed tension. We dress Poppaea in yellow, moving in tandem, keeping total silence. She stands still as a doll, though I see her brow pucker with dislike when she watches me straighten her hem. Then she moves to her dressing room to have her hair curled, the favourite maid trailing after her. I move swiftly. While Henna and Frida make the bed, I pretend to straighten the table with her most personal belongings, including a small pile of letters and poetry written by her husband. With a quick glance to make sure Henna and Frida are busy, I slip Lucan's verses in among them.

Then the three of us leave, stepping out into the corridor to return to the servants' corridor. The rising sun pours through the windows, lighting up the marble. It is done. All I can do now is wait.

In the palace gardens, some of the slave children are playing, shrieking between fountains and shrubs. They are an exotic collection Poppaea has gathered from across the world, and when she remembers their existence, she enjoys dressing them in colourful clothes, or feeding them sweets, like pets. Henna, Frida and I have been left to look after them for the afternoon, and it is a painful task, though one that helps distract me from brooding on Lucan's scroll. Some of the children cling, desperate for a mother figure, while others are feral, distrusting every adult they meet. None act like the Iceni children I remember. I think of Senovara, the way she stopped my mother's chariot, her utter fearlessness. These slave children are better fed, yet they are brutalised. Henna and Frida chase the littler ones round and round the pond, while I sit on a bench, holding a crying boy who has clambered onto my knee.

Over the noise, I become aware of another, more distant, commotion. It is screaming, gradually growing louder. The knot of anxiety in my stomach tightens at the sound. Then a gaggle of Poppaea's maids spill out onto the green, scattering like a murmuration of starlings, drawing the children into their hysteria. The little boy turns to look at me, eyes wide with curiosity, then he scrambles from my knee. My hope rises as I join the chaos. Can Poppaea have been banished already? Everyone is so eager to know what is happening I do not even have to draw attention to myself by asking questions.

"The Empress is dead," one of the girls tells Henna, breathlessly.

"She had a blazing row with Nero," another girl adds, gleeful at the gossip. "We all heard them screaming. Then Fabius says he shoved her so hard, she tripped and fell all the way down the stairs." A couple of the maid's companions try to shush her, but the girl is in full flow and ignores them, raising her voice instead. "Now he's crying about it, threatening to kill himself with remorse."

I do not have to disguise my shock. I wanted to be rid of Poppaea, but not like this. I imagined Nero would keep his child and divorce her, perhaps executing his wife later, like Octavia. This feels like a shameful way to have killed my enemy.

Frida sees my expression and puts her arm around me, mistaking my guilt for sadness. "Remember Ressona," she whispers. I glance at the other women. A few are genuinely crying, Poppaea's favourites who either loved her or enjoyed their position, but most are dry-eyed, their hysteria closer to excitement than grief. None of the other maids plotted Poppaea's end as I did, but few will mourn her death either.

"Yes," I say to Frida, steeling myself against remorse. "Ressona."

She nods, pleased I have understood, a fierce look in her eyes. I think of Frida's kingdom, Germania, and of all the suffering she must have seen Rome inflict. She will have prayed for vengeance, just as I did. I am wrong to pity Poppaea. I called upon Andraste the Indestructible to free me, and I cannot question how the most brutal of all the gods chose to answer my prayer. My enemy is dead, and I survive. The thought brings me a surge of savage satisfaction, as dark as the rage I once felt riding down the defeated soldiers of the Ninth. *May the bones of my enemies rot un-mourned.*

Guards are now coming into the gardens to quell the wailing, ordering everyone back inside. I walk with the other enslaved women and children, tilting my head to look up at the sky. A flock of birds fly across the blinding light of the sun, black as crows. Boudicca is dead, but I have brought my mother's vengeance to the heart of Rome.

43

PAULINUS

"You have little respect for the Empress to come for her belongings while her body is barely cold." Tigellinus looks haggard in the lamplight, picking fretfully at his cloak.

The study where they sit is all too familiar to Paulinus, the inlaid marble walls as immovable to his petitions over the years as the wretched man sitting before him. Yet this time Paulinus's opponent has lost his most valuable ally. Tigellinus must be feeling weaker now Poppaea is gone, a vulnerability Paulinus intends to exploit.

"I have every respect for the Empress," Paulinus replies. "All of Rome mourns her. But nobody here will miss one of her maids, especially at such a time. I'm sure Nero must have no desire to look at Solina and be reminded of the woman she no longer serves."

"I will think on it."

"No." Paulinus's voice is cold. "You have had long enough to think. I respected the Empress's claim to Boudicca's daughter but there is no reason for you to insult me now. Or are you careless of every remaining ally in Rome?"

"Are you threatening me over a concubine?" Tigellinus sneers.

"My loyalty to Caesar is beyond reproach," Paulinus says, allowing his anger to show, not because he has lost control of himself but because he means to intimidate. "I left Britannia without fuss, even though my recall was groundless, and I retain the respect of the legions who served with me. If Rome were threatened, I would again answer the call to defend her. My demand for Solina is wholly reasonable. Why do you obstruct my request?"

Tigellinus stares into the middle distance, as if considering. "You can have her for a hundred thousand sesterces."

It is an absurd price for a slave, but Tigellinus knows that is not what Solina represents to Paulinus. This is a hostage payment to return a lover, and like all such demands, there is no clear limit on what a man might give. As it is, Tigellinus profoundly underestimates Solina's value. "Very well," Paulinus says. "You can have a first payment of ten thousand, now, in promise of the rest." He brings out a pre-written deed of sale, scratching in the total sum and his own signature, before handing the tablet to Tigellinus. "I will wait here for her to be brought to me."

"It's the evening!" Tigellinus protests, sour at realising he could have demanded more. "She will have no time to prepare herself."

"While I appreciate your concern for her welfare, we have now agreed that she belongs to me. I intend to take her immediately."

Tigellinus makes a petulant gesture at his scribe, who has been observing their deal in silence. The man leaves to fetch Solina. "What *is* it about her?" Tigellinus asks, still curious after all this time. "She's interesting enough, but not exactly a beauty."

"She is Boudicca's daughter. Perhaps I am vain and require

a constant reminder of my victory. Or maybe I will have her train my horses."

Tigellinus looks at Paulinus sharply, as if he cannot quite believe someone so dull is capable of sarcasm. "Well, so long as you understand this whole affair was not personal. I hope we can be sensible about it, now you have the girl back again."

Paulinus smiles. "But of course."

Tigellinus smiles back, no doubt aware the former legate would cheerfully step over his dead body in a ditch.

Having waited so long, the final moments before he sees Solina are almost the worst. Paulinus is obliged to sit with Tigellinus, listening to the man's nonsense, since the prefect clearly intends to amuse himself by observing an emotional reunion. At last, the door opens, and Paulinus rises to his feet. Solina's face is blank; the only sign of fear is in her widened eyes.

"You're here," she says, her tone abrupt.

"Yes," he replies, his voice equally calm. "I've come to bring you home." Solina walks over in silence to take his hand. He realises she is shaking and grips her more tightly so Tigellinus cannot see.

"Half a million sesterces!" Tigellinus murmurs, regarding the seemingly passionless pair standing before him with a look of incredulity.

Paulinus nods, walking from the room. "You will have the second payment tomorrow."

Solina does not speak when they are in the carriage. She sits rigid beside him, clasping his fingers so tightly it hurts. When they have left the palace complex, she takes in a deep, shuddering breath.

"It's alright," he says gently. "They won't stop us. I promise you, it's over."

She tries to recover herself, wiping her hand hard against her cheek, as if ashamed of crying.

"Solina," he says, taking her face in his hands. She is in shock, and it takes her a while to focus on his eyes. Then she smiles. The joy he has been carrying like a precious, fragile object from the moment she walked into Tigellinus's room is finally safe to set down. He holds her in a crushing embrace, dizzy with relief.

"We are going to your house," she says, her voice muffled by his tunic, even though her excitement is palpable. He releases her, reality tempering his euphoria. *Pliny.*

"My house is being rebuilt after the fire," he says. "We will stay for a while with one of my dearest friends." Paulinus thinks of Pliny, who might still be in the library, where he closeted himself earlier in protest at the prospect of his new house guest. Hopefully Pliny will be more sanguine about Solina in the morning.

He looks at the woman he has fought so hard to regain. Tigellinus was spiteful to say she is not beautiful. She has the most remarkable face he has ever seen, every aspect of her is so vibrantly alive. "How did you know what to say to me before, *dearer than oak*?" she asks.

"I asked a Briton what you might have said to me in Gaul, trying to remember the sound of it." He is pleased she remembered his words. It suggests she has not lost all affection for him.

"You have not yet learned to speak all my language?"

He laughs at the *not yet*. "No."

"I will teach you," she replies, confident of his acquiescence. Paulinus is not sure he will find her determination so endearing if she persists with this idea, but right now everything about her delights him. He had felt uncertain about what might happen when he regained possession of Solina, for so long she has only been an idea rather than a real woman to him. But all he feels is happiness.

They arrive at Pliny's house, pulling up on the moonlit street. Paulinus helps her out of the carriage, knocking for the doorman. Solina gazes up at the tall front of the villa, which is almost blank, like so many Roman houses, giving little sense of the wealth within. The tall wooden door opens inwards, and Paulinus guides her over the dimly lit threshold.

Being here is not like taking her to his own home. Not least because he is unsure how their host will behave. He tries to see the place through Solina's eyes – the walls are painted with scenes from the fall of Troy, the pool in the centre of the room is surrounded by carved marble pillars – but the place is so familiar to him, it is hard to imagine this atrium afresh. Solina stands close, still holding his hand, dark eyes wide in her pale face. She seems shy, which does not displease him, although he knows that mood is unlikely to last long. "Would you like to eat?" he asks. "I know it's late, but we can ask for something."

"I would like to be alone with you."

Her expression is hard to read; it will take time to understand her again. Paulinus does not want to assume Solina is looking at him with desire, even though he hopes she might, in time. "Of course," he says. "You must be tired."

His room in Pliny's house is on the ground floor, its now shuttered windows facing the garden. Paulinus leads Solina over the mosaic of twisting black vines, and they both wait in silence while one of Pliny's servants lights the oil lamps, sending the flames flickering over red painted walls. Then the maid leaves, closing the door. Paulinus feels uncharacteristically nervous. After wanting Solina for so long, he hopes she is still as fond of him as he remembers.

"I'm very happy you are here," he says, struggling to express the intensity of his feelings.

Solina bursts into tears. Paulinus is frozen with dismay. He thinks of Tigellinus's reluctance to hand her over. Was he too hasty in taking her? Had she given up on him after so long and grown attached to someone else? She is still gripping his hand, so he pulls her closer in a tentative embrace. Solina responds by flinging her arms around him.

"You are not sorry to be here?" he asks, kissing her forehead and smoothing her hair.

"I'm *relieved*, you fool."

Her rudeness is so much like the woman he remembers he laughs, and after a moment she starts to laugh too. Paulinus leads her to sit beside him on the bed. Once there, he is less sure how to behave. His memories of Solina as a lover are contradictory, much like Solina herself. She pursued him aggressively but had also seemed afraid at times, making him worry some of her behaviour might be bravado.

"Do you not want me?" she asks, after a moment's awkward silence.

"Of course," he exclaims, annoyed that he keeps blundering. "But I didn't want you to feel obliged, if it's too soon. I haven't seen you in so long."

"You asked me to marry you."

"If that's still what you want?"

"Why would it not be?"

Solina has twisted the bedclothes in her hands and looks anxious. He did not remember her being this vulnerable. "Then there's no rush, is there?" he says pleasantly. "We have plenty of time. Why don't we just go to sleep tonight?" He turns his back to get undressed, to spare them both embarrassment, and climbs into bed. Solina does not move. "You can always keep the dress on, if that's more comfortable."

"How could this ridiculous outfit ever be comfortable," she snaps. "But if we're both naked in bed together, I will want to lie with you, and it will be very annoying if you just fall asleep and snore."

Paulinus wants to laugh, but she looks so truculent he doesn't dare. "I promise that won't happen," he says seriously. Then he turns away, pretending to adjust the oil lamp, so she doesn't feel self-conscious undressing. Solina gets into bed beside him. His sudden awareness of her body, so close to his, makes it difficult to think of anything sensible to say. Fortunately, he does not have to, as she leans over to kiss him.

"I am also happy to be here," she says, as if she has weighed this up carefully. Then she kisses him again.

PART 4
DOMINA

"Only let them moderate their anger, and give their hearts to those to whom fortune had given their persons."
Livy, on the rape of the Sabine women, *History of Rome*

"I had horses, arms, men and wealth: what wonder if I was unwilling to lose them? If you wish to command everyone, does it really follow that everyone should accept your slavery?"
Caratacus speaking to the Emperor Claudius, as imagined by Tacitus, *Annals*

44

SOLINA

I wake before Paulinus. His hand is still warm and heavy on my flank, and I run my fingers over his arm where it lies against my body. It would be so easy to get drunk on my freedom, to imagine that because he loves me, I am safe. But I am not and never will be. He is still the same Paulinus who gave me to Poppaea and destroyed the Iceni kingdom. I would be a fool to forget this. If I am to survive marriage to such a man, I must always keep some part of myself separate, the way the Iceni used to bury our most sacred treasure deep under the earth as an unseen offering to the goddess Andraste.

I press closer to Paulinus's sleeping body, enjoying his warmth, and look about the room. It must be dawn. The light spilling from the shutters is watery and pale. Shadowy painted figures are just visible in the dim light, nymphs chased by satyrs, seemingly eager to be caught. It is exhilarating to be here, not trapped in the palace. I have wanted to escape for so long, I can scarcely believe this is real, that I never have to go back. Then I think of Frida and Henna rising alone in the room we have long shared and feel a pang of guilt. There was hardly time to say goodbye. They will imagine my escape is nothing more than chance, that it is solely down to Paulinus. I never told them of my part in Poppaea's downfall.

He shifts slightly and I glance down. I like the look of him when he is sleeping. If he were not Roman, I would not be ashamed to own such a man. I kiss him impulsively on the brow, then the cheek, then the nose, so that he wakes, at first startled and then laughing. Paulinus kisses me back, much gentler than I have been with him, and I enjoy the comforting feeling of being held.

"I'm fortunate to have such an affectionate wife," he says.

"You are very fortunate," I agree. "We must make a sacrifice to Nortia, in thanks." I pause, taking in the implications of what he has said. "Am I *already* your wife?"

"I consider you to be my wife." Paulinus traces the line of tattoos down my arm, the way I remember from before. "But it is legally complicated. Pliny is looking at all the possibilities. At the very worst, I can formally adopt our children and protect you financially. And after a man and woman have lived together a year, any union has even greater weight."

"Is this how many Roman marriages work?"

He pauses, looking uncomfortable. "No," he admits. "Only when there is a significant difference in social standing. Would it bother you very much if other people did not consider us to be married, but I did?"

I do not have to ask him whose standing other people consider to be higher. Poppaea taught me it means nothing in Rome that I am the daughter of a king. "No, it does not bother me. By Iceni custom we are already married."

Paulinus looks smug at this, and I regret giving him so much, so quickly. "You have considered me your husband all this time? Even when we were apart?" He tries to squash me in a complacent hug, but I wriggle away. "You cannot pretend not to care for me." He laughs. "Caratacus didn't only teach me how to say your words, he taught me their whole meaning."

"Caratacus was the Briton you saw?" I stare at him in astonishment. "The rebel leader?"

"Not so rebellious. Claudius pardoned him after he was brought to Rome and gave him a pension. His house was almost bigger than mine, until the fire. Sadly, he was one of its many casualties."

I try to hide my shock. I had wondered about his fate, when Caratacus never visited Poppaea in her second pregnancy, but it is still upsetting to hear he is dead. I disguise my emotion, not wanting Paulinus to realise I knew him. "What did Caratacus say?"

"He insisted no Briton would have said such a thing to me, that I must have misheard you." Paulinus is smiling, and I feel exposed, wondering what Caratacus must have thought of me, making such a sacred promise to the Roman general who defeated my mother. "He also said I would never fully understand the meaning, that there is no equivalent in Roman thinking. It isn't so much an expression of love, but of an inviolable bond, such as a parent says to a child, or a man to his wife." I feel my face flush and turn away. "What's wrong?"

I am too distressed to answer. Caratacus was my last link with my mother, and I had hoped to speak with him again one day, to understand whatever relationship the two of them shared. Now I will never know, and it feels like I have lost another part of her. And to make it worse, the last thing Caratacus ever knew of me, Catia's daughter, is that I had made a Roman man my family. Manipulating the enemy is one thing; caring for them is another.

Paulinus moves me gently so that I am facing him again and pulls my hands from my face. When he sees my expression, he smiles, mistaking my grief for shyness. "Don't be embarrassed,

Solina. There's no reason to be ashamed. I feel the same way about you too."

He does not understand that this is impossible.

We take bread and sweet wine in our host's winter dining room, both ravenous with hunger. It is a bright, pleasant space, covered in paintings of wild birds. Pliny himself is yet to appear. I have washed in water the maid brought but am still wearing the strange fantasy robes from my life at court, since Paulinus did not think to buy any other clothes ahead of my arrival. The sight of my tattoos seems to make him anxious, and he keeps fiddling with the fabric of my dress, trying to hide them, until I snap at him to stop, and he holds his hands up in apology.

"Does Pliny always sleep late?" I ask.

"No. He barely sleeps at all. I expect he's been in the library for hours already."

"You have been friends a long time?"

"For a lifetime."

His tension is contagious, and I am about to tell him to stop jogging his leg in such an annoying way when our absent host finally appears. Paulinus is instantly on his feet, so I also rise.

The moment I see Pliny, I know. This man is blessed with the sight. I gawp at him, never having seen a Roman marked out by the gods in this way before. "This is Solina," Paulinus is saying, ushering me forwards. Pliny turns to me, and his eyes are dark mirrors to the Otherworld.

"The Druid," he says, his voice unfriendly.

"My wife," Paulinus corrects him.

"You *are* the Druid," I say to Pliny, lapsing into my own language without thinking.

He turns to Paulinus, irritated. "You said she spoke Latin?"

"I do," I say flustered. "It's just you look like...." I stop. Romans are never pleased to be compared to Druids. "You look like my father." It is the closest I can get to the truth, even though their features are nothing alike.

"How touching," Pliny says. "Though since Prasutagus was surely older than me at the conquest of Britannia twenty years ago, not all that flattering."

Paulinus looks from Pliny to me, too flummoxed to add anything. "My father had the sight," I say to Pliny. "He was gifted in divination."

"I prefer observation, myself. It tends to be a better means of getting at the truth than slicing open livers. At least in my experience." Pliny smiles, watching me with his strange, unsettling eyes. "But *you* have the gift of sight, do you not? You have promised my friend a son."

"*Pliny*," Paulinus says, a note of warning in his voice.

This man knows I lied, that much is obvious. But he is also a Druid who is blind to his own gifts, so he will be left stumbling after me in the dark. "It is true," I say, staring Pliny down. "I will indeed give Paulinus a son."

Pliny looks ready for a retort but Paulinus interrupts. "Solina told me she would be delighted to answer any of your questions about Britannia or its artefacts," he says, even though I have said no such thing. "And I'm sure she would be fascinated to see the library."

Pliny looks as enthused by this idea as I feel. "Very well."

"I will join you both shortly," Paulinus is still addressing Pliny rather than me. "I need to pay Tigellinus. And I will instruct one of your maids to buy something sensible for Solina to wear. I suppose your neighbour Gaius might lend me one of his wife's maids to dress her hair."

I have no great interest in clothes, beyond a

never-to-be-fulfilled desire to wear trousers again, but it is still galling to have two men discuss how I must dress as if I were not even here. It reminds me of Poppaea, the way she treated me like a doll. Pliny looks me up and down, nodding in agreement. "Blue would suit her," he says.

I flush with annoyance, feeling certain Pliny must know the Roman insult *blue-faced Britons*. "I want to choose my own clothes," I say to Paulinus.

He kisses me on the head. "Next time. But you cannot go out dressed like this." He strides off into the atrium, leaving me choked with frustration.

Pliny looks even less friendly now Paulinus is gone, if such a thing were possible. "I don't know if you have ever been in a library before," he says. "But I would ask you not to touch anything."

I cannot think of a polite reply, so I stay silent, and follow him as he heads towards the gardens. His library is the entire length of one of the colonnades, huge and floodlit from high windows, like a vast, beautiful temple. To my surprise, as soon as we enter, I see a chunk of my father's carved door is mounted on the wall. "That is mine!" I exclaim, laying my hand on the wood.

"It once belonged to your family," Pliny corrects me. "But given your relationship to Paulinus, it is rightfully his. And since he gave it to me, that now makes it mine." He sounds pedantic rather than malicious but is no less annoying for this. I glare at him. Pliny raises his eyebrows. "Perhaps you would prefer to wait for your husband elsewhere, since my company is clearly so disagreeable."

"No," I say, curious now to see which of my family's other treasures might be here.

Pliny looks sceptical, but ushers me out of the way, so that he can reach into a chest of drawers. He brings out a golden object. My mother's torc. The sight of it makes me gasp. "Paulinus told me this belonged to your mother, but he had nothing of interest to add beyond that. Would you be willing to describe its significance?"

"What do you mean?" I stare at the torc, both longing and dreading to hold it in my hands.

Pliny sighs. "Its *meaning*. Symbolic, mythological and political."

I gesture for him to hand it over. The gold is heavy in my hands. I think of my mother wearing it – how it shone in the flames when she sat laughing beside my father at the hearth, the flash of it as she carried the torch to burn the temple of Camulodunum, the sight of it around her neck, the last time I saw her alive. "*Forgive me*," I murmur, the only words I have ever felt able to say to my mother's spirit. I speak to her in my own language, so Pliny cannot understand.

My eyes smart, but I cannot cry in front of my enemy. With my fingertip, I trace the thick gold threads which are woven together to form the torc. "These represent the five highest qualities of mortal life," I say. "That is honour, courage, truth, loyalty and wisdom. My mother possessed all these gifts. The pattern of the rope also represents a warrior's duties to family, the gods, the people, and the land, as these are the sacred ties that bind us as one. The two spheres at the end of the torc represent our mortal world and the Otherworld, close together but not touching." I look up from the gold in my hands to stare at Pliny. "You ask for its political meaning. The torc is always open as a statement of freedom. Only a slave would wear a closed collar around the neck."

"That is interesting." Pliny stretches out his hand for me to return the precious relic of my mother. I hesitate before giving it to him, reluctant to let go. It is so heavy. I realise it is the weight of my own failure. The kingdom I was born to protect lies in ruins, its people enslaved. Nothing I do will ever atone for this. "The craftsmanship is exceptional." Pliny holds the torc up to examine it. "Truly exquisite."

I feel a flicker of warmth towards him for his admiration. "It was made on the Street of Gold, in our capital city. For generations, the most skilled of the Iceni jewellers crafted treasures there."

"Your capital was the City of the Horse?" I nod in agreement, before realising Pliny is reaching curiously towards the mark of the horse on my arm, as if I were no less an object than the torc in his hands. At the press of his finger on my skin, I flinch.

"*Do not touch me*," I hiss, instinctively raising my hand in warning that I will strike him.

Pliny steps back, red with anger and embarrassment. "Paulinus is one of my dearest friends. I was curious about the design, that is all. You cannot imagine I would ever insult him by attempting anything improper."

"You miss the point," I snarl, so full of rage he takes another step back. "You insult *me*."

I storm from the library, running across the garden to shut myself into my husband's room. Before I can reach it, Paulinus himself calls to me from the atrium.

"Solina!" he exclaims, hurrying over. "What is it?"

"Ask Pliny." My arm shakes with anger as I point to the library's open door.

Paulinus hesitates, his hand resting on my shoulder, as if he doesn't want to leave me alone. "Very well. Wait here."

I do not obey him. When he is inside, I creep over to listen to their conversation.

"... *of course* I know you meant nothing by it," Paulinus is saying. "But you must understand Solina can be very innocent, even naïve. And she takes her loyalty to me extremely seriously. In her eyes I have been her husband ever since we first lay together. I imagine it's some Iceni custom or other, that I am the only man entitled to touch her."

This is utter nonsense. He has completely garbled what I attempted to tell him earlier. But I am reassured he is at least defending me, even if he has not understood *why* I was offended. Pliny on the other hand, is unimpressed. "*Innocent?*" he scoffs. "The girl has ridden into battle alongside hundreds of men. And anyone who wasn't completely infatuated would understand she must have lain with Nero, Tigellinus and who knows how many others. She is deceiving you."

"I don't believe she is deceiving me," Paulinus says calmly. "I would be surprised if Solina has had other lovers, but in any case, why should it matter? Does Vespasian care about Antonia's past? If this were important to me, I would have chosen a different woman."

"You cannot compare the two," Pliny says. "Antonia is highly intelligent and has been nothing but discreet. Solina was publicly and infamously dishonoured. Her rape is the reason her mother started a war."

His words set off a ringing in my ears. The horror of the attack is suddenly so close, and so overwhelming, it is like a wolf at my throat. I don't want to be here, I don't want to hear this, but I cannot move. I reach out to touch the wall and slide down it, unsteady on my feet. "She was a defenceless girl," Paulinus is saying. "I do not hold her responsible for what happened. It pains me to hear you speak this way."

"I don't doubt it was entirely tragic, and she is to be pitied. But you cannot imagine such an atrocity left her with her honour intact…"

"Enough." Paulinus finally sounds angry. "I love you as a brother, but I cannot hear you speak of my wife in this way. I ask you to apologise to Solina as you would have done to Fulvia."

I should move from the door so Paulinus does not know I have been listening, but I am crying too much and cannot stand. I see his boots through my tears, then he is crouching down to lift me to my feet. "You should not have heard that," he says.

We walk back to his room, and he closes the door. I curl up on the bed in a ball, unable to look at him. Everything hurts. I have never spoken to Paulinus about the attack, and part of me hoped he didn't know. The darkness I have tried so hard to lock away has just been ripped loose, all the ugly fragments scattered around me, tainting everything they touch. I feel the bed dip as Paulinus sits on it. I want to tell him that I was unarmed, that I was outnumbered, that I do not even remember most of what happened, but I cannot form the words or the will to say any of this. Paulinus lies down and holds me, so I can feel his presence but do not have to face him. "It is not true that I have no honour," I manage to croak out. "I regained it. Weeks later. I killed one of the men who attacked me."

"Please, Solina, don't speak of it. I wish you hadn't heard."

It hurts me that he does not say he knows I am not dishonoured. I turn to face him. "And I did not have any lovers at court." As I say the words, I almost wish that I had. I wish I had married an Iceni warrior when I was free, I wish Paulinus were not the man I have chosen. He gathers me close, misunderstanding the reason for my grief.

"Hush," he says. "I believe you, my darling. Don't upset yourself." I cry into his chest, soaking his tunic, his love both a cause and comfort for my distress. "I did not know you had killed one of the men," he says, and I go still, wondering if he will guess this was the body he discovered on Andraste's altar. Paulinus holds me tighter. "I hope his death was agony."

45

SOLINA

It is so long since I walked freely down a street. As Poppaea's slave I was confined to whichever palace in which she wanted to store me, an object like her silk dresses or the chests of my family's gold. Even though it is years since I left Britain, it is not until after my marriage that I truly see Rome. As soon as dawn breaks, when I hear the wooden shop fronts clattering open, I want to be out of the house. At first Paulinus is indulgent of my excitement. He walks with me early in the morning, before he leaves for the Forum or to oversee the rebuilding of his house, enjoying my happiness, describing everything we pass so that I might understand it all.

The street where we are staying grows familiar to me. Stepping outside Pliny's heavy wooden doors, I face a nest of snakes on the opposite wall, a colourful painting to mark the entrance of a shrine to Salus, Goddess of Safety, which billows incense onto the road, and sometimes into the hallway of the house. The pavement is crowded, and people call to one another from balconies above, which hang with pots and flowers. Everything is colour and noise, everyone has something to sell. Sometimes Rome reminds me of the lost Town of the Wolf – the same press of people, the same sense of so many lives. And yet it is different. When Paulinus takes me to a goldsmith, buying me a ring of two interlocked hands to show I now belong to him, I cry. He holds me, thinking it is because I am moved by his love, but it is not. I weep because I am reminded of the Street of Gold, all the beauty and skill that was destroyed.

After a week, he takes me to the Forum, because I am eager to understand what he does now he is not a warrior. It is a mistake. I am not awed by the basilica after living in the palace, and I dislike being surrounded by so many men. They have sneering faces, hidden behind smiles, and I know they are laughing at my husband, that even though I am swathed in the clothes of a Roman matron, they only see a savage. Paulinus grips my hand, and I know he feels it too, that perhaps he is ashamed, not of them but of me.

He does not take me out as often after this. I am obliged to ask one of the slaves to go with me when he is working, because it is not considered proper for me to be out alone. My suffocation builds. We are guests in a house where the host despises me and the truce Paulinus arranges does little to improve things. Pliny apologises for offending my sensibilities, repeating my husband's absurd ideas about Iceni modesty, and I feel obliged to accept. This allows Paulinus to believe I should be pleased to wear the cumbersome robes he buys which hide every inch of my body, as if I had not spent most of my life on horseback wearing tunics and trousers. He cannot understand why I hate it so much. But the clothes are more proof there is no role for me here. Women in Rome are not like the Iceni. They cannot be warriors, or Druids, or leaders; their only domain is the home. And this one is not mine.

*

In the evenings, the three of us dine together. Listening to Pliny and Paulinus gossip, I learn Nero has married Messalina, but shortly afterwards he causes outrage by castrating a boy who looks like Poppaea, calling him Sporus or *seed* in mockery of his mutilation, and dressing him as his dead wife. I imagine this is poor Fabius. Pliny and Paulinus debate this scandal at length without asking for my opinion, even though I know Fabius and have surely seen more of Nero than they ever will. Sometimes I wonder what the two men would do if they discovered I had a hand in Poppaea's death. It is not a secret I will ever tell.

One evening when they begin to lament the fate of Octavia, I cannot resist interrupting. "I brought Octavia's head to Poppaea," I say, startling them both. "She asked for it to be given to her on a gold platter."

"Why you?" Pliny asks.

I am busy helping myself to the roast pigeon, so have an excuse not to look at him. "She wanted the other British girl to bring it, because Ressona had been one of Octavia's maids. I offered to go instead, to spare Ressona distress."

"That was brave of you, Solina," Paulinus says, and I can hear the pride in his voice.

"I suppose a human head would not be such an unusual sight for you as a Druid," Pliny remarks, making me wonder if my husband's affection has provoked him to spite.

"Nobody uses the *head* for divination," I retort. "Any power of prophecy lies in the heart." I realise from his smile that I have blundered straight into a trap, as Paulinus now looks disgusted. I feel infuriated with them both. "You despise what you cannot understand," I say, stabbing angrily at my food.

"Then perhaps you would like to explain your sacred rites to us," Pliny says. "I am keen to be enlightened."

I look at Paulinus, expecting him to intervene, but he is

gazing at the glass in his hand. "I am not ashamed of anything I have done to serve the gods," I say. "Nor do I feel the need to explain myself to those who will not hear me."

"But you have never taken part in human sacrifice," Paulinus says, looking up at me. "Have you?"

His mouth is drawn into an anxious line, and I wonder how long he has sat with this question. My heart beats faster, knowing how much of his regard for me might rest on the answer. I lay my hand over his. "I swear to you by the sacred memory of my parents, that I have only ever killed in the same way you have, in armed combat, or in the heat of battle." Paulinus nods, looking reassured if not delighted.

"Well, that's heartening," Pliny says. "The only men to die at your hand were our countrymen slaughtered in a rebellion against Rome."

"Enough now," Paulinus says wearily. "Please. Can the pair of you not be civil?"

We finish our meal in silence. I know Paulinus is annoyed with Pliny, but this does not feel like a victory. The more Pliny demeans me, the more I fear my husband will come to see me through his friend's eyes.

One of the few places I experience a sense of peace in this house is in the gardens. The Romans do not revere nature as the Iceni do. They try to tame it into obedience, until it holds only a pale shadow of its true power, but even this is better than nothing. I sit by the painted roses on the colonnade, looking out over neat rows of mint and lavender. When I close my eyes and breathe in, I can almost believe I am truly outside, rather than trapped in this strange indoor version of a field. I crush some of Pliny's herbs together, then hold them to my nose, inhaling their scent. It helps with the nausea.

Driven by the need to feel closer to him, I have lain with Paulinus almost every night. I expected to fall pregnant quickly, but this still feels like a shock, just two months into our life together. It should make me happy, yet I am afraid. I do not want to have a child here, in my enemy's house. Pliny may not understand the powers he holds as a blinded Druid, but I do. His hatred will carry a weight beyond that possessed by other men. Anxiety makes the roiling in my stomach even worse, and I crumple more herbs, desperate to get rid of the nausea. I feel much sicker than I did for the last pregnancy. I will have to tell Paulinus soon, or he will guess.

"*You have a visitor, domina.*"

It is the voice of Secundus, Pliny's steward. I open my eyes to find him hovering like a hawk. I do not trust the man; he is always watching me with his sharp eyes. "A visitor?" I repeat. "That is impossible. I have no friends."

"It is Polla Argentaria."

Lucan's widow. I stand up, flustered. The last time I saw her, I was enslaved and used her as the means to destroy Poppaea. "Where would it be proper for Paulinus's wife to greet a woman friend?" I ask, not caring that Secundus will guess my ignorance of Roman customs. I do not want Pliny to have any cause to tell my husband I have shamed him.

"The garden is entirely suitable on such a fine day," he replies. "You have no need to move."

I sit back down, gripping the edge of the stone bench, as Secundus goes to fetch Polla. At the sight of her, I rise again, holding my hands out in greeting as I once watched Poppaea do. I hope it is not a gesture of superiority. Polla takes my hands and kisses me three times on each cheek. I am a little startled, since we were only slight acquaintances before, and I was far beneath her. As we both sit, a large satchel she is carrying thumps into my thigh. "Congratulations on your marriage," she says.

"Thank you." I am uncertain what is expected from a visit like this. Polla is no less strange looking than before, with her huge eyes and dream-like air, but rather than repel me, her manner is reassuring. Part of her oddity means she has never seemed to hold the same prejudices so many Romans have towards Britons.

"I will bring refreshments," Secundus says, since I have forgotten to request any.

"I hope your husband is kind." Polla watches the steward leave. "And that this was both a marriage and a man that you wanted"

"Yes. I care for him." Polla's remark is blunt, but I like her better for it. And answering her reminds me I *do* want Paulinus, that my life is infinitely better than it was at court.

"A good husband is beyond price," she says, her eyes filling with tears. "Although the loss of mine is made more painful for knowing this."

I disliked Lucan immensely but still pity Polla's loneliness. "It was a great loss. I am sorry."

"I know you understand grief," she says. "You have lost so much yourself. All your family. I cannot imagine the pain. It is why I chose to listen to you that day, when you commanded me to live."

I'm so stunned by Polla remembering my family, for acknowledging that they matter, it takes me a while to recover myself. Perhaps Paulinus understands the weight of grief I carry, but if so, he has never mentioned it. "I know it is often considered more honourable to die," I say, reaching to take her hand. "But I have come to believe it takes greater strength to live, and to face whatever the gods may bring. Especially when one is alone."

"Survival can be a burden," she agrees. "But it means I am now preparing Lucan's work to live on after him, just as you foretold." She opens the satchel she has been carrying, bringing out a scroll. "I have had a copy made for you of the first book of his great epic on war, the *Pharsalia*. After praying to Lucan's spirit for guidance, I have woven my own reflections into the poem, based on conversations I had with you. I do not believe my husband would mind."

"Reflections based on our conversations?" I am both touched and surprised. "Like what?"

"You made me think of what war means for those who try to master it," she says. "It is an unending evil, devoid of glory, which makes monsters of men. Nobody can remain uncorrupted by its power."

I gaze at Polla, who seems to speak to me from another time. Her words conjure up the spirit of my sister. *All this suffering. All this death.*

A clinking sound makes us both jump. One of the maids, sent by Secundus, is setting out pastries on a small table by the bench. I watch the girl set out the plates.

"I wish you had met my sister, Bellenia," I say, when the maid has finally gone. "She shared your feelings. You would have made her feel less alone." At the thought of Bellenia, I find myself blinking back tears. I turn to Polla, who is gazing at me in concern. She takes both my hands.

"You make *me* feel less alone," she says, squeezing my fingers. "Daughter of Boudicca."

Polla embraces me as I weep, and in that moment, she could be Vassura, she could be Bellenia, and even though she is neither, her kindness brings my family closer.

*

I stay sitting in the garden, holding Polla's scroll close to my body after she has gone, just as I once held the scrap of Lucan's verses. Before she left, Polla recited some of the passages she has written, and the words made me think of my mother, of what war might have meant to her. All those questions I will never have the chance to ask. Looking at the tight, cramped script as Polla held the parchment, I knew I would not be able to read it myself. My Latin is not good enough. Yet even if I cannot read it, this scroll is priceless. It is the first possession I have owned since my capture which was not given to me by Paulinus. Polla's gift reminds me I am not wholly in his shadow, that even in Rome, I can be a separate being. My past still holds its own power.

The shadows lengthen, the blue sky darkening above Pliny's red slanted roof, and I decide that I do not want to wait for my husband here, swathed in uncomfortable clothes. There is no reason I should remain in public areas of the house out of politeness to a rude host. I head back to the bedroom, setting down Polla's scroll on the desk, and get rid of my heavy robes, so that I am in nothing but a short, sleeveless tunic which leaves my arms and legs free. Immediately, I feel better, and pace about, working off some of the energy that constantly builds inside me in this house where I cannot move. Pacing back and forth dredges up ugly memories of when Paulinus held me prisoner, but I force them away. The past is mine, but it does not own me. I have chosen to close this door, nobody has locked me in, and I will not be brought to Paulinus, he will come to me.

When he finally arrives, he is startled to see how I am dressed and startled too by the passion of my greeting. He kisses me back, tightening his grip on my waist when I do not release him.

"What are you doing in your shift?" he asks, perplexed rather than cross.

"I am too warm," I say, leading him to sit down beside me on the bed. I place his hand over my stomach, finally allowing myself to feel the excitement which should have been mine the first moment I knew. He immediately understands.

"Are you certain?"

"Yes."

Paulinus hugs me so tightly it hurts, but I do not stop him; I want to feel his happiness. "Nortia is rewarding us for fulfilling our vow," I say, when he has released me. He nods, his expression full of such admiration and joy, I know I can take the power of this moment to change my life. "Your son cannot be born here. I need to give birth to him in the house where your mother gave birth to you."

"In Pisaurum?" Paulinus looks surprised.

I had not remembered the name of his hometown, but do not want to admit this. "Yes, in Pisaurum. That is where I need to have your child."

"Most of the slaves from my household in Rome are there," he says. "As well as the estate staff. But the villa still won't be as luxurious as this, even if I send word ahead. Are you certain?"

I think of Pliny, of what it would be like carrying a baby to term in this hated house. Whatever state the other place is in, it will be mine. "I am completely certain."

Paulinus cups my face in his hands to kiss me. His tenderness tells me my gamble has paid off, even before he speaks. "Then we will go," he says.

46

PAULINUS

He is deeply relieved to arrive. Concern about leaving his legal practice meant Paulinus delayed the journey from Rome, and now Solina is so far along in the pregnancy, every jolt on the road to Pisaurum made him feel afraid. He helps his wife down from the carriage, touched by her excitement to see his childhood home. The villa looks more dilapidated than he remembers. Its walls are peeling paint, revealing cracked plaster beneath, and the two large pine trees at the entrance have crept their ragged arms over the red tiles of the roof. A lump forms in his throat. He grew up alone here with his mother, and even though she died many years ago, her absence from the house is difficult to endure.

"It is beautiful." Solina stares at the villa with a look of wonder.

"It needs a lot of work," he says, secretly pleased by her reaction. She walks ahead to one of the pines, laying her hand against the bark, closing her eyes and inhaling the tree's scent, a blissful expression on her face. Even dressed like a Roman matron, she looks utterly savage and peculiar. The tangled knot of emotions Paulinus feels towards his wife pull tighter around his heart. Marrying a Briton has brought him society's disapproval, which he sometimes regrets, yet her difference is also a source of desire, and increasingly, a sense of respect.

He resists the urge to stop Solina from touching the tree and walks over to rest a hand on her shoulder. "If you like the pines, then you will enjoy the forests along the coast."

"We will ride there together," she says, turning to him in excitement. "Like we did in Gaul."

"Well, maybe someday, but not *now*," he looks down meaningfully at the swell of her stomach.

Solina beams up at him. "It will make our son brave, to ride a horse. All Iceni women ride through pregnancy, but out of respect for you, I will stop riding when it is closer to his birth."

"I will have to think about it. I'm not convinced it's safe."

Aulus, the estate steward, has joined them, standing back respectfully until Paulinus acknowledges him. Paulinus steps away from Solina to greet his freedman. "*Thank you for preparing everything at such short notice,*" he says, unthinkingly slipping into the Etruscan dialect.

"*We're all very happy to see you home again,*" Aulus replies politely. "*And we are delighted to meet your new wife.*"

Solina looks between them both, confused. "I cannot understand," she says.

"It's the regional dialect," Paulinus apologises. "Aulus and I will speak Latin in future."

"We are all very pleased to meet you," Aulus says slowly to Solina, his accent almost as strong as hers. He turns to Paulinus, lapsing straight back into Etruscan as if no promise of Latin were ever made. "*Your mother's shade will be happy you have brought your family here. Nothing would have pleased her more than a child in this house.*"

Paulinus does not want to talk about his mother. "Thank you," he replies in Latin. "Please see everything is unpacked."

He takes Solina's hand and leads her inside. The hallway is dark, with a lingering scent from the pines, the atrium a bright space beyond. Walking into this house is like stepping back in time. His mother's old loom is still in one corner, now being worked on by a slave woman. Flaking scenes from the legend of Hercules line the walls, and Paulinus remembers the hours he spent as a boy, looking at these same pictures, wishing he too were brave enough to fight monsters. He lets go of Solina and walks to the pool in the centre of the floor, which sits beneath the square in the ceiling, open to the sky. A familiar mosaic of a dolphin ripples beneath the water. He squats down to dip his fingers in the pool as he used to do as a child, and the gesture takes him back unexpectedly, not to his own past, but to Solina's childhood home in *Lukodunon*. He squatted like this at the centre of her parents' empty roundhouse to take a silver brooch from the cauldron, which is now locked away in his desk. His wife will never return home like he can; he burned it all to the ground.

Guilt is an unwanted and increasingly familiar feeling for Paulinus. The more he loves Solina, the more conscious he is of how he has harmed her. He rises, turning to look back at his wife, almost expecting to see hatred on her face. But she is gazing curiously about the room, one hand resting on her stomach in an unconscious gesture of protection towards their child. She smiles and walks over to join him.

"This is the right place for us to be." She speaks with that strange, fierce certainty she has.

"I thought you might like it in the north." He lifts the veil from her head so it is draped around her shoulders, setting her hair free. "And since it is colder here, we wear *braccae* which are a little like your trousers. Well, the men wear them. But it might be safer for you to wear more familiar clothes whenever we ride, so I will find you a pair." Solina is staring at him in such complete astonishment, he wonders if he made a misjudgement. That perhaps the mention of trousers offended her. "Though you might think that unsuitable…"

"No!" She grips his hand, as if afraid he might withdraw his offer. "I will wear them." She leans close to him, and he puts his arms around her. "Will you show me the gardens now?"

Paulinus wonders why she does not want to see the house first – it seems eccentric to go straight back outside again – but he decides not to contradict her. Perhaps he does that too often. "Of course."

They have dinner in the winter dining room, with the brazier lit. Its fire casts a warm orange glow. It is only September but there is already more of a chill in the air here than in Rome. Paulinus sits upright, since Solina claims she gets indigestion from reclining now she is pregnant. She is cross-legged on the couch, as he made the mistake of explaining the mosaic beneath them, and now she does not want to touch it with her toes. Lifelike images of bones and scraps of food are tiled all over the floor, in an imaginary offering for the *lemures*, the dark spirits which haunt every house. Solina hated this idea. He finds her extreme reaction both endearing and exasperating.

"This is where you would eat with your parents, as a child?"

Solina is tucking into the uninspiring vegetable stew, which she appears to be enjoying much more than he is. He puts down his bowl. "Just with my mother."

"Your father died?"

"No, they were divorced."

"Why?"

Paulinus thinks of his mother, and the violence she suffered at the hands of his drunken father when he was a child. It is not a story he likes to share. "Many different reasons," he says.

"You have no brothers or sisters?"

"My father had two other sons and a daughter with his first wife." He takes a sip of watered-down wine. "One of my nephews shares my name and is the consul this year."

"Why have I not met them?"

"Families can be complicated," he says, irritated by her persistence. "We are estranged."

"It is not that you are ashamed of me?"

Her question makes him feel contrite. "No, of course not." He hesitates. "My father chose not to take me from my mother and raise me, which is unusual in Roman families. It is something of a snub to the child. My grandfather was my *paterfamilias*, but he died when I was seven, so I don't remember him well. He supported my mother in her decision to get a divorce. She was his only surviving child, and sole heir."

"Your mother divorced your father?" Solina looks surprised. "I did not know Roman women could do this."

"Don't get any ideas." He laughs, seeing her expression. "And I'm afraid you cannot divorce me, if that is what you are plotting."

"I know, Pliny told me this," she says, calmly dipping bread into her stew, to wipe around the sides of the bowl. "He says you own me completely, because you married me by manus."

"*With* manus," he corrects her, slightly perturbed Pliny would have said such a thing to his wife. Whatever possessed him? "It was the only way to marry you. I didn't do it to…" Paulinus trails off, unsure of the word he wants. "I didn't do it to give you less freedom; I did it to make our children legitimate." He realises how hollow that sounds, given he took Solina from her own people by force and held her captive. "I could not love you more than I do," he says. "You understand, my darling, don't you? Whether you were Iceni or Roman, it doesn't matter to me."

Solina smiles at him, and he is hopeful that she is going to say back the words he has waited for, ever since he married her. She leans over to kiss him. "Etrusci," she says gently.

"What?"

"You are not Roman. You are Etrusci." She says it with immense pleasure, without the slightest idea that she has just delivered an insult rather than a compliment. "I asked Aulus what dialect you speak. He told me: Etrusci. Like Nortia's people. They are your ancestors. This is why she favours you." Solina sighs with contentment. She puts down her empty bowl and nestles close to him. Paulinus wrestles with the overwhelming urge to reprimand her, to stress he is *Roman*, not Etrusci, but he is aware that his wife seems to like the part of him he considers a source of embarrassment, so instead he puts his arms around her and kisses her. Solina murmurs something in her own language, then translates it before he can ask what it meant. "My beloved," she says.

"*Mi un tura*," he replies, a phrase he has not spoken since he was a child. Words his mother once said to him.

"This has the same meaning in your language?"

Paulinus has the urge to tell her it is not his language, his language is Latin, but he refrains. "It means *I love you*." Again, he hopes she will say the words back to him, but Solina simply squeezes his hand.

47

SOLINA

The twisted branches float past, slow as creeping mist, their shaggy tops obscuring the sky. I have no fear of falling – the placid mare Paulinus has given me picks her way carefully over the path through the woods, her footfall as slow and steady as my heart. Yet even a horse this plodding can be roused by an experienced rider, and I have no doubt that if I chose, I could make her rival Tan's speed, if never his passion. The movement of the mare's muscles, the sense of her power aligned to my body, makes me feel alive. I glance to the side, where Paulinus rides. He looks away immediately, embarrassed to be caught staring, keeping up the pretence that every moment he sees his pregnant wife upon a horse is not agony. If such knowledge would reassure him, I would tell him my mother experienced her first labour pangs with me when she was out riding. Disaster did not ensue; she calmly returned to the Town of the Wolf to give birth to her daughter. In everything she did, my mother was a warrior.

    I lay my hand over the child who I pray will become my own firstborn. My mother's line will not die. When I speak to Paulinus about our child, I speak of the strength he will have, the courage and the resilience. I do not say, *You will be father to the heir of Boudicca*, but this is what I believe. Perhaps he has also thought this; it would be strange if not. Roman legends are full of gods and heroes who are overthrown by their own children. I try not to dwell on what Paulinus will think of my visions if our baby is a girl. Now that I know him better, I understand he only ever wanted a *child*, he did not care whether it was a boy, and I trapped myself in a lie for nothing.

"Perhaps we should head back?"

Paulinus is no longer able to master his anxiety. I turn to smile at him. "I want to see the marshes. It is healthy for me to move."

He wants to say no but does not. I think of the first time we met in the woods, when he pursued me through the trees, how he appeared to me as nothing more than a blur of black and gold, the way he cut in front with Viribus, barring my way, ready to see me die. For all the crimes I hate Paulinus for, I do not hate him for that. I would have pursued my enemy too and fought him to the death. In this way, we are alike.

Clear, cold sky cuts through the thinning trees, the dark pines fading, then we are at the very edge of the marshlands. I rein my mare to a halt. The first time I saw the salt marshes here, I wept. I had not imagined I would see a landscape so like the Iceni kingdom again. Now I sit on my placid horse, listening to the sigh of the reeds, watching their strange rippling waves, the endless blurring between land and sea. Paulinus came from this place, he was born here, and I find it painful knowing he wandered these marshes as a child, calling them home, yet he could not see the beauty in mine.

"It will soon be the Feast of Darkness," I say to him.

"Is that an auspicious festival?"

"It is the most powerful."

Paulinus is beside me, so close he blocks the full force of the wind. His face is inscrutable as he gazes out towards the sea. I want to ask him if he ever went to the far north, if he ever saw the Iceni salterns, but I am afraid I might hate him more for his answer.

"It is too cold here," he says, his patience frayed to breaking point. Every day I push him a little further, forcing him to concede more to me. It was enough to get to the marshes this morning.

I smile. "Then we will return home."

The afternoon is overcast, and it is too dark for weaving. Paulinus has been surprised by my abilities at the loom – I don't know if he imagined that because Iceni women know how to fight, we cannot also sew. I sit in the atrium, heaped in blankets, embroidering a coverlet I have woven for my child, a design of red horses my aunt Vassura once sewed for her son Aesu. Resistance takes many forms. I have no kingdom, no birth family, yet some part of the Iceni will live on through my own children. Aulus's wife Tita sits beside me, spinning thread. She cannot speak much Latin, and I will never learn the language of the Etrusci, so we communicate only in smiles and nods. I find this companionable, although having been enslaved myself, I know Tita's own feelings towards my company will be different.

In my old life, I was loved by many. My family were a forest, planted the length of the kingdom, strong and dependable, stretching back through the ages, covering both the mortal and Otherworld. Now I only have Paulinus and Polla. My friend writes to me here, describing her quiet days in loving detail, and I find her letters a comfort. Paulinus reads them aloud, and I dictate my replies to him, while I learn how to improve my written Latin. At first, I was unsure if I wanted to invite him into this friendship, but I have decided it is good he understands he is not the only living person to value his wife.

A sudden pain startles me as I try to rethread the needle. I hold myself still, scarcely breathing, and it fades. I carry on sewing, time passes, lulling me into thinking it was nothing, then the pain grips again. I wait for it to pass. There are two expensive midwives from Rome in the house – Paulinus is not taking any chances with this child, and they have both warned me what to expect when labour starts. I rise from the seat, placing my sewing carefully upon it, when another pain hits. I wince and Tita looks up in concern.

"Baby?" she asks, the first Latin word I have ever heard her speak. I nod in reply, and she gestures for me to stay, rushing off to fetch help.

It has never felt lonelier without my family than now. I imagine how my aunt Vassura would be in the birthing room, with her soft voice and kind hands, or my mother with her fierce encouragement. Instead, I am surrounded by foreign midwives and their attendants, and however much my husband is paying these women, I do not trust them. I have heard how Pliny speaks of the Britons, and it reminds me of the way the midwives look at one another when I ask them questions, or when they pretend not to understand me.

The birthing chamber is the room that once belonged to my husband's mother. A brazier is burning incense, but even this cannot dispel the smell of damp and disuse. I wanted Paulinus in here with me, but this is not allowed, so I have demanded Tita. The old Etruscan woman is not my friend, but I do not believe she despises me. I pace the room with Tita holding my hand, and I pretend she is Riomanda. The waves of pain grow steadily stronger, the moments of peace between them shorter, until it becomes hard to move.

Sweat coats my skin, and I want to cry out whenever the agony hits, but I stay silent, doubling over and gripping Tita's hand so hard, she winces. It is increasingly difficult to think; every other feeling shrinks as the pain grows larger, even my fear for the baby's safety. The midwives finally interrupt my pacing, forcing me to the birthing chair, and I am too weak to resist. I just want this torture to be over.

It does not end; it gets worse. I cannot stay silent. When the pain strikes now, I scream, no longer a woman but an animal, writhing to be free. I am being split apart, with a violence more shocking than any I faced in battle. My Latin leaves me; I can only speak my own language, and I focus on Tita, the kindness in her voice, even though her words are utterly incomprehensible. One of the midwives takes my face roughly in her hands, forcing me to look at her.

"Push as the pain hits," she shouts, repeating the phrase to make sure it sinks in. I obey and to my shock, the agony lessens. "You are very close now," she says. "Your husband is waiting for his son."

Her last words are meant to inspire me, yet they make me furious. I push down in anger when the vice of pain grips, knowing that this child is Iceni, this child is *mine*. It still isn't enough. I call upon my mother, asking her to give me her strength. When the agony builds again, I imagine her shouting beside me, demanding that the baby show himself. This time I feel my child move, physically pushing out of my body, as if answering my mother's call. The suffering eases, though I am still on fire, and I am also staring, amazed, at a wailing red creature in the midwife's hands.

"A boy," she says, pleased.

I no longer care about the sex, or any of the lies I have told.

I simply want to hold my child, to look at his face. I reach for him, but they are hustling me over to the bed. If I were not so exhausted, I would fight them. Tita tries to restrain me, her voice no longer soothing. The midwife brings me my son as soon as he is swaddled, perhaps alarmed by the way I keep scrambling out of the covers.

"He is healthy," she says, mistaking the cause of my distress.

"Give him to me," I demand. She does as I ask, and I draw him close, this strange tiny person, my child, with his pink, scrunched-up face. "*You are Cunovindus,*" I say, wanting our own language to be the first he hears. "*You are the youngest warrior of the tribes of the Wolf and the Horse. May Esus protect you, may the gods guide you, every day of your life.*" He stares back at me with his startled blue eyes, looking as fragile as a baby bird that has fallen, naked, from its nest. I hold him tighter, anxious suddenly that he might be cold, that perhaps the birth hurt him, or that this new world is too large and alarming for such a small being. "*I love you,*" I say, my voice softer, my eyes filling with tears. "*My little one, dearer to me than oak.*"

As I speak, holding my son, I know my mother is beside me. And I know too that this is what she felt for me, her daughter, the day I was born. I have been so afraid of her judgement, yet there was no need. Whatever terrible choices I have made, whatever humiliations or failures I have endured, I understand my mother wanted me to live, she wanted me to survive. Because there is no world in which I could ever wish harm upon my child.

"Solina."

I look up to see Paulinus, whose eyes are bright with tears. I did not hear him enter the room, but then I have been unaware of anyone but our son. He sits down on the bed beside me, gazing at the tiny, rumpled creature in my arms, struck dumb. If Paulinus had demanded to hold Cunovindus, or claim ownership of him, I would have felt resentment, but instead he simply reaches over and gently strokes our child's head, as if he were almost too precious to touch.

"You must hold him," I say, understanding Paulinus is the only other living person who will love Cunovindus as much as I do.

"Please." He sits even closer to me, so that our baby will not feel distressed from being moved. The look of wonder on my husband's face makes me wish so much that he were not Roman, that I could love him without guilt. He begins to speak softly to Cunovindus, and I realise I cannot understand him because he is speaking Etruscan, the language his mother once spoke to him. Then, even though I suspect he wants to hold our child for longer, he hands him back to me.

"*Dearer than oak*," Paulinus says. His face shines with the silver lines of his tears.

48

PAULINUS

The atrium is chill, and Paulinus has been here since dawn, wanting to spend time with his son before he leaves for the Forum. Lucius totters across the newly laid mosaic in his freshly built house, taking wobbling steps over the vast tiled body of the city's founding wolf, with Romulus and Remus almost completely hidden behind her shaggy legs. It is a famous image of Roman patriotism, but Paulinus suspects that is not why Solina chose it. Lucius reaches the wolf's snarling jaws, then lurches onto his knees, seeking out the familiarity and speed of crawling. Paulinus scoops up his son before he can tip head first into the freezing pool at the centre of the atrium: he is a fearless, chaotic creature. Lucius reaches out a chubby hand for the water he has been denied, a woeful look on his face. The baby's tragic expression makes Paulinus laugh, and at this, his son also begins to laugh, easily distracted by merriment.

The sight squeezes Paulinus's heart so tightly, it hurts. He loves this child so much. It is as if his own heart were now wandering over the earth, lurching into pools, chasing bees, and resting safe and warm in his arms, like this. Paulinus had always known he wanted to be a father; he had not realised it would completely upend his world. Lucius is wriggling, unmoved by his parent's sentimentality, wanting to explore. Paulinus wraps him in his cloak, walking into the garden. A slave is already out here, sweeping up the twigs and debris from last night's storm, restoring the courtyard to its pristine condition. At the garden's heart is a tiled shrine to the goddess Nortia, where Paulinus lights incense every evening in thanks for the great honour Fate paid him, singling him out for blessing over other men. He stops before the altar now with Lucius, murmuring a prayer. This place is nothing like the ragged orchard his child knows in Pisaurum, and Paulinus takes time to explain everything, while his son reaches out to pat statues or scrunch leaves. When he frowns like that, Lucius looks just like Solina.

"Do you think he might be cold?"

Paulinus never hears his wife creep up on him, as silent as if she were a scout. She must only just have risen from their bed, since her hair is not dressed yet. Solina presses her hands around Lucius's small toes, testing their warmth. "I think he's fine," he says, amused at her concern.

"Yes." Solina nods, as Lucius reaches for her red hair, always a source of fascination, and Paulinus relinquishes the baby to his mother's arms. The sight of them together fills him with gratitude. His marriage is not always easy, but he no longer cares for anybody else's opinion. Let people think what they like. Even the peculiar British name Solina gave their son no longer bothers him.

"I have asked the cook to prepare the boar the way Polla likes," Solina says. "But I think you like it too."

"That's fine. And anyway, the court hearing will go on until sundown," Paulinus says. "You should both eat without me." It is as well he likes Lucan's widow as the woman is almost a permanent presence in his house. His wife is intensely attached to her eccentric friend, and he feels certain it was Polla who put her up to the garish fresco of Amazons conquering Scythia in the dining room, without an Achilles in sight. Solina cannot have read Herodotus, but he is sure Polla has.

Paulinus still misses his old home, and misses the traces of his first wife, Fulvia, even more. He felt guilty when he asked Solina to help design the new place, as if this were disloyal to Fulvia's memory, but it would also be unfair to deny Solina things simply because he was married before. In Rome he visits Fulvia's grave every month, an observance Solina has never questioned, and the *lunula* remains around his wrist, wherever he is.

Lucius is squirming, wanting to run around, so his mother sets him down. Immediately he is off, straight into a flowerbed. His parents look at him fondly, as he brings them both small piles of soil, his hands getting muddier with each trip. "Maybe fetch a stone next time." Paulinus squats down, brushing the mud back into the flowerbed. "Like this?" He holds up a pebble for his son to see, and the little one obliges, copying him. He feels the warmth of Solina's hand, resting on his shoulder.

"He is clever," she says proudly. "He will be an intelligent man, like his grandfather."

Paulinus looks up at her, amused. "Not like his father?"

"You are not stupid," she allows, which makes him snort with laughter.

He straightens up, happy to see the way she is smiling at him. "What would be perfect is if you give me a daughter, as blunt as you." Paulinus says it lightly, but his longing for more children is real enough. Solina asked him to avoid pregnancy for a year, and was disconcertingly knowledgeable about how this must be done, but he is hoping she might unbend now Lucius has had his first birthday.

Solina takes his hand, not deflecting him from the topic as usual. "Yes," she says, her tone also light.

Paulinus pulls her closer, not wanting to ruin the moment by demanding too much. They stand together, watching their son add to his ever-growing pile of pebbles.

Two men, most likely witnesses in a case, sit on the white marble steps of the Basilica Julia playing *Latrunculi* as Paulinus heads into court. The lines of the game are deeply etched into the stone, the black-and-white playing pieces the men's own. Paulinus has lost count of the number of times he has come across witnesses passing their long wait to be called at this spot, but this morning the white player is missing a move so obvious, Paulinus cannot resist stopping. *Latrunculi* has always been his favourite game of strategy; he used to make Agricola play it in Britannia to learn military tactics.

"You can take his piece, there," he says to the white player, pointing to a black counter.

"Fuck's sake," the other player protests, rounding on him. "Why would you interfere?"

"How do I take it?" the white player asks eagerly, but Paulinus only shakes his head and laughs, leaving the two men to argue it out for themselves.

"Amusing yourself this morning?"

Paulinus turns as he reaches the top of the steps. It is one of the rising orators of the court, a young lawyer, perhaps Solina's age. Pliny has faced him a few times. "Who doesn't enjoy *Latrunculi*?" he asks.

The younger man smiles. "Galba certainly seems to."

Instantly, Paulinus is on alert. Every serving general in the Empire has declared their loyalty to Nero against the rebellion in Gaul. Every general except Galba in Hispania.

"As a military man, I would expect him to enjoy the game," he says pleasantly. "We're all fairly predictable."

"Galba seems to be spending a long time calculating his next move," the young orator replies, trotting to keep pace with Paulinus's giant stride as he enters the basilica. "Or perhaps he is weighing up the courage to do what is necessary."

"In *Latrunculi*, as in life, it rarely pays to be rash."

"You think the other generals are rash to have declared for Caesar so quickly?"

Paulinus stops. He stares down at the younger man, at his perfectly waxed hair, and his slight, handsome form. "No," he says coldly. "But perhaps you are, for starting this conversation."

The orator flushes. "Well, we have no doubt where *your* loyalty lies. I suppose Caesar was most generous in gifting you a wife."

Paulinus is unmoved by the insult to his marriage – this fool would hardly be the first – but he feels rage at the young man's recklessness. He imagines grabbing the boy by the shoulders and forcing him to look back out at the city. To ask if he wants to see the white marble run red with blood, if he wants to see Rome sacked, if he understands what rebellion *means*. Not the removal of Nero, but civil war. Instead, he smiles. "Did you not hear? My wife was gifted to me by the Goddess of Fate." The orator stares, perhaps wondering when the former general lost his mind. "If you will excuse me, I am due to advise the judge on the next hearing."

Paulinus continues walking, leaving the irritant behind, but the monumental interior of the basilica, with its soaring walls and shining marble, does not bring him the usual sense of calm. The rebellion is small – it has not gathered much support, and even Nero is not reported to be especially anxious. But Paulinus has fought enough campaigns to understand everything can turn on a hair, and everything can be destroyed. Even a temple to justice.

When he returns home, it is evening. Solina is sitting beside the cot, her hand resting on their sleeping son. The tips of her fingers brush the golden *bulla* around Lucius's neck, the same one Paulinus wore as a child. "He keeps waking when I move," she whispers, looking up at him. "And then wailing."

Paulinus walks over, and Lucius snuffles under his blankets. Most nights they give up, exhausted from all the crying, and let him sleep in their bed, as the child is never happier than when he is sprawled across both parents. Tonight will likely be the same. Paulinus thinks of today's long hearing, which was dull but reached a satisfying conclusion, and he thinks of the excitable young orator, eager to set fire to society. Paulinus would do anything to defend the stability of Rome, to defend his son's peaceful life – even uphold Nero.

"Perhaps now his father is here, he will stay asleep," Solina whispers, removing her hand, slow and stealthy, as she might have once moved through the forest. Lucius stirs but does not wake.

With a last look at their precious child, they both get into bed as quietly as possible, blowing out the light. There is no space between himself and Solina by the time she has made herself comfortable. It is eccentric for all three of them to sleep crammed into one room, but his wife grew up in a roundhouse and dislikes the idea of sleeping alone or leaving Lucius to the nurse. She has become very physically affectionate since they married and seems to find it hard to drift off unless he is holding her, complaining bitterly if he moves away. Between his wife and son, Paulinus often has no room in the bed at all.

"I remember when you were the spikiest woman I ever

met," he murmurs. "I could barely persuade you to let me hold you for a moment."

"That is not because I did not want you to hold me," she says. "It was—"

She stops, her body stiffening, and guilt hits him in a nauseous wave. He does not need to ask why she moved away when she wanted to be held; it is suddenly obvious. Solina used to be afraid of him. Or else she hated herself for loving him. He is not sure which is worse. "You're not still afraid of me, are you?" he whispers.

"I don't want to talk about the past."

"I could not love you more than I do. I—"

"I know you love me," she interrupts him. "I never doubt that you do. Please, I don't want to talk about it."

Paulinus holds Solina tightly, kissing her on the top of her head. He says nothing more, but that does not mean his mind is not full of painful memories. As a legate, he still believes he acted justly in Britannia. Yet as a man, he is aware that he hurt his wife in ways for which he cannot even begin to ask her forgiveness. Now he is trapped, reliving the sight of her standing in her father's hall, lifting the sword against her cousin. He remembers telling Solina that he would kill her if she tried to escape, making her beg for the lives of her own people, keeping her captive for months, burning her childhood home. The nausea is so severe he wants to get up and pace the room, to *beg* her to forgive him, but he has given his wife enough pain to carry – she does not need the burden of his guilt as well. Her body is still tense in his arms, and he realises she must also be trapped in the past. He wishes he had not said anything – he never seems to learn.

"My darling," he whispers. "If you cannot sleep, would you like me to read to you?"

She grips his hand. "The light might wake Cunovindus,"

she says. "But you can tell me a story from memory. About Camilla. Just be sure to whisper. You have such a loud, booming voice."

Solina's own voice is much louder than his, but he is always reassured by her rudeness. It means she is not afraid of him. She holds his hand over her heart, and he caresses her palm as he murmurs stories he remembers about Camilla, Italy's mythical warrior queen, until he knows from her breathing that his wife is asleep.

49

SOLINA

The statue is breathtaking. Taller than any figure I have ever seen, its burnished bronze skin glows in the sunlight, and the ripples of its muscles are so lifelike I almost expect the giant to step down from its plinth. The colossus has Nero's face, staring out over the city he once ruled. I stand beside Polla, gazing upwards. This echo of Nero is even stranger to look upon now the man himself is dead, overthrown by his own army, replaced by one of his generals.

Polla pulls me aside as some drunks approach, making obscene gestures at the statue, shouting and laughing. All around us, other curious day-trippers have come to wander through the vast pleasure gardens of the Golden House, and the atmosphere is growing increasingly raucous. Everything has been thrown open to the public as a gesture of goodwill. Above us, the new Emperor Galba is installing himself in the Golden House pavilion on the Oppian hill. I can remember once walking through its foundations, when Nero and Poppaea were alive.

"I do not believe such a man as Nero will have had the courage for suicide," Polla says, glancing back at the golden figure who killed her husband. One of the drunks is now taking a piss at the statue's marble base. The fool gestures at us both, as if *he* is the sight we have turned to watch, and she hastily averts her eyes.

"You are right," I say. "Either he was murdered, or he ordered a slave to do it. He was always a coward." I know the manner of Nero's death is deeply personal for Polla. She was with Lucan when he killed himself, holding her husband's hand while he bled out, unable to intervene. She has only spoken to me of that day once, but I know how much it haunts her.

"Didn't Nero flee with that slave boy he castrated?" she asks. "Perhaps the eunuch killed him. I've been told the boy was present for the death, but not Nero's wife."

"I hope it was him. That would be fitting." I think of all the violence Fabius himself endured and am not surprised to hear Messalina stayed away. Paulinus once told me of her distress at her first husband's enforced suicide, and I wonder what Messalina truly felt for Nero, if it was ever love or only fear. "What do you think the new one will be like?" I nod towards the glittering marble façade on the Oppian hill.

"Galba is old," Polla replies, looking around to see who might be listening. "And if the army was persuaded to betray one Caesar, who knows if their loyalty could be bought yet again by another."

This is what Paulinus has also said to me. I had expected my husband to rejoice, as I did, in the fall of such a hated leader as Nero, but he is treating the whole affair as a tragedy. Now that the new Emperor Galba has arrived in the capital and the streets are filled with soldiers, I am beginning to understand why he is afraid. I have always thought of Rome as a monster, uncrushable and insatiable, devouring the lands of other people, never suspecting it is a serpent which might also devour itself. "Shall we go to see the lake?" I ask Polla, taking her arm.

My friend looks around uneasily at the increasingly boisterous gardens. "No. I think we should leave now." She gestures to her steward, Silvanus, who accompanied us for protection, along with three other male slaves from her household.

We walk through the gardens of the Golden House, a complex so vast it is a city within a city, then rejoin the streets. There are even more armed men loitering out here than when we arrived earlier. Galba's legions continue to flood into Rome. A soldier barges past us as we wait to cross the road, shoving his elbow into my stomach without apology, almost knocking me from the pavement. Silvanus shouts as if to remonstrate, but I stop him. The atmosphere feels as if it might be turning. I am relieved Paulinus persuaded me to leave Cunovindus home with the nurse. "My house is closer than yours," I say. "I think you should come back with me, until the crowd thins out."

"Yes." Polla nods.

It is hard to walk briskly when the pavements are so crowded. Silvanus goes ahead with one of the slaves, while the other two follow behind us. Polla grips my arm, and I know she is frightened. She is not used to seeing Rome's armies as a threat, though they have long been monsters to me. I think of the last time I rode through The City of the Horse with my mother and sister, when the Romans left us with blackened ruins and looted homes, and I wonder what is restraining the men from inflicting similar violence here, or how long that restraint will hold.

We keep to the broad colonnade, where the shops are expensive, and the soldiers less likely to cause trouble. Many people seem unaware of the danger. A group of women dawdle outside a clothes store, picking over fabrics, oblivious to the armed men watching and laughing from the other side of the road. As we draw closer to home, I realise the only route back to my street is a side alley. Silvanus stops us before we take the turning.

"We will walk quickly, mistress," he says addressing both Polla and me. "And we will keep close together."

The alley is narrow, darker than the main street. I know there is a busy cookshop in the middle of it, and as we approach, my heart sinks to see a commotion going on outside. Silvanus ushers us over to the other side of the road, but I cannot help looking back. A group of soldiers are waiting to be served, amusing themselves by tormenting a girl. One of them grabs hold of her, pulling at her tunic, while the others laugh and the shopkeeper frantically protests, trapped behind his counter and the crush of people. I stop, and the slave behind bumps into me.

"There is nothing we can do for her," Polla whispers.

I know my friend is right, but I cannot move. These men are like the ones who came to my father's house. The shopkeeper is screaming now, and I realise he must know the girl. Some of his neighbours have gathered, pleading with the soldiers, but none dare get too close.

"Let the girl go." My voice cuts across the noise, ringing with command.

It momentarily startles the soldiers, then they see who shouted and guffaw. "Jealous are you, bitch?" one of them yells. "You should get your husband to fuck you, if that's what you're after."

"Solina, please," Polla whispers.

I ignore her, and stride towards the soldiers. People part to let me through, curious at the prospect of a scene. On the counter, just within my reach, I see a long, cruel knife, used to carve portions off the joint of meat. The sight emboldens me. I look at the man holding the struggling girl, flicking my eyes up and down his body with contempt. "I said let her go."

The soldier straightens up, stepping towards me, and it is there, in the fluid arrogance of his movement, in the violence of his gaze. The dark memories I have long buried. "Or what?"

My rage ignites. I seize the knife on the counter and hold it out to him in warning. "Or I will slit your throat like the dog you are."

His face flushes. I tear the veil from my head as he draws his sword, hating the foreign robes that bind my body. People scatter, shrieking in alarm. Silvanus steps forward, trying to intervene, but I gesture at him to stay back.

The silver of the soldier's blade catches the light, twisting as he points it at me. "You will apologise," he says, still gripping the girl by the wrist.

"I command you to release her," I shout. "Or by the will of Andraste, I will cut out your heart."

He finally does what I ask and lets the girl go, but only so he can lunge at me with his sword. It is years since I have fought, and I am dressed in the absurd flowing robes of a Roman matron, but my body still remembers enough to dodge a blow. He hits the counter, unbalancing himself, perhaps drunk, and I swing round with the knife. Before I can strike him, the shopkeeper gets in first, upending a vat of stew. "Leave my daughter alone, you bastard," he shouts.

Boiling liquid hits the soldier in the chest, and he yells in pain. In his shock I am momentarily forgotten. He swings for the shopkeeper, leaving himself exposed, and I press the knife to the side of his throat.

"Drop your sword," I snarl. His eyes swivel towards me. I can hear the other soldiers shouting, but in this moment my rage is so all-consuming I do not care. My enemy and I stare at each other. "I said drop it," I repeat, pressing on the knife until it draws a bead of blood. There is the clatter of iron on stone as he obeys me.

"What the fuck is this?" A loud angry voice cuts through the yelling. "What are you doing?"

I maintain the pressure on my enemy's neck, tilting my head to see. A centurion is striding over, and he looks furious.

"What is this?" the centurion shouts, not at me but at his own soldier. "Why are you being held hostage by a fucking woman?" He turns to me. "Release him." With reluctance I lower my blade. Immediately Polla grabs my arm, pulling me backwards, hoping to escape. "No," the centurion says to us both. "You will not leave."

From the corner of my eye, I see the shopkeeper hurry his sobbing daughter into the darkness of the kitchen, safely out of sight. His neighbours have melted away. Where once there was a crowd, now it is only me, Polla, Silvanus, her frightened slaves and a large gang of soldiers. My friend starts to cry. "It will be alright," I whisper, watching as the man I fought rubs his hand against his neck. He looks at the blood smeared on his palm in disbelief.

The centurion gestures to several of the soldier's companions. "Take Gaius back to camp, I will discipline him later." He turns to Polla and me. "Well, *ladies*, what happened here?"

His address is sarcastic, and I do not let go of the knife. "One of your men was abusing a girl."

"And this outraged your moral sensibilities as a married woman, did it?"

I look at the centurion with contempt. "He deserved far worse than he got."

"Solina," Polla begs. "Please *stop*."

"You sound foreign," the centurion says to me. "Who do you belong to?"

"I am the wife of General Suetonius Paulinus, former Legate of Britannia."

The centurion raises his eyebrows. "In that case, I will leave it to your husband to discipline you. Allow me to escort you ladies home." His tone sounds courteous, but I am in no doubt this is a command, not an offer. I do not move, distrusting his motives. He looks meaningfully at the knife in my hand. "Put down the weapon and come with me."

"Do what he says," Polla says. "Please." I glance at my friend who has bundled her cloak across her front, trying to hide the shape of her body. I feel guilty, suddenly understanding why she is so frightened, and the terrible danger I have placed her in.

"If you harm us, my husband will take his vengeance upon you all," I warn the soldiers, laying down the knife.

The centurion smiles. "As he did upon the rebels of Britannia. But then you would know all about that, wouldn't you?"

Paulinus is used to masking his feelings, but even he cannot hide his surprise at finding his wife surrounded by soldiers in his own atrium. I see him take in Polla and her servants huddled to the side, clearly not the focus of hostile attention, then his eyes flick between me and the men. I know he is calculating his odds of taking them all on. It does not look good.

"What brings you here?" he asks, his voice calm.

"That depends, general," the centurion says. "I have heard two versions of events. In the first, we defended your wife and her friend from brigands, earning your gratitude through whatever payment you might care to give us. In the second, your wife took up arms against a soldier of Rome in full view of a street of witnesses. An especially regrettable situation, given her past as an enemy rebel." He smiles. "I am sure as a former commander and now learned jurist, you will be able to tell me which version is true."

I do not believe anyone present, not even Polla, will be able to see how angry this has made Paulinus. "My gratitude, always, to a fellow soldier of Rome," he says pleasantly. "I hope you killed the brigands who made an attempt upon my wife, otherwise I am sworn to execute any who harm her." He holds out his hands to me as he speaks, and I walk over, clasping them. Then he pulls me closer as if in a loving embrace, whispering in my ear: "Go to the strongbox in the study. Bring whatever payment you believe this merits." Paulinus releases me. "My wife would like to fetch you the reward herself," he says as I hurry from the atrium.

The strongbox is under piles of tablets and papyrus beside the desk, as Paulinus always makes a terrible mess when he is working. My hands shake as I unlock it. The payment the centurion's behaviour merits is a sword in his guts, but I am beginning to understand how much danger I have placed my family in. I pray the nurse keeps Cunovindus safely upstairs. I have already counted the number of soldiers, and after a moment's hesitation, I take enough denarii for them to have five each. The centurion can either split the money or keep more for himself. I hope his companions murder him over it.

When I walk back into the atrium, Paulinus is smiling and talking, while the centurion looks edgy. I wonder what has been said. I head over to the man, giving him a leather purse. Then I return to take my husband's hand in silence. "My thanks again," Paulinus says to the men. "I hope you see yourselves safely back to camp, given there are brigands on the streets."

"Our thanks and respects, general," the centurion says, clearly wanting to open the bag to check the bribe but not quite having the nerve.

I watch our steward Cosmus shut the door on the men and bolt it. Paulinus is still holding my hand but does not speak to me. Instead, he turns to Polla. "I cannot apologise enough for the shock you must have had," he says. "If you go to the dining room, one of the maids will look after you, and I know Solina will want to join you in a moment."

Polla looks anxious, perhaps worried I might need her help in dealing with an angry husband. "I won't be long," I reassure her. With a last look over her shoulder, she leaves.

"What did you do?" Paulinus sounds calm, but I know his anger wasn't only for the centurion.

"One of the soldiers was going to hurt a girl outside the cookshop. I couldn't bear it. I told him to stop, and when he wouldn't, I took a knife from the counter and disarmed him."

"You *disarmed* a serving soldier?" Paulinus is incredulous. "But you haven't trained in years!"

"It was mainly luck."

Paulinus gazes at me. "Or perhaps you are a natural." The words are familiar, and I realise he has remembered the excuse I gave him all those years ago after disarming one of his own men. For once, the memory of our shared past does not distress me.

"Perhaps," I say. We stare at one another. He reaches over, tilting up my chin to kiss me, and I kiss him back. Then he breaks off, brushing my lips gently with his thumb. "You had better look after your friend," he says.

I watch Paulinus walk back to his study. My heart hurts,

flooded with emotions I cannot even name. I close my eyes, trying to calm myself, then I go to join Polla.

50

SOLINA

It is night. Cunovindus is sprawled over me in a warm, snuffling heap, with one arm flung out to rest against his father's chest. Our son is the only one asleep. I used to feel safe when the three of us lay bundled together like this, but there is no longer any safety in Rome. The shadow of civil war hangs over our house, and even though this is not my country, I am afraid for my family.

"There was so much blood," Paulinus whispers. "Even when he was dead, they kept hacking at his body. More like animals than men." He closes his eyes. My husband cannot seem to stop reliving the horror he witnessed earlier. His life has been steeped in violence, but I suppose he still never expected to see his Caesar being torn apart in the Forum by soldiers from his own guard, like starving dogs falling on a carcass. "Galba was murdered by the Fig Tree," he says. "Almost at the steps of the Basilica Julia, the greatest monument to justice man has ever built. It is impossible to explain the desecration."

I want to tell Paulinus that I understand. How can I not, when I heard his men rip apart the sacred grove built by my father? Everything the Iceni suffered was a desecration far beyond the death of an Emperor. But I say none of this.

There was a time when I would have relished my husband's suffering at the disintegration of his kingdom, in rightful payment for mine, yet now I cannot. "There is nothing you could have done," I say, stroking Cunovindus's soft cheek, as if my love might protect our son from the horrors his father describes. "You were unarmed and outnumbered. What were you supposed to do, attack them with a scroll?"

"I am sworn to defend Caesar. I stood there like a coward and watched him die."

"You didn't even like Galba."

"It's not the man, it's the office, and all it represents. The army has overthrown two Caesars in a matter of months. Now we will have Otho, an Emperor who began his rule by murdering his predecessor, or else we will have Vitellius, if the fool fulfils his threats to march on Rome. *Vitellius!* The man is a drunkard unfit to run anything but a tavern."

In his agitation, Paulinus has raised his voice. "You'll wake him," I warn, as Cunovindus moves, grasping fretfully for his father. Paulinus holds our son against the warmth of his chest, soothing him until he settles. "I can't send you both to Pisaurum," he whispers, his voice quiet again. "Vitellius will attack Otho from northern Italy. The estate is even more dangerous than here."

This chills me far more than which fool will be the next Caesar. I know how little mercy soldiers have for children when they sack a city. Paulinus has started training in earnest again, recognising his body is unused to combat. I want to train too, to stand some chance of defending our son. Yet even at my strongest, I know I cannot withstand a mob. I lay my hand on my husband's shoulder. Paulinus is older than me, and although he is nothing like as old as my father compared to my mother, it still makes me feel afraid. Roman soldiers are wolves – they respect a commander for his strength, little else.

He tenses. Somebody is knocking at the door to our room. "I'm sorry to disturb you," Cosmus calls. "A woman has arrived at the house in distress."

Paulinus carefully hands me Cunovindus, then slips out of bed. He opens the door to speak to his steward. "What name did she give?"

"It is Verania. The widow of Licinianus."

"Why did you let her in?" I hiss. "Otho will be furious if he thinks we're harbouring a traitor. He just had Verania's husband murdered!"

"Tell Verania I will see her in a moment," Paulinus says to Cosmus, closing the door before the steward is drawn into an argument.

"Galba named Licinianus as his heir." My whisper is as loud and angry as I dare. "You said Otho was even more eager to kill him than the old Emperor! So why is a traitor's widow now at our house?"

"It will be about Licinianus's remains," Paulinus whispers back, stumbling around to get dressed, before opening the shutters to let in some moonlight. Freezing air rushes into the room. "Soldiers have been parading the man's head around the city all day. Verania will want her husband's remains back, to bury him. The poor woman must need somebody to intercede for her."

"Why should that somebody be *you*?" I say, although I already know the answer. My husband's integrity is widely respected in Rome – he has expressed no personal ambition for power and has kept himself scrupulously removed from any plotting. For all these reasons, Otho might listen to him. If I were Verania, perhaps I too would beg Paulinus for help.

"I will be back in a moment," he says, heading out, before remembering the shutters and turning round to close them. "Please try and sleep." His tall form is briefly silhouetted in the doorway, then he is gone. I hold Cunovindus close, not sure if I am stroking my son's hair to soothe him or myself.

Verania gets her husband's head back to bury, for a hefty fee. Otho does not despise Paulinus for interceding on his enemy's behalf, but perhaps it would be better if he did. This Caesar is desperate to shore up his reputation after such a bloody beginning, and having little integrity himself, he wants to leech the shine from others who do. No Roman woman whose virtue was under siege from a lover was ever sent as many gifts as my husband now receives from Otho. For once I am allied with Pliny, who watches this attempted seduction with alarm.

"He will expect you to lead his armies," Pliny says, stepping into our atrium mere moments after the arrival of another gift.

This one is an expensive painted horse, studded with gems or glass, that runs on wheels. Otho is now targeting my husband through my son. Cunovindus wriggles free from my arms, running over the wolf mosaic to seize it. "Neigh!" he exclaims, before rattling it across the floor, aiming straight for his father's legs.

"I'm well aware of what he wants," Paulinus replies, deftly side-stepping his son's attacks. "But I haven't served in the military for years."

"You should never have agreed to go to that dinner at the Golden House the other week," Pliny sniffs.

"How am I meant to decline an emperor's invitation?" Paulinus retorts. He bends down to talk to our son, sending him off to fetch some "hay" for the horse from the garden, then he straightens up again, as if the conversation had not been interrupted. "Especially one who has half the Empire's legions roaming the streets. At least I found an excuse to leave Solina safely at home."

"Maybe you should have taken her," Pliny says. "To scare Otho off." This annoys Paulinus so much he storms from the atrium, swearing loudly, in a rare display of temper. "I didn't intend to be offensive on that occasion," Pliny says to me. "I was attempting to be humorous."

"I know. But he's afraid. And he's never afraid, so he doesn't understand the feeling."

"He's afraid for you and Lucius."

"Yes, and maybe also—" I stop, remembering this is Pliny, not Polla.

"Go on," Pliny says, waving a hand. "I am interested." The pompous way he says this is extremely irritating, but I have also been longing to speak with someone who cares for Paulinus as I do.

"All his life he has had an idea of what it means to serve Rome. And civil war threatens it. Because he is facing a choice without honour. Whatever he chooses, it will be dishonourable. He's not used to thinking that way about himself." I do not add that *I* am used to it, that much of my life has been about making appalling choices.

"You *know* him," Pliny says, as if this were an astonishing discovery.

Cunovindus has returned with handfuls of herbs from the garden, and dumps them at my feet, before fetching the horse to eat his dinner. "Did you only just notice?" I ask Pliny. "Maybe you should try divination, to help you see what lies within the human heart."

To my surprise, Pliny laughs. Then he stares at me with his dark Druid's eyes. "Or maybe I will make a sacrifice to Nortia, so she can bless me with a vision."

Pliny's knowledge of my deception almost makes me glad

Caratacus is dead. At least Pliny will never be able to prove to my husband that the prophecy which shaped his life, which still gives him an unwavering belief he is a man blessed by Fate, was a lie.

"I shouldn't have been so rude just now." Paulinus has returned, making me jump. He looks between Pliny and me. "Have the pair of you simply been glowering at one another in silence this whole time?"

"Of course not," I say. Cunovindus is tugging at my dress for attention, so I bend down to admire the new horse.

"Do you want to discuss the case now?" Paulinus asks, leading Pliny to the study. "And you are very welcome to stay to dinner."

The men disappear and I squat on the floor with my son. "What shall we name him?" I ask, speaking our own language now we are alone. I stroke the wooden animal, whose gem-encrusted bridle reminds me of the decorative mail Iceni horses wear into battle. This horse is painted chestnut, the same colour as Bellenia's stallion. "I think he should be called Kintu." I smile, trying to hide the grief I feel at saying the name of my sister's horse after all these years. "He is *Kintu*."

"Kinnu," says my son, patting the horse. Then he runs back and forth across the atrium, every now and then shooting me a proud glance, to make sure I am admiring his speed.

The evening I am finally obliged to attend one of Otho's banquets falls shortly after the enforced suicide of Tigellinus. I think of my old enemy as I recline beside Paulinus in the octagonal dining room of Nero's Golden House, no longer here as a slave but a guest. After a lifetime of spinning lies, the thread of treachery finally ran out for Tigellinus: his decision to support Galba over Nero left him vulnerable to Otho. After so much scheming, the old spider died as venomously as he lived.

On the central couch, Rome's new Casear is laughing, his face pink. I remember the first time I saw Nero, how unimpressed I was by his stature compared to Paulinus, but Otho is even more pathetic. He is short and balding, and his attempts to ingratiate his guests make him appear even weaker. Fabius reclines silently beside him, dressed in silks I recognise as Poppaea's, and he is glassy-eyed, perhaps drunk. Otho was married to Poppaea before Nero forced him to divorce her, and I suppose he likes using Fabius as a toy to remember his late wife, just as Nero did. The resemblance in their features is uncanny, yet I do not see my former mistress when I look at Fabius. He has none of her vivacity or cruelty.

Paulinus is listening politely to the senator who is closest to us, his wine untouched. "It was an obscene amount of money," the man is saying, "but it is hard not to find this impressive." He gestures at the room. "What sort of marble *is* that?" I look where he points. Translucent stone lines every surface of the room, glowing with light, as if we were trapped inside the moon. Above us, the constellations are painted on a revolving ceiling, which occasionally drops dried, scented rose petals on the guests, fluttering down like pink snow. A clump plops into the senator's outstretched glass, splashing his wife, and a slave rushes to replace it.

Paulinus is distracted, peering over my shoulder. "Otho has just sent out several of the Praetorian Guard," he says. "He seems agitated, look." I glance over. The Emperor is engaged in intense conversation with one of his guards. "Excuse me for a moment," Paulinus says to the senator and his wife, rising from the couch. I watch him cross to Otho, who appears relieved to see his approach.

My companions begin arguing in angry whispers. "I *told*

you it was a mistake to come," the woman hisses. "He's lured us to the palace only to murder us all!"

I see Otho get to his feet, as Paulinus walks back towards me. "My most honoured guests," Otho declares, speaking loudly over the hubbub of voices. Silence falls, and in the quiet I finally hear it – a muffled roar, the sound of distant shouting. Other guests hear it too, and people murmur in alarm. "There has been some misunderstanding among my men," Otho says, his attempt at a smile looking like a grimace. "The troops mistakenly believe a coup is being staged against me. When they arrive, I must reassure them that all is well. It may be best if you leave for your own safety. I cannot apologise for this enough."

"They are storming the palace!" someone yells. "They have broken into the gardens!"

There is a mass stampede for the doors. Guests and slaves jump over couches, smashing crystal glassware to the floor, shoving and kicking in their desperation to escape. Paulinus catches hold of me as the senator's wife barges her way past. "Otho has commanded me to stay," he says, raising his voice over the noise. "When the soldiers arrive, say nothing. Do not look in their eyes, do not antagonise them. Just keep close to me."

Paulinus is unarmed, as am I. If Otho cannot calm his men, we will be slaughtered. I think of our son, alone and unprotected, the future he faces if both his parents die. It fills me with panic. "What will happen to Cunovindus if—"

"Pliny would adopt him," Paulinus says. "It's all in my will. But that is not going to happen. We will return home, just stay calm."

The thought of Pliny raising my son does not make me feel calm, but I try to master my anxiety. We are not the only guests left. A few other military men and their wives, and a handful of the bravest – or most foolish – senators remain. We look round at one another, afraid but not wanting to show it. The shouting grows steadily louder, there is the ring of iron, then armed men burst into the banqueting hall. They surge towards the guests, instantly surrounding us. A soldier is pointing his spear straight at my face, and I feel the nudge of a sword against my waist.

"Traitors!" the soldier with the spear shouts. "You mean to kill Caesar!"

"We are here to serve Caesar, like you," Paulinus says calmly. "We are your friends."

I do not frighten easily. I have killed men and survived battle. But this is too much like the attack on my father's house. The feeling of being surrounded and unarmed, knowing Paulinus is powerless to defend me – just as my mother once was – is terrifying. The soldier senses my fear and jabs his spear closer to my face. I do not cry out, but drop my eyes, not looking at him.

Otho's voice rises over the screams and chaos. "My fellow soldiers!" he cries. "I know you are here out of love for me, but please calm yourselves: these are my dear guests, not traitors." The Emperor is so short he cannot be seen above the heads of so many men. The crowd parts slightly and I see Otho scramble up onto a couch to give himself some height. Fabius is cowering near Otho's feet like a wounded animal, arms over his head. Otho speaks again, pleading with his men to release us, even weeping as he implores them to put down their weapons, but I can no longer follow everything he says, my fear is too overwhelming.

The soldier who jabbed his spear at me is distracted, mouth agape, listening to Otho, his weapon slightly lowered. I turn to Paulinus, burying my face in his shoulder so I do not have to see, while he grips hold of me. I close my eyes and then

I am in darkness, listening to the steady thud of his heart, pretending we are both elsewhere.

51

SOLINA

Otho manages to calm his men, but Rome is not the same after that night. The relief I feel at making it home is short-lived. We are under siege, and a restless, violent army rules both the city and its Emperor, ebbing and flowing through the streets, a dark river volatile enough to burst its banks at any moment. Polla flees for her cousin's estates in the south. I rarely leave the house, and when I look out onto our road, half the shops are boarded shut. Rome's armies destroyed my home and everyone I loved once before, and now they are coming for my family all over again.

Two weeks after Otho's fateful dinner, Paulinus suggests we spend the night alone together. I dread what is coming. I know the choice he faces; I have known ever since Otho started courting him, but I am not ready to hear his answer. Whatever decision Paulinus makes will place Cunovindus at risk. We get ready for bed in silence, and even though I am expecting the conversation, it is still a shock when he finally speaks.

"I have agreed to lead Otho's army in his campaign against Vitellius."

He sounds abrupt, as if expecting me to argue, but I sit down on the bed, too upset to reply. Paulinus sits beside me. "I don't have a choice," he says, his tone gentler. "Neither Otho nor Vitellius is fit to be Caesar, but if the battle happens outside Rome, at least the city will not be sacked. We might even avoid fighting altogether. The two rivals are still communicating, and if I advise Otho towards restraint, perhaps they will come to terms."

"Do you really believe that? Given how ungovernable the troops are?"

"What else can I hope for?" he replies. "I truly believe Otho is a lesser evil than Vitellius. But even if I did not, Otho will assume I am a traitor if I refuse him."

I grip his hand. "Is part of you flattered to be asked?"

Paulinus is silent for a while. "Yes," he admits. "But I swear to you that is not why I have accepted. Civil war is wholly without honour, Solina. If it does come to battle, I will be killing my own. In the end, I have tried to make the choice that will be best for my country and for you and Lucius."

He looks so earnest. I want to beg him not to leave, to tell him I cannot bear this, but my parents raised me to live first as a warrior, not a wife. "*If* I agree to this," I say, "then you will make me a promise. If you are defeated, you will not fall on your sword. While any chance of survival remains, you will do whatever it takes to come back to your son and to me."

He starts to protest. "Sometimes it is a question of honour—"

"No," I say, raising my voice in anger. "I am not some Roman woman who does not understand what it means to fight in a war. Do you think I have no honour because I surrendered to you? Or do you imagine it takes less courage to survive humiliation than to die? You took everything I had,

Paulinus, and you *owe* me this promise. You owe me your life."

I have never spoken like this to my husband about what he did, although the weight of it is always between us. He takes my face in his hands. "I will never forgive myself for—"

"No," I say again, removing his hands, stopping him. "I don't want your apology. I want your promise. That is all I will accept."

He hesitates, looking down. I know how deeply ingrained the idea of a noble suicide is for Roman men and wonder if I have pushed him too far. He meets my eyes again. "I swear to you on the life of our son that I will do everything in my power to come back to him, and to you. I will do whatever it takes to survive." The relief of hearing the words almost makes me cry, but Paulinus has not finished speaking. "My only condition is that you and Lucius move in with Pliny while I am away. It will be much safer." I am about to protest, but he raises his eyebrows in amusement. "Think of what I just promised *you*," he says. "The death of my honour, if that's what you demand. All I'm asking is that you put up with Pliny for a while." I nod, and he embraces me. "I love you, Solina," he murmurs. I tighten my grip on him but stay silent.

All these years, I have never said that Latin phrase back to him, even though I know he longs to hear it. If there were ever a moment to speak, it should be now. Yet I still cannot bring myself to say the words.

My husband has left Rome. I am back in the house where I did not wish my son to be born, staying in the same room I once shared with Paulinus. At night, his absence is particularly painful. I try not to think of what might be happening in the war, or the danger hanging over my family. Instead, I focus on Cunovindus. We play in the large gardens, and although he shrieks a great deal, running alongside the library for hours, Pliny never complains.

Watching my son scamper about, I see so much of my little sister in him. He has Bellenia's exuberance. I remember playing with her outside our home in The City of the Horse, and how she would demand that I chase her, just as my son does now. Cunovindus has Bellenia's temper too. Sometimes he flings himself onto his front in rage, and he looks so funny it is hard not to laugh, even though this makes him even crosser.

When I hold my son in my arms, his body small and warm against mine, it brings me closer to my own mother. I remember the comfort I once drew from her strength. I can see her as she looked in my childhood, long before the war, the way she used to throw back her head and laugh, the stories she told, the way she danced. I remember sitting on her knee, her arms encircling me, allowing me to handle a knife for the first time, helping her skin the pelt from a wolf she had hunted. How proud I felt that day. I think this may even have been the same wolfskin she wore the last time I saw her.

I do not know how many of these memories I will ever share with Cunovindus. He is not only Iceni; he has the dark hair and olive skin of a Roman child, because that is who he is too. When he chatters to me in accent-less Latin, the golden bulla shining around his neck, he is very much Paulinus's son. And he has his father's smile. Sometimes it is almost a shock, how much they look alike, but I never love Cunovindus less for this. I will always feel guilt for the choices I have made, yet I cannot regret them, because I cannot regret anything that led me to my son.

*

It is Cunovindus who begins a thaw between Pliny and me. Once Pliny starts venturing from his library more, like a crane cautiously wading into water, he proves surprisingly patient with my child, delighting in teaching him simple tricks or ideas. Occasionally, Pliny almost reminds me of Paulinus – he has the same gift for storytelling, and Cunovindus is soon trotting after him, demanding entertainment from his "uncle" or to be carried about. I have always thought of Pliny as old, but seeing him laugh so much, it makes me realise he must only be a similar age to my husband.

A fortnight into our stay, Pliny asks if I will dine with him after Cunovindus has gone to bed, and my heart does not sink as it once might have done. Since there are only two of us, we sit at a table, which is much more comfortable than reclining in the main dining room. This room is simpler, painted with images of pigeons, geese and swans, trussed up as if we were in the market. Pliny rests his elbows awkwardly either side of his bowl, his tunic lop-sided, trying to pick out the soft meat of the sea urchins in his broth.

"I am thinking of having my sister come to live with me, and to adopt her son," he remarks. A slave silently places more bread upon the table, as Pliny has eaten so much mopping up his broth. "My nephew is a dear boy, a little older than Cunovindus, but delightful."

"Did the boy's father die?" I ask.

Pliny shakes his head. "No. He is violent. I don't think my sister should have to endure such a man. The situation is not unlike that which Paulinus experienced with his father as a child. His mother took him to his grandfather for similar reasons." Pliny is watching me keenly, and will have seen my surprise, so I do not bother to pretend I knew this.

"Paulinus never told me."

"It's why he doesn't often drink," Pliny remarks. "Paulinus

doesn't want to be like his father." He contemplates me for a moment, then goes back to picking at his sea urchins. "I was against your marriage, as I'm sure you know. I believed you wished Paulinus harm. Well, I admit now, I may have been partially mistaken." He does not look at me. "You tell the most dreadful lies, but I suspect you love him more than Fulvia did."

"He adored Fulvia." I am disinclined to trust the waspish Pliny's opinion.

"I cannot believe it has escaped your notice that Paulinus is astonishingly sentimental about women. All the times I've had to listen to him telling me what an innocent you are..." Pliny chuckles. "Fulvia clearly married him for his money."

"She seems to have cared for him a great deal, from all he's said to me."

"Yes, in the *end* she cared for him. Women always do fall in love with Paulinus eventually, if he sets his heart on one. It's remarkable. They cannot seem to resist him. Look at you."

"Are you in love with him?"

Pliny puts down his spoon. "Do you have any idea how offensive that question is?" His words are harsh, but his expression is not. It is close to amusement.

I shrug. "That's not an answer."

"Because your question is too impertinent to warrant an answer."

I smile. Whether or not Pliny is in love with my husband doesn't matter to me; I like him better for his evasion. It reminds me so much of my father. "It is true what I once told you," I say. "If you were Iceni, you would be a Druid."

"Like you?"

I nod. "Like me."

Pliny gestures at the two slaves waiting on us. "Leave us for a moment please." I watch, curious but not alarmed, as the servers do as he asks. "Paulinus gave me permission to share this information with you, if I thought it might assuage your anxiety during his absence."

My heart quickens. "What is it?"

"He has not merely gone to lead Otho's armies, but to gather intelligence on behalf of another, in the hope we might have a better Caesar than either of those currently on offer."

"*You?*" I ask in astonishment.

Pliny snorts with laughter. "Don't be ridiculous. I am speaking of the current governor of Judea, our friend Vespasian."

"Why has this man not launched his own campaign? Why would he expect Paulinus to spy for him?"

"Because, unlike the other two, he has a genuine regard for Rome and its people. A bad emperor is almost always better for a country than a long civil war. Vespasian will only strike if he is certain of winning."

I am still suspicious of Pliny. "Why did Paulinus not tell me this himself?"

"Acting as a spy carries certain risks and he did not wish you to worry. I argued that you are well used to war, that surely your mother must have shared her counsel with you. But he does not like to dwell on this side of your past." Pliny is staring at me, and I can tell there is more he wants to say, but for some reason he is struggling. "Solina," he says at last. "I am aware your marriage cannot have been uncomplicated for you." *Uncomplicated.* I think of the tension I have lived with for so long. All the rage I have supressed, the love and hatred constantly knotted around my heart, the toll of having married Paulinus, who will always be two men in my mind. Pliny is watching my face, as if he wants to read my thoughts. "I don't believe you know that your husband's first act when he returned to Rome from Britannia was to prosecute the former procurator," he says. "By that I mean the man who ordered your…" He breaks off. "Well, anyway, Paulinus asked me to prosecute the man. Which we did. Successfully."

"You prosecuted Decianus?" I am not sure how to feel about this. It is confusing to think Paulinus wanted to take vengeance on another Roman who harmed me, while he has never acknowledged the harm he did to me himself.

"It was Paulinus's case. I merely presented it." Pliny still looks uncomfortable, shifting in his chair. "I hope knowing this might help you understand him better, that is all."

"Thank you."

"It doesn't mean I trust you," he says, some of his old waspishness returning. "Your prophecy remains the most audacious lie a woman ever told."

"I promised Paulinus a son, and the Goddess of Fate granted us a son. There cannot be a clearer sign of divine favour than that."

"It was luck. A roll of the dice that fell in your favour. We both know this."

"And what is Fate herself if not the Queen of Luck?"

Pliny smiles, as if he sees through me, yet does not wholly dislike what he sees. He inclines his head in polite agreement. "That I will allow. There is no greater god than Chance."

52

PAULINUS

The streets of Gaul's capital Lugdunum have changed since Solina rode through here on Viribus, and Paulinus is grateful she is not present now as he retraces the route they once travelled. His own clothes have been taken, and he is dressed in a slave's filthy tunic, his hands bound. People jeer as he passes, relishing the chance to throw rubbish at a defeated general. His fate has not yet been decided by Vitellius, so Paulinus is at least permitted to ride upon a horse, unlike the condemned centurions who stumble on foot behind. Otho is not among the prisoners, he already died by his own hand.

The humiliation of disgrace burns, as does the guilt Paulinus feels knowing he once treated Solina like this. He forced her to wear a whore's green dress and paraded her before her own people to destroy her reputation. For years he has assuaged his guilt by telling himself that he did not love her then, that it was not personal, it was war, and yet now he understands how deeply painful it is to be shamed, he cannot believe he ever did this to her. Or how his wife has learned to look at him with anything but hatred. He imagines how alone and afraid she must have felt, and he wants to go back in time, to protect her from himself.

Riding in front of Paulinus is Vitellius's victory parade. The cavalry is masked in bronze, the horses' harnesses shining gold and scarlet, an imposing display of Rome's glory, even if they serve a worthless Caesar. Vitellius himself is too far to the front to see. Defeat is the nadir for any commander, yet today is not even the most disgraceful part of this campaign for Paulinus – everything about it has brought him shame. Within days of leaving Rome, he understood nobody intended to take his advice. Otho brought him to serve as a scapegoat for any failings, steadfastly ignoring every strategy his general asked him to consider when it did not suit his desires. Paulinus had to watch as Italian towns and villages were sacked, the soldiers indiscriminate in their slaughter, only to end by leading men into a battle he knew they could not win, which he had *repeatedly* told Otho they could not win.

They arrive at the city's forum, stopping in front of the palace where he was once a guest, the cavalry fanning out in a giant circle, and Paulinus is forced to stand among them. None of the men look at him, as if he were a spirit trapped between the worlds of the living and the dead, likely to bring them all bad luck. Vitellius dismounts from his horse, climbing to sit on a raised platform looking out over the crowds, cheered by people who have packed into the marketplace to see their new Caesar. They would have cheered for Otho too, or any other man crowned with laurel and backed by an army. As it is, Vitellius is less fit for the office than almost anyone Paulinus could imagine. The Emperor's six-year-old son is brought to his father in triumph, wrapped in a general's cloak, and Vitellius proudly lifts his child up to show him to the cheering crowd.

The boy looks slight for his age, his face fearful, and Paulinus thinks of Lucius. Sons often pay for the crimes of their fathers, even when they are defenceless infants. Paulinus knows he is strong enough to face his own death, but if Vitellius finds him guilty, he is terrified soldiers might then take his child. Panic surges through his body. He twists against the fetters on his wrists, trying to stay calm, forcing himself to put Lucius from his mind. Even contemplating his son being harmed is agony.

A hush has fallen. Paulinus realises that the captured centurions are being led forward for execution. Guilt and shame sicken him. He was their commander, yet he has survived to watch his men die, unable to intervene. The marble stones of the Lugdunum's forum are soon slick with blood, and Paulinus prays to Nortia Goddess of Fate, closing his eyes to conjure the image of the Etruscan statue as he remembers her in Volsinii. The goddess marked him out for divine favour, and he draws strength from this; Paulinus cannot believe that Nortia would have given him a son, only for the boy to be killed in childhood. There must be a way to survive, and to keep Lucius safe.

The room where Paulinus is brought already houses another prisoner: the eunuch with Poppaea's face who Otho took on campaign as a bed-mate. The boy shrinks against the wall, keeping as far away as possible from the guards when they enter. To Paulinus's intense relief, one of the soldiers undoes the painful fetters on his wrists, but then Fulvia's *lunula* catches the man's attention.

"What's this?"

"It belonged to my first wife." Paulinus places his hand protectively over the charm. "It is sacred to her memory."

"It's solid silver," the man retorts. "You should have surrendered it to the Emperor already. That will be worth something, melted down."

Paulinus has not removed the *lunula* since he first put it

on, after Fulvia's death. His grandfather's seal ring and the gold band that matches the one he gave Solina have already been taken, but the lunula was left out of respect for the dead. "I cannot believe that Caesar would need such a trinket," he says.

"You will give it to me, unless you want to lose the hand as well," the soldier replies.

Paulinus kisses the crescent moon while it is still bound to his wrist, asking for Fulvia's forgiveness, then he removes the necklace. His wrist feels naked without it, but he hides his distress. Nothing invites cruelty more than vulnerability.

The guard pockets the *lunula* and locks the door. Paulinus turns to look at the eunuch, who is still huddled into a ball with fear. Solina told him the boy's real name once, but he cannot remember it. All he can remember is the name Nero gave his concubine in mockery of his castration: *Sporus*. "You have nothing to fear from me," Paulinus says, wanting to put the boy at ease. "I think you knew my wife, Solina. She served Poppaea for a while."

"You are the man who rescued her?"

Paulinus has never felt more undeserving of such a description. "I married her."

"They are going to kill me," Sporus whispers, obviously unable to think of anything beyond this awful looming reality. "In the arena. When we get to Rome."

Sporus looks so broken, Paulinus cannot imagine how two Emperors ever lusted after him. The boy's short life must have been a hell beyond comprehension. "If it is a gladiatorial show, you will have the option to kill yourself first," he says, unable to offer any comfort beyond this.

"You are certain?" The look of hope on Sporus's face pains him.

"Yes. I promise you."

Sporus sighs deeply, covering his face with his hands. "Thank the gods."

"How did you learn your sentence?" Paulinus is uneasy to hear that Vitellius is in a vindictive enough mood to be using the arena as punishment.

"Caesar is making people beg for their lives. If they come up with something inventive enough that it amuses him, then he spares them." Sporus looks crushed. "I couldn't think of anything to say. My mind went blank."

This is the most useful information anyone has given Paulinus since his capture. "Perhaps Vitellius will spare you later," he says, trying to comfort Sporus with a lie. The boy gives him a tight smile and turns away.

Paulinus squats down on the floor – there is nowhere else to sit – and starts to think of what desperate tale he might spin. Solina made him promise to do whatever he could to survive – now he has a chance to do as she asked.

Vitellius keeps him waiting days for an audience, no doubt intending to break his prisoner's spirit through anxiety. Paulinus had not appreciated how profoundly exhausting captivity can be, and he often thinks of Solina, no longer wallowing in guilt for what he did to her but instead drawing inspiration from her example. He feels amazement at her self-possession, at the strength she must have had not to give in to despair. It makes him feel close to her. His wife has shown him what courage looks like when every power you once held is lost, when your reputation is destroyed, when all that remains are your wits.

If it were not for Solina, Paulinus might have felt too crushed by humiliation to think clearly when Vitellius finally calls upon him. He is led into the centre of the dining room while the Emperor holds a banquet, to plead for his life in front of men who were once his peers. Paulinus pretends that he is not unshaven or in a filthy tunic, darkening the glittering mosaic beneath his feet like a stain. Instead, he stands with the same poise he would have shown at the Basilica Julia when advising a judge. After all, he remains the same man.

Vitellius smirks, picking at his dinner, a quivering plate of eel. "What do you have to say for yourself?"

It is obvious from his voice that Vitellius is drunk, and therefore surely more volatile. Paulinus crushes the anxiety this provokes and bows low in submission. "Caesar, I have come to beg your forgiveness for my implacable treachery towards Otho, your enemy."

There is a murmur of confusion. "Your treachery to *Otho?*" Vitellius slurs.

"Yes," Paulinus nods. "I lost the final battle on purpose."

"How can you expect us to believe such nonsense?" The question is from one of Vitellius's companions, his general Caecina, who Paulinus had roundly defeated in an earlier skirmish.

"I was a hostage to Otho in Rome, unable to refuse his demand that I serve him. Yet once on campaign, I did everything in my power to ensure that he failed." Paulinus delivers his lie with utter conviction, borrowing the authority he once held as a respected jurist. "You all witnessed his final defeat. Who but a madman would have agreed to battle on such terms? What sane general would have committed his troops to such an exhausting march before they entered the field? What fool would have fought without waiting for the reinforcements which were known to be on the way?" He speaks with passion, and this part of his speech at least is true. Only a fool would have done these things, and Paulinus argued against them all, but he was overruled by Otho. "I would ask you to consider my reputation in Britannia. I have never been reckless in war. I abandoned London rather than fight a battle I knew I could not win. For Otho's entire campaign, I sabotaged him without remorse, hoping in this way to bring about the glorious victory of our true Caesar, Vitellius."

Paulinus sees the men exchange glances, but he keeps his own face impassive. "And this is your final plea?" Caecina asks.

"Yes. I humbly beg Caesar to believe my treachery and acquit me of the charge of loyalty."

At this Vitellius laughs. "Acquit you of *loyalty*? Has any man ever made such a plea?" The Emperor looks round at his guests, who all smile, eager to show that they share Caesar's amusement. "Very well, you may live. I believe you lack loyalty, that you ran the campaign of a madman. What great glory this judgement brings you." Paulinus's knees are weak with relief, and it is hard to supress his emotion. Lucius is safe. He opens his mouth, ready to make a speech of thanks, but Vitellius stops him. "We must see you drink to celebrate your good fortune. I think ten glasses of wine would be a fitting mark of gratitude."

Vitellius has not forgotten Paulinus's reputation for sobriety. His life has been spared, but he must pay for it with further humiliation. "I would be honoured to drink your health, Caesar."

Paulinus watches a slave fill a glass with wine. He has barely eaten in days. Ten glasses will see him collapse, a laughing stock to all those watching. The glass is cold in his fingers as he takes the goblet, and wine sloshes against the rim, red as the blood Nortia accepts in sacrifice. Paulinus knocks back the drink without hesitation, and as his throat burns, he understands at last why the Goddess of Fate chose him over other men. Solina told him once that a person's destiny is held within their name. He has always hated his own – it was chosen by his father to mark the low place he held within the family, and Paulinus has spent his life trying to resist rather than fulfil its meaning: *humility*. Yet now the fate his name promised will save him.

53

SOLINA

I do not think I will ever grow tired of the sight of my son with his father. Paulinus has come back from the campaign thinner, and with Fulvia's bracelet missing from his wrist, but whatever he may have suffered, our child is unaware of it all. He makes Paulinus play for hours, wanting to hide and be found, or race with Kintu the horse, or simply clutch his father's hand, chatting to him endlessly and making him laugh with his funny childish phrases. Whatever darkness Paulinus brought home, its grip is lessened in the light of so much love.

When we are alone together, he tells me of the lie he gave Vitellius which saved his life and destroyed his reputation. He says he not only acted to fulfil his promise to me, but to protect our son, and I feel proud of Paulinus for this. After his first night back, we do not often speak of the campaign. Some of the humiliations he suffered clearly bring him too much shame to share, and there are times he almost seems shy of me, but I pretend not to notice, persisting with my affection until he understands it is not only Cunovindus who is happy he is home. I am too.

*

Life in Rome remains unstable under Vitellius. The new Emperor tries to win favour with the people by throwing endless shows in the arena, but after Vespasian declares himself a competitor for the principate, there are food shortages, and the price of everything rises. Whatever Pliny and Paulinus think of their old friend, I am suspicious of a man who sits in Egypt, using his power to limit the supply of grain to his own capital. Everything Paulinus learned of Vitellius, any weakness he spied in his camp, is all fed to Vespasian through Pliny. I would have preferred my family to remain as far from danger as possible, but Paulinus is passionate in his support for Vespasian, claiming his friend will be the most honest Caesar in a generation. Since I have a low opinion of all Rome's Emperors, this does not move me.

The city prepares for the Saturnalia, even as Vespasian's troops begin to mass outside its walls, led not by the man himself who is still in Egypt, but by one of his generals. People cope with their fear by ignoring it. Evergreen garlands for the festival are hung between balconies, and families crowd into shops to buy gifts as if nothing were amiss. Cunovindus is three, old enough to understand the excitement, and he constantly pesters his father to take him to the Via Sigillaria to buy terracotta figurines for the holidays. Paulinus is uneasy at the idea of our son being out on the streets at such a time, but I persuade him to go. If Vitellius decides to strike early against Vespasian's suspected supporters, the house will not be safe for Cunovindus either.

Our son sits perched up high on his father's shoulders, trying to touch the green garlands as we walk along the busy street. We make for the oldest shop on the Via Sigillaria, where Paulinus once came as a child. Cunovindus's excitement makes me smile. His father sets him down with strict instructions not to touch anything, a rule he struggles to obey. Polished counters hold an abundance of figurines of Roman gods. The cheapest are plain red clay, designed for children, but on higher shelves, there are exquisite statuettes in glass or marble, gilded and colourful. The shop is busy, full of children laughing or making querulous demands. Paulinus asks Cunovindus to cover my eyes with his small, sweaty hands, so I cannot see the gift he chooses for me, and our son is delighted by the subterfuge.

"The horse one!" he cries, ruining the surprise, making us both laugh.

The journey home is even busier, but as we push our way up the hill, the atmosphere becomes less festive. People seem afraid rather than excited, struggling to shove past one another as swiftly as possible. Paulinus stops a man to ask what is happening.

"There is fighting on the Capitol," the stranger replies, before plunging back into the crowd.

The thought of street warfare is like a cold blade pressed against my heart. I have no idea how to keep Cunovindus safe. If this city is truly to be sacked, the way I once sacked Camulodunum with my mother, then we will have nowhere to hide. The doors of our house would not stand for long against soldiers or fire. A vivid memory of the British woman in the baths takes shape in my mind – the way she ran screaming for her children before she was cut down, her blood spreading across the tiles. I grip Paulinus's hand, and he glances down at me.

"We will keep him safe," he murmurs, guessing my thoughts.

We push through to the corner of our street, only to realise armed men are waiting outside the house. Paulinus bundles Cunovindus from his shoulders, almost throwing him at me in his haste to hide our son from view.

"Take him," he hisses. "Go back to the shop, or anywhere you might hide in a crowd."

I am about to do as he asks, but one of the soldiers has already seen my husband's recognisably tall form and shouts for us to stop. People clear the pavement to let the armed men through, only too glad it is not them who have caught the soldiers' attention. I hold Cunovindus close, trying to hide him in my cloak, but he struggles, protesting loudly.

"You are Suetonius Paulinus?" one of the men demands.

"I am." Paulinus steps in front of me and I press myself and my angry child into a doorway, trying to be as unobtrusive as possible.

"You will return to your house and stay there, if you have any regard for your family's safety."

"What has happened?"

"Rebels have taken the Capitol. We had been told you were among them. Fortunately for your wife and child, that is not the case." The man pauses to look over my husband's shoulder at Cunovindus, who has managed to struggle free of my cloak. "You should get your son home," he says. "Traitors have no regard for children."

I understand from his cold expression that this is not said out of concern for my son's safety. It is a threat.

The soldiers are thorough. Overnight they guard our house, along with the homes of other suspected allies of Vespasian, ensuring none can join the rebellion. All night I lie awake, terrified in case the fighting spreads and the soldiers decide to kill my family rather than risk Paulinus escaping. But the relief I feel when the armed men finally leave in the morning is short-lived. We discover the ancient Temple of Jupiter on the Capitol has been burned to the ground, and Vespasian's brother is dead. As rumour of the calamity spreads, people gather on the streets, some openly weeping. It is a disaster beyond the scale of most Romans' imagining. The temple was held sacred, and the horror of its fall brings home how much danger we are all in.

Paulinus is frustrated to be denied the chance of serving Vespasian as a soldier but is still determined to defend the city. "We should secure the road," he says, pacing the atrium. "Once the fighting spreads, Vitellius will try to hold the city street by street. The slower the army's progress, the better."

"Do you think our neighbours support Vespasian?"

"It hardly matters. People will want to defend their homes and businesses from attack. And if too much of the city is destroyed, there will be little left for Vespasian to rule."

"I will help you," I say, even though I have privately vowed to have no hand in this war between Romans.

Paulinus stops. We stare at one another over the giant body of the tiled wolf. I know what my husband is thinking, as I think it too. There is a great deal of strangeness in defending a city together. "Thank you," he says at last. "I will be glad of your help."

It is hard not to think of Camulodunum while I help shift furniture to block the road. I can remember the feeble barricades my mother burned at that colony's victory arch, and I remember too the measures Paulinus once took against the Iceni forces in London, destroying the bridge to halt our progress, using boats to shelter families out of our reach. Perhaps some of those Londoners were British women who chose to have families with Roman men. I had thought them traitors back then. I even told Bellenia their children were better off dead. I try not to think of that now.

Sleet is falling, making the task of barricading the streets even harder. Other women work alongside me, and we load up a blockade of amphorae, all of us anxious for our families. I help an older woman struggling with her jar, the pair of us shuffling together over freezing slush. My weapon lies on the pavement, snowflakes dampening the wood. Paulinus has given me a spear, as it will keep attackers further at bay than a sword – a sensible choice, given I am out of practice. There are ominously few soldiers on the streets. Rumours have reached us that Vespasian's troops are already invading the outskirts of the city; Vitellius must have sent all his forces to meet them. I pray the battle is over before they get this far.

Even though we are on alert, some keeping watch while others build defences, the fighting still bursts upon us unexpectedly. Our attackers are silent, surging in from a side street, killing one veteran who has no time to draw his sword. I stand ready with my spear, without knowing which Emperor these men are fighting for, or if they might simply be looters taking advantage of the turmoil. They try to smash into a boarded-up shop, but Paulinus and other men from the Night Watch repel them until they run off.

"You need to get back in the house," Paulinus shouts, seizing my arm. He hurries me up the street, and we bash on the door, calling for Cosmus. We already agreed I would stay inside as a last defence to protect Cunovindus, and to give Paulinus cover.

Cosmus opens up, and after a rushed kiss goodbye, Paulinus is gone. I leave the spear in the atrium and hurry upstairs, climbing up onto the roof through the garden window. A heap of tiles sits ready for me to throw. Now that I have left him, I am sorry not to fight alongside my husband, although I know this is a better strategy. On the street below, I can see him in a group of other men, waiting by one of the barricades. Even though there is a battle in progress a few streets away, the city cannot decide how to respond, with some shops boarded up, and others still open, braving attack rather than miss a day's trading before the Saturnalia.

It is freezing on the roof, and I try to hide my hands in my cloak, not wanting them to become uselessly numb. Another dark figure on the gable opposite shows me I am not the only woman up here. From my vantage point, I can see soldiers advancing upon the street from some distance away and hurl a tile before the barricades in warning. A river of black, shot through with silver, is slowly eddying towards my home. People rush out to defend their shops, and other scouts, mostly women like me, hurl down tiles at the advancing soldiers, in an even more savage flurry than the sleet. I am not in the heart of the violence as I was at Camulodunum, yet my fear now is greater. It is not for myself, but my son. The walls of my house will be no shield to determined attack, and I try not to think of Cunovindus, locked inside the study with the nurse. At such a moment as this, love is a weakness.

The enemy is now directly below me. To my frustration, I see Paulinus putting principle before sense, trying to shout at the approaching soldiers. Their answer is to hurl a missile at him, which he ducks. I throw a tile in response, striking a man's head. It is satisfying to watch my enemy fall. Our street is swiftly engulfed in fighting, the sound of screaming, the ring of metal and the smash of tiles rising to the rooftops. I am reassured to see Paulinus's savagery: he is a butcher with the sword, coldly slaughtering his enemy, red trailing in his wake.

The attackers soon give up, perhaps surprised by the resistance, but then others arrive. This time, their assault is more aggressive, and they smash through the barricades, like a river churning up debris in a flood. The fight is pushed further up the street, and to my horror, I see Paulinus is trapped, held back by a smaller group of the soldiers who intend to finish him off. I manage to knock out three from above, but do not dare aim at the remaining two for fear of killing my husband by mistake.

Even though I promised to stay in the house, I cannot stay here and watch as these men murder Paulinus. I scramble back inside, rushing down the stairs to the atrium, where Cosmus and some of the other servants are armed and positioned by the door. I seize my spear and advance on them. "Let me out!"

"But the master's instructions…"

I point my weapon at Cosmus. "You need to let me out. Otherwise, he will die."

After a moment's hesitation, the steward stands aside, and I lay my hand on the bolt. "Keep watch through a crack when it's open," I say. "And be ready to let us in swiftly. But if we are both killed, you must lock it again to protect Lucius."

I draw back the bolt, opening the door wide enough to see where the fighting is, then slip through. Snow is falling, and the wreckage looks much worse than it did from above. The pavement outside my home is slick with reddening slush, and bodies darken the road like stepping stones. Paulinus is leaning against our neighbour's wall. I realise he is struggling, unable to use his sword arm properly. He must be injured. One of his attackers has even abandoned the fight in favour of jeering, confident Paulinus is now no more than easy pickings. They are the only people here; everyone else must be locked inside or caught up in the battle several houses ahead. I move silently, approaching from my enemies' blind spot. Paulinus sees me but does not immediately react. Then, trusting I will understand what he is doing, he moves so that he is dangerously exposed, yet the assailant is easier for me to hit. I act instantly, thrusting the spear through the man's neck. The second attacker shouts in rage and surprise, and while his attention is on me, Paulinus strikes him, sending up a spray of blood. I skewer him when he is down, to be very sure he is dead.

Paulinus takes my arm, and we stagger to the house. Cosmus locks the door behind us.

"Your injury," I say, helping my husband to the bench. "How bad is it?"

"I have no idea."

The padded tunic he is wearing as makeshift armour is already soaked with blood. I wrestle the fabric free. "It is a long wound, but not as deep as I feared," I tell him. "We should dress it, then I will bandage it to stop the bleeding." I turn to Cosmus. "Bring wine, honey and vinegar. And something for the bandage."

Paulinus watches me. "Thank you," he says, laying his hand over mine. "I have never been more grateful to have married a disobedient woman. I do not believe there is another man in Rome whose wife would have been capable of using the opening I just gave you to kill."

I look at his face, splashed red with our enemies' blood. "If I had not realised what you wanted me to do, you would be dead now. How certain were you I would understand?"

"Completely certain."

"But we have never fought together."

Cosmus has returned with the supplies. I take the wine first, pouring it liberally over the wound. My husband does not flinch, though I know how much this must hurt. I follow with the vinegar, which is worse, then soak a piece of fabric with honey, wrapping it round the cut, followed by another, much tighter, to stop the bleed. Paulinus flexes his fingers after the final knot is tied. "I knew you would understand what I was doing because I have seen you fight," he says. "You threw a pot to unbalance an opponent once. And you survived several battles. That doesn't suggest a warrior who misses many chances."

We look at each other, both remembering the past. I cannot think of a worse history. Yet for all the horror of our beginning, I suspect Paulinus now understands me better than almost any other man might have done. My father's words return to me: *I have seen Solina's spirit rise above the rooftops of Rome.* His prophecy came to pass in ways he could never have imagined.

54

SOLINA

We escape the sack of Rome unscathed. Vitellius is killed on the first day of fighting, and although some stragglers continue to loot and riot, Vespasian's army slowly tightens its grip, restoring order. The day after his injury, Paulinus seems to be recovering well, my bandages controlling the bleed, and the day after that, Pliny joins us for dinner, to celebrate their friend Vespasian's victory. I feel confident my family is as safe as they can be in such a turbulent city.

That same night, after Pliny has left, I wake sweating, and realise it is because Paulinus is burning up beside me. He is feverish. In the darkness I scramble out of bed, stumbling towards the shutters to let in the moonlight and the cool air. The bottle of vinegar glints on the table. Perhaps we have grown complacent, not applying it often enough. I peel back the bandage on Paulinus's arm, my heart thudding, and slosh liquid onto his wound. It drenches the bed, and he wakes, crying out in pain.

"You're so hot," I say, clutching the bottle. "I'm trying to treat the injury. I think it's infected."

"Shit." He winces as he moves. "You put the vinegar on?"

"Yes."

"Then get back into bed. Hopefully the fever will break overnight."

He is asleep again almost instantly, but this does not reassure me. His breathing sounds shallow, and I am frightened it is not healthy sleep, but sickness which has knocked him out. I lie beside him, wide awake. In the dim light, I keep peering at his arm, hoping each time it will look less swollen and red.

In the morning, he is worse. I try to talk to him, to rouse him into coming back to himself, but he is shivering and keeps losing his train of thought. I have seen too many warriors die from infected battle wounds not to understand what is happening. Paulinus is gravely ill.

I send for the doctor, an army surgeon Paulinus trusts, but he has very little to recommend beyond frequent dressings of vinegar and honey. When I follow the man from the bedchamber, to press him for more help outside my husband's hearing, he reluctantly gives me a paste to try and draw out the puss.

"Either his body will prevail, or it will not," the doctor says, speaking with the bluntness of one who has seen countless deaths on the field. "There is little anyone can do besides pray. If the fever begins to break and the inflammation goes down swiftly, then he stands a good chance." I listen in silence. This man does not understand that Paulinus is not just another patient, to be dismissed so easily. He is an entire world, and he is mine.

I will not allow anyone to look after Paulinus except me. The fever burns, but I continue to dress the wound and force him to drink honeyed water, even when he is half asleep. In desperation, I send for Pliny, in the hope that he might have more knowledge than the doctor. He does not. Instead, he stands there uselessly, laying his palm to Paulinus's hot forehead, frowning. My husband does not even understand that his friend is present.

"I cannot advise anything beyond what the doctor has told you," Pliny says quietly. "We have to wait for the fever to break."

"I cannot allow him to die. You must do something. You must *know* something."

"Solina, I do not hold power over life and death. Nobody does."

"But all those books you've read," I shout. "There must be something! Or maybe another doctor…"

"No," Pliny says firmly. "Another doctor will waste your money and may even make him worse. Paulinus trusted the army surgeon for good reason, because he knows the man will not sell nonsense to desperate relatives."

Paulinus stirs, muttering to himself, and for one hopeful moment I think he is going to speak, that he is going to remark on his wife and friend arguing as he has so many times before. But he does not open his eyes. I sit beside him on the bed, my anxiety so severe I feel that I might suffocate. "Pliny is here," I say, taking his unresisting hand. "You must wake and greet him." He does not answer so I bend lower to speak more loudly. "Wake up! Please, wake up!"

"Solina, stop." Pliny lays his hand on my arm as I start to cry. "I know you love him, but you cannot become hysterical. You must show endurance. Loss is a natural part of life."

"What has my life been if not endurance in the face of loss?" I scream at Pliny through my tears. "The gods cannot have Paulinus. He is *mine*. I cannot lose him after losing everyone else. I cannot bear it—"

Pliny grips my arm, stopping my tirade. "Enough! This will not help."

I breathe deeply, trying to calm the panic that is rising in my chest, threatening to overwhelm me. Pliny is right, weeping will not help. I must think clearly. We are in the middle of the Feast of Darkness, the time when the veil between worlds is thin. If medicine cannot help Paulinus, perhaps I can. "At your house, among the gifts my husband gave you, is a silver Iceni mirror," I say, my voice calmer. "It belonged to my father. Two crescent moons are engraved upon it, back-to-back, and the horse of Epona is between them, inlaid with gold. The doctor told me all we can do now is pray. I ask you to bring me this mirror, so that I may do as he asks."

"Superstition will not—"

I interrupt Pliny before he can start some pompous speech about the non-existence of the gods. "Feel free to believe this is nonsense," I say. "I ask you to bring this to ease my suffering."

He does not wish to obey me, yet I know my distress has rattled him. "The mirror is all you will be using?"

"I will also be sacrificing several of the servants," I retort, and he almost smiles at the sarcasm.

"Very well. So long as you understand I do this purely for *you*, not because I believe it will help."

"I knew this without you having to tell me, but yes, I understand."

Pliny realises he is still holding my arm and lets go, giving me an awkward pat. Then he leaves. As soon as he has gone, I call for the steward, Cosmus. "How is Lucius?" I ask, using the Latin name Paulinus gave our son.

"He still calls for you and his father, but the nurse is keeping him entertained."

"Thank you. I will see him in a little while. But first, please go to the apothecary to get me some mistletoe. I know they sell it at this time of year."

"In the current chaos, many of the shops are closed. But I

will do my very best, *domina*." Cosmus bows and unlike Pliny, he does not ask what the mistletoe is for.

I am left alone with Paulinus, who is now deeply asleep, no longer stirring. I do not know if this is a good sign or not. His hand feels hot in mine, and I bend to kiss him, stroking his hair.

"I forbid you to leave me. Do you hear me? *I forbid it.*"

He says nothing in reply, so I climb onto the bed beside him, to hold him, as he has so often held me. The walls around us are painted with scenes from the life of the female warrior Atalanta, including her victory at the Calydonian boar hunt. Paulinus chose these. He said he first understood he loved me when I killed the boar to save his horse, as brave as Atalanta of legend. Whenever I am with my husband, his crimes lie between us, so heavy they can never be forgiven. Yet in this moment, when I am close to losing him, I cannot think of the terrible things he has done. Instead, all I can remember are his many acts of love, the care he has shown me every day since we married. I hold Paulinus tighter, painfully aware that I have never told him that I love him, even though I have always known how much he wanted to hear it.

The mistletoe is dried. In my fingers, it is so brittle I'm afraid it will disintegrate before the sacrifice, and I doubt it was gathered from an oak tree at midnight. Yet in leaner years my father also had to make do with old herbs like these to lift the veil between worlds. I open the bedroom shutters, letting in the cold. The sky above Rome's rooftops is black, the moon a sliver of silver. I light the mistletoe in the incense bowl which Cosmus took from Nortia's shrine downstairs, wafting some of its smoke outside, so that the offering can rise to the heavens. While it burns, I raise the mirror to reflect the night, chanting the song of Epona, whose words I last sang in the presence of my living family. It is an incantation which has the power to send the living to sleep and to wake the dead. My husband lies between both worlds, the most perilous place for mortals, and this song should call to him above all other souls who hear me.

When I have finished, I tilt the mirror towards the sky so it will not reflect my face. I speak into it, not to see a vision of the future, but to reach my family. I call for them in turn, then I close my eyes, trying to visualise their beloved faces.

"*I ask you to forgive me for the one I have chosen, but I beg you, let him return to me. Tell him he must leave the Otherworld, tell him he cannot stay with you. I beg you, if you loved me in life, ask Epona to bring him back to the mortal world.*"

I set down the mirror, reluctant to let go of this precious link with my past. It is easier to believe in my own power when I hold it.

On the bed, I can see Paulinus's sleeping body and walk over to sit beside him. My song should have woken his soul, but that does not mean I will find the right words. In the dim light, Atalanta is chasing after the boar, a blurred but familiar shape on the wall, a memory that makes Paulinus think of me fondly. I cannot tell him when I first loved him, because I do not know. I buried the feeling under guilt for so long, pretending it was not real.

"Lucius misses you desperately, and he loves you," I say. "Come back for him. He needs his father."

My voice sounds cracked in the darkness. I know Paulinus loves our son more than any other being, as I do, but it is not Cunovindus who lifted the veil, and the message must come from me. "I love you, Paulinus," I say in Latin, almost expecting him to rise from his bed in shock at hearing the words. Yet he does not stir. I say it again, over and over, unable to bear that I may be too late.

When I wake in the morning, I feel a surge of hope that the incantation will have worked, but when I scramble upright to check on Paulinus, he is still deeply asleep. I lay my hand on his chest, and it is hot. The fever has not broken. I press my knuckles against my mouth to prevent myself from sobbing, trying to contain my grief. The thought of losing Paulinus is unspeakable, and I experience a rush of rage and self-pity, furious that the gods are so implacable in what they take from me.

When I have recovered myself, I send for Cunovindus. I had hoped to spare him the distress of seeing his father so sick, but it will be worse if Paulinus dies, and he has not seen him.

The nurse brings Cunovindus in, and he runs to me, wanting to climb up onto the bed. I lift him into my arms. "Your father is sleeping," I say, amazed at how normal I sound.

"Shall I wake him?"

"I think he is very sleepy and may not wake."

I allow Cunovindus to scramble over his father as he would usually do, only protecting Paulinus's wounded arm. "He is very sleepy," he agrees. "*You* will have to play with me instead." My son has a child's blithe selfishness, unaware that he might be about to lose a parent.

"I will play with you soon," I say. "But for now I need to stay here with your father until he feels better."

A worried frown creases my son's forehead, and he carefully pats his father's face. "Feel better," he whispers, before turning back to me. "Will he hear?"

"Yes," I say, thinking of my own father. "Always."

Cunovindus hugs me and slides from the bed. I watch as the nurse leads him out.

The day is endless, and yet I don't want it to end, because I don't want Paulinus's hours to spill through my fingers like sand. I still give him water, and dress his wound, and I talk to him constantly. I tell him I love him, and I tell him about my family, about my life before, sharing more of myself in one morning than I have in all the years we have known each other. I speak as if he were not the Roman general who destroyed my home, but only the man I married.

I am still talking, describing the ride Bellenia and I would take through the woods by the salt marshes, my eyes closed to see it more clearly, when I feel him stir. He has moved fretfully before, so I turn to look without much hope. To my shock, his eyes are open, and he is squinting to focus on me. "Water?"

I almost knock over the glass in my eagerness to give it to him. He reaches for the cup instinctively and gulps it down, then I put it back on the table. "You are awake," I say, amazed.

"It would seem so."

He looks rumpled and completely exhausted yet perhaps not as pallid as he has been. "How is your arm?"

Paulinus grimaces as I hurry to inspect the dressing. "It's been better."

"I think it is less red," I exclaim, unable to restrain my excitement. I press my hand to his chest, startling him with the sudden movement. "You are not as hot."

He is looking at me with a mix of amusement and affection, unaware of all the terror I have felt. "I'm still tired," he says, laying his hand over mine. "I might sleep a little more."

I want to argue, to keep him awake, but he closes his eyes and has soon drifted off again. I don't want to move his hand from where he has placed it, so I stay frozen, watching his chest rise and fall, feeling the thud of his heart, reassuring myself that he is getting better, and this is not the cruel burst of life that sometimes occurs just before death.

When he wakes again, Paulinus is more alert, he even asks for food. I have Cosmus bring up some broth and call for Cunovindus. Our son has no idea of the danger his father has endured and makes no allowance for his exhaustion. He fetches the terracotta figurines he was given for the Saturnalia, insisting Paulinus tell him a story in the character of the goat god Pan, and while his father talks, he steals some of his bread. My attempts to take over the figurine storytelling are rejected – it is true I cannot spin a tale as well – and I reluctantly allow the nurse to take Cunovindus away, because I can see that Paulinus is struggling to keep up with all the demands.

When we are alone again, I scarcely know what to say. I have talked myself hoarse while he was sleeping but cannot imagine being as intimate with him now that he is awake. Paulinus is watching me, a curious expression on his face.

"In my dreams I thought you were telling me about your family."

"I was," I say, and he looks down at the bedclothes, the same blanket Fulvia made which he took to Britain, which we slept under while I was still in captivity. "I also told you that I love you," I say, in case he is embarrassed to ask if he dreamed this. "Because I do. Very much."

He takes my hands, and I expect him to tell me he loves me too. "Do you forgive me, Solina?"

I stare at him, too shocked to speak. There is such yearning in his face, and I realise that he has not been waiting all this time for me to tell him I love him, which he must have guessed years ago. He wanted something else entirely. "I love you," I say, gripping his fingers. "More than you could ever imagine."

"But do you forgive me?"

My husband is frail, and I am still anxious for his recovery. Yet it is impossible to give him what he wants. "No. I will never forgive you. What you did, the suffering you caused, it is not even mine to forgive." It is such a relief to admit this, that even though I am afraid to cause Paulinus pain, I carry on, unable to stop. "I cannot forgive all the people you killed, the towns you burned, I cannot forgive you for watching me execute Diseta, I cannot forgive you for not only destroying the Iceni for one generation, but forever." I am crying, both in relief that he is alive but also grief for what he did. "I know if it had not been you, it would have been another Roman general. I know all these terrible things would still have happened. I have told myself this often, and yet—"

"And yet, it *was* me," Paulinus finishes my sentence, and I nod. "I will never ask for your forgiveness again. I understand this is impossible. But would it make it easier for you to know that I could not regret what I did more bitterly?"

I realise that does make it easier. Not enough for me to forgive him, but at least it lessens the guilt I feel for loving him. "Yes," I say. "That means something." I lean forward to cup his face in my hands, kissing his forehead. "Would it be too painful to hold me?"

"No," he says, embracing me. I cannot tell if it's true that it does not hurt him, because I suspect Paulinus would endure any agony in that moment rather than push me away.

55

SOLINA

Nortia's face is implacable, cold as the tiles that shine upon her throne. The Goddess of Fate stares at me as I sit in my garden, and I think of my husband's ancestors, the Etrusci, a brilliant people defeated and enslaved by Rome. Paulinus has told me of their history, the mix of pride and shame he feels, the regional accent he has tried so hard to lose, and the fierce devotion he has towards Nortia, the Etrusci's most destructive of gods. I wonder whether Paulinus's ancient family still lives in his heart, and I wonder how much of the Iceni will live on in the hearts of my children.

I walk over to Nortia's shrine, and her dark eyes watch me. Her altar is crimson, red as the wine we pour for her in offering. I knew long before Paulinus confessed it that Nortia once demanded the human heart in sacrifice. Like Andraste, she is a goddess of blood.

"*Thank you for bringing him back to me,*" I say, speaking my own language to the goddess who turned my lie into truth, granting me the fate I demanded.

"Solina."

I turn at my husband's voice. Paulinus is watching me from the colonnade, his hand resting on a pillar. He is recovering well, though still weakened, and I hurry over, alarmed by his expression. "Is anything wrong?"

"There is something I should have shared with you years ago," he says. "I was too much of a coward back then. But after everything that's passed between us, I know I must tell you."

"What is it?"

Paulinus sits on a cold marble bench, and I sit beside him. He hands me a purse. "I have kept both these objects since I served in Britannia. I believe one of them is rightfully yours."

I tip out the purse, my hands shaking. Sitting on my palm is a half-melted coin and a tarnished silver brooch. Suddenly I realise what I am seeing. I gasp. This is the brooch my aunt Riomanda gave me on my naming day. The one I sent to the Town of the Wolf with Senovara.

"How did you get this?"

"Towards the end of the campaign, I went to *Lukodunon*. It was completely deserted; I think it had been for some time. We destroyed the town, but first I searched the great roundhouse at its centre. This brooch was in the pot hanging over the hearth."

I start to sob. Paulinus reaches for me, but I shake him off. My heart feels as if it will break. I feel grief that my husband kept this from me for so long, but most of all I feel overwhelming relief that Riomanda survived. I did not completely fail the Iceni. Senovara reached The Town of the Wolf, bearing my message. Perhaps hundreds of people were saved.

"I am so sorry, Solina. I wish I had told you this earlier," Paulinus says, his voice cracking. "I believe many people from the Iceni's most northern settlements must have survived. I saw some when we left, watching from the woods. We did not pursue them. And although this cannot atone, and I do not ask your forgiveness, it was because of you that I let them be."

My beloved aunt was there in the woods; I am sure this is who Paulinus saw. Riomanda was waiting for me to make my way back to her. And I never came. I get up from the bench, walking away from my husband, wanting to cry for Riomanda out of his reach. My fist is clenched around the brooch, and I can feel the other object too, which I had forgotten. I open my fingers to look at the melted coin. Then I hold it out to Paulinus, who has risen to his feet. "What is this?"

"It belonged to a child who was burned to death in the temple at Camulodunum. He wore a *bulla*, like Lucius. I buried him, along with several other children, then carried his coin with me throughout the campaign. I told myself everything I did was in vengeance for his murder."

Whether or not Paulinus is trying to make me feel guilty, I do. I remember the way the temple burned, the screams of those trapped inside drowned out by the chants of my mother's warriors, her face lit red in the flames. I believe that is when the war destroyed what remained of Bellenia's spirit. I close my fingers around both brooch and coin. "I am glad you finally told me all this." I look at Paulinus, my beloved, yet also still the legate. "I want to be alone for a while."

Riomanda lived. *Did her child live too?*

Part of me wants to try to find them now, to spend the rest of my life searching, yet I also know there is no going back. Britain is convulsed by another civil war, and my aunt will have melted into the woods with whatever remained of our people. She will not want to be found. Returning to my family as a Roman general's wife would place them all in terrible danger. And although she loved me, I know deep in my heart Riomanda would not forgive me for who I married. Some choices in life are irrevocable. You cannot atone. You cannot even ask for forgiveness.

A bang makes me jump; it is the door whacked against the wall of my study. Cunovindus charges inside, clutching something in his grubby little hands.

"What's this?" I say, smiling at his excited face. "Show me." My son trots over, opening his fingers. It is an empty snail shell, shining black and gold, as precious as a jewel. "How beautiful," I exclaim. "Where did you find this?"

"Beneath Nortia. She left it for me."

I lift Cunovindus onto my knee, holding him close. Far across the plains and cold seas of Rome's vast Empire, perhaps Riomanda is also holding her child close, the surviving son or daughter of my beloved uncle Cunominus. I could not fully call my own son after him, as Cunominus means *Little Hound*, the name for a younger brother. My son is *Bright Hound* and Lucius also means *Bright*, a fitting name, since Paulinus told me Lucius Cunovindus is destined to be the light of both his parents' lives.

"What is this?" He points to an object of shining gold on my desk. It is the most precious of all the treasures Pliny has returned to me. I lift my mother's torc and give it to my son. The gold is heavy for him, its precious ropes almost as wide as his fingers, yet he is a child of the Wolf Tribe and does not drop it. In his hands he holds the power of our stories, of our shared history, of everything it means to be Iceni.

"This belonged to your grandmother."

"Can I meet her?"

"She is in the Otherworld. But I know that she loves you, and her spirit guards you always."

"What was she like? Was she like you?"

I take the torc from him, turning it to catch the light. My mind is full of memories, shining as bright as the treasure before us both. I see my family, stronger and dearer to me than oak. There is so much love there, and courage, as well as pain. One day, I will have to tell Lucius Cunovindus how I met his father. I will have to tell him what happened to the Iceni, and I will have to tell him that his grandmother was Boudicca.

But for now, this is the story I want to tell my son. About the time before she was Boudicca.

When she was a woman called Catia.

When she was my mother.